REMF

Vietnam Was Only the Beginning

A Novel Based on True Events, the Psychological
Challenges Facing a Vietnam Veteran

RAY DYER AND STEPHEN DWYER

Visit Us At:
theremf.com

For information regarding permission, please write to:
info@barringerpublishing.com
Barringer Publishing, Naples, Florida
www.barringerpublishing.com

Cover, graphics, and layout by Linda S. Duider
Cape Coral, Florida

ISBN: 978-1-954396-21-0
Library of Congress Cataloging-in-Publication Data
REMF: Vietnam Was Only the Beginning
Ray Dyer and Stephen Dwyer

Printed in U.S.A.

This story is dedicated to the 58,220 men and women who died in Vietnam and to all of the men and women who came back wounded physically, mentally, and spiritually, those who are still suffering, those who have recovered and those that took their own lives.

Twelve thousand helicopters were put into service in Vietnam. About five thousand were lost, mostly to ground fire. Forty thousand helicopter pilots served in Vietnam. Nearly twenty-two hundred pilots were killed.

FOREWORD

"REMF" (Rear Echelon Mother Fucker)—A term grunts in the field called anyone stationed in the rear who had it easy—too easy.

The following is a matter of record:

General Maxwell Taylor was Chairman of the Joint Chiefs of Staff. In 1962 he sent his observations to President John F. Kennedy. This was among them:

> *"South Vietnam was not an excessively difficult or unpleasant place to operate. While the border areas are rugged and heavily forested, the terrain is comparable to parts of Korea where U.S. troops learned to live and work without too much effort."*

> —*Vietnam Magazine*, August 2018

TABLE OF CONTENTS

PROLOGUE

There was the cold and brutal beauty of Lake Erie on a winter morning. The gray choppy waters extended to the northern horizon of the inland sea. Broken and jagged ice piled up and created mini-mountain ranges that packed the barren shoreline and empty marinas. Two long breakwalls constructed of thousands of boulders jutted out into the lake, stopping the massive ice packs blown in by the fierce winds escaping from Canada. On the lee sides was open water where the icy ravages of nature were considerably less. One foot of snow lay in the low areas, but only a few inches around the wind-blown grounds of the treatment center. There was no one to be seen anywhere outside. A solitary lone gull landed on the shore now and then.

Gary Dyson had dragged a lounge chair up close to a window and sat scanning the scenery. Dressed in donated blue jeans, sweatshirt and sneakers, he deeply inhaled the smoke of his Camel cigarette. He had just come out of a six-year relapse. This was his fifth time in treatment for alcoholism.

1968

I III I

HOME BACK THEN

Dyson's earliest recollections were of towering trees, sunshine, ponds, and cows, and of his boyhood home in the country. It was an isolated life with him, his mom and dad, and a few years later, his younger brother, Len. Winters brought deep snow for making snowmen and snow forts, and frozen ponds with ice skaters. He loved the seasons and their changes, trees budding, rolling New England hills of green turning to yellow, red, and brown. His family visited the seashore many times. The boys loved the sand, waves, and tidal pools full of starfish, minnows, and hermit crabs.

His mom was a homemaker. Back then, all mothers were homemakers. The family was supported by his dad's pattern shop, making all kinds of industrial quality control jigs for the aircraft industries all over Connecticut. There were prosperous years and lean ones, too. The family finances went up and down.

Elementary school marked the start of many years of long friendships. He was not the brightest student but fit somewhere in the middle of his classmates. His teachers said he had the potential to learn but lacked the drive or the interest. When disappointing report cards started coming home, it was the beginning of tension and resentment between him and his dad.

Gary and Len hunted pheasant, grouse and woodcock which thrived all over Tolland County. The streams and ponds had plenty of trout, bass, crappie, and pickerel. Gary loved being in the woods. Sometimes he brought along a novel to read with his back against a tree. He developed a love for nature and a respect for life.

During high school, the push was on to go to college. In his senior year, he pulled up his grades enough to get into college. Like many young men at that time, he was unready and unsure of making a career decision. Consequently, he went to the local community college to continue his education and to avoid the draft. Neither he nor any of his classmates wanted to go to Vietnam, especially after watching the news on TV. He loved going to college—new friends, beautiful girls, great music, frat parties, drinking Budweiser, and smoking pot. He preferred the social scene over studying. His grade point average dropped every semester.

His dad died suddenly in 1967, bringing their family to financial ruin. He also flunked out of school. The college notified the draft board he no longer had a student deferment. He was classified as 1-A, eligible for military service effective as of January 1968.

I IIII

INDUCTION

It was 4 a.m. He hadn't slept much. He, his mom, and his brother were driving to the Amtrak station in Hartford for the connection to New Haven. He didn't care much for Hartford. To him it was the city and he was a country boy. His brother parked the car in the train station lot. There was litter everywhere, and the sidewalk was spotted with the usual wrappers, old chewing gum, and hawkers. He had the train ticket given to him by the local draft board so they bypassed the line at the ticket window and walked out onto the platform. Other guys there were his age. He nodded to one or two of them. Like him, they all had an overnight bag with the underwear, toothbrush, and shaving materials the draft board recommended. Off to the side were some Korean and World War II vets proudly wearing their baseball-style hats displaying the treasured American Legion and VFW logos. They had hot coffee and fry cakes for the draftees. One vet who offered him coffee was an amputee.

"Thanks, man," Dyson half mumbled.

"Good luck," the older man said softly and glanced at him without any emotion whatsoever visible behind gray, vacant eyes.

A blue-uniformed conductor announced that all those bound for the New Haven Induction Center should board this car and that car. It was time to say goodbye. Already the specter of the war hung over the crowd, staring down from the unlit spaces and grimy steel girders above—the same specter that had hung over previous wars. His mom teared up as he gave her a hug.

"It's too early to worry about it, Mom," he said. "I may luck out and be sent someplace else."

"I hope so," she said as more tears flowed.

"Take care of Mom," he said. He and his brother shook hands. Then he turned and got aboard.

He found his assigned seat by the window on the west side of the train, but couldn't see his mother and Len on the platform. After a 15-minute delay (unusually short for Amtrak) the train started rolling, headed south slowly. He turned and shook hands with the guy next to him.

"I'm Gary Dyson."

"Al Dwight. Nice to meet you."

‖‖‖

BRAVO COMPANY, BASIC TRAINING CADRE

There were four drill sergeants for the company—one for each platoon. They wore Smokey the Bear hats and a brass badge on the front of their right shirt pocket. Dyson's drill sergeant was Staff Sergeant Grimm—good name for someone who could make your life miserable. Then there were three buck sergeants back from Vietnam. They had the CIB (Combat Infantryman Badge) and highly polished helmet liners. One of them had a large C-shaped pink scar on his right cheek. The drill sergeants were gung-ho Army, the buck sergeants were not. There were also two second lieutenants right out of Officer Candidate School on their first assignments. They called one of them "The Stork" because that's what he looked like.

While three of the drill sergeants were combat vets, Grimm was not. He was a Nebraska Cornhuskers college grad out of Lincoln, had been a baseball and football star all through school, was real smart, and had volunteered for Vietnam but hadn't heard any approval for that decision. He wanted to go and told us so. He was patriotic, and he was devoted to getting us ready for combat.

"I'm hard, but fair," Grimm said. Dyson liked him.

All three buck sergeants were good guys, just biding their time until discharge. The one with the scar, Sergeant Martino, could be aloof and testy at times. Occasionally, they would speak to the guys in a low voice and offer a word of advice. "Buddy-up with someone," "Keep tabs on your buddy," "Cover for each other." Also, "Watch out for booby traps," "Don't trust *any* of them—not even the goddamn kids." They used terms like "gooks," "dinks," and "slope heads."

These people were getting men ready for a war and one war only. Vietnam.

"Everything bad you heard about the place is true." There were false rumors and false stories, horrific stories based on fact, and real stories that were very scary. "And always remember—they can crawl like snakes."

▌▐▐▐▌

Week 3

At 03:00 hours, everyone was rudely awakened two hours early. "What the hell!" Moans and curses started when SFC Grimm announced a change in plans. "EVERYONE is going to pull KP today!"

More moans and curses. "Did I tell ANYONE to talk? DID I? Do you want TWO days of KP?" Everyone shut the hell up. "Now get dressed, make your bunks, and be ready to fall out."

Whenever they went through the chow lines, no matter what mess hall it was, there were always trainees pulling KP. Their faces were not happy. KP was usually a 20-hour day. Dyson remembered hearing about KP from vets when he was a kid. Without fail, some mess hall NCO was screaming at someone about something. Chow was not home cooking by any stretch of the imagination. Just once, it would have been nice to have a casual meal in a mess hall.

"Fall out! Fall out! Move, move, move!" When the cadre, the company NCOs, screamed, everyone in the bay double-timed it from their bunk area out into the company street. "Fall in! Fall in! Come on, people, let's move! You are too slow."

"Dress it up, dress it up!"

"Did you shave this morning? Don't lie to me!"

"You! What platoon are you standing in? Get the fuck behind the guy in front of you. Is this your first day here, asshole?"

"GET SQUARED AWAY, PEOPLE!"

Finally, all was deemed ready and First Sergeant Richards yelled, "Ten-hut!"

Everyone stood at attention, motionless and silent. The sergeants went through the ranks looking for things to bitch about and took a headcount.

"First Platoon all present and accounted for!" a sergeant barked along with a bunch of other military bullshit.

"At ease," the field first yelled. "Listen up, people." Shit, he sounded like he was getting ready to deliver some bad news. Was it that the entire company was going to Vietnam?

"Last night, Robert Kennedy was assassinated."

No one had seen a newspaper since the start of basic training. No TV, no radio. Nobody even knew how the baseball season was going. Now the only news was bad.

"I'm sorry I'm the one to have to tell you people. We don't know a lot right now. But Mr. Kennedy is definitely dead."

▌▏▌▏▌

Week 5

Rush, rush, rush all the time. Yell, scream, curse, insult, push, shove—lots of up close and personal in-your-face "counseling."

He was convinced Army life was not for him, but he chose to

play the game. He had a few incidents with the drill sergeants, but nothing major like some guys encountered. The physical training, long marches, running, and the diet were getting him in better shape than he had ever been. Seventy-seven rungs on the overhead ladders to get to the mess hall. If you fell off, they messed with you. The fat boys were running laps around the mess hall. Leave nothing on your tray when it's turned in. They were "rewarded" by having Sundays off. Sleep in, go to the PX, stop by the beer hall and drink 3.2 beer. Just don't get in any trouble. They had two radios in the sleeping bay. The music helped sometimes.

He knew the break from all the booze and pot was good for him. He wrote his mom and Carol, his girlfriend, once or twice a week, and they wrote back. He and Carol seemed to be getting closer. The prospect of going to Vietnam hung over every trainee, over the entire fort, like a phantom, up there in the sky randomly pointing down, selecting those who go and those who don't.

Gook, dink, and slope head were becoming part of their vocabulary. The bayonet dummies were dressed up in black pajamas and a "non la"—a conical straw hat that is part of the traditional, Vietnamese peasant garb. Simulated ambushes were sprung by training personnel dressed like peasants or with khakis and a pith helmet to look like the North Vietnamese Army enemy. To paraphrase the infamous Indian fighter general, Philip Henry Sheridan, "The only good Indian is a dead Indian."

There was even a class on venereal disease with a movie showing grossly infected genitals. It was far worse than the first-aid movies in high school. The instructor held up a big plastic penis for a teaching device. Then he showed how to put on a rubber. It ripped. He tried another—success. "Use these things, men, and never go bareback!"

I III I

JULY

Graduation

It was the middle of July. First, a wet spring and then the start to a hot summer. The trainees were dressed in khaki uniforms with their little National Defense ribbons and marksmanship badges. Those who had been promoted, Dyson among them, wore their Private (E-2) stripe ("mosquito wings"). Two graduating companies marched into a huge auditorium. Their Bravo Company was on one side, Alpha on the other. Proud parents, wives, siblings, and kids filled the bleachers.

There was a sense of relief at the end of basic. But then what next? Relief and dread at the same time. Now, after completing their Basic Training, they would receive their orders for AIT (Advanced Infantry Training) after the ceremonies. Infantry? Artillery? Armor? Amputee? Killed in Action? Missing?

They were finally ordered to line up in formation in the company street. Duffel bags were packed and on the floor in the barracks next to their bunks.

"All right, all right! Listen up. When I call your name, answer 'Here,' go grab your gear, and form up in front of the Orderly Room." He started on the A's, breezed through the B's and C's, and started going down the D's.

Bingo! Dyson's name was called. "Here!" he barked as he double-timed it over to his duffel bag. Dwight's bag was still there—they had been split up. He almost ran in to SSG Grimm on his way out of the barracks. "Where we going?" He was astonished he had blurted out the question and had not used Grimm's rank, like he was asking some longtime school buddy.

Surprisingly Grimm seemed OK with it—no screaming, no pushups for penance. "You guys lucked out. You're going to Fort

Eustis, Virginia, for Helicopter Maintenance/Crew Member School." A miracle. Grimm even extended his hand for a handshake. "Get ready to be shot at—a lot. Good luck, Dyson. Now get the fuck outside and get in formation!"

I III I

Fort Eustis

All the men going to Fort Eustis filed onto the Trailways bus as an NCO called their names. Their duffel bags were stowed in the luggage compartment. As an added bonus, they all stopped at a New Jersey Turnpike rest area for a meal, paid for with U.S. government vouchers. Over the years, many soldiers from Fort Dix had eaten there under the same conditions.

Around 19:30 hours, the bus stopped at the main gate of Fort Eustis. MPs checking the vehicles entering the fort waved the bus in. After half a mile, they pulled into the Fort Eustis Replacement Center. An NCO who looked like an oversized Boy Scout with a clipboard stepped up into the bus real close to the driver and shouted, "All right, all right. You people are STILL trainees and will obey my orders just like back in basic, understand?"

I III I

AUGUST

It had been four, long weeks of KP, pointless formations, rumors, harassment, police calls, and Charge of Quarters duty, which was sitting in the orderly room to answer the phone from 23:00 hours until reveille. Then there was unarmed guard duty where one man was dropped off at each rifle range to patrol that night to make sure it wasn't vandalized or whatever. Sometimes the men were told what they would be doing the next day, sometimes not. The thirtieth man had joined the class last week and still no orders to start school.

Weren't they in a big hurry to get helicopter crews to Vietnam? Where was the sense of urgency? Hurry up and wait . . .

Their class, designated Bravo Three, began a new routine. Reveille for the entire post was at 05:30 hours followed by falling out for a headcount and inspection by SSG Dodge. Then off to the mess hall, back for Company Formation of all seven classes, and march to the athletic field for PT and calisthenics. There were police calls and work details scattered all over the post, but no KP because it took up too many hours to fit into the school schedule. Thank God. After the noon mess, it was: finish the work details, back to the barracks, class formation, march to class (or a bus if it was too far away), evening mess, more classes until 21:30 hours, back to the barracks, and lights out at 23:00 hours; it was like working evening shift back in the civilian world.

▌▐▐▐▌

SEPTEMBER

Briefing

In the background of all this was the presidential campaign. President Lyndon Baines Johnson had announced he would not seek re-election. LBJ's vice president, Hubert Humphrey, won the Democratic nomination to run against Richard Nixon, the Republican. Dyson's mom sent him an absentee ballot with a stamped-addressed envelope—most GIs voted for Nixon because he said he had a top-secret plan to end the war in Vietnam. It is still top secret; Nixon took his plan with him to the grave.

▌▐▐▐▌

Maintenance/Crewmember School ended the last Friday in September. At 23:00 hours, they were all in their barracks getting ready to turn in. The rumors didn't quit. Some were simply ridiculous, others fucking frightening.

ⅠⅠⅠⅠ Ⅰ

OCTOBER

Of the many euphemisms, acronyms, mottos, and sayings in Army jargon, the prime message was "Hurry up and wait." It was apropos for scores of situations in military life. If you didn't remember this you could go nuts. The men were awakened at 05:30 hours to be somewhere at 09:00 hours. They were double-timed to the dispensary only to stand outside for an hour until the medics were ready. They were marched to begin a new class to find out it was intended to start the next day. One time, they were rushed to eat morning chow, get in formation with full gear, and then double-timed five miles to a rifle range, just to be told the ammo truck would not arrive until 11:00 hours.

Now Bravo 3 was in the fifth week of waiting. The Company had finished AIT and was awaiting leave and assignment orders. The news had been full of big battles and figures of American KIAs and enemy body counts. The generals were pushing hard for more troops to be sent over. Dyson and everybody else wrote home telling their folks they didn't know what the holdup was. Homesickness and frustration were rampant.

ⅠⅠⅠⅠ Ⅰ

NOVEMBER

They had been at Fort Eustis since July, waited to start AIT, then completed that training, and they still did not know when they would get leave and where they were assigned. Would they be home for Thanksgiving? Seven men in the company were AWOL.

It was getting surreal, like a Kafka story, or was it the Twilight

Zone? At PT, the guys were quiet and distant. The Daily Dozen calisthenics were done in a fog, certainly not crisply and uniform in perfect cadence as before. Orders were here, but they weren't. Hurry up and wait.

I III I

Leave

It was the third Wednesday in November. Dyson's orders gave him ten days leave at home. He had to report to the Overseas Processing Center at Fort Dix on December 1, 1968. As a Private E2, he made $113 a month, so he had enough money to fly home. His mom and Len were overjoyed he would be with them for Thanksgiving. They picked him up at Bradley Field in Granby, Connecticut.

He would call Carol first thing in the morning and make plans.

Days would be spent hitting the local bars with his buddies Roy and Bill, drinking shots and beer, an occasional lunch at a pub with great hamburgers, then pile in a car and tour the beautiful Connecticut countryside smoking pot. Nights would be with Carol.

I III I

Dyson tried to spend a respectable amount of time with his mom. His brother joined in the partying with Roy and Bill. He and Carol were together every night. They'd met in high school. They would sneak off to her girlfriend's apartment and use a bedroom. He sure hoped she wouldn't get pregnant. The day before he left, they spent the whole time together at the apartment.

"I'll be with my mom and brother tonight."

"This isn't goodbye, Gary."

"I'm hoping you'll write."

"You write, I'll write. You write, I'll write." She looked into his eyes as she reached up to touch his cheek. "I'm not leaving you."

The time came to leave for LaGuardia Airport.

I III I

DECEMBER

Clipboards and Headcounts

It was dark when the taxi dropped him off at the Fort Dix Overseas Processing Center.

Finally, they were loaded aboard buses to the airport.

At 10:35 hours, the jet was cleared for takeoff. They were flying nonstop to San Francisco.

After setting down in San Francisco, it was on to the next jetliner, this one to Honolulu. Most guys set their watch back three hours.

I III I

They landed in the dark of night in Hawaii and, at 06:45 hours, they boarded again bound for Japan, an eight-hour flight to a one-hour layover. Then came the twenty-four-hundred-mile trip to Vietnam—a one-way trip for some of them.

"Gentlemen," announced the pilot, "we will be landing at Bien Hoa Airport in fifteen minutes." There was no cheering or anything when the landing gear hit the runway.

Someone opened the aircraft's exit door, and the cool air of the cabin was immediately sucked out and the humid, stinking heat of Vietnam saturated the plane. He would remember that putrid smell for the rest of his life.

I III I

Welcome to Vietnam

Sweat soaked their uniforms and poured down their faces. What was that stench? It smelled like smoldering fires and septic tanks. A blue haze hung from thousands and thousands of motor bikes.

I III I

At a supply depot, they were issued their jungle fatigues—the standard in-country work uniform—along with OD (olive drab) socks, boxer shorts, T-shirts, a baseball cap, and a field jacket. They were fitted with jungle boots, a combination canvas and leather with a steel plate in the sole supposedly for protection against stepping on a punji-stake. Then, it was to another supply company for the field gear to wear until they were with their assigned companies—steel pot, helmet liner, flak vest, and utility belt. The last leg of the circuit was where they got their personal M16s, but no ammo. The rifles all showed wear and tear. No telling what their histories were.

"OK, you FNGs," boomed an NCO. "You guys are FNGs. Fucking new guys. Remember that!" There would be a lot more Army jargon to learn. "First rank, in order, head to that aircraft."

The waiting Caribou was a big, goofy-looking cargo ship with a loading ramp in the rear, overhead wings, and two prop-driven engines. It had no seats or benches, you sat on the belly of the plane between the aluminum ribs and struts of the fuselage. The pilot put the plane in a steep climb after takeoff to get above any ground fire and finally leveled off at five thousand feet.

The landing gear hit hard and bounced off the tarmac as they touched down at An Khe. The second time they touched they stayed on the ground and the plane shook with jarring little bumps, like riding on a gravel road, the result of the perforated steel planking used to construct the runway. Sitting on the skin of the aircraft, they felt every single bump as they taxied to a stop. The loading ramp opened and the engines were shut down. They had arrived at Division Headquarters.

I III I

An Khe

An Khe was a sprawling, segmented camp with rolling hills and copses of woods inside the base perimeter. Rocky, rutted roads of laterite, the hard, red clay-like soil that covered large areas of South Vietnam, twisted and turned among the compounds of different brigades and battalions.

A deuce and a half truck ferried his group to the Division Replacement Center at the base of the mountain. It reminded him of pictures of the Wild West towns that sprung up during the gold rush.

The FNGs carried their duffel bags to the company street where a roll call was taken. A stern-looking Master Sergeant addressed the group:

"All of you will remain here until you are transported to your units. When you get in your barracks and your assigned bunk, dig out your shot record. Then you all will be processed into the 2nd Airmobile Division. Welcome."

The 2nd Airmobile Division was infamous for its battles with the North Vietnamese Army and Viet Cong; for burning down entire villages in Zippo parties, named after Zippo lighters; and as baby killers. Back home, the Hells Angels said that any member of the 2nd Airmobile Division was welcomed as an honorary member of their gang.

I III I

Now it was the Friday morning formation, this one led by a Sergeant First Class. "All right, listen up, people. When I call your name, answer 'Here,' and fall out and form up over there," he pointed. No one knew what this list was for. He read about ten names and then called, "Dyson!"

"Here," Dyson said and joined a group that would be flown out to Phuoc Vinh, Division Field Headquarters. They would leave at 11:00 hours on a Chinook cargo helicopter.

I III I

Phuoc Vinh

They headed southwest for the two-hundred-mile trip. He was thinking how they had headed northeast two hundred miles to get to

An Khe from Bien Hoa. Afterwards, he would find out Phuoc Vinh was about twenty-five miles west from Bien Hoa—it took almost three weeks to get there.

The ship set down at Ban Me That for refueling and then continued on to Phuoc Vinh. He remembered reading in history courses that the United States should never get involved in a land war with Asia—a warning trickling down all the way to the individuals now serving in Vietnam.

At last, the ship began a steep descent as they approached Phuoc Vinh, a sprawling camp surrounded by a no-man's land and forests. The ship slowed to a hover just feet off the ground, sending up the usual swirling cloud of choking red dust and debris. A ground crew member guided the pilot down until the wheels touched earth.

I I I I I

They were escorted by an SP5 to a battalion Control Point, or Orderly Room. A few moments later a sergeant and the battalion Sergeant Major came out. The sergeant went through the roll call. All present. The sergeant major was all Army and scanned the men critically.

"Welcome to the 137th Assault Support Helicopter Battalion. Some of you will be assigned here, the rest to different companies in our battalion. Sergeant Baker will sort you out and show you to your barracks. Again, welcome." At least he was decent in talking to the men.

They followed SGT Baker. They stopped at a hootch with its own wall surrounding it and the bunker. "You guys sleep here tonight. There's your bunker. Tomorrow, you will fly to your assigned companies."

Dyson said, "All I see is Hueys. Is this a Chinook outfit?"

"No, it's a Huey battalion. Why?"

"I went to Fort Eustis for Chinook training."

"You know what a tech manual is, don't you?"

He nodded yes.

"You'll be fine. You didn't learn anything in AIT anyway."

So, all the weeks and bullshit didn't mean anything. He was trained, sort of, on Chinooks, and sent to a Huey company.

They went to chow shortly after 18:00 hours. There weren't many guys in the mess hall. Some were still on the flight line, working on ships. Come to find out, this mess hall was open about twenty hours a day because of flight crews and pilots coming and going around the clock. After filling their trays, they sat down among the men already eating. "New guys!" one proclaimed. Brand-new fatigues and looks of bewilderment marked new guys.

"Where are you guys assigned?" asked a hillbilly-looking Spec 4.

"A Company."

"B Company," said Dyson.

"Oh, man. B Company, at Long Thong," said another.

"Why, what's there?" asked Dyson.

"They call it Rocket City." Sounded bad. But it really was just the old guys trying to scare the new guys. Half truth, half bullshit.

"Anyone from California?" asked one old guy.

"I am," said an FNG.

"Well, just keep your hands on the table," and some snickering. "Just kidding, man."

"We're glad you guys are here. We always need more mechanics. Come to think of it, we need more of everybody." It all seemed cool. The chow was good and the milk cold.

After eating, they got ready for tomorrow, wondering what Long Thong was really like. Rock music floated around the area. Some Doors here, Janice Joplin there. The sun was setting over the Cambodian border twenty-five miles away on the Fish Hook and Parrot's Beak region that was the NVA's backyard and stomping ground. Red and orange clouds with gold outlines. He told himself he must start taking pictures of these beautiful skies.

‖‖‖

Darkness brought more music. Dyson and another FNG, Robbie, walked next door where men were smoking cigarettes. "Hi, new guys," said one of the men, shirtless and wearing a headband. They started shaking hands and giving names. There was small talk of assignments and duties and then "Come on in."

In the hootch, thick, blue, pot smoke hung in the air. There was a hard-to-get TEAC reel-to-reel tape recorder playing a jam tape—Hendrix, Spirit, and Creedence.

"Aren't you guys afraid of getting busted?" Robbie asked.

"Nah. You'll see. At night, the lifers stay in the NCO club drinking and the officers stay in their club drinking." Some hootches were smokers' hootches, others were drinking hootches. "You can tell by the music. Country it's drinkers, rock for stoners." They would see it was true, everywhere.

Most of these guys wore trip glasses, headbands, peace symbols, and beads. A Sherlock Holmes-style pipe was passed around packed full of glowing Golden Triangle pot. The gooks called it "dinky-dow" (dien cai dao) The world's best. It came from the triangle at the borders of Laos, Cambodia, and South Vietnam. Everyone got stoned on their first hit. They also used the phonetic term "dinky-dow" to mean "crazy." Seems like most times they went together hand in hand.

Dyson had never smoked anything like this stuff. He just sat back and let others do the talking. He didn't want to do anything to ruin it. Smoking with no worry about being caught. Jim Morrison was singing "The Crystal Ship." Dyson lit a Camel. He drifted into the conversation, then out of it. Something was hilarious but he wasn't sure what. He laughed at Robbie laughing. Robbie's laugh made everyone laugh. It was contagious.

It got to be 23:00 hours. Dyson joined Robbie headed back to their hootch.

"Man, that stuff was great. Did you get off?"

"Did I get off!? I am fucked UP!"

In a few minutes, Dyson was in his bunk. He slipped into sleep. That night he had Cecil B. DeMille, cast of thousands, multi-technicolor dreams in a deep, restful slumber. The hell with the war. If every night could be like this . . .

At 05:50 hours the Charge of Quarters (CQ) officer woke up the transients. He turned on the row of fluorescent lights hanging above the center aisle. "OK, FNGs, let's go. Time to get up. Shave, eat chow, get all packed up, and we are going to fly you out of here." He was the first guy ever to wake them up without being an asshole about it. That was wonderful, and Dyson realized he was still pleasantly half-stoned.

On the way to the mess hall, he noticed the flood lights on the flight line with men working on the Hueys. Did they work all night?

There was plenty on the chow line—French toast, scrambled eggs (powdered), hash browns, grits, oatmeal, toast, orange juice, coffee, and cold milk. They sat near some guys who had been working and were sooty with red dust, grease on their skin and T-shirts. They got few murmurings of "hi" and "hello." Everyone knew they were transients.

"Where you guys going?"

"A Company."

"B Company," said Dyson.

"Oh, shit. Long Thong. Rocket City." It was the second time he'd heard that. The chit-chat remained friendly. One guy had a peace symbol on a necklace. Another wore root-beer-colored trip glasses. It made him smile.

Suddenly, there was a loud WHUMP! and everyone jumped. For a split second it seemed like the place was suspended in air during the lag time of hearing and reacting. All the men in the entire dining area were up and running when the second WHUMP hit. Ten men made it through the same door in just a couple seconds. Then WHUMP. WHUMP. WHUMP-WHUMP-WHUMP!

Mortars. Enemy mortars. They were in the bunker now. The cooks had beat them to it. At least twenty mortars had landed. More kept coming, louder and closer, making flashes on the sandbags outside their bunker. WHUMP! WHUMP. WHUMP-WHUMP-WHUMP!

"Oh, shit."

More rounds, with some impacting real close on the rock-hard red clay, detonating, spitting shrapnel ground level and higher.

Then they stopped. It was quiet except for the ringing in his ears.

A couple of the cooks started to leave. "No, man," someone said, "stay here for a while."

After three minutes, they came again. WHUMP! WHUMP! WHUMP! At least six exploded close by. Remember to remain in the bunker after "the last round."

It was ten minutes until someone yelled, "All clear! All clear!" How the hell did this guy know it was all clear? Did he know that the gooks had fired their last round? But he was right and gradually people came out of the bunkers. Lifers went around making sure everyone was accounted for. The sun was rising and so was the humidity.

Most of the mortars had landed on the hard earth. But a few hootches had major damage. The rounds pierced their metal roofs and exploded. When they got back to their hootch, they saw where one round landed inside the wall running around their place, between the barracks and bunker, sending shrapnel through the clapboards and tearing into two wall lockers, a footlocker and two bunks. One of them was his.

What if he and Robbie and the rest had still been in the hootch? What if they had been walking in the open to the mess hall?

The Battalion area took forty-four hits with no casualties. The neighboring company sustained sixteen hits with two KIAs and four wounded. Two men were medevac'd. What's with this getting hit in the early morning? At breakfast? In the mess hall? As long as they were under the open sky everyone was in danger. Anywhere. Anytime.

Long Thong

The CQ, SP5 Darrow, rounded up the transients and took a roll call. "OK. Dyson, Ellis, Garrett, McMann, Peters, Stevens, and Williams, you guys go to Bravo Company, Long Thong-Rocket City." Third time he heard that nickname. "The rest of you go to Alpha Company, Lai Khe. Hang loose around this hootch until I come get you."

"You guys in Bravo Company, get all your gear outside and we'll truck you to the flight line."

The sun was up, and it was getting hot. Dyson was still a little stoned. Somewhere nearby, the Chambers Brothers were doing "Time Has Come Today." A three-quarter-ton truck from the motor pool picked them up along with Darrow. Instead of having the new guys carry their gear a quarter-mile, this time there was transportation. Dyson felt he was becoming part of a unit. The truck stopped along a line of Hueys. There they were—the Bell UH-1s. He didn't know shit about these utility helicopters. But then again, he didn't know shit about the Chinook either. Some ships were being worked on, some running up, some idle, and some had pilots making pre-flight inspections. Shacks were scattered around the tarmac. A big steel building in the center of the camp just off the flight line was used for a hangar. It looked like four ships were undergoing major work in there. Rotors were off and much of their skins removed.

SP5 Darrow checked his notes and pointed. "OK, you guys, you are going on this ship, *024* (pronounced "zero-two-four," as all tail numbers are). And listen up. Whatever you do, stay away from these tail rotors. Ya hear? Stay away from the tail rotors! They are killers. Keep your wits about you. Look where you're going. It is so easy to walk into a practically invisible tail rotor while you're walking around these things. It happens everywhere, guys walking into the tail rotor and they're dead—no survivors. It happens in camp; it happens in the field. These things have killed enlisted men, NCOs, officers, medics, 11 Bravos. Everyone, everyone, everyone. Ya hear?"

They all said they did. They saw he was dead serious, but some guys would never learn.

"Hang loose right until the crew lets you know when to board. Goodbye, guys, and good luck." As he walked away, Darrow hoped to God all the new guys had listened to him.

They watched ships come and go. There was another aviation unit at the far end of the flight line. He could plainly see that those Hueys were armed with different combinations of armament—rocket pods of different sizes, fixed electric miniguns, and crew-served M60 machine guns, the standard weapon of helicopter door gunners. One ship had its rocket pods painted like Schlitz beer cans. Another had a pair of Texas longhorns mounted on its front. Some of the pilots wore black Stetsons, like cavalry officers of the old West.

A crew chief and door gunner in their flame-retardant, Nomex, flight fatigues touched base with the guys and confirmed they were going to Long Thong. The entire crew was poking into everything: rotors, drivetrain, engine. They had a conference outside the cockpit. An aircraft commander and co-pilot were dropped off by jeep and they too started going over the ship. The AC had a cool, waxed, handle-bar mustache and a pearl-handled six-gun for a sidearm.

The pilots got in their seats. The crew chief and gunner checked and loaded their M60s. They had their flight helmets on. The crew chief motioned to the guys to come over. "OK, you, you and you sit here, here and here."

The gunner had instructions for the guys beside him. "Sit like this. And don't worry about falling out."

The AC yelled, "Clear!" and the ship started to run up. The crew members communicated with each other through their flight helmets. The engine reached the proper RPMs, the ship taxied on a route to the flight line. The nose was facing down the airfield at a hover. They got the go-ahead from someone somewhere and proceeded down the line, gaining speed. The steep ascent started toward five thousand feet for the thirty-mile trip to Long Thong. Here he was, flying in a Huey in Vietnam.

As they gained altitude, more and more of the beautiful countryside stretched before them. He saw a large town and villages of different sizes separated by rice paddies. Rice paddies everywhere, many of them centuries old. And unending bomb craters of various sizes. One end of a village looked like it had been wiped off the map. Was that intentional? What happened to the villagers? They passed a few U.S. bases and the air traffic picked up. Hueys, Chinooks, and fixed-wing aircraft everywhere. And then two huge bases, Bien Hoa and Long Binh. They were flying over the city they landed in three weeks ago. Amazing.

Their ship flew right over Long Binh, astounding with its permanent buildings of steel and concrete, rows of shiny metal barracks scattered about like housing developments back home, three- and four-story buildings, concrete sidewalks, airfields (not just one), and artillery companies in massive concrete and sandbag revetments. The huge outdoor amphitheater was where Bob Hope and other celebrities put on USO shows. To Dyson, it was nothing short of amazing how permanent everything was here to stay.

The 93rd Medical Evacuation Hospital was festooned with large red crosses on white backgrounds. Open twenty-four hours a day, seven days a week, no cover charge. Hueys like theirs were landing with wounded GIs from some battle somewhere.

On the descent, the new guys shifted in their seats. The land below them was pock-marked with hundreds of craters. Now, they were a couple hundred feet over the perimeter around Long Thong. He could still see Long Binh, but his gaze was now checking out the camp defenses. The tree line stopped two hundred meters from camp, but closer at the other end. Rows and rows of concertina wire lay on the ground like spilled Slinky toys, with metal stakes holding them in place. The green line—the camp perimeter—was a bulldozed earth berm. There were machine gun bunkers of all sorts every hundred feet or so. One in every five or six bunkers was a watchtower made of railroad ties, steel, lumber, and sandbags. At one was a deuce and a half with four .50 caliber Browning machine guns mounted in a single unit called a Quad 50. They descended to a few feet above the ground, continued to a designated area, and set down. A four-by-eight-foot hand-lettered sign in big letters said, "Welcome to Long Thong—Rocket City."

"OK, you guys," shouted the crew chief. "You all get off this side, walk STRAIGHT toward that shack."

After days and days of bullshit, work details, and KP, the FNGs had finally made it to their unit. It was Christmas Eve, 1968.

‖‖‖

Bravo Company, 137th ASH BN

A Spec 4 joined them. "Hey, new guys. I'm Jensen, the company clerk. We'll go to the orderly room first, over there." And they all headed off again, lugging their gear, duffel bags, and weapons through the midday heat and humidity. Leave your gear here but take your M16s. No ammo, right?"

Everyone confirmed they had no ammo.

"Don't leave your M16 anywhere but in your wall locker. They are really big on finding an M16 somebody left somewhere. You'll get an Article 15, busted down one grade, pay a fine, pay for the M16, and fill many sandbags. Got it?"

Everyone confirmed they got it.

"This is great," said Jensen, "no one else is here," meaning the orderly room was empty. Everyone was either at work or getting ready for Christmas. He had them sign into the company on some sort of log-roster. There were forms about next of kin, religious preference, and life insurance beneficiaries. They verified the serial numbers on their M16s on the company inventory.

"I'll take you guys to your hootches," Jensen said. "I got a list here of who goes where according to where you're going to work. Follow me." They all carried their equipment to a first hootch. "Garrett and Peters, you guys are here in the Avionics hootch." Two hootches down he said, "Dyson, Ellis, and McMann, you're here in Maintenance for now. Maintenance is the biggest section we have, but we're in for a change of some sort."

"Dyson, you're at the end." Nice, he thought. "Garrett, there, and McMann, over here. Get settled and hang loose. Someone will be here in a while to show you around. I'm glad you guys are here. There's a lot of work to do all the time, but this isn't a bad company to be in at all, believe me. For your mailing address, just copy that sign over there," he pointed. It read, "Bravo Company, 137th ASH BN 2nd Airmobile Division."

I III I

This chicken coop of wood and metal would be their home for the next year. They could finally unpack for good and spread out. They had some stability and would be performing work every day instead of pulling details and KP.

Dyson distributed his field gear like the others in the hootch, which was neat and orderly. The concrete floor had broom trails on it with random designs outlined in the stubborn red dust. There was a thin layer of it on just about every surface. And it settled in all the pores. In one direction were the latrines, outhouses seating six each. The other way was a company shave and shower station. It had a row of sinks and mirrors, and a room with six shower heads. The gravity-feed water was pumped from a water truck into a large steel shipping container from a gas-turbine helicopter engine. Amazingly, a kerosene field heater underneath heated the water so there would be no ice-cold showers. Sandbagged walls and revetments were everywhere. Big bunkers, little bunkers, and trenches. The mess hall had pipe chimneys poking through the roof. The company command post displayed an amateurish hand-painted sign that proclaimed "Bravo Company, 137th ASH Battalion, Killer Bees" and a crude cartoon of a killer bee made to look like a Huey. The supply building, heavily bunkered and sandbagged, incorporated the ammo bunker. Down near the flight line was the motor pool. Companies of various sorts were scattered all over the camp that looked to be a half mile across and a half mile wide.

Jensen stopped by. He said the first sergeant wanted to see all the new guys who came in today. "Make sure you're in full uniform," he said. They all headed to the orderly room. Outside the door, he said, "Form a rank right here facing this way."

First Sergeant Roland Peterson wore immaculately pressed jungle fatigues and spit-shined boots. He had a close military haircut and a finely stenciled mustache. He was kind of overweight and looked like he could be a prick. He stood centered in front of them and eye-balled each man.

"At ease, men. I'm Bravo Company First Sergeant Peterson. This is a working company. We put in a lot of long days keeping these Hueys in the air. They never have enough Hueys. I hope you guys are up to working like this, along with the duty roster of guard duty and KP." KP again.

"Keeping the Hueys airborne is the primary mission of this company. The work comes first. But you will also play by the rules. I know today and tomorrow are holidays, so I will give you until Friday to get all insignia, last name, and rank sewn on your uniforms. Friday, understand?"

Everyone said they understood.

"Jensen will fill you in on getting that done." He went down the rank to each man, shook his hand, asked his full name, sometimes asked where they were from, and said welcome to Bravo Company.

"Your section chiefs will get you started working tomorrow. Now go get some chow."

In the mess hall, a couple of cooks with a keen sense of the obvious announced their arrival.

"Hey, it's the new guys."

"Look, FNGs."

Only a few others were eating just yet. The hellos and small talk were friendly and upbeat. The cooks wore white T-shirts, white hats, and white aprons. A black cook said, "I'm Floaty. Everyone calls me Floaty." Right away Dyson liked Floaty.

Dyson and Robbie sat at a table next to some sooty, grimy mechanics. There were a couple handshakes and questions like where you from? When did you get in-country?

Everyone heard about the mortar attack at Phuoc Vinh the night before. "You guys know what mortars sound like now?" asked Floaty.

Another guy said, "Now you'll have to learn what rockets sound like. They come in quicker than mortars. Mortars go like WHUMP and rockets go like SSSSS-KA-BOOM."

Was he kidding or serious?

"They have been getting more active around here lately," said a mechanic named Kranicki. "We didn't have anything for a long time, and they've started their shit day and night."

"Last week, a Huey approaching camp got shot up pretty bad."

"Then a one-o-seven came in, and that was it." That was a 107mm rocket, used along with 120mm rockets—the two main Communist-made rockets that the NVA and VC fired on Americans by the thousands.

"They may make a big attack on these ships sometime," someone said softly.

The menu listed "beef patty" for the main course. There were debates all over Vietnam just what this patty was made of. They came in OD coffee-can-size cans, dehydrated, stacked like buffalo chips, and almost white in appearance. They had a circular grain pattern getting smaller and smaller down to nothing in the middle. The meat looked like it was cut out of the asshole of the steer. When tasted without gravy, it could have been chicken, beef, pork, turkey, horse, who-knows-what?

More men were coming into the mess hall. Among them was the mess sergeant, Sergeant First Class Broyer, who waddled around behind the chow line. Everyone called him Pops. He looked way too old to be in the Army. He was an alcoholic, drunk most of the time. The booze had aged him more than a few years.

Music was drifting from the barracks. Janis Joplin from one, Jesse Colin Young and the Youngbloods from another. Some guys only had a towel wrapped around their midsection as they headed for the showers. And an exclamation or two like, "Hey, new guys."

Then it started.

"Fifteen days, motherfucker!" yelled one guy.

"Thirty-one days," yelled another.

These guys were "short" and going home soon. Everyone kept a running count of exactly how many days they had left in-country. Some guys updated the number on their steel pots, some kept calendars on their wall lockers, some just had a large numeral they changed daily. Dyson had more than three hundred days to go. He would figure it out exactly sometime real soon—the number of days until December 7, 1969. Pearl Harbor Day.

When Dyson, Robbie Ellis, and Allen McMann entered their hootch, someone said, "Hey, new guys. Merry Christmas." His name was Benson. He was an SP4. Everyone called him "Spook." He had a big, smoking bowl of Golden Triangle pot. It was a bamboo shoot three sections long with an empty brass 40mm grenade shell for a bowl, and it was packed. "Here," he offered. The three new arrivals each took a hit as Hendrix started "All Along the Watch Tower."

"Sit somewhere," Spook said. "Pick yourselves up some folding chairs at the PX when you can." For now, they sat on footlockers and on empty wooden shipping crates. Three more men had entered the hootch and plunked down near them. "Aahhh . . . my favorite time of the day," said one. Now two big bowls were going around. Just the smell of this stuff was enough to get you high. Introductions flowed.

"Dyson," he said.

"McMann."

Spook pointed out three other guys. "That's OD. That's Ramirez. And that's Super Chicken, Soup, for short. And this is our hootch." There were handshakes and nods. Dyson took another toke, a big one, on the Super Bowl, as the bamboo pipe was called. God this stuff was incredible.

They slipped into casual talk, using the hippie and rock music jargon of back in "the World." The World was back home, the U.S.A.

"You're gonna meet Brady tomorrow," Spook said. "He's our maintenance chief NCO-SFC Tommy Brady. He's also in charge of our hootches." There were eight maintenance hootches with about ten men each. It was the largest section in the company.

"What's he like?" asked McMann, exhaling a thick cloud.

"Well," Spook said, "he can be a prick when he wants to be. Getting the work done is the main thing. And keep the barracks about like this, you'll be OK."

Dyson was seeing what he heard about. The lifers stayed in their clubs at night drinking, and the men stayed in their places smoking and drinking. The songs on this reel-to-reel of Spook's seemed endless. It looked like only about a quarter of the tape had been played so far. He could faintly hear Patsy Cline when there was a gap in their music.

"Can you believe it's Christmas, man?"

"No, man."

"I mean, if you told me last Christmas I would be here for this Christmas, I'd say you were damn crazy, man."

"Fate."

"Let's talk about fate," said OD.

"Yeah, like who determines fate?"

"Do you believe in karma or anything like that?"

Some guys chose to sit back and stay out of this topic. Others were brought up and then discarded. The minutes ran into hours.

"OK, everyone, let's stay up until midnight. Just to see the start of Christmas."

"I'll try, but I don't know."

"I'm going outside for a while," said Robbie, standing.

"Yeah, let's." Dyson rose. The others got up and walked outside. Two guys brought their lawn chairs, the rest sat or leaned on the revetment. Three very different sounds came out of the nearby hootches—Hendrix, Tammy Wynette, and Marvin Gaye. There wasn't a Christmas decoration in sight.

It was a moonless night. But the stars were out, millions of them. Close to the equator like this, many, many more stars were visible than up north. Bright starlight illuminated the camp. Dyson gazed upward. God, look at them. Clouds of galaxies he never saw before.

No one was talking much. Dyson bummed a cigarette. He would buy Camels tomorrow at the PX. He knew it would help disguise the smell of any pot smoke on him.

"Wish Tyler was here," OD said.

"Who's Tyler?" McMann asked.

"One of you guys is Tyler's replacement in this hootch. A couple weeks ago, the gooks mortared us. Tyler got killed by the first round." He pointed. "Right over there. On his way to chow."

"Tyler was the most liked guy in the company. He always knew what to say."

"Yeah, and he was funny. Once he called a full-bird colonel 'Duck.'"

Everyone chuckled. They had started to talk about fate.

❙ ❙❙❙ ❙

Christmas Day, 1968

The CQ, Private First Class Peter Green, made damn sure each of them was awake. "Come on, Dyson, it's time to get up. McMann, you awake, man? Come on, come on."

No one was bitching. It was Christmas. As was usual each morning, Ramon Ramirez lit a Salem cigarette before getting out of bed. Pot pipes and big bags of gold grass lay everywhere out in plain sight. The tops of the footlockers looked like they had been sprinkled with gold dust crowned with big buds of pot. Nobody worried about getting busted.

"OK," said Green. Having a permanent CQ worked best for everyone. A new CQ every night of the duty roster was a pain in the ass. PFC Green got to know where every man bunked, exactly who had to be awakened every morning and at what time. Plus, he was a good man. "You guys can work today, or you can go to Long Binh for a Christmas service. Deuce and a half will take you if you want to go, but I need a headcount first of who wants to go."

Two SP4s in the hootch, Maris and Abbott, said they would go. Not so much for the service, but to get out of Long Thong for the day, four or five miles away. There was plenty of opportunity to get stoned for the trip.

No sooner had Green left than SFC Brady entered. It was the first time McMann, Robbie, and Dyson saw him. He was a powerful little NCO, with big forearms and a bull neck. He got right down to business, like he didn't even see the pipes and the pot. He shook hands with the new guys.

"Glad you're here, we need you." He seemed likable but he was still a lifer in their book. "OK. Maris and Abbott are going to Long Binh for Christmas. The rest of you down to the flight line and start breaking in the new guys."

Before leaving for the next hootch, Brady said there was a big holiday breakfast this morning and then special mess that night, with no Vietnamese day laborers. The local civilians worked on practically all U.S. bases. They were hootch maids, laundry workers, barbers, tailors, and massage ladies. Their hootch had a maid named Tug who made the beds, changed the linens, swept, and dusted the place, and made sure the laundry was done. She also would get all their insignias, names, and ranks on their uniforms before Friday.

Some of the locals performed duties in the mess hall, but KPs from the company were needed for early morning and evening assignments as the day laborers did not live on post. They were paid once a month by an NCO managing and monitoring their work. This system with Vietnamese civilians freed up the GIs for their missions. Many, many Vietnamese depended on the U.S. military one way or another for income. Dyson would soon find out the massage ladies were almost all prostitutes.

▌▐▐ ▌

"Listen," said Spook. "We'll all eat together and leave together, come back here, have a toke or two, and go to the flight line."

As they walked to the mess hall, the guys yelled "Merry Christmas!" to another group.

"Merry Christmas, assholes," they replied.

"And Merry Christmas to you, too, you son of a gook whore!"

"I like when your mom leans over my bathtub, teat-fucks me, and garfs my gas bubbles!"

"Your momma is so fat, she can kick-start a B52!"

It was all good-natured. The more obscene the insult, the funnier it was.

Overnight, the cooks and KPs had transformed the mess hall. Tinfoil garlands ran everywhere, laundry soap was piled in places like snow, a dummy Santa Claus clutched an M16, and *Playboy* centerfolds had homemade Santa hats taped to them. The chow line was really special: fresh eggs done to order, pancakes, hot oatmeal, bacon, sausage, ham, grits, warm toast, orange juice, coffee, and cold milk. Someone even made non-alcoholic eggnog. Wow, this was really nice. There were a couple of KPs, but not like his previous experiences. Sure, it was still clean, clean, clean, but here it was slow-paced and low stress.

The mess sergeant, SFC "Pops" Broyer, continued stumbling around behind the chow line. Specialist Jessers, known to all as Floaty, was really the man responsible for everything that was good about the mess hall. Jessers, an Alabama-born black guy from a long line of sharecroppers, was the cool, down-to-earth supervisor of those pulling KP.

The mess hall was a large wood-framed building with a metal roof, screened above chest level, and sandbagged and bunkered outside. In one corner, two tables were isolated by a chest-high wall for the semi-private dining of the CO and his cadre. In the back was an open area beneath a metal roof. Kerosene heaters provided all the hot water needed, and KPs would work there out of the sun and rain. The mess hall also had chimney pipes sticking up into the air that could be a target for Communist mortar and rocket and teams. The hangar, water towers, and any visible antennae were also targets. It was said that VC rocketeers could put a 107mm or 120mm rocket down a mess hall smokestack from one mile out. Asians had been using rockets in warfare for two thousand years.

The men filed out and joined up at their hootch. "Let's get a buzz on before we go," said Super Chicken as he produced a big bowl ready to fire up.

"I got these menthol Marlboro Greens," Ramirez said. Marlboro Greens were one of the many items on the black market. Dope dealers would carefully open the cellophane, remove the cigarettes, blow the tobacco out with a bicycle pump, fill the empty cigarettes with Golden Triangle pot, and reseal the cellophane to look like the Marlboros were factory direct. A pack went for the outrageous price of two dollars, MPC. Mocked as "Monopoly money," Military Payment Currency was issued to all U.S. military personnel in place of American greenbacks and was only worth a few pennies on the dollar.

"I've got this opium-laced Cambodian red hash," Spook said.

"Hey, save that for later when we don't have to work." said someone.

"Yeah, that may be a good idea."

Dyson, Ramirez, and OD shared a Marlboro Green. The others fired up their bowl.

"Merry Christmas" was exchanged again and again.

❙❙❙❙❙

At the flight line, the group split up. Spook and Ramirez took Dyson under their wing that day. There were mechanics everywhere working on the Hueys. There were guys mostly on engines, but also new parts installations, electric and hydraulic work, and a tail rotor replacement. It was 06:45 hours and already getting hot. Guys wore T-shirts or no shirt at all. Many exhibited the red soil-colored tan GIs got from working in the sun. Dyson couldn't wait to get tan. Some wore necklaces of beads and peace symbols, some had colored trip-glasses on, and others had the military-approved, stylish, Ray-Ban aviator-framed sunglasses—the only ones authorized by the Army.

"Sergeant Brady floats all over the place," Spook said. "He really does know a lot of these things and knows the tech manual like the back of his hand. He will probably be giving you new guys a tryout." Dyson learned that drill at Fort Eustis.

Spook looked around to see if it was safe and lowered his voice, "We usually don't smoke down here. Too many lifers floating around all the time. Smoke someplace else and be careful during the day. But nighttime, shit, everyone does their own thing. Drink, smoke, whatever."

Dyson saw that the men worked diligently. It was Christmas morning, but these ships had to fly and others coming in needed work. A whole day off with no maintenance or repairs could put a real hurt on the missions. This was serious business.

Spook and Ramirez took Dyson from ship to ship, looking at the work, pointing out this, that, and the other thing, introducing him to the guys in maintenance at Avionics and the "body shop" where the Hueys' aluminum skins were repaired or replaced and painted. At the Operations office, guys were on the radio communicating with everyone involved with the missions. Emergencies were common. These guys had to be sharp in receiving and relaying messages. Misstating an aircraft tail number or a six-digit location on the map could kill people. Ramirez introduced him to SP5 Taylor. "Gator" Taylor was the number one man in company operations, recognized all over the battalion for his professionalism and keeping cool under pressure. He could remember tail numbers and call signs from days before. He had a memory like an elephant. And he liked to smoke pot, but off-duty only.

Like every day on the flight line, there were no signals for mealtimes. Everyone went to chow when they could break away. The guys decided to skip lunch in the mess hall and go back to the hootch for a bit, have a cold beer or two, a smoke, and then some more orientation. During the blazing afternoon, Spook, Ramirez, and Dyson walked down to the green line, the camp defensive perimeter, which was manned at all times, especially at night. Under Spook's direction they headed for one large bunker.

This was the part of the defensive perimeter assigned to Bravo

Company. It was a command bunker from which an officer of the guard would oversee the two bunkers to the left and the two to the right. It was built right into the six-foot berm bulldozed around the entire camp, walled by sandbags and fifty-five-gallon drums filled with dirt. The roof was made of steel tarmac panels, thick wooden timbers supplied by the engineers, and layers of sandbags. Three guards were stationed, and one could take a nap while the other two were on watch, taking turns dozing on the folding cot. The guards could stand up and peer over the firing port sill while manning an M60 or M16.

"Spook, my man," greeted an SP4 named Gilbert. "Hey, new guys." He seemed friendly enough.

"This is Dyson," Spook said. "This is Gilbert, that's Rollie, and that guy napping is Truly." Then he added, "Yours Truly."

"Good to meet you." Dyson shook hands.

"Anything going on?" asked Spook.

"Not a thing. Not a thing."

"Oh, yeah, well how about this?" Ramirez produced another Marlboro Green.

A quick look outside confirmed the coast was clear. Two joints were lit and passed around between the six men.

"Ooohhhhh . . . stingy, huh?" A third was lit. Two men per joint. Not a bad ratio.

An M60 was resting on the firing port sill, aimed at the woods. Bare red sunbaked soil stretched all the way to the woods. Rows and rows and rows of coiled razor wire were strung around the entire camp. Steel fence stakes held the wire in place. There were dozens of Claymore mines (from the Scottish Gaelic *claidheamh* "sword" + *mòr* "great") and hundreds of trip flares. The bunker's mine detonators, which looked like staple guns, sat at both ends of the firing port. There were also plenty of hand grenades and smoke grenades.

"Fuck this stupid war."

"Amen, brother."

The talk drifted casually between what's happening back in the

World, to where you from, ever been to, and how we heard this and that.

"Boy, not many guys went to Long Binh today."

"No, not many at all. Top said only eight guys." (Top was a nickname for a 1st sergeant.)

"They still having big demonstrations back home?" one of the guards asked Dyson.

"Yeah, they're all over the place. They take over university headquarters now. Even pour blood on Selective Service files."

"You're shitting me."

"No. Someone broke into a draft board and poured blood all over them."

"Hot damn. Ain't that a bear."

They decided to all try to meet up at the mess hall around 18:00 hours for the Christmas dinner.

"I know for a fact that Gator and Floaty have been working their asses off for our dinner tonight," said Spook.

"Ya gotta love them guys," Ramirez added.

And out the three men went toward Bravo Company area, stoned in the sunshine.

▌▐▐▐ ▌

They hadn't had a meal since breakfast and the pot gave them the munchies. The company area had guys walking all over it—to the mail room, to the showers, and to the mess hall. The guys were in a good mood. There were Merry Christmas greetings along with the usual good-natured taunts and insults. The ever-present sound of aircraft and artillery was in the distance.

The guys were greeted in the mess hall with handshakes from the CO, Major Kendall Sliman, and the 1st Sgt. "Merry Christmas. Merry Christmas. Hey, new guys," MAJ Sliman said, "glad you're here." Dyson and the guys all had red eyes and probably smelled like pot, but neither Top nor the CO seemed to notice, or they didn't care.

"Nice to be here, sir," said Dyson.

"I'm gonna get with you new guys tomorrow morning for a bit. I like to know my men and who they are." He seemed genuine.

"Looking forward to it, sir," said McMann, almost emotionless.

The Christmas dinner chow line was an impressive spread for a drab mess hall in Vietnam. Frozen turkeys had been sent to these sites all over South Vietnam. Floaty and Gator knew exactly how to prepare the birds, serving and carving two at a time. There was piping hot white and dark meat, savory stuffing, and wonderful thick gravy. Gator supervised the making of the mashed potatoes, sweet potatoes, and green peas. There was cranberry sauce, honest-to-goodness fresh baked rolls, and butter. Not oleo, but real butter. Just for today.

For dessert, Floaty baked deep-dish apple pies in 18-by-24-inch baking tins, and they turned out perfect. Gator kept busy making sure everything was available to everyone so no one missed out on anything. Pops was stumbling around in his habitual alcoholic daze doing next to nothing.

Along the chow line everyone was showing their pleasure and amazement. This was a dinner, not "chow." There were still men working on the ships, but there was plenty of food so no one would miss out. As the first men through the line sat down with their food, a chaplain entered the mess hall.

"Men, can I have your attention please?" The place quieted down. "OK," . . . said the chaplain, "it's impossible for everyone to be here at once, but we will say grace." He looked around, then began, "Bless us, O Heavenly Father " and went on to thank God for this food, their loved ones back home, the safety of the men, and those who prepared the meal. An "Amen" from everybody followed.

"Seconds! Seconds!" came a voice from behind the chow line. "Come on guys, we have plenty. There are still some birds we haven't carved yet." The food was fantastic, a sensational boost to morale, a godsend.

Tonight, Dyson would write his mom and tell her of this wonderful Christmas meal and not to worry. Then he would write

Carol his longest letter yet. But right now, he and his friends were finishing dessert along with a cup of hot coffee. They made it a point to go and shake hands with Gator and Floaty.

"Thanks, man. This is fantastic."

"Love you, man."

"If you ever need anything."

"God bless you, Gator."

The CO and 1st sergeant were oblivious to the fact Floaty and Gator had made the Christmas dinner—not drunken, old-man Broyer.

Outside now, Dyson lit a Camel and heard some familiar music with a message just right for the moment. It was the guys in the Avionics hootch singing, a cappella, to the tune of "Oh, Christmas Tree."

"We like it here, we like it here,
You're fuckin' A we like it here.
We shine our boots, we shine our brass,
We ain't got time to wipe our ass.
Although we get malaria,
we still maintain our area.
We like it here, we like it here,
You're fuckin' A we like it here."

▌ ▌▌ ▌

After Christmas

Reveille was at 05:30 hours every day for the mechanics' hootches. Green, the CQ, woke the men up without being an asshole about it. "Five-thirty, guys, five-thirty." Then he would turn on the fluorescent lights running down the center aisle. "Come on, don't go back to sleep." He made sure each guy was awake as he went down the lines of bunks and out to the next hootch. The guys were swinging out of bed and getting dressed. Ramirez lit up a Salem. Most mornings Brady would walk through the hootches saying good morning and also making sure everyone was up. The camp was stirring.

As soon as they were ready, some of the men headed for the mess hall for morning chow. One guy had a towel wrapped around himself heading to the showers. This was Private First Class Dan O'Grady from Pittsburgh, a big guy with red hair and ruddy complexion.

Someone yelled, "Hey, Grady. Let's see that thing," and a chorus went up, "Yeah, whip it out!" What the hell was this about?

"Ready?" Grady says.

"Yeah, do it!"

Grady held the towel up with one hand and with the other swiped the towel away and grabbed his cock. It was enormous! Dyson had never seen one that big in his life—nor, it seemed, had anyone else. "Holy shit!"

Grady wrapped his hand around the base of it and started swinging it. It had a huge head overhanging the shank. Some guys cheered. Dyson could plainly see the veins in the darned thing, as round as a big cucumber. He became conscious of staring at it and looked toward the mess hall.

"Just wait," said Spook, "you'll see what a star he is around here."

"He's got all kinds of stories about women seeing that thing."

"When are the whores coming back?" asked Ramirez. He was referring to the prostitutes who were "smuggled" into camp.

"Saturday," said someone.

"Just wait till you see Grady and the whores."

"Wait till you see him sleeping with a hard-on," Spook said, with a laugh. "Oh, man."

The camp was getting back to normal after Christmas, but the chow line would feature leftover turkey for a couple of days. Gator and Big Floaty were doing their usual to make sure the guys ate well.

"Thanks for yesterday, man." Those words were said over and over.

"Did you like that?" Gator said without looking up.

"Yes. Thank you," said Dyson. He and "Georgia" Gator shook hands.

When they got back to the hootch, Brady was there. "Right now," he said, "before you go to work, you guys need to move the bunks around any way you want and set up two new bunks and wall lockers. The bunks are outside leaning against the hootch. They'll be here this afternoon sometime." Then he left.

They were getting two more new guys. "Oh, man." Put the new bunks on the end? Anybody want to move their bunk? Ten men were perfect for this hootch. Twelve would be getting tight. The problem was all the footlockers.

"I'm gonna stand mine up," one guy said.

That would work. While they discussed the details, someone put Deep Purple on a reel-to-reel. A bowl was lit and passed around. SP4 Burt Maris was getting his mess kit together. He'd have his breakfast in the hootch. He sprinkled some cleaned pot onto his mess kit aluminum bowl and poured orange juice from the mess hall all over it. He stirred it and crushed it and turned it over and over to get it saturated and soft.

"You eat that shit?"

"Yep."

"Oh, man. What's that like?"

"Well," said Maris, "it takes a while to get off, but when you do, wow." He didn't say that it tasted awful. Or that he could be eating bugs, too.

Cream's "White Room" was playing. The hootch was rearranged, the guys got a good buzz on, and it was time for Dyson to go to work in Bravo Company.

Brady was on the flight line talking to the Maintenance Officer, Captain Irwin Horstall, son of an Air Force General. He was "Captain Horse" to a lot of guys.

"Three new guys, sir," Brady told him.

"I'm Captain Horstall. I'm your head of maintenance." He shook hands with Dyson, Robbie, and McMann. "Glad you're here. We always need more mechanics. They can't get here fast enough." Wonder why. Dyson was led off with Super Chicken and OD to work with them.

"Drink a lot of water when you're working. And use salt tablets."

It was hot, over a hundred degrees. As soon as he moved, the sweat would start pouring down his head, neck, arm, and torso. There were Lister bags of water hanging every five ships or so and ice chests from the mess hall. He needed a headband, aviator sunglasses, Camels, and one of those folding lawn chairs. At lunch time, a lot of guys would go to the PX in camp, rest in their hootches, have a cold beer or two, and/or get high—again.

"We were working on this ship here," said OD, "and we will finish up this afternoon. For now, use the tech manual to install this servo. We'll be with you every step of the way."

Besides guiding him through his mechanical work, Soup and OD gave him instructions for finding his way through the Huey tech manual and filling out the "necessary" forms. Forms, forms, forms for everything done on the ship.

Everyone on the flight line was working. No one was just standing around. SFC Brady went from ship to ship, job to job, carrying a clipboard of forms and personal notes.

CPT Horstall was there, on and off. He kept darting between the ships and the air-conditioned Maintenance bunker. Out for five minutes, back for ten, out five, in ten. "He doesn't like the heat much."

Pilots and crew members conferred with the mechanics, detailing problems, and discussing performance. The pilots, or aircraft commanders, were either warrant officers or commissioned officers. The warrant officers had been to flight school at Fort Rucker, Alabama, and then Fort Wolters, Texas. They were mostly Warrant Officer 1s, Chief Warrant Officer Twos, CW3s, or CW4s. One of the WO1s told the guys how bad the in-flight training had been, with student pilots causing accidents and "taking people with them." Slight mistakes can be fatal in these ships. A pilot's mistake was called "pilot error."

It was good to finally get to work, a job with a purpose instead of pulling endless details and KP. There were still duty rosters for guard duty and KP that he had to check constantly for his name, but from what he had seen and heard, it was low key compared to life as a trainee or an FNG in transit.

At midday break, he walked with OD and Soup to the small PX a quarter mile away. He had to get used to this heat and living and working in the blazing sun. The PX was the size of the mess hall. They walked around looking at the snacks, toiletries, a few cameras, *Playboy* magazines, some stereo equipment, and a bunch of LPs. He bought three packs of Camels, flight sunglasses, and a lawn chair.

"Don't buy any cameras here," OD said. "We'll go to Long Binh sometime soon and you can get a good 35mm there. Take the pictures and send the film home undeveloped." Dyson appreciated that good advice.

That afternoon, Dyson was told that three maintenance pilots who, besides inspecting work, would take the signed-off Hueys for test flights. These pilots were Captain Phil Spentser, First Lieutenant LeRoy Jones, and Chief Warrant Officer Two R.C. Riley. WO2 Riley was an all-right guy, everyone said, and he seemed so. 1LT Jones was an athletic-looking black guy and always looked immaculate. He could be a prick when he wanted to. CPT Spentser was the one to watch out for. He was surly, volatile, and unpredictable. He had been counseled a few times for his inability to get along with the enlisted men and for his drinking. Whenever a ship was ready to just fire up the engine or go for a test flight, everyone tried to get Riley or Jones first. But there were times when only Spentser was available.

On this day after Christmas, a Huey with tail number *084* was inspected and certified after a lengthy stay in maintenance, longer than any ship anyone could remember. It had needed everything in repairs and replacements and right now Spentser was the sole maintenance pilot around. "Oh, crap."

After conferring with Brady as they both went over the ship's records, Spentser grabbed a flight helmet to run up the ship. The test flight would be done later after a complete crew was put together.

"Watch this. Spentser's been drinking," OD said to Dyson and Soup. Some of the other guys knew what was going on. Did he just stagger a bit?

Opening the swing-out door, he had trouble getting himself up into the pilot's seat. He was moving around in his seat, turning on this, that, and the other thing. Then he yelled "Clear!" It was a required warning to anyone near the ship.

After twenty seconds the engine was exceeding normal RPMs. It sounded wild and straining.

"Shut it down, asshole! Shut it down." But he couldn't hear anything above all the noise.

"He just oversped the engine," OD explained to Dyson, "A big no-no."

Now Spentser was shutting down the Huey. The blades coasted to a stop. People stared at him. Brady was peeking from around from the back of a CONEX shipping container. Spentser sat in the cabin for a few minutes.

"He knows what he did," said OD. "Well, it's back into maintenance for *084*."

Finally, Spentser got out. He kept his flight helmet on with the sun visor over his eyes. He didn't look at anyone. Horstall was nowhere around and Brady was hiding. Spentser walked toward his barracks. He needed a drink.

During the following days, Dyson learned the company's routines, schedules, operations, missions, and some of the hidden agendas under the official radar of Military Assistance Command Vietnam (MACV) and U.S. Army Vietnam (USARV). It was defending democracy and patriotism on top, and dark and sinister on the bottom. The public back home, and even many GIs in Vietnam, did not know of the horrific underside of the American presence in Vietnam. Some of it, Dyson saw plainly. Other things needed to be explained in depth.

He soon noticed three NCOs who were always together, always had clean and pressed uniforms, shaves, haircuts, and shiny boots. They had more military bearing than most officers. Dyson saw them around the Orderly Room talking with the CO, sitting in the mess hall with a couple of officers, and once riding in a jeep with two MPs up in front. One time a Huey landed on the flight line and the three of them got off.

Dyson and Ramirez were leaving the mess hall and came face to face with the three NCOs on their way to chow. After a few steps Ramirez said, "You know about those guys?"

"No. Don't they work anywhere?"

"Not now. They got nailed selling shit to the gooks."

"What kind of shit?"

"Fracas was a motor pool sergeant. He sold batteries, tires, spark plugs, I forget what else. The other two were selling about everything: C-rations, uniforms, boots, bunks, wall lockers, even a CONEX." After a few more steps he added, "They're up for court-martial."

Dyson was starting to see that low-level drug dealing and alcoholism were rampant. He heard—and eventually believed—every time a GI bought drugs or paid a Vietnamese prostitute, he was supporting the Viet Cong, pumping U.S. money into the Communist war effort.

I IIII

Many of the Vietnamese day laborers who came on post almost every day were undoubtedly a part of the local Communist war effort. Some drove tank trucks and delivered water to the installations. These drivers brought in prostitutes and drugs. They also gathered intelligence for the Viet Cong, like mapping targets and pacing off the distances from landmarks. At Long Thong, the camp's regular water truck driver was known as Little Han. He was friendly, spoke good English, smoked Marlboro menthols (which were unavailable in the PX), and said he had been born in North Vietnam.

A couple of hours before sunset every day, Han drove his filled tank truck up to the main gate. The GIs on guard duty (larger installations had MPs or SPs) would eyeball him and his truck and wave him in. They never climbed up on the running boards to look inside the cab. It was simply understood that he could bring in girls and dope to the compound and take out who-knows-what. Similar mutual arrangements were in effect all over South Vietnam.

Han would drive into the company area, all the way down to the water tower at the end of a row of barracks, nose the truck between two hootches so the passenger side door was out of sight, and the girls and drugs were dropped off. He would then back up and unload his water into the shower's holding tank. After a few minutes, someone from the last hootch would set up a small TV on the sandbags as a signal that the girls each had a bunk and were ready for business. The guys from other hootches would bring their lawn chairs down there to watch TV. A mama-san would greet each GI at the door and conduct business. "Five dollars clothes on, ten dollars clothes off, fifteen dollars for BJ." Rubber or no rubber, it did not matter. Sometimes, all the guys would get up and move down a seat as they watched TV and waited their turn.

"Wanna go down there and check it out?" Spook asked Dyson and McMann.

"Yeah, OK," and down they went. The smell of pot was everywhere. Spirit's "I Got a Line on You" was the soundtrack of the moment.

Spook took them between the bunker wall and the wall of the hootch. They peered through the insect screen. Four prostitutes scattered on different bunks. Right in front of them was a bunk and a girl. She had just finished screwing a guy and got up, took a few steps to a steel pot on the floor, squatted down over the helmet and splashed water on her twat for a douche. A couple splashes and she was done. Dyson now got a good look at her. She looked like a little girl—small, thin, with tiny teats, and next to no pubic hair. She wore heavy eyeliner and bright red lipstick, but still looked like someone's little sister back home. The others looked about the same.

"Hey, you want to . . ." started Spook.

"No thanks."

"Maybe after you've been here a few months. I haven't yet, either."

They returned to their own hootch. Dyson couldn't get over it.

They looked like little girls.

As sunset neared, Han and the girls sneaked into the truck and headed for the main gate before nightfall when the gate closed.

"Han. Get us some more of that good stuff you had," someone called out as they drove by.

"Yes, yes. I get, I get," Han said with a wave.

Soup had mixed the jam tape that was playing on his big TEAC reel-to-reel. It was song after song and no one knew what would come next. A few mellow numbers followed by a rocking, stomping hit. The dozen men of this hootch were here now, and the two newest guys fit right in like Dyson, Robbie and McMann had just a few days before.

SP4 Tony Kranicki from another hootch came in and announced to all, "You ain't gonna believe this one, man."

"OK," said OD, "what happened?"

"You know Ossman?" SP4 Dan Ossman worked in avionics and was known as a good trouble-shooter.

"Are you ready?"

"Yeah, what is it?"

"Ossman was the last guy out of the hootch and ATE out one of those whores!" Moans and groans of shocked disbelief.

"You gotta be shittin' me!"

"No, man. Banks and Cusler seen him do it!"

"Aaaaarrrgghh . . . that's sick!"

Dyson couldn't believe it. Picturing it in his mind was revolting. He was creeped out. An imagined taste slithered onto his tongue. "I wish you never told us."

"Yeah, man. First, he asked the mama-san how much it would be, and she said, "No, number ten, no do!" ("Number ten" meant something was bad. "Number one" was great.)

"Oh, God."

"He paid her ten dollars, climbed on top of her, put it in, then pulled it out, threw her legs over his shoulders and . . ." He was cut short.

"Stop! Stop! STOP!"

"Oh, man, I can't stand it."

"I think I'm gonna be sick."

It put an instant downer on everyone. Can you imagine? Can you get VD that way? Did you ever hear of the "black-bull-head-clap?" Or the "black-bull-head-tongue?"

They guessed it was time to watch Ossman for a while and see what happened. Almost every morning there would be guys from all over the camp getting penicillin shots at the medics. Dyson swore he would never get the clap.

❙❙❙❙❙

Happy New Year, 1969

It was a good idea every day to check the bulletin board in front of the Orderly Room. It was two feet tall, four feet wide, and three feet above the ground with a small metal roof and a clear plexiglass door hinged on top. There were official notices and schedules and the duty roster—DD Form 6—for guard duty and KP. Guard duty meant all night on the camp perimeter with some time off the next morning. But many guys knew the importance of their work and would go right back to duty on the flight line. KP was eighteen to twenty hours, but it was low stress, slow paced with breaks during the day. Guys volunteered for guard duty New Year's Eve. As luck would have it, Dyson was scheduled to pull guard that night. Besides all the New Year's Eve parties all over camp, there was always a big party on the green line. "You'll like this," Spook predicted.

Tuesday, December 31, 1968, was hot, even by Southeast Asian standards. Dyson loved being in the heat and the sunshine. He followed advice and made sure he drank plenty of water and wore his fatigue OD soft cap off and on as needed. Working on the Hueys was always top priority. He was always alongside his teachers, the guys who had been working there months longer than him and knew the ropes. Dyson enjoyed his new trade and learned a lot more and much faster than he had at Fort Eustis. The guys were right. They didn't get taught much in AIT. Almost all the enlisted men got along. They ate together, worked together, partied together, showered together, and even seemed to write letters home at the same time. If there were any conflicts, it was when they were drunk. There would be drinking tonight for sure.

Men pulling guard duty would strap on their gear and weapons and form up outside the Orderly Room for guard mount. They would stand in ranks while the Officer of the Guard and the Sergeant of the Guard inspected each man. Dyson had his M16 and the bandoliers of loaded clips for it. Their arsenal included M60 machine guns, M79 grenade launchers, some 1911A-1 .45 semiautomatic pistols, fragmentation grenades, and black, baseball-like concussion grenades. Trip flares and Claymore mines were planted in front of their bunkers. Fifty-five-gallon steel drums filled with aviation fuel— nicknamed "foo gas" barrels—were scattered a hundred feet in front of the bunkers, buried in the soil with only the top quarter exposed. The defenders could fire tracers into the barrel and ignite the foo gas like a napalm fireball. It seemed like very daunting protection, but the enemy was capable of attacking and destroying formidable defenses like these. Very capable.

Also tucked away and well-hidden in their field gear was another powerful form of ammo: Golden Triangle dope.

I IIII

When Bravo Company pulled perimeter defense, there would be three men per bunker. The Sergeant and Officer of the Guard would rove through the bunkers and guard tower. Smoking was permitted out of sight. No radios or music were allowed between sunset and sunup. But tonight, it was New Year's Eve. There would be extra people on the green line. They usually piled into the bunkers and behind the berm after 23:00 hours. It was now 21:00 hours.

He was assigned to a bunker with two SP4s from other parts of the company, Vic Romano and Paul Roberts, who seemed like good guys. Roberts had only a month to go. The three of them were standing and leaning, looking out through the firing port. There were two folding cots opened in the rear corner of the bunker, for napping or sitting. The only light was from the quarter moon behind them combined with the amazing starlight of the tropics. Keep watching the area in front of you, he kept telling himself. Keep your eyes moving. Don't stare at anything.

The whole damn world knew it was New Year's Eve. The Americans were armed to the teeth and ready to celebrate at the stroke of midnight, so would the enemy try anything? Who knows how many of them were sitting in the woods right now concealed under cover and waiting to see the show? Could anyone imagine both sides putting down their arms and joining in the celebration? Like the spontaneous Christmas cease-fire in World War I, when the Germans and the Allies forgot about the war somehow, left their trenches, and celebrated together, if only for a little while. Fat chance here. Besides, it was our New Year celebration, not theirs. They had their own celebration of the New Year known as Tet. In fact, at the beginning of 1968, on January 31, using the celebrations surrounding Tet as distractions, the VC and NVA had launched all-out attacks on U.S. positions and camps while starting a strong, destructive, urban battle in the city of Hue.

Right now, unfortunately, the only music they could hear on the breeze was from a country-western hootch, "Together Again." Who the hell sang that? The smell of pot wafted through the darkness. He couldn't get over the incredible high he got from smoking this stuff. He had never gotten off anything like this with the pot they scored back home. And here the stuff was everywhere, and so cheap it seemed to be free the way it was passed around. Everyone always had some, like magic.

After a while, two more guys entered the bunker. They didn't have any field gear, but they did have their M16s and bandoliers of ammo. They were from another hootch in Maintenance.

"Can we welcome the new year with you?"

"Sure can," said Romano. The two visitors leaned against the firing port with them. It was 23:15 hours.

A jeep pulled up outside the bunker. Roberts looked out the rear entrance.

"Four more partiers."

Dyson took a break and stepped outside the rear of the bunker. Four guys were sitting in the jeep and there were other jeeps with their riders at other bunkers. There were also men with weapons huddled in little groups behind bunkers and the berm. A bottle of liquor was being passed in one group. He could hear rock music faintly in the air. He couldn't see anyone who resembled the Sergeant or Officer of the Guard anywhere.

Dyson leaned against the jeep. He recognized the riders from the flight line. "Hey."

"Hey, Dyson. Ready for the show?"

As they were getting out of the jeep, Dyson could see one guy had an M60 and wore two two-hundred-round belts, while the other had an M79 40mm grenade launcher and a bandolier of ammo.

"What time is it?"

"I got 11:55. That's civilian time, man."

Everyone was openly milling around the bunkers and the green line. Weapons were being loaded and checked. Big smoking bowls and cigar-sized joints were in motion up and down the line. There didn't seem to be any lifers around. Look at all these armed kids, Dyson thought. Could you imagine a bunch like this back in the World? A big Sherlock Holmes pipe full of smoldering Golden Triangle pot came his way. He took a hit and passed it on.

It was 23:59 hours. Suddenly the beginning notes of "Purple Haze" blasted from the nearest barracks. Cheering went up. Everyone pointed their weapons toward the woods. The mechanical sounds of locking and loading were everywhere.

"Ten. Nine. Eight . . ."

More and more joined the countdown.

"Seven. Six. Five . . ."

The jeep riders all brought their weapons up.

"Three. Two. ONE!"

At least a hundred guys opened up on the tree line. The roar was deafening. Thousands of tracers laced through the sky and woods. Guards set off Claymore mines in no-man's-land, and some threw hand grenades. A tracer set off a barrel of foo gas that lit up everything like a napalm bomb. Down the line was a duster, a self-propelled vehicle originally designed as an anti-aircraft weapon and armed with a 40mm Bofors automatic cannon that was firing what looked like a solid stream of tracers up over the tree line. The tracers stopped and seconds later the flashes from their explosions a mile away silhouetted the tree line. A side mounted M60 machine gun erupted with another set of tracers that arced up into the sky and then downward.

Dyson emptied clip after clip. He looked around. The entire three-hundred-sixty-degrees of the green line was firing. Men were yelling at the tops of their lungs.

"Fuck this stupid war!"

"No prisoners!"

"Kill for peace!"

The firing went well beyond the typical "mad minute," when people soon began shouting, "Cease fire! Cease fire!" The shooting sputtered out when clips were emptied and belts expended but for a few single shots until the firing stopped completely. Smoke hung in the air like a fog.

"Wow, man. Wow!"

"That was something!"

"Happy New Year!" That call was echoed by dozens of voices.

Dyson's ears were ringing like never before. This time it was two high-pitched tones in both ears, increasing and then ebbing, up and down. His ears had rung after the mortar attack at Phuoc Vinh, but that went away. He had no way of knowing it then, but this was the beginning of the hearing loss that would be with him for the rest of his life.

Briefing

There were more than 500,000 U.S. service members in South Vietnam.

By the end of 1968 more than 40,000 U.S. service members had been killed in action in Vietnam.

Hundreds of U.S. service members had been killed in Laos and Cambodia.

Pot smoking was rampant all-over South Vietnam and use of 95 percent pure "China White" heroin was steadily on the rise.

While many troops began to question orders, they still obeyed them. It wasn't until later in the war that they started disobeying orders.

"Search and destroy" missions became "search and avoid" missions.

Assassinations of officers and NCOs by enlisted men were also on the rise. It was called "fragging," for the fragmentation grenades used in many of these killings.

1969

I III I

JANUARY

On the morning of January 3, there was a mandatory formation for all members of Bravo Company. Everyone was there except the radio operators on duty in Operations. There'd been a rumor for a month that something big was going to happen with the aviation units in the 2nd Airmobile Division.

"I heard we're moving."

"I heard we're going up next to the border."

"Bullshit. Where'd you hear that?"

"No, they need us down in the Delta."

"At ease, men," instructed MAJ Sliman, the CO. "The Division Commander, General Richards, believes there have been too many aircraft crashes due to mechanical failure. Some of these crashes were the result of a lack of regular maintenance, some due to sloppy repairs and replacements, some for unknown reasons. Even though the paperwork said the work was performed, obviously it was not. Losing these ships and their crews is unacceptable."

The mechanics and crews could vouch for that. They dealt with the pressure of getting the ships back in service. Blame could be passed around to the mechanics, their inspectors, and test pilots. But sometimes things just happened.

"General Richards and his staff are reorganizing the maintenance and flight units into combination companies consisting of mechanics and flight crews. There will be mechanics who will become flight crews, and some crews will become mechanics. Those Hueys will be your babies."

"We are staying here. Alpha Company is moving next door to us where the Aussies moved out," the CO said, referring to the vacant company area that had been occupied by Australian troops that moved to another camp. "The transition will not be easy, as missions will continue without interruption. Bravo Company and Alpha Company will have joint responsibility and workloads. We need the full cooperation of everyone. And one more thing: Bravo Company has the best maintenance record in the Division." Cheers went up from the men. "Dismissed."

"That wasn't so bad," said Spook.

"I think we lucked out," Ramirez said. "Maybe our maintenance record helped."

The men headed back to the flight line, but along the way they went through their hootch to get a few tokes of the good stuff.

I IIII I

With the two companies' assets combined, there were a lot more men on the flight line, in the hangar, in the mess hall, everywhere. And now twelve men were in the hootch: Dyson, SP4 Tony Kranicki, SP4 "Spook" Benson, SP4 Thom "OD" O'Dayle, SP4 Ramon Ramirez, PFC Del "Soup" or "Super Chicken" Trone, SP4 "Florida" Miami, PFC Dan "Iron Cock" O'Grady, SP4 Randy Medina, SP4 "RJ" Gray. SP5 "Gato" Riaz, and SP5 Larry Rector. Rector amused us all by using an old-fashioned straight razor that he would always strop before shaving. Rather than going to the showers and shaving in front of one of the mirrors, Rector would bring back his steel pot full of hot water from the showers and shave with his straight razor while standing in front of the mirror hanging from his wall locker.

Everyone in their hootch smoked pot and drank beer, and they all got along just fine. In chalk, someone wrote across the door headers: "Work Hard, Play Hard." In the evening, most of the twelve were there when Bobbie, the Weather Girl, was on American Forces Vietnam TV. Bobbie would never have made it back in the world as a weather forecaster, but over here she was a big hit. She was blonde, had big boobs, and always showed a lot of leg. Her dialogue could be suggestive, which routinely drew rude, crude, and socially unacceptable suggestions from the men. She liked to dance to rock music and finished every forecast with a big kick with one leg. What talent!

Working seven days a week, it was easy to forget what day it was. Usually, it didn't matter much. But Saturdays were special. That's when the whores were "sneaked" into the company area. There was one group for the enlisted men and another entirely better bunch for the officers and NCOs who had more money. The first group were not the best-looking girls. They were small, with thin, tiny boobs, some makeup, and they didn't have the best hygiene. The others were better looking by far. A few of them were of French-Vietnamese descent. Most had nice bodies and bigger boobs. Some even had records of their shots to keep them clean. A mama-san acted as the pimp, negotiated a price with each man when he selected a girl, collected the money, and enforced the rules.

O'Grady got off work at 16:00 hours. This time, six guys were tagging along with him, going from hootch to hootch looking for the right girl. He rejected them all until he came to the Avionic shop's hootch. The mama-san met him at the door.

"Hey, GI. You want boom-boom?"

"Yeah, I want boom-boom, but can any of your girls take this?" he said, and without undoing his pants, he grabbed his cock showing the mama-san the size of it. It looked like he had a kielbasa in his pants.

"That Number one dickey! Number one!" Then she yelled, "Annie! Annie, come here!" A short, cute, little lady with some meat on her bones appeared. They spoke quickly. She stepped up to O'Grady and put her little hands on his love muscle. With her small hands, it looked like she was examining a rolling pin. "Ooohhhhh," she cooed. "No problem, no problem. You want suckee-fuckeee?" The guys who had come along to watch got all excited.

"Now you're talking," said O'Grady. He gave the mama-san ten dollars. Like they say, "Five dollar clothes on, ten dollar clothes off, fifteen dollar stand on head." Annie took him by the hand and led him to a bunk with some poncho liners and blankets hung around it for tent-like privacy. The guys were listening outside of the hootch.

"Come on, Annie, make it big," they heard O'Grady say.

"Number one dickey!" she said and a little later, "OK, GI. OK, we boom-boom."

The whores were known for not moaning and groaning during sex. Most seemed preoccupied. But Annie was grunting like during heavy exercise. The guys were snickering. Two minutes later, there was silence.

"OK, we done now," said Annie.

O'Grady came out putting his wet cock back in his pants. Apparently, he had gone bareback.

"She took the whole thing in—no problem," he said. He was as amazed as everyone else.

He told stories of women back home wanting to screw, but when they saw the size of the thing they said no way. He bragged about one lady who even jumped out of his bedroom window.

As Dyson and some of the guys walked to evening chow, they passed a big guy going the other way. He was six feet tall and about forty pounds overweight. He had soft milky-white skin, a baby face with no need to shave. He wore big, black-rimmed glasses with Coke-bottle lenses and a CIB. He looked like a stupid, mouth-breathing, live-at-home, Baby Huey loser.

"Who was that?" Dyson asked.

"That, gentlemen, is PFC Llewellyn Earlywhile, formerly of Spokane."

"He was in the infantry?" Dyson found that hard to believe.

"Yep. He was in the First of the Fifth Infantry for about two months. He couldn't keep up at all. One day out of the blue he just appeared here with orders. People say his CO couldn't see keeping him in the field—almost guaranteed he would get it sooner or later or maybe even take someone with him because he couldn't function."

"You might get to work with him some time or other," Ramirez told Dyson. "You'll see, he's just about worthless. I don't think he has any friends here. He keeps to himself. Some of the guys keep bustin' his balls about being cherry."

The three NCOs—Fracas, Hill, and Doyle—were going to be court-martialed soon and rumor had it that the Bravo Company CO, MAJ Sliman, and 1SG Peterson were both under investigation. Their names came up often in the court-martial testimony. The black marketeering was so open, so widespread, so SOP (standard operating procedure) that getting prosecuted was the result of higher-ups taking revenge for not collecting their cut of the profits. Sliman and Peterson must have pissed someone off.

But Sliman looked out for his men. At formation one morning, he told the company he was going to promote all private E2s to private first class E3s and E3s up to E4s. He wanted his men to earn more money for the work they were doing.

The Division Commander, Brigadier General Roland R. Richards, wanted the entire division to become "stateside." That was a term to describe the strict Army regulations of just about everything—uniforms, personal appearance, barracks conditions, military courtesy, and enforcement of regulations—that was expected back in the states. The men dreaded the change to stateside, but now things were too lax for a lot of lifers to bear. Many of the guys needed haircuts, didn't shave every day, and worked shirtless. A lot wore beads and necklaces and nonregulation sunglasses. No one ever shined their boots. In the barracks, some guys had hammocks instead of steel bunks. Enlisted men and officers were working alongside each other, and a lot of saluting and military courtesy had fallen by the wayside (though some officers insisted on salutes). Overall, it seemed to be a great working environment. With the combination of companies, all that was going to change.

I IIII I

At the morning, company formation on January 3, MAJ Sliman announced a meeting with the NCOs and officers in the mess hall. Among those attending would be the Alpha Company CO, Major "Ben" Bentworth, and First Sergeant "Honey Bear" Hollingsworth. They were pricks of the first degree. Both were ALL Army, with more than twenty years of service, and chomping at the bit to get these men into and under strict Army regulations.

"Well," said Spook, "all good things must come to an end, my friend." From an unseen sound system, Eric Burdon's "Sky Pilot" floated through the company area. That song was corny and fitting at the same time. Guys would join in and shout out the chorus as loud as they could to the heavens above. Dyson wondered, could they, would they ever reach the sky?

As they walked to the flight line, they passed one of the six-seater latrines—you could smell it before seeing it. PFC "Stinky" Rivers was the company's permanent shit burner. He was tall, gaunt, aloof, and no one would shake hands with him. Rivers was a draftee and seemed like he could have mental issues.

Besides burning shit, Stinky filled sandbags, ran errands for the Orderly Room, and drove trucks to Long Binh to pick up supplies. Because he volunteered for the shit-burning he was exempt from the KP roster.

"There's a meeting in the hangar. Something's up," said a mechanic joining the group. The flight line, maintenance, and shop personnel were gathered at the open side of the hangar, out of the sun. Beams of sunlight, forming brilliant Jacob's Ladders, shone through shrapnel holes in the metal siding.

"OK, men, please listen up," said CPT Horstall, the OIC of Maintenance who called the meeting. "You can smoke if you want to." Guys lit up. "OK. As you know, we have combined with Alpha Company. All of you mechanics—not the shop personnel—will be assigned to a section of mechanics and crew members. Mechanics will learn crew member duties, and crew members will learn to perform maintenance and repair. Each section will be assigned six to eight ships to maintain, repair, and crew. Each section will have a pool of aircraft commanders, test pilots, maintenance officers and NCOs." Horstall looked around at everyone. "Most of you guys are good mechanics. Our record proves it. We think the transition will run smoothly. Alpha Company ships and personnel will be integrated onto this flight line. Teams in each section will be assigned jobs on specific ships by Sergeant First Class Brady from Bravo Company and Master Sergeant Cosko from Alpha Company. You guys that are old hands will be breaking in new mechanics, and you, in turn, will be broken in as crew members. Any questions?" Everyone was silent. "Let's get to work."

I IIII I

Brady called out to Dyson. "I want you to start today working with the guys on replacing some damaged sheet metal on a couple of ships."

"Damaged" meant damage from ground fire. The work crew was doing the bodywork on two ships, *084* and *077*. A few panels had been removed and there were 15 bullet holes scattered around the engine compartment and the tail fuselage. There was also one hole through the aircraft commander's plexiglass.

Brady introduced Dyson to the crew—nothing but last names. "Dyson, this is Blunt. That's Holgerson, and this is Devaney." There were handshakes all around. "Guys, show him the ropes."

"OK, watch me start removing these rivets," said Blunt as he began drilling. "We'll remove what we have to, figure out the sizes we need, and go cut the pieces in the hangar."

They talked while they worked and listed to AFVN radio. It was already roasting. Most of the guys were in T-shirts or shirtless. Some wore bandanas. The talk gravitated toward hometowns, high school sports, and time left in Vietnam. Dyson had figured his out. Three hundred twenty-five days to go—depressing.

About twenty minutes into the repair, Dyson happened to glance over at a ship being worked on sixty yards away. For a split second he was aware of a dark form streaking downward through the air just above the Huey. Time seemed to stand still. The ship tilted sideways onto one skid and was silhouetted against a cloud of red dust and gray and black clouds. One of the mechanics had his back turned toward Dyson and he was in midair like he was sitting in a lounge chair, arms out, head back. Another mechanic was also suspended in the air, three feet off the ground. Neither of his legs was visible. The third mechanic, who only had his heels on the ground, was leaning backward. The right side of his torso and his arm and head had been shredded. Finally came the WHUMP! of the mortar round.

Somebody yelled, "Incoming!" No shit. A few guys hit the ground and stayed down. Others hit the ground, then got up and ran. Some guys ran straight to the bunkers. Dyson followed his bunch toward a bunker but stopped behind the revetment wall. He looked at the blown-up Huey. Two guys ran to check out the men who'd been hit, and then back behind the wall.

"They're all dead."

"You sure?" asked some lifer.

"Jesus Christ, man, go look for yourself!" The lifer stayed put.

Belatedly, a siren sounded the alarm, a "red alert." Another siren joined in. The entire camp was waiting for more mortars or rockets. Minutes went by. The sirens continued. After fifteen minutes, people started yelling, "All clear." How they knew it was all clear was a mystery.

Men drifted out to the flight line. Dyson, John Devaney, and a dozen others went over to the downed men. Two of them had their dog tags around their neck. Just as many other airmen did, as a precaution, one of the mechanics had knotted his second dog tag into his bootlaces to aid in identification in case the first one went missing. Didn't matter this time. Just about everyone knew the guys who died. They were co-workers, hootch mates, friends. Here one minute, KIA the next. That shell had their names on it. Dyson found himself staring. The scene of the three men frozen in the blast stayed in front of him all day and into the night. And then was permanently burned into his brain.

I IIII

After evening chow, Dyson rejoined the crew at *084* and *077*. They went over the work and required forms with SFC Brady and CPT Horstall, who inspected and signed off on their work. Both ships were ready for another crew to work on the hydraulic systems. It was 20:00 hours. It was agreed they would get up at 04:00 hours and start work.

When Dyson entered the hootch, most of the guys were done for the day and were listening to tunes. "Here, man," Ramirez said, offering an oversized smoking bowl. Dyson took a big toke, then another and slowly exhaled in a long cloud. Morrison was singing "Waiting for the Sun."

"Reminds me of California," someone said.

None of the guys killed that day were from their hootch, so it wasn't necessary to clear out their missing comrades' gear and personal property. Theirs would have no empty bunks awaiting FNGs for replacements. The Company commander would sign a freshly typed form letter to the next of kin, stating what great soldiers the men had been, how saddened he and the other soldiers were, and that they were killed instantly and never suffered. Many, many times the soldier died in agony. Dyson would learn that those who die in extreme agony at the height of insurmountable fear do not look like they are at peace. They have ghastly expressions on their faces. Those are the faces that haunt. They never go away.

More music, more talk, more music, more smoke. Medina was lying on his bunk. He put his hands up and moved them gracefully through the air, like an orchestra conductor. OD looked at Dyson and said, "He's been doing heroin."

"Really? Shooting it?"

"Yeah. Shooting it."

Dyson would find out soon that some guys—not many—in the company were using heroin, shooting it, snorting it, or smoking it. Ninety-five percent pure China White heroin, a small Rosebud Matches box full for two bucks. Two dollars for what would cost hundreds back in the World.

"I'll never do heroin," he said.

"Yeah, there's him and his two buddies. One of them is gonna OD here pretty soon."

I III I

Every day after 16:00 hours everyone could stop by the mail room, which was a CONEX refitted to serve as a small office. The Bravo Company mail clerk was SP4 Lenny Kosski, a Polack and proud of it. Mail went out and mail came in daily via Huey. Kosski held the mail not picked up or he would walk around and hand it out. On this day, he handed Dyson letters from his mom and Carol. Kosski, like a lot of guys, wore sunglasses to conceal his red eyes. He looked like one of the *Campbell Soup* Kids—blonde, blue eyes, and baby-faced, and quick with the funny and sarcastic comments at exactly the right time.

"Here you go," Kosski said.

"Thanks, man. I'm Gary."

"Ron." They shook hands. "You need a nickname. Got any?"

"None that I know of."

He had received six letters from his mom and four from Carol since arriving in Bravo Company. He always read Carol's the first chance he got. She didn't douse her letters with perfume like many girls did, but he could still pick up her scent. God, he missed her.

A PFC named Hiller was showing the picture of his newborn son to three guys in Maintenance. They called him "Hiller the Killer" because he said the dumbest things that made people laugh like hell. He was a tall, beefy hillbilly from West Virginia. He had a head shaped like a bowling ball with a flat side, one eye-socket higher than the other, and big cab-door, pistol-grip ears—ears like handles to grip when getting a blow job.

"Wow, man, look at that little guy," said Kosski. Dyson followed suit. He said the kid looked like a real bruiser.

"I'm gonna buy some cigars," said Hiller. He might have to go to Long Binh to buy cigars. The camp's PX didn't have a lot of anything.

After he was a good distance away, Kosski said, "Did you ever see such an ugly baby?" The kid looked just like his dad, but he had Elmer Fudd ears. The ears were the first thing everybody noticed.

Someone said Hiller named the kid after himself, Harold H. Hiller Jr. Very fitting.

▌▐▐▐▌

Briefing

Peace talks began in Paris on January 25, 1969. The months since Richard Nixon's election as president marked the start of preparation for an about-face in American policy in Vietnam. The new administration announced a coming end to U.S. combat in Southeast Asia and a simultaneous strengthening of South Vietnam's ability to defend itself.

Close to fifty ground combat operations were undertaken from the time of his election. During this period, the following being a few of the most important:

(1) *Operation NAPOLEON* in the Dong Ha area initiated previously (in 1967) by Marine units, terminated on 9 December 1968.

(2) *Operation WHEELER WALLOWA* by 3d Brigade, 1st Cavalry Division and 196th Infantry Brigade (Light) in north-central Quan Tin Province. This ended on 11 November.

(3) *Operation MACARTHUR* initiated by 4th U.S. Infantry Division in II Corps tactical zone terminated on January 31, 1969.

(4) *Operation SEALORDS,* the acronym for Southeast Asia Lake, Ocean, River, and Delta Strategy, a joint U.S.-South Vietnamese operation intended to disrupt North Vietnamese supply lines in and around the Mekong Delta. It was launched on November 5, 1968, The U.S. Navy's role in this operation officially ceased in April 1971.

(5) *Operation GIANT SLINGSHOT* started on December 6, 1968, to disrupt the enemy infiltration of materials from the "Parrot's Beak" area of Cambodia. Air defense operations continued to be important with 60,000 sorties flown.

▌▐▐▐▌

On January 24, 1969, Military Assistance Command Vietnam announced 1,000 helicopter pilots had been killed in combat in Vietnam.

I IIII

FEBRUARY

FNGs continued to trickle into Bravo Company. On February 1, a new Spec 5 arrived. Richard Strickland was from northern California. This was his second tour in Vietnam and wore a CIB with crew member wings for being a door gunner. He also wore two different 2nd Airmobile Division patches to show he'd been in the 2nd on his first tour. He bristled when anyone called him a lifer and said he had been suckered into a six-year re-enlistment by a lying re-enlistment NCO. He landed in the hootch next to Dyson's, and he smoked pot with the guys at night, so he was OK in their book. He knew a lot about Hueys and was assigned to Maintenance. Nobody knew it at the time, but he had a special skill.

Dyson saw right away that Strickland had working man's hands—and he smoked Camels. They were working with Ramirez and Soup on *066*, a well-worn, battle-scarred crate to look at, but dependable as hell, like all the Hueys. It was in maintenance because two aircraft commanders said they felt a vibration when banking to the left. Writeups like these could be difficult to correct and trying to find the source even harder.

"Hey, where were you on your first tour?" asked Ramirez.

"All over Quang Trị; at the end of the Khe Sanh-Lang Vei fiasco; Camp Evans; Mai Loc; Ba Long; and my personal favorite, the A Shau." These were places of big battles, fierce campaigns to win territory—only to be deserted and then retaken months later, the war of attrition. Strickland didn't seem to mind talking about it. Everyone back home knew about Khe Sanh and the months-long siege there. But not many knew of the A Shau Valley, a North Vietnamese Army stronghold and highway from the Ho Chi Minh Trail to South Vietnam.

"You're lucky," said Ramirez.

"Yeah. I only got this." He pointed to a ragged-shaped scar on the front of his upper left arm where a bullet had ripped through his bicep but missed the bone. "They go in kinda like that," he said, "but really kickass on the way out," revealing a huge crater of torn scarred muscle where it exited the back side. "There were so many dead NVA up there that when you flew over the place at five thousand feet you could still smell the fuckers rotting."

"Glad you're here, man," said Ramirez.

"Yeah, I am too," said Strickland.

"Got a name or a nickname you like to be called?"

"Lotsa people call me Rick.

As the guys worked on the drivetrain, linkages, and mounts trying to find the source of the vibration, the talk went from this ship to others, to the pilots, and the companies combining, the bullshit and dogma of the Army, plus things going on back home. "I'd love to be in an anti-war demonstration and see guys burn their draft cards, and us guys dumping our medals in the trash," said Ramirez.

Around 11:00 hours, SFC Brady stopped by the group to make an announcement. "All you guys who have hammocks to sleep on, take them down and a steel cot and mattress will be provided to you at 16:00 hours today. No more sleeping in hammocks allowed, as set forth by the Commanding General." The conversion to "stateside" had begun.

▌▐▐▐▌

Kearny

Dyson, Soup, SP4 John Devaney, and another SP4, Sancho Alvarez, from Mesa, New Mexico, were all scheduled for KP duty on Monday. That meant having the CQ wake them at 05:00 to get the mess hall up and running under the supervision of Floaty, Gator, and Pops, who would still be drunk or hung over from the night before. Those on KP would work in the mess hall until 08:00 when the Vietnamese civilians would take over for the next eight hours. Then the four would return to the mess hall, serve evening chow, and clean up and close down. This system freed the men up to work on the ships during the day.

The work force of sixty Vietnamese hootch maids, barbers, tailors, "massage" ladies, and various day laborers arrived daily at 08:00. The maid for Dyson's hootch was "Tug," short for a name no one knew. Some Americans treated the Vietnamese badly with name calling, insults, even physical abuse, and treating every woman like she was a whore. Dyson didn't like it. He would visit with Tug on his way to the flight line. While she did the laundry, cleaned the hootch, made the beds, and shined boots, Dyson got to know and like her. Her husband had joined the Army of the Republic of Vietnam, (the South Vietnamese, which everyone called ARVN, pronounced "R-vin"), was sent to northern South Vietnam and never heard from again. She had three baby-sans at home in Long Thong village. Dyson would give her bars of soap, toothpaste, candy, and anything else to take home to the kids. Tug (and the other laborers) told those who would listen that even though they were paid by the American government, the Viet Cong in their villages levied taxes on them. It took a lot of her money. Being executed by the VC was the only way to stop paying.

Every company had an NCO in charge of paying the Vietnamese laborers. The sorry-ass lifer for Bravo Company was Staff Sergeant Tommy Kearny. He had been in the Army more than twenty years and was only an E6. SSG Kearny was five-foot-eight, thin as a rail, chewed on Beech Nut tobacco, smoked Pall Malls, had rotten teeth, and a sneaky, rodent look about him. He acted like he had the power of life and death over the women he supervised. Why this was tolerated was unknown.

Dyson and the other KPs had worked through the day and were walking to the mess hall when they heard the hootch maids all over camp squabbling. You didn't need to speak Vietnamese to know they were really upset. When Dyson, Spook, and OD walked through their hootch, Tug was sitting on a footlocker, crying, and rocking back and forth.

"Tug, what's wrong?"

Tug burst out speaking Vietnamese, then caught herself. "Kearny is a bad man. Number ten! Number ten! He no good!" Tug didn't have a big English vocabulary like some of them did.

A couple of other hootch maids joined in. They said pretty much the same thing.

"What did he do?"

"Kearny say if we want our money, we have to have boom-boom with him. We no boom-boom for anyone! We work and want our money!"

"What a sorry-ass motherfucker," said Spook. The guys in their hootch were pretty decent toward the hootch maids, but some of the others liked to make it tough on them.

"When's payday?" Dyson asked Tug.

"Tomorrow and I no boom-boom. I want me money!" she cried. The others noisily agreed.

"Tug, let us see what we can do about Kearny, OK?" Dyson said.

"Yeah, let us do something," OD added.

Besides being a sorry-ass lifer, Kearny was suspected of stealing a lot of personal stuff while the men were working on the flight line and while supervising the hootch maids. OD suspected Kearny stole his brand-new *Playboy*—a precious and unforgivable loss. Lots and lots of little stuff had turned up missing during Kearny's work hours.

"You GIs number one!" said Tug, "Number one!" The others joined in and some patted the guys.

"OK, OK," said OD. "But let's keep quiet."

Just what was going to be done hadn't been decided yet. The hootch maids left to catch their ride home and the guys headed over for KP duty.

What a rotten son of a bitch," said OD. "How'd you like your mom to have to go through that shit?"

"But don't go running to Sliman or Peterson about this. They don't want to hear it," said Spook.

Kearny had proven himself incompetent at every other job. He'd been worthless in maintenance, the supply room, the motor pool, and the mess hall. Sliman thought being the boss of the hootch maids was a job Kearny might be able to handle.

That evening, Floaty and Gator made the guys fried chicken, mashed potatoes, gravy, green beans, canned pears, and chocolate cake with white frosting.

"Damn, look at this spread." Words like it were heard up and down the chow line.

Spook and OD were scalding the metal trays and utensils when Dyson told them Kearny was in the mess hall, eating.

"Thanks," said Spook. He looked through the doorway from the galley into the dining area. Kearny was by himself with his back toward most of the men. There were only two dozen or so men in the mess hall. Kearny was the only lifer.

Spook made his way purposely toward Kearny. Had word spread through the company about Kearny's bullshit? It seemed like that because all the guys stopped eating to watch what was about to happen. Kearny never saw it coming. Spook was a much bigger man and put his full weight down on Kearny's head, pushing his face into the metal tray of chicken, mashed potatoes, and gravy. Spook made sure to wipe Kearny's face left and right, forward and backward through the mess.

"No boom-boom, Kearny. You hear me? No boom-boom!"

Kearny couldn't break Spook's grip and he couldn't get up.

"Say something, Kearny. You hear me? No boom-boom!" Kearny waved his hands as in submission.

"Say 'No boom-boom,'" Soup ordered, his voice getting louder. The guys in the dining room all watched, some silent, some snickering.

"No boom-boom," Kearny finally sputtered.

Spook let go and Kearny sat up. He was a mess. Spook had his hands on his hips now, towering over Kearny.

"I don't want to hear that again about you, understand?"

"Yeah, I hear you," said Kearny through his gravy and potatoes.

He wouldn't look at anybody. He turned in his tray and left the mess hall. Spook was shaking.

"Wonder what will happen now."

"I don't know and I don't care," said Spook.

This was an early lesson in Dyson's education about life in a war zone in the Army. Back home, SSG E6s were gods with the power of life and death over trainees. You did not sass, insult, answer back, question, disobey, or piss off an SSG or any other higher-ranking soldier. But over here, he would see time and time again enlisted men telling NCOs and officers to fuck off. This was the first he had seen an enlisted man actually put his hands on a lifer—and get away with it. Clearly, Kearny did not report the assault.

❚ ❚❚❚ ❚

One of the guys in the hootch got hold of the January edition of *Playboy,* already well-worn from being passed around. A small crowd was looking over Spook's shoulder as he opened the centerfold. "Oooohhhh . . . Lorna Boccacelli, a dago!"

"Wow. Tan and dark hair. I love that."

"Too skinny!" said OD. "Take her out back and shoot her."

"Too skinny?" hissed Ramirez. "What do you like, fat mamas?"

"No, just something with some meat on their bones."

"Let me see." The magazine was handed to Ramirez. Now the guys hung over his shoulder. The latest *Playboy* was always an event. Joining the guys ogling the centerfold was an SP4 from another hootch. Cochise Toohany was a full-blooded American Indian. He grew up on a reservation in the Southwest—New Mexico or Arizona. (His 201 File showed he was one of thirteen kids). He had dark skin with terrible oozing acne and was an alcoholic, almost always drunk on Jim Beam. (2nd Airmobile Division regulations forbade enlisted men procuring, possessing, and drinking hard liquor, but it was everywhere.) He was known as the "Electric Indian" since the 1st sergeant assigned him to keep the company's diesel generators operating. He didn't say much and spoke only when it was important.

Right away Dyson liked him.

"Anything on the reservation look like that?" someone asked.

"Nope." Classic answer.

"Toohany, what are Indian women like?"

"Fat, ugly, no hair on their twat, but hair under their arms," he said and smiled.

"Ever have a white woman?"

"White women talk too much" was Toohany's answer.

It was getting dark. Time to turn on the music and pass the bowls around. One end of the hootch was playing "Waiting for the Sun" by the Doors, the other had on Big Brother and the Holding Company's *Live at the Fillmore*. Dyson and Toohany joined the Doors crowd around the doorway facing the next hootch. The two new friends talked about their lives back in the World. Dyson recalled his high school days, party life at college, his 1938 Ford Woodie, and hunting pheasant, grouse, and woodcock. Toohany told of deplorable schools, unemployment, alcoholism, poverty, and knife and gun fights.

"I'm gonna stay in the Army," said Toohany. A statement like that usually started some name calling and derision of all kinds. Dyson could see his point. It seemed like there was nothing good to get back to. Toohany took a great big hit which was on top of what he had been drinking. "I have to check on the generators." He walked out. The marijuana and music continued.

I III I

Incoming

Around 22:30 hours guys started hitting their bunks, stereos were turned down, and barracks put out the lights. Dyson was in his OD green boxer shorts, stoned, and hoping for some colorful, vivid dreams, maybe one of Carol.

From the barracks next door, someone yelled "Incoming!"

Dyson thought, "Incoming?" Then WHUMP! A mortar hit fifty feet away. More rounds were falling fast and everyone was stooping while running for their bunker. WHUMP! WHUMP! WHUMP-

WHUMP-WHUMP! They rained down at a rapid rate. There had to be at least two mortar tubes, maybe more, in the woods someplace. Every explosion produced a flash of light and hundreds of sparks of molten metal shrapnel—not seen in daylight blasts.

"Jesus Christ, man."

The intensity of the bombardment increased. Dozens of rounds were falling. Some exploded at the same time. Rockets joined the destruction, deadly 107mms from Red China. The camp's useless sirens started up. Dyson tried counting how many rounds fell in ten seconds. He couldn't. The guys in the bunkers could hear a Huey running up on the flight line. Two Huey gunships, the reactionary team, would fly out and hunt down the enemy mortar and rocket teams. Along the south perimeter guards in their bunkers were firing into the woods with M60s and .50 caliber Browning machine guns. The rockets were visible blasting off in the woods and arcing toward their target. Salvos of shells landed close, just outside their sandbag wall, as if their hootch was the main target.

"Little people, this tall." Yes, they were short compared to Americans, usually only chest tall and ninety or a hundred pounds.

"It ain't Tet yet."

"Welcome to Rocket City."

"Who the hell yelled 'Incoming?'"

As the Hueys reached full RPMs, the explosions diminished, then stopped. The VC mortar and rocket teams did not want to be spotted from the air, even at night. The sirens faded out. The gunships were up in the air now, cruising and looking for a target.

Dyson became conscious of the ringing in his ears. Everyone stayed put waiting to hear either more incoming or the "all clear." Ten minutes went by, then fifteen. No one had declared "all clear" but the men came out of the bunkers.

"Holy shit! Look at the Avionics hootch." It took two direct hits. Half the metal roofing was blasted off. Walls were blown out and splintered. If the guys had been in their bunks sleeping, it would have been a disaster. There were casualties in other companies in camp. Alpha Company just to the north sustained three men killed and nine wounded. The attack also took a toll on the rear end of the mess hall (with its smokestack targets), the mail room (the entire CONEX would have to be replaced), the supply room, the avionics, and shops. A six-man latrine was almost obliterated. However, the water tower (a landmark for VC fire teams) remained intact.

Smoke hung in the air like blue fog. Everywhere were craters and the remains of rocket nose cones, dozens of them. Each looked like a jagged, lethal king's crown. There was a roll call at each section. One man from the radio shop was unaccounted for.

Someone said one wall of the hangar was "Swiss cheese."

"You should see the flight line." It was a dangerous place to be, anytime.

The first mortar round hit there, killing two mechanics, and destroying one ship. Four men were taken to the dispensary. One was being prepared for Medevac. A gunship would take him to the 93rd Evac Hospital in Long Binh. Ninety shredded 107mm rocket nose cones were collected in Alpha and Bravo Companies areas. The number of mortar rounds was unknown. The man from the radio shop was found unscathed.

Word was that Strickland had yelled "incoming" before the first round had even hit. Even with all the diesel generators roaring Strickland was still able to hear the first round way before anyone else. This was another fact that was never recorded in his official records. Rick Strickland never got a citation for the lives he saved.

The two most important abbreviations in every enlisted man's mind were DEROS and ETS. The first (literally Date Estimated Return from Overseas) was for tour of duty, and the date leaving Vietnam. ETS was the Expiration of Term of Service, the date of discharge from the service. Everyone counted the days left in-country and had a daily countdown knowing precisely how many days were left. When someone had thirty days and less in-country, they were "short timers." The Army allowed enlisted men to extend their service in Vietnam until six months before their ETS for a six-month early discharge. Many draftees had to extend only one or two months for a six-month early discharge. It was something to think about.

Many GIs extended their tour in Vietnam simply for the cheap, abundant, and powerful drugs. Some preferred to be discharged in Vietnam and live as a civilian again, with all the drugs. Those guys later came out of the woodwork when the Communists started conquering South Vietnam.

Dyson kept a daily tally on his wall locker. He had 288 days left, a long way to go.

▌▐▐▌

It was Saturday, February 22, and Dyson, Spook, OD, and O'Grady were all scheduled for guard duty on the perimeter.

That month in Long Thong saw a rise in the number of stand-off rocket and mortar attacks on the camp, both day and night, in a campaign of VC and NVA attacks up and down South Vietnam. Though none had the ferocity of the 1968 Tet Offensive, there had been five nighttime probes of Long Thong's defenses by the local Viet Cong, tests of the camp's defenses rather than all-out ground attacks. Alpha and Bravo Companies continued their mission of keeping the Hueys up in the air despite the continual bombardment and casualties.

At 20:00 hours, the four guys relieved the guards in their assigned bunker. There was an M60 machine gun resting on the sill of the firing port. The guards picked up their weapons and gear and moved out. The guys set down their gear and were leaning at the firing port, gazing out at the no man's land and the woods beyond. This part of the green line was the closest to the woods and had the narrowest no man's land, only two hundred feet to the woods. Sunset was at 18:50 hours. Now it was dark. The moon wasn't even half full, but the starlight was, as always, magnificent.

At 21:00, First Lieutenant Donald Papp entered the dark bunker. He was Officer of the Guard that night. Everyone liked Papp. He was soft-spoken, intelligent, a realist, and no-nonsense. He wore a CIB, an Airborne badge, pilot wings, and a Special Forces patch. He started out as a career officer in 1963 and had a hell of a record. But like all the others with common sense, he had become disillusioned with the insanity of the war, the military leadership and hierarchy, along with the blatant lies of the administration in Washington. He was counting down the eight months he had to go until his last enlistment ended.

"Hey, guys," he said and sat down on one of the folding cots. "Who we got here?"

The guys sounded off their last names with O'Grady last.

"O'Grady!?"

"Yes, sir."

"Well, keep that thing in your pants tonight." The guys giggled and after a little chit-chat, the lieutenant got serious. "Listen up. There are confirmed reports of several VC units in the area. On February 19, a deserter told the ARVNs the VC were going to launch a big attack on Long Binh on February 22. That's today. A big ground attack. Long Binh, of course, did not get the word until today."

Long Binh? Are they sure they got the right information? Disney Land? No one would launch a ground attack on Long Binh. It's too big. Too many artillery pieces, too many gunships, and an out-of-this-world, most heavily fortified perimeter in Vietnam. That included dusters (vehicles with automatic 40mm grenade launchers) and Quad 50s (deuce and a halfs with four-barrel .50 caliber machine guns).

"Fuck. What do they mean 'in the area,' sir?"

"Long Binh's four miles north-northeast of us. There are two VC battalions within striking distance of us tonight. This side here," meaning where they were right now, "is probably where they will attack."

"'Will' attack, sir?"

"I bet they do something here tonight." Papp knew how they operated, having shot it out with them in the field so many times. He had seen it all. "Commo check the landline, Spook." Every bunker had a crank-up landline connected by wire to a CP (control point where the officer of the guard was stationed). Spook declared the line was working.

"Listen, guys," Papp said as he got off the cot, "don't smoke tonight." And he was referring to drugs, any drugs. "You can smoke your cigs down, out of sight as always, but don't smoke dope tonight."

"You bet," they promised and off he headed to another bunker. Nobody wanted to jeopardize their working, or personal, relationship with Papp. He didn't fuck over the guys at all like most lifers did. Mechanics sought him out when a test pilot was needed. Papp started out as a lifer—now he wasn't.

"Great guy," said OD.

This time all four would stay on guard scanning the field of fire in front of them. No one was napping on the cots. At 23:30, they heard distant booms in back. OD went out the rear entry for a minute or so.

"Looks like Long Binh is getting hit."

Sure enough. They could see flashes followed by delayed sounds of explosions. Tracers arced through the sky. Usually, the guys on this side of Long Binh would set up their lounge chairs, smoke, drink, get high, and listen to tunes while watching Long Thong get hit. Now it's the other way around.

"Keep watching, man," said OD. "Don't let that distract you."

After a while, they could hear some cheering from the area to their rear. O'Grady looked out there.

"Oh, man. Spooky is over Long Binh, pissing on them!"

"Spooky" was the call sign for the C-130 gunship in this area. The Douglas AC-47 ("A" for attack) gunship was first designated "Spooky" by the Air Force. After a while, the ground troops gave it the nickname "Puff the Magic Dragon." The C-130 Hercules airframe was later selected to replace the AC-47 because it could fly faster, longer, higher, and had increased munitions load capabilities.

Up in the sky over Long Binh a steady stream of red tracer rounds exploded out to the ground from an unseen C-130. At the distance of six miles, it sounded more like a chainsaw than military weaponry. The C-130 was equipped with down-facing electric Gatling guns (miniguns) along the left side; each pouring five thousand rounds a minute, every fifth round a tracer, and all that could be seen was solid tracers. In 1969, a 20mm rotary autocannon and a 40mm Bofors cannon were added. Incredible firepower. Every time the gunship let loose a stream of firepower, cheers rose from the camp. Dyson, Spook, OD and O'Grady returned to their firing port and scanned the grounds in front of them.

"Wonder if they're out there?"

They all had heard about the incredible feats of the VC and NVA sappers—little guys weighing about ninety pounds soaking wet who would cover their body in axle grease and, crawling like snakes, slide through coils and coils of razor wire, neutralize Claymore mines (sometimes turning them around to face the Americans), disconnect trip flares, and with lengths of bamboo saplings slide a Bangalore torpedo up to a bunker. They were proven to have slipped in and out of installations undetected. It was not impossible for them to overrun a camp—even a big one.

A few minutes after midnight, the sound of C-130 engines got louder.

"Hey. Hear that?" OD looked from the rear entry. "Can't see him, but he's close." It was still getting louder. Papp came by.

"Spooky's coming. Recon units say there is a VC battalion making their way south and they're passing close to Long Thong to the east right now."

They all looked at the woods to their east-southeast. The forest was black with only the tree line visible against the starlit sky. Now the gunship was right over their camp. It had no running lights on, but you could see its silhouette. It was difficult to estimate how high it was. Maybe three thousand feet? The cheering started all over again as the pilot circled the target at 120 knots and rolled 30 degrees to port.

Two parachute flares flew from the ship, each ignited and drifted under a parachute while illuminating the ground for the crew.

Spooky corrected itself a little and, using a gunsight over the pilot's left shoulder, opened up on the woods with the miniguns from a half mile away. It sounded like a huge chainsaw as two solid streams of red tracers pissed on the forest like big fiery garden hoses. Thousands and thousands of rounds rained down. The ship dragged its impact area with it, seeming like someone pulling gigantic magenta sparklers through the woods. Tracers ricocheted in every direction. Some shot upward forming brilliant arcs in the sky.

"Yeah! Piss on 'em!"

The guns stopped and the ship let go two more parachute flares. From one of the barracks someone cranked up "Purple Haze." The pilot was moving his killing zone further south. The ship banked again and another fusillade began. It was mesmerizing, like something out of a movie.

With firepower like this, why haven't we won the war already? Did we even put a dent in the number of enemy soldiers? Did we really need half a million U.S. servicemen in South Vietnam in 1969? Why were we fighting over the same areas time and time again? How come the Army of South Vietnam wasn't swarming all over the countryside overtaking the Viet Cong? Why were so many draft-age Vietnamese not in their military? Could Washington really see the light at the end of the tunnel?

▌▐▐▐▌

MARCH

Briefing

During March 1969 there was major activity in the III Corps area. One was Operation MENU, when U.S. Strategic Air Command bombers covertly bombed Communist forces in eastern Cambodia. This was an escalation of the tactical air attacks that had started in 1965 under the Johnson administration and entailed bombing rural sanctuaries and base

areas of the northern People's Army of Vietnam and the Viet Cong in
Cambodia along the South Vietnam border.

The 1st Cavalry Division launched Operation MONTANA SCOUT
from March 29 to June 23 against elements of the 1st and 7th NVA Divisions
along the southern boundaries of War Zone C in Tay Ninh Province on the
border with Cambodia. It used small-unit patrols and ambushes along the
enemy lines of communication extensive coverage by aerial reconnaissance
and surveillance. 1st Cav troops could watch the bombing and see the mile-
high black curtain of debris the mass of B52 strikes produced.

❘ ❘❘❘ ❘

It was 05:00 hours, Sunday, March 2.

PFC Green awoke the hootch. He always got them up by going
from bunk to bunk, like a gentleman, shaking each guy and turning
on the fluorescent lights.

"Come on, guys. Don't fall back to sleep. The lifers are around.
Come on, get up. Get up."

Ramirez lit up his first cigarette of the day. Tobacco smoke that
time of the morning almost nauseated Dyson, but Ramirez was a
good guy and a friend. There was some giggling. A couple of the guys
were looking at O'Grady. He was still asleep and had the enormous
hard-on sticking straight up with purple veins bulging. God, was
that cock big! It must have had a quarter-inch blow hole. "I wonder
how much cum shoots out of that thing," someone kidded. Try not
to stare.

Almost every man in the company had been issued an M16
but each hootch had one man assigned an M60. Some of the guys
who were also qualified crew members had been issued .45 Colt
semiautomatic pistols. All had ammo for their weapons—VC and
NVA infiltrators were not out of the question. Weapons and ammo
were obvious when wall lockers were open.

While the men were getting ready for the mess hall or the
shower room, the Commanding Officer, Major Sliman, and his
Executive Officer, Captain Birch, strolled through all the barracks to

see how things were going. When they entered the hootch, Florida yelled, "Tens-hut!" Everyone casually came to attention.

"Carry on, men. Carry on." Everyone went back to getting ready. Then Sliman spotted Rector shaving with his straight razor. It was pretty rare to see anyone using a straight razor daily, but they did produce wonderfully close shaves. The CO and the XO continued through the hootch and out into the company area.

"Captain Birch . . ."

"Yes, sir?"

"Write up an Article 15 for Rector—possessing a deadly weapon," said Sliman.

"Yes, sir."

"We can't have the enlisted men using things like that. What's he plan on doing anyhow, cutting someone's throat?"

I III I

His mother and Carol kept writing him letters, Mom more than Carol. He read Carol's over and over. On March 4 he got a letter from his mother saying that Brian Cromwell, a guy in his high school class, was MIA. All that was known was the helicopter he was riding in was shot down and crashed with all bodies recovered except his. Had he been a crew member? Had he been in an infantry unit on their way to a landing zone? Was the ship really shot down? Or was it a case of faulty maintenance? News stories could be such misstatements of facts. Sometimes the grapevine could be trusted, other times not.

I III I

They spent days and days working on the Hueys. Every twenty-five flying hours, a ship was inspected and gone over with a fine-tooth comb. Rotor blades, drivetrain, engine, linkages, controls, hydraulics, electric, avionics, and internal communications. Fifty hours was a more demanding inspection, and one hundred hours was the biggest inspection and tear-down of them all. None of Alpha and Bravo Companies' ships were gunships. There was only an M60 machine gun on each side for the door gunner and crew chief. The gunships had much, much more to inspect, service, and replace.

The gunship company in Long Thong had some unauthorized and custom-painted ships with rocket pods painted like Schlitz and Budweiser beer cans. "Give them the Schlitz!" and "This Bud's for you," could be heard over the radios when they fired their rockets at the enemy. There were ships painted up like World War II bombers with nose art and names like *Good Ghoul, Poltergeist, Widow Maker, Purple Haze,* and *Iron Butterfly.*

The company also had two LOHs (pronounced "Loaches"), light observation helicopters. They were small Volkswagen Bug-like helicopters—a four-seater, two in the pilot cabin and two in the passenger area. Most LOHs were unarmed except for door gunners, but these two had small rocket pods on each side and/or a minigun. The pilots would fly low and slow to entice enemy gunners and engage them or just mark the enemy position with smoke rockets. Then, the gunships would come in and do their thing. The guys in gunship companies were in a class all by themselves—brave, itching for a fight, fatalistic attitudes, and loved to pulverize the enemy with rockets and miniguns.

Reveille was officially 05:00 hours, but many guys worked second and third shift like back in the World. There were usually twenty Hueys. With the combination of the two companies, forty ships had to be kept in the air. But having a constant number was impossible. It took time to replace missing ships. The flight line, hangar, and operations sections were a beehive of activity, always. The busiest times were dawn and dusk when ships and crews departed for missions and, hopefully, returned from them. All returning ships needed service and often repairs. There was a grapevine of information between the operations personnel and the maintenance men.

Everyone knew when a ship was fired upon; fired upon and hit; hit but continued flying; or hit and downed. Inside the Operations Bunker was a detailed map of their AO (Area of Operations) with red-headed pins where anti-aircraft fire was encountered and the time and date. A pin was removed after forty-eight hours. There were red-headed pins in every direction around Long Thong, some very close to the camp.

On Thursday, March 6, the 137th Assault Support Helicopter Battalion was inserting troops into Tay Ninh, one of the Cambodian border provinces. Fifteen ships left Long Thong, picked up the troops in Phuoc Vinh, and ferried them to a valley near the border. Five ships at a time off-loaded their troops and then lifted off. In the last wave of Hueys, NVA gunners opened up. Mortars rained down on the LZ and the men as the enemy fired on the ships with machine guns and RPGs. Two of Alpha and Bravo Companies' ships were destroyed on the ground. Although the remaining three were shot up, they were still managed to fly out of range of the gunners. Artillery and gunship support were called in with some degree of effectiveness. The all-important enemy body count that would be used by most military and governmental world leaders to both justify and quantify the assault was a total of seventy NVA KIAs. And for this, we sacrificed twelve American KIAs and forty WIAs. Dyson still wished he could be flying as a crew chief or gunner.

The two ships destroyed were *065* and *067*—one crew member from *067* survived. He said he believed the ship was downed by a captured Claymore mine the gooks had set up in a treetop. *071, 072,* and *077* made it back to Long Thong. Two wounded crew chiefs and two door gunners were Medevaced to Phuoc Vinh. They were expected to survive. The bodies of the KIAs were taken to Graves Registration. Damaged ships could be repaired. Destroyed ships had to be replaced. Four aviator officers and three crew members had to be replaced—replaced with men like Dyson who wanted to fly and risk being KIA, WIA, or MIA.

▌▐▐▐▌

On March 7, the PVT E2s like Dyson were promoted to PFC E3s—Private First Class at one hundred fifty-five dollars a month.

Dyson got a letter from Carol. Two little boosts to his morale. Carol wrote that Pete Harley, a classmate of theirs, said, "Hello and take care of yourself." Dyson and Harley had many of the same friends and drank at the same bar occasionally. It was a nice gesture, he thought, to relay that through Carol. She said she missed him terribly. That gave him a pang of regret for not staying in school. Too late now.

One particular afternoon, Dyson, Spook, and SP4 Beeler and SP5 Ferrier were on a team replacing the main rotor blades on two ships. Dyson had watched blade replacement a few times and knew generally how it was done. They had stopped in their hootch for their noon break, touched base with Tug, drank a beer, and took just a couple of tokes of Cambodian Red. (Every batch of pot had a name, real or not.) This pot had been cleaned and was red like the dirt and damp with resin from the buds. It looked potent. A small bowl was packed and passed around. Dyson took just one decent-sized hit, and he could feel himself getting stoned. They put on their sunglasses, lit up cigarettes, and headed for the flight line. Dyson really enjoyed smoking a Camel after taking a hit or two of the other-worldly marijuana buds.

In front of the hangar were the three ships that made it back. *071* had holes everywhere on both sides. *072* was wounded with a gaping hole through the cowl under the engine exhaust, clear through. The forward part of *077* took a few rounds on its belly and through the lower front plexiglass panels, but the pilots were unscathed. Lucky. A closer look at *071* revealed dried black blood on the floor of the cargo area. Some of the troops had been hit by fire before jumping off. The two main targets for Communist gunners were a Huey's tail rotor and the pilot's cabin—the heck with the main rotor and engine.

Not surprisingly, it was Papp who brought *077* and its crew back. As always, cool under pressure.

I III I

In the evening, Alpha and Bravo Companies could watch a movie outdoors on an eight-foot-tall, sixteen-foot-long white plywood "screen." There was a small stage in front of it for an occasional show or band. The men sat on rows of old rotor blades for benches or brought their lawn chairs.

Next to the movie area was the Bravo Company Enlisted Men's Club. It was like a heavily sand-bagged chicken coop with a bar and tables and chairs, big enough for about thirty men. You buy cold beer, snacks, and cigarettes at the bar or through a service window. Beer was twenty-five cents a can. An unseen tape player in the back flooded the place with rock music. There was a sign above both entry doors that read, "NO WEAPONS ALLOWED—THIS MEANS YOU." Three men staffed the club from 15:00 to 22:00 hours. They enforced the "no weapons" and "no fights" rule.

Second Airmobile Division regulations stated enlisted men could drink beer only—no hard liquor, but it was everywhere, just hidden out of sight. The rule was flouted daily. Some men drank liquor only. Of course, there were guys who simply could not handle their liquor and got out of hand—usually the same drunks over and over again. Hootches were known to be either a drinker's hootch or a stoner's hootch. Theirs, of course, was a stoners'.

Dyson got a letter from Carol on March 14. She wrote about the winter back home, who she had seen around town, the upcoming St. Patty's Day, and her new hairdo. Couldn't she send him a picture? Dyson carried her high school graduation picture in his wallet and a picture of both at a big beer-bust picnic. He missed her so much.

Two hundred sixty-nine days to go.

▌▏▎▌

Olsen

That evening, Dyson, Florida, and Super Chicken got stoned in the barracks and had to decide between going to the EM Club or the movie. The movie was "Love Story," which they didn't care for—a movie with no shoot-outs, no karate, no sexy scenes—so they chose the EM Club. They got the last three chairs at a table with two other mechanics, SP4 J.R. McGinty and the newest FNG in Bravo Company, Private Richard Pauley. Just about everyone in the club was stoned or drunk or both. The atmosphere was like an old saloon out West with plenty of loud talk, belly laughs, bragging, and a thick haze of cigarette smoke. Dyson noticed someone had used a bayonet or K-bar knife to carve "FTA" (fuck the army) on their tabletop.

Around 23:00 hours, SP4 Rich Olsen, a crew chief dressed in a Nomex flight suit and wearing a 1911-A1 .45 in a holster, came in. One of the guys staffing the club, Sergeant Millard, was just inside the door.

"Whoa, whoa. Stop, stop, stop right there. No weapons allowed. You know that, Olsen." Olsen took another step forward and Millard said, "Stop, stop. You can't come in here with that weapon!" Now he had his hand on Olsen's chest.

Olsen was already drunk; his walk was unsteady. He and Millard had known each other for months and they never had an incident before.

"Turn around, leave, and come back later with no weapon."

"Fuck you, Millard. I'm staying." He side-stepped Millard, "Gimme a beer." They both shuffled left and right, Millard blocking Olsen and Olsen trying to get around Millard. Their movement put them next to Dyson's table.

"Look, Olsen. Give me the gun." Millard was offering to let him stay, but without the sidearm.

"Fuck you, Millard. You and your mom." Now he was drooling.

"OK, dickhead. Turn around and walk out of here."

"Hey, you want my gun?" and he pulled it out of its holster. A few men seated near the door hurriedly got up and left. "Here, go get it," and he tossed the pistol spinning end over end into the air over Dyson's table.

At that moment, you could see the gun suspended in the air, hammer down, muzzle pointed up at a forty-five-degree angle. It froze there; time seemed to stop. Dyson had experienced moments like this before, such as when the mortar killed the three men on the flight line. It was as if he even had time to think in complete sentences. He saw the checkered grip, the engraving on the slide, the iron sights, and the primary safety in the "fire" position.

Every eye was on the weapon in midair.

Hammer down, it struck near the center of their table. There was a POW! and the muzzle flash—a yellow-orange mini-explosion four inches long. To Dyson the gunshot was quiet. He saw individual sparks streaming outward. Time froze again with the flash. Pauley had both hands on the table, palms down, and a hole in his forehead over his left eye. It looked like a red cloud had just erupted out the back of his head—a cloud of blood, skull fragments, brain matter and scalp. Dyson was talking to himself in that millisecond "He's got a hole in his head . . . eyes open . . . look at that . . . ejected shell hanging in the air . . ."

Pauley's head snapped backward, his arms at his sides. He slouched in the chair with blood gushing from his massive exit wound onto the wood floor. He was dead. The .45 was on the floor, hammer back ready to fire the next round, and the slug was buried dead center in a two-by-four stud behind Pauley's chair. The empty brass shell was twelve feet away on the floor. The newest FNG in the company was dead.

The club quickly began filling up with lifers, some of them drunk. People gathered around Olsen, hemming him in. When Brady saw Pauley, he scurried outside and puked. Visibly shaken, Sliman looked at Olsen and his empty holster and ordered Olsen locked in the Mail Room CONEX for the night. He would be transferred in the morning to Long Binh Jail ("LBJ" it was called everywhere) to await his court-martial.

The word was out all over Vietnam. "You don't want to go to LBJ." It was notorious for its raw treatment of prisoners. One man was killed during a race riot ignited by black inmates protesting conditions.

The guys never saw Olsen again. Private Pauley was not alone. By the war's end there were approximately ten thousand noncombatant deaths of U.S. servicemen in South Vietnam.

A letter from the CO would be sent to his folks. How would he explain his death to them?

▐ ▍▍▍

Rumors had been swirling all over the country about a massacre of Vietnamese civilians by U.S. troops in March 1968. There were wild estimates about the body count, different locations where it occurred, rumors and more rumors. Then it was confirmed. It was a village called My Lai, two hundred forty miles north of Long Thong. When the guys heard about the slaughter, the overall attitude was, "So what? It happens all over Vietnam."

Fracas, Hill, and Doyle were all court-martialed for black marketeering in separate trials the same week on charges of theft, falsifying records, misappropriation of government goods, coercion, the list going on and on. All three staff sergeants later stated they could not have had access to the U.S. government goods they stole if it had not been for the aid of MAJ Sliman and 1SG Peterson. The court-martial board dug into Bravo Company's motor pool, supply, and mess hall records. It found discrepancies with Sliman's signatures and determined that Peterson was the person responsible for ordering much of the stolen goods. The proceedings were supposed to be confidential, but word spread everywhere.

▐ ▍▍▍

St. Patrick's Day

March 17, Saint Patty's Day, was an excuse for enlisted men to declare their Irish roots, real or imagined, party, and get drunk. The only true Irishman in the battalion was SP5 Ian O'Donahue, from County Cork, Ireland. To get his U.S. citizenship, he enlisted in the Army for three years. Later in the year, he and other immigrants in the service planned to attend a big Naturalization Ceremony in Hawaii. It was going to be a television news event. CPT Horstall had given O'Donahue and O'Grady the day off—O'Donahue so he could celebrate and O'Grady to watch him.

"Christ," Dyson thought. "Who's going to watch who?" All day long the two Irishmen harassed the hootch maids for boom-boom.

By 06:00 hours, Dyson, Spook, Soup, Florida, and Ramirez had already eaten chow. Back at the hootch, they were getting a buzz on before going to work. Joining them was SP5 Andrew "Andy" Morgan, a crew chief from Alpha Company assigned to the ships in their section.

"You got a nickname yet, Dyson?" asked Florida.

"No, not yet. None that I know of."

"How about Mister D?" said Ramirez. It had a nice ring to it, better than some of the derogatory nicknames around like Little Cock, Botch, Clam, Skimmer, Beggar, Moochie, and Shitty Pants.

"Yeah," said someone, "Mister D. Sounds nice—respectful."

"You like that, Mister D?"

"OK, I'll be Mister D. I'll smoke to that."

"Mister D, it is."

┃ ┃┃┃ ┃

"You going up today?" someone asked Morgan.

"Not unless they call me." He had been in-country eight months and had always been a crew chief. Morgan had many Air Medals. Every twenty hours in flight earned one. Morgan was sharp, married with one kid on the way.

"I want to be a crew chief or gunner," said Dyson, exhaling menthol-flavored smoke from pot repackaged in the Marlboro Greens.

"Believe me. It's not what it's crapped up to be," warned Morgan. "You can be dead in a heartbeat."

"Or you could die in the EM Club," Ramirez said.

┃ ┃┃┃ ┃

Brady assigned Dyson, Ramirez, SP4 Don Bratton, and SP5 Steve Conley to work on the hydraulic problems written up by the aircraft commanders for slow responses, controls too tight, and not enough lift when approaching maximum weight. They were common issues but sometimes hard to diagnose. Conley had a lot of experience. This was his second tour. A mellow guy, he said he liked it over here—the sun, the heat, the scenery, and the pot. He was both mechanic and crew chief and had survived some pretty hairy missions under fire.

Dyson would be tutored by Conley, while Bratton and Ramirez did routine parts replacements. Conley sorted through the writeups and maintenance forms. He was a fallen-away Mormon from Utah. Dyson was a lapsed Catholic. There were Mormon services in Long Binh and Catholic services here in Long Thong. Neither guy attended any of them.

Right now, they would work on *080*. The pilot had written up "spongey-ness" of one of the foot pedal controls and a slow response to lifting off. Conley knew right away what the problems could be and ran through the probable causes. He put the Huey tech manual on the ship's deck and opened it to a specific page.

"OK, let's see you remove that access panel." They talked as Dyson followed the steps in the book. "You stoned?" Conley asked.

The question kind of stunned Dyson. . . . "Uh . . . no."

"Yeah, you are."

"Yeah, but I . . ."

"No-no-no," Conley said. "I smoke, too. But I wait until midafternoon." So now, Dyson had another friend.

Conley continued instructing his student who was half listening while noticing how sensual the heat and the sunlight were beginning to feel on him.

Conley talked about life in a devout Mormon family, Dyson about being brought up Catholic. Conley went on about the strict family upbringing and the community-based Mormon structure. Dyson recalled not eating meat on Friday, giving up something for Lent, the relentless and punitive catechism classes, confession, penance, Holy Communion, high mass, and worshipping an angry and punishing God. Conley said when they wanted him to do his two years of missionary work in white shirt and tie, bicycling around the country preaching conversion, it was his time to leave home, and he did. Dyson said his dad quit going to church because of some resentments and he himself stopped when he went to college.

"You believe in God?" Conley asked.

"Well . . . yeah. I believe in God."

"You believe in God, but . . . what."

"If there's a God, why does he allow all this pain and suffering? I mean, look at this place. All the damn deaths. Thousands and thousands killed. Thousands and thousands wounded, disfigured, maimed, missing—for centuries and centuries." Dyson had seen only a tiny tip of the iceberg so far. Even to himself his words sounded corny, like an answer a dumb blonde Miss America contestant would give. "I have a problem with that."

"Well," Conley said, "the way it was explained to me, we live in the world created when Adam and Eve disobeyed the Lord. From then on, man had to live in a world of sin and disease."

"The Garden of Eden. Do you believe there was such a place?"

"There's two ways to read the Bible. One is to believe exactly what it says happened, as written. But the other way is to look at the stories like allegories."

"What's that?"

"An allegory is a statement that may or may not be true, but it teaches a lesson."

Dyson would remember that for the rest of his life.

O'Donahue and O'Grady's celebrating could be heard all the way from the Company area. It was only 11:30 hours and they were already smashed. O'Donahue was singing at the top of his lungs. "Give Ireland back to the Irish. . ."

Dyson, Conley, Ramirez, and Bratton went to noontime chow. Bratton had an ice chest from the mess hall so he invited the three others to his hootch for a beer. Dyson opted out of the midday beer. He'd wait until after work. He did have a quick toke, though. For the rest of the afternoon, Conley and Dyson talked about many things, but nothing more about God and religion.

From one of the nearest barracks, the Beatles sang "Why Don't We Do It in the Road?"

| ||| |

When Green woke them up at 05:00 hours on Monday, he said the usual morning formation at 06:00 hours was mandatory, in full uniform, for everyone, including personnel working on the flight line, in the hangar, and at the shops. Only guards on the perimeter would remain at their posts.

"Oh, boy, I wonder what this is about."

At 06:00, FSG Peterson called everyone to attention and turned the formation over to MAJ Sliman. But he didn't have them stand at ease, the point being that everyone was to listen to the message without distraction.

"OK, men, I am going to make this short and sweet. Starting immediately everyone, and I mean everyone, is to always be in full uniform. At work, at mess, at the PX, at the movies, in the EM Club. Everywhere except your own personal area where you bunk. Full uniform means boots, pants, T-shirt, blouse and headgear. When at work or on detail, EMs can only strip down to the T-shirt and it MUST be tucked in . . . No more shirtless GIs."

"Fuck this . . . balls . . . stateside bullshit" were whispers in the ranks.

"Yeah," someone said, "a fuckin' thief wants us to follow orders."

"Being in uniform means with dog tags, haircut, shave, and shined boots. No more necklaces, beads, or head bands." And then came the classic lifer taunt: "Is that clear?"

"Yes, sir," came the formation's half-hearted response.

"Also, everyone will have a steel cot and mattress. No more hammocks. And everyone, I mean everyone, will have a mosquito net over his bunk. By this evening, the cots, mattresses, and mosquito nets will be distributed to all barracks. There will be a walk-through inspection tomorrow morning to make sure everyone is only using the authorized sleeping gear." (More pissing and moaning in the ranks.) "And get rid of any 'FTA' graffiti you see. Paint over it, scrape it off, bury it, or piss and shit on it, but get rid of it! Is that clear?"

Only about half the men made a faint-hearted "Yes, sir."

I III I

Communist activity was heavy in the three border provinces, Tay Ninh, Binh Long, and Phuoc Vinh. Lying undiscovered for months was a system of three major supply and troop trails—highways really—running from the border sixty kilometers to the south. One trail west of Phuoc Vinh reached Bien Hoa and Saigon. The middle trail was east of Phuoc Vinh and ended in its heavily wooded area. The third was further east and also ended in War Zone D. Some parts of the trail were six feet wide underneath jungle canopy. The entire way was loaded with hundreds of thousands of sandal tracks and rutted lanes from an unending progression of bicycle tires. A VC was shot and killed walking a bicycle loaded with seven hundred pounds of rice. The 137th ASH Battalion flew in and out of the area every day.

The 137th ASH ships were being fired on and hit at an alarming rate, so there were plenty of Hueys to work on. The past week was the busiest Dyson had seen. Now half of the battalion's ships were on the ground for work. Division and Battalion Operations were hot on getting them back in flight. The men were working in three shifts, like a factory back home, and many guys were voluntarily putting in twelve to sixteen hours a day. Floaty and Gator brought sandwiches and drinks to the hangar, shops, and flight line. Pops never would have thought of that. He was off drunk somewhere.

Floaty walked up to the ship Dyson and Conley were working on. He had an insulated jug with ice and fruit drink.

"Hey!" What a voice Floaty had. He must have been the star tenor in his Baptist church's choir. Somewhere the Four Tops were singing "Don't Walk Away Renee."

"Hey-hey yourself," said Dyson.

"Hear the latest?"

"Good or bad?"

"Good. Sliman and Peterson have both put in for emergency

leave back home. Do you guys know Bennington at Battalion?" Neither of them did because Bennington was hardly ever seen out of the air-conditioned Battalion Headquarters, but he handled a lot of confidential paperwork for the Battalion Commander, Lieutenant Colonel Bannon, and Sergeant Major Jensen. If anyone would know anything it would be Bennington, the clerk. "He couldn't give me any details but he said Sliman suddenly had a seriously ill wife, and Peterson's family has two hospitalized siblings."

"What a coincidence."

"Yeah, and since they both have less than sixty days to DEROS, they won't have to come back to finish their tour." Unbelievable. What timing.

"And Colonel Bannon is expediting both requests with help from Division. They're all helping them get out of this investigation." Of all the goddamn . . .

"This stuff goes all the way to the top, this black-market shit," said Conley. He had seen enough of it on his first tour, and now here. "Of course, it would be a black eye for Division if they were tried."

"Did you ever see such a thing?"

"Well, if that don't beat all . . ."

The news went from the cooks to a couple of mechanics, on to the flight line, shops, and barracks. Everyone knew about it now. Bennington may have told Floaty, but Jensen told everybody in the NCO Club the night before that they were getting emergency leave for Sliman and Peterson and the investigation would be over. A bunch of NCOs in the club visibly breathed a sigh of relief as they listened to Tammy Wynette singing "Stand By Your Man."

I IIII

The last day of March. Kosski was making the rounds, handing the workers their mail. Incoming mail was priority No. 1. It was accepted all over the country that everyone could stop whatever they were doing to read their mail.

"Here you go, Mister D."

He noticed right away the envelope felt light. Usually, it was packed with maybe four sheets of folded writing paper. This was a single page. "Not much going on . . . Dad retired . . . deep snow . . . party at Nora's house . . . Billy got busted for pot . . . have to go now."

Not much going on is right. Maybe she didn't have a lot of time to write. Maybe just a small list of things to write about. But the tone of the letter was nothing like all the previous ones. Where was the "missing you very much" part? Well, he knew sometimes he had to grope for things to write about, that's all.

I IIII I

APRIL

The 137th ASH Battalion had been working around the clock as Hueys flew in and out of War Zone D. Charlie and Delta Companies combined had lost four ships, six aviators, and eight crew members since March 6. Alpha and Bravo Companies in Long Thong had lost seven ships, four aviators, and seven crew members. New Hueys would come in a few at a time, but not as fast as they were shot down. New aviators, crew members, and mechanics trickled in. Aviators underwent a one-week pilot orientation in An Khe to get familiar with 2nd Airmobile Division Operations before being sent to their units. Mechanics and crew members were stuck in a senseless circuitous routine of being sent up north to replacement camps, pulling KP, filling sandbags, another replacement camp, more KP, burning shit, another replacement camp, ending up in their unit only miles from where they first landed in Bien Hoa.

Dyson and some other men who all came into Bravo Company about the same time were being recognized as dependable hard workers who could pull long hours and perform their duties without a whole lot of supervision.

"Give Dyson a tech manual and a few instructions and he gets it done," CPT Horstall said. The whole company knew him as "Mister D." He and the other dependable PFCs were on a list to be promoted to SP4—a pay increase to two hundred fourteen dollars a month.

It was April Fool's Day. By sunup, the flight line was already at full capacity. Same for the hangar and shops. Battalion and Division needed constant updates on ships and availability. The Operations Center was almost a madhouse, but SP5 Brandon Taylor kept things running smoothly. The wall map of the Battalion's AO had so many pins in it showing ground fire, it sparkled like rubies when the sun hit it. Dyson, SP5 "Paco" Riaz and two other mechanics were working on *080*. It needed another four hours.

There were a lot of new faces around. FNGs everywhere as well as new officer-aviators checking on their ships. Horstall was walking with the company XO, CPT Birch, and a major no one had seen before. Floaty came around with hot coffee. He even had creamer and sugar—not many guys could drink mess hall coffee black. The three officers had stopped next to the sign, "NO SMOKING ON THE FLIGHT LINE." Horstall seemed to be pointing out the flight line from left to right for the major.

"See that major over there?" Floaty said. They peeked that way. "He's your new CO."

"New CO? When's this gonna happen?" The guys knew Floaty had inside information at Battalion HQ.

"It already happened, man. Division was rushing like mad to get rid of Sliman and Top as fast as they could to stay away from the investigation." Somebody snorted in disgust. "They even had the Red Cross 'verify' their emergencies back home."

"I wonder what kind of deal that was."

"Unbelievable."

Sliman and Peterson both had sent a lot of money home for months. There were limits on how much money a GI could send home, but with a waiver from commanding officers it was easy to send over the limit. They would have gotten away with that and gone home, but the court-martials mentioned their names repeatedly.

"They're gone?"

"Yep," said Floaty, "Sliman flew home yesterday. Top flies home today."

"What about the Change of Command Ceremony?" asked Riaz. That ritual was always a big to-do with an outgoing commander and the incoming commander formally changing command in front of all the company formations.

"There is none," said Floaty. "It's all said and done. Major Brisco, that man over there, is our new CO. A new 'first shirt' (another name for a first sergeant) is at Battalion HQ right now."

"Do you believe that shit?"

"Amazing. If the people back home could only see."

| ||| |

The next day was another mandatory morning formation. The new Commanding Officer of Bravo Company was indeed Major Donald J. Brisco, a West Pointer bound to be a general someday. The new first sergeant was J.M. Enrico, a man with twenty-five years of service. Everyone was stunned at the no-warning transition of the command. The company sign outside the Orderly Room had been taken down and was somewhere being updated. First Brisco then Enrico said they were looking forward to working with the men. 1SG Enrico had a Spanish accent, so thick it was hard to understand some of his words. Then it was back to work for everyone.

In the days that followed, inspections made sure every man had a steel bunk, wall locker, and footlocker. The damn footlockers took up so much room in a hootch that they hindered evacuating it during an attack, but the footlockers remained.

The uniform regulations laid down by Sliman were enforced. Haircuts—"high and tight"—and daily shaves were monitored and mustaches could not extend beyond the ends of the lips. That was funny because a major in the gunship company, part of the 2nd Airmobile Division, had a classic handlebar mustache, sculpted, and waxed. He also strolled around wearing a pair of polished nickel

Colt .45 six-guns like an Old West sheriff and black Stetson cavalry officer's hat.

SP4 Kevin Sparse from Oklahoma was still the CO's permanent driver. Like everyone there who worked in the sun, his skin had turned a reddish tan from a combination of the tropical sun and the red dust and clay soil of Vietnam. He had sandy-colored hair and a mustache. When he wasn't driving, he was reading. In the rear of the jeep were books like *The Waste Land* by T.S. Eliot and *Absalom, Absalom* by William Faulkner. There was more to Sparse than met the eye. His DEROS and ETS were in May.

Kosski made the rounds with the mail. Sparse was outside the Orderly Room, reading in the shade when he opened the letter from his fiancé. "That motherfucking whore!"

As it eventually came out, his fiancé had written faithfully and Sparse faithfully sent practically all his money to her to get their new life together—a place to live and a car. Not a hint of anything wrong until today. She had hooked up with another guy, married, and spent all his money.

"Dear John" letters were delivered all over, just about every company got them occasionally. Suddenly Dyson was wondering about the change in Carol's letters.

IIIII

April was a busy month in III Corps. On April 10, the 1st Infantry Division launched *Operation ATLAS POWER* around Saigon to destroy the NVA and VC infrastructure and supply lines. And on April 12, the 1st Cavalry Division began *Operation MONTANA RAIDER* in Tay Ninh Province.

The 137th ASH flew daily to a cluster of LZs in the three border provinces: LZ Dot, LZ Dolly, LZ Barbara, LZ Betty, and LZ Grant. These were all camps manned by infantry and artillery, chiseled out of the woods. Army Engineers cleared the sites with bulldozers and piled a ring of earth in a berm all around. The woods were cut down as far away as possible for a no man's land beyond the green line. Each camp was an anthill of bunkers, trenches with sandbags, and guard bunkers dotting the perimeter. LZ Grant was within sight of 3,200-foot Black Virgin Mountain (Nui Ba Den in Vietnamese), an extinct cinder cone heavily wooded and covered in large basalt boulders. Inside Nui Ba Den was a honeycombed NVA stronghold of tunnels, trenches, and machinegun bunkers and spider holes—camouflaged foxholes for one man. Supplied by helicopter for much of the war, the Americans "controlled" the top to boost radio communications while the Viet Cong controlled the bottom and surrounding foothills.

It was common knowledge that the enemy constantly monitored each camp's activities and enemy gunners ringed those camps twenty-four hours a day to maintain target priorities. If a ship flew in and out, it would be fired upon. Troops leaving the camps for search and destroy missions almost always engaged the NVA and VC, from small firefights to full-scale battles requesting artillery and close air support. In some circumstances CH47 Chinook helicopters were deemed too slow and too big a target for the enemy gunners so Hueys flew in and out—ferrying in FNGs, ammo, hot meals and C-rations, mail, and sling-loaded Lister bags of water under the ship. Outbound they would carry mail, WIAs, and KIAs. The WIAs could either be lightly wounded or partly stabilized by medics, or clinging to life with a medic feverishly tending them in flight. The KIAs were not always hidden in body bags. These rides were not for chickens or the squeamish.

I III I

Medevac

For a few days, Dyson was conscious of a slight toothache, but as the days passed it became a major one. Like anyone needing medical attention he went on "sick call" and went over to the dispensary for Alpha and Bravo Companies. When the medic looked in his mouth he said, "Oh, man. You've got an abscess on the gum next to a molar." He put down his flashlight and said, "You gotta go to Phuoc Vinh—now."

"You're shitting me."

"No, man. If that thing breaks open, you'll get so sick you could die." The medic went to the landline and called Operations for a Medevac to Phuoc Vinh. He put the phone down and said, "Captain Boyle says to get to Operations right now. Go."

Boyle was standing in front of the Operations CP, waiting. "Hey, Dyson. Over here. Let me see, open up." He knew how bad abscesses could be. "Holy shit! See *086* over there?" He pointed to a Huey already running up. The aircraft commander motioned to come aboard.

SP5 Morgan, the crew chief, had him sit centered on the bench seat facing forward. They taxied above ground to the flight line, then took off down the flight line, quickly gaining speed. The ship climbed as rapidly as possible and headed northwest toward Phuoc Vinh, forty miles away. At five thousand feet the ship leveled off and they were cruising at 100 knots.

By now his gum was throbbing, but that didn't keep him from marveling at the countryside. Stretches of forests, areas thick with bamboo and elephant grass. Villages with acres of rice paddies, some centuries old. And everywhere bomb and artillery craters. Big craters, little craters, and one superhighway-size path of immense craters from B52 strikes. Some craters were filled with blue water like swimming pools. Dyson yearned to be a crew chief.

Phuoc Vinh was in sight before long. They descended rapidly to over the flight line, taxied toward a ground crew member waving them in, and set down. Morgan motioned for him to jump off and pointed to a jeep with a Red Cross symbol on it. The Medevac then lifted right off for another mission.

"Dyson?" asked the jeep driver. He jumped in the front seat. The 2nd Airmobile Division Field Dental Facility was a big bunker, a combination of sandbags and fifty-five-gallon barrels filled with dirt. The roof was layers of sandbags on railroad tie-type beams. Over it a canvas tent had been pitched to keep the rain out. Two air conditioners stuck out through one wall. A medic was waiting.

"Dyson? Let's see, open up. Wow, man, you're lucky."

The field dentist's chair where Captain Vincent Waller operated was the most ominous one he had ever seen. It had a rudimentary movable spotlight, and the spitting and rinsing fountain spat back. It looked like a torture device. Of course, it was OD green. The cushion seat and backrest had been repaired with green duct tape. The medic sat Dyson in the chair, put a bib on him, and tilted this crude seat back almost horizontal. "The doc will be here in a minute."

CPT Waller hurried in. "Open up," he ordered. No introduction, no small talk. He shoved his fingers into Dyson's mouth. "Where is it?" he hissed.

Where is it? You got to be kidding me! No one else had any trouble spotting it. Dyson pointed. The dentist was sweating profusely. He had a pockmarked pudgy face with tiny red veins on his nose, and yellow teeth. "Medic!" he yelled, and the same guy came in to assist.

"I'm gonna numb ya," the dentist said and produced a stainless-steel syringe with a thumb plunger, finger grips, and a long, stout needle—like in the horror movies. Taking quick aim, he inserted the needle in the hinge joint of the upper and lower jaw. It felt like his jaw was connected to house current, a hundred and ten volts. The needle had hit the mandibular nerve. Damn that hurt. After a few seconds, Waller pulled it out. This guy had left his bedside manner stateside.

The medic put gauze on the gum on each side and readied a suction tube. The dentist picked up a small lance and burst the abscess. The medic cleaned the whole mess up.

"I'll be back," the dentist said.

The medic bent down and said in Dyson's ear, "He doesn't like to be out of his air conditioning." And as if that wasn't bad enough, "He doesn't like enlisted men." They waited for the painkiller to take effect. "Feel numb? Here? Over here? OK." He stepped out of the little room and called, "OK, Doc."

The dentist hurried back. Dyson opened his mouth wide and faced him directly. Waller roughly adjusted Dyson's head this way and that. He began pushing away the gum below the infected tooth and tried moving it with his fingers. It didn't budge. "Shit," he said, now sweating bullets. The medic handed off a tool and the dentist began pulling on the tooth.

Dyson could feel the pressure, but not the tooth moving. Now Waller was getting impatient. He applied more force and wound up breaking the molar off at the gum line. "Fuck!" he said and tossed the bloody tool onto a tray.

"Scalpel," he barked to the medic. He began to cut away the gum to get the root of the tooth exposed. Dyson shut his eyes. He could feel the cutting here, cutting there, this side, that side, lower over here, a little further down here. Finally, there was enough tooth exposed to pull the whole mess out. The medic began suctioning him out. Dyson moved his tongue around the spot. He opened his eyes. The dentist was gone and so was his tooth and much of his gum.

"Sorry, man," said the medic. "He's the only dentist we got." The medic packed the gum with gauze, cleaned around his mouth, and removed the bloody bib. "Come on," he motioned. At his desk, the medic offered a cup of water and a big pill. "Here. Take one of these now." Dyson downed the pill. "I'm only supposed to give you four of these, but I'm giving you twelve. Take one every four hours. That thing's going to bleed for a while. Rinse with salt and water, and here's some gauze to take with you. And don't smoke for at least forty-eight hours if you can."

"OK, bud. Thanks." They shook hands.

"The driver will take you to the flight line. Good luck."

For years and years after that day, whenever a dentist looked into Dyson's mouth, he would ask, "What the hell happened in here?"

I III I

Monday, April 7—two hundred forty-five days to go.

The guys were working seven days a week—as many hours as they could. Lives depended on these Hueys being in the air. The work was punctuated with a cold beer here, a few tokes there, music sporadically in the background, and a little party-time before going to sleep. It was great not having to spend time on laundry, cleaning the hootches, and shining boots. The hootch maids took care of that. The only contact Dyson had with Tug was during the midday break after lunch in the mess hall when the guys stopped in the hootch for a quick high. Tug was always glad to see him. This time he had a little bag for her to take home—a bar of soap, toothpaste, new toothbrushes, a comb for each kid, and packages of gum. "Thank you, Mister D. You number one." Why did so many of the guys treat these people like they were shit? One young hootch maid in Bravo Company was very pretty with long black hair. Many of the guys talked to her like she was a whore. It disgusted him.

He and Tug chitchatted for a bit. She was like any single mother back home. "It is hard to feed little ones when VC take most my money." The VC levied taxes on villagers. It was an open secret that some of the day laborers were, in fact, Viet Cong, gathering intelligence. "VC in Long Thong last night," she informed him under her breath as she quickly turned away and went back to her work.

There was a new problem to worry about. Rotary wing pilots all over Vietnam reported a grave malfunction. It seemed when a Huey was loaded near or at maximum capacity and climbing, picking up speed and banking (as it often did when flying out of a hot LZ) the ship would lose lift, stall, and then fall out of the sky like a rock. Those killed took the cause of the crash with them.

All the divisions and MACV had repeatedly, but so far unsuccessfully, tried to reproduce the malfunction. The word was put out to 137th ASH flight and maintenance personnel that if anyone could discover what the problem was, they should notify Division Headquarters immediately.

Vickers

April 9 was hotter than usual. The flight line was like a giant griddle. The pressure was on to get the ships up and out because of all the communist activity in War Zone D, at the Iron Triangle and the Ho Bo Woods, both just a few short miles north of Saigon. Dyson and Rector (who'd been punished with an Article 15 for possessing his straight razor) were replacing the drive chain on a tail rotor. Two other mechanics were working on the front of the aircraft. SP5 Strickland and another guy were on the next ship on the line.

A stereo of some sort in a hootch had Arthur Brown singing "I Am the God of Hell Fire," one of those infamous one-hit wonders. Dyson was bobbing his head to the beat when he happened to make eye contact with Strickland. In that instant, Strickland glanced skyward and yelled, "Incoming!" Guys immediately hit the dirt.

WHUMP! A mortar landed at the entry of the nearest hootch. Now everyone was up and running. Dyson headed toward the bunker at the hootch that was hit. Someone yelled, "Medic! Medic!" at the top of his lungs. The sirens started. A wounded man lay on the ground. Someone rushed up and knelt beside him. Dyson ran to the downed man. There was always the overwhelming urge to help.

The kneeling man had lifted the wounded man's head off the ground with one hand and had his other hand on the man's shoulder. The man's body, from his boots up to his collar bone was shredded. His fatigue pants were bloody rags. The remains of his T-shirt hung around his shoulders and neck. His midsection had been blown open and his lacerated organs glistened. Blood quickly collected in pools at his sides. His hands were up in the air and he was violently shuddering and screaming. How in the fuck could he even be alive?

"Oh, my God! He's gonna die," one asshole cried.

"Will you shut the fuck up!" Strickland said, pushing the asshole away, causing him to spin to the ground.

The guy was wide-eyed and screaming. What in the hell *can* you do? Strickland knelt beside him. "Vickers! Vickers! Listen to me. You're gonna be all right, you hear? Stay with me, Vickers . . ."

A medic, SP5 Corelli from the dispensary, and two litter carriers arrived on the grisly scene. Phil Corelli had seen it all—gunshot wounds, head wounds, sucking chest wounds, traumatic amputations, snakebites. Closing his eyes, he bowed his head slightly and silently shook it "no," but he kept on regardless.

"Hey, Vickers," he yelled as Vickers continued to scream and convulse and refused to die. "Vickers! We're taking you to the dispensary. You're gonna be all right." The guys stooped down and deftly transferred Vickers and his guts onto the litter. His screaming was dying down, fading away. The three of them rushed him to the dispensary. He was dead before they got there. A single mortar shell with his name and serial number on it had fallen right at his feet. Was it by coincidence? By chance? Or was it simply that his name finally arrived at the top of "the List?"

SP4 Donald Vickers was an auto worker from Detroit, a draftee. He wasn't in Bravo Company very long before people realized he didn't like to work. He wouldn't do even the bare minimum, constantly going to the latrine, back to his hootch, to the Orderly Room for personal business, and he always took his sweet time doing it. He learned how to go on sick call, often. He'd been bounced around from section to section. Nobody wanted him.

Now Brisco and Enrico joined them at the scene. "Anyone hit?" Brisco asked.

"Yes, sir. Vickers is KIA."

"Vickers?"

"Yes, sir."

"Humph. Didn't know him."

▌▐▐▐▌

DEPARTMENT OF THE ARMY
MILITARY ASSISTANCE COMMAND VIETNAM
2ND AIRMOBILE DIVISION
137th ASSAULT SUPPORT HELICOPTER BATTALION
COMPANY B

April 10, 1969

Dear Mrs. Vickers,

Please accept our deepest sympathies and sincere condolences on the death of your son, SP4 Donald Vickers. He died as the result of a mortar attack from hostile forces at our base in Long Thong, South Vietnam. I want you to know Donald did not suffer from his wounds and was killed instantly.

As you know, Donald had been in our Company seven months. He was a soldier of the highest order. He adapted quickly and very well to these difficult working conditions and performed his duties as a helicopter mechanic, exceeding many of his fellow soldiers in his job performance. His high degree of military bearing was an example to the entire Company.

Over the course of seven months Donald gained the respect and admiration of many men and he gained many new friends. These men will miss him very much.

Donald was a credit to himself, his unit, and the U.S. Army.

Enclosed are his awards of the Purple Heart, United States Army Commendation Medal, and Good Conduct Medal. We hope you will display his awards proudly to show all the hard work Donald did toward achieving democracy and peace in South Vietnam.

Again, my most sincere condolences and I remain,

DONALD J. BRISCO
Commanding Officer
Bravo Company, 137th ASH Battalion
2nd Airmobile Division, U.S. Army

I III I

April 15. The IRS filing deadline for income tax. Right. Come and get it. At 20:15 hours the three mechanics decided it was time to call it a day. Dyson, Florida, and Riaz had been working since 06:30, breaking only a half hour for a noon chow of Sloppy Joes, baked beans, and potato salad. By 21:30 they had showered and were hanging around Riaz's area with a few other guys, listening to music, and smoking some potent grass. For a change they chose Simon and Garfunkel to mellow out. Considering their surroundings, it was nice.

"Wow, man," said R.J., "I wonder when it's going to slow down around here."

"Not until the monsoon starts," Riaz said. "When the rains come and all their roads and trails turn into mud and their tunnels and caves fill up with water." He had seen it before. The monsoon season didn't start until the end of September—a long way off.

Men were working on the flight line under portable flood lights, serenaded with the ever-present sound of aircraft in the sky and artillery off in the distance. There was artillery in Long Thong, too—a couple batteries of 105mm cannons arrayed in bunkers and revetments for camp defense and supporting units in the field.

"Well, 05:00 comes early."

"Yeah, I guess it's time to sleep." They broke up and went to their bunks. It was always great to lie down stoned and drop off to sleep. Dyson had vivid dreams that took place in civilian life. Other times his dreams were Army-oriented. The people and places would be real, but the circumstances would be crazy and out of place.

Some bunks in his hootch were empty as those guys preferred to work nights. Only one guy remained up. Spook was listening to music with his headset on. Dyson stared at the underside of the metal roof and gradually fell asleep.

A "WHACK!" jolted him. Then another, "WHACK!" He looked up at the roof. He couldn't believe his eyes. Two warheads of two large mortar rounds were poking through the sheet metal. Are those eight-deuce mortars? Delayed action? Were they duds? Did he have to run for cover? Before he could think any further, twelve more 107mm and 120mm rocket warheads pierced the metal roof. What the fuck! These can't all be duds, he thought. Then some big, fat, grotesque lifer with two bloody stumps for arms leaned over him and yelled, "Run, you stupid motherfucker! Run!"

He sprang up from the bed and yelled "Run! Run! Run!" while trying to shake off sleep. He was panting and sweating like he had just run a mile. He could feel his feet on the concrete now and he was awake, mostly.

Rector, Florida, Spook, and Riaz were now saying, "Hey, Dyson . . . Mister D . . ."

"Easy . . . easy . . . You musta had a dream. Easy."

Jesus, that was so real. He looked up. No nose cones, no warheads, no holes, just a plain corrugated and completely intact metal roof.

"You OK now?"

He exhaled. "Yeah. OK." He had dreamt about the room he was sleeping in and it was very difficult to tell if he was still dreaming or not. When he awoke, he would always ask himself, "Did that really happen?" This was the beginning of his many years of nightmares.

He could fall asleep in a place he had never been before and have a dream about something happening in that room. It would get to the point where he felt he could only go to sleep drunk or stoned. But he wouldn't be sleeping; he would be passed out, two entirely different things.

Dyson didn't sleep for rest of that night.

▌▐▐ ▌

Ships from the Alpha and Bravo Companies were again flying missions into the three border provinces, inserting troops in the Communist sanctuaries, carrying in supplies, taking FNGs to their units, hauling mail to and from the field units, performing Medevac missions, some of them quite hairy under fire, and flying out KIAs to Graves Registration points. Bloody decks and bench seats were the norm. The troops left behind a myriad of different things on the ships—ammo, grenades, field packs, canteens, cigarettes, dope, and sometimes a bloody body part from a wounded or dead grunt. Once there was a big headless snake. The snake was later put in a mechanic's bunk for a joke.

▌▐▐▌

In the early days of the war, troops would spend three to five days in the field and return to base. As the war dragged on, three to five days became seven, ten, thirteen, three weeks, a month or more. One LRRP (Long Range Reconnaissance Patrol) came back in after sixty-some days along the Cambodian border. The Division paymaster had them listed as MIA and there wasn't any pay for them.

Some LLRP teams went into the woods and were never heard from again.

▌▐▐▌

After three weeks, he finally got a letter from Carol—a single page, filling just half of it. She didn't talk about much at all, only how she was tired of seeing the war on TV every night and signed off "More later." Pen pals could write better letters. Could she have depression or something? He wrote back asking if there was anything wrong and told her how much he missed her.

The grapevine from the Operations Center went from the pilots and crews to the flight line. Everyone knew and talked about the battles going on in the three provinces, day and night. On AFVN TV in the evening, guys would faithfully watch Bobbie, the Weather Girl and also news of what was going on in-country. It was a new experience learning about stuff before it got on TV. The latest scuttlebutt had to do with the attacks on LZ Grant in Tay Ninh Province.

It was 17:00 hours and he could see he would be working late into the night again. *074* had returned early from its daily missions because the pilots reported a slight delay in pedal response. Dyson, Spook, and Ramirez were assigned to dig into the problem. The aircraft commander met with them. CW2 Scavelli looked maybe sixteen. He was five-foot-ten, had a boyish face, some acne, and only needed to shave to keep his sideburns straight. Officers and crews said he was a good pilot. They also kept a list of bad pilots.

The two pilots left and their crew chief, SP5 Aaron Dell, and door gunner, SP4 Bob Anderson, joined them for a bit. *074* had some new bullet holes.

"Where'd you guys go today?"

"Back and forth between Phuoc Vinh and LZ Grant, back and forth." Dell looked tired.

"Did you get these at Grant?" asked Spook about the holes.

"Two holes one time and four another time. They're shooting at everybody flying in and out of Grant." Dell and Anderson were staying there to give their M60s a good cleaning.

"We exchanged fire with people we couldn't see. Even a tracer coming out of the trees doesn't pinpoint exactly where the fucker is."

"It took Chinooks three days to get a battery of six 105 Howitzers into camp. They had to do it with gunship support every single time." Anderson was on an extension of four months for a six-month early out. Dyson did not have to extend as the Army took its sweet time sending him over here. Lucky. Two hundred thirty-four days to go.

Four other ships were coming in now off their missions because of mechanical issues or damage from ground fire. One crew member suffered a minor wound when an enemy round went through the top of his flight helmet and put a slice in his scalp. Lucky.

Dyson, Spook, and Ramirez worked until 20:00 hours. They finished filing all their maintenance forms, touched base with Brady, and headed to the mess hall.

"God, I'm hungry."

The guys took one look at the chow line and could tell both Gator and Floaty were absent. Floaty was on R&R to Singapore, Gator on sick call. Pops made tonight's mess.

"Oh, my God."

It was supposed to be Sloppy Joes but it was more like grease con carne. A steel ladle for serving ran through two inches of red grease and into the ground meat. The stale buns had been left out all day, the potato salad had formed a crust, the cake with frosting was hard like the buns were, and the milk machine was dried up.

SP4 Gerson was on KP. Ramirez asked in a low voice, "Where's Pops?"

"Drunk." Gerson and the KPs had nothing to do with the food preparation. No one knew where Pops was. The cooler was padlocked so there was no filling the milk machine. Many lifers got away with murder.

I III I

Around noon the next day, *072* returned to Long Thong desperately in need of repairs for damage done while dropping supplies off to LZ Grant. It was all over Long Thong that there had been a fierce ground attack on LZ Grant overnight. The crew from *072* would be given the first available ship. The pilots walked to the Operations Center and the two crew members began talking with some of the ground crew, Super Chicken among them. Soup motioned for Dyson to come over. "You should hear this."

"It was unbelievable," the crew chief was saying. "It looked like someone took a big steel rake and just shredded the ground and the trees on one side of the camp. The gooks had overrun one part of the camp and were trying to divide it in two." Here was another account of NVA and VC breaching formidable defenses into a U.S. camp and overrunning it. "But the artillerymen leveled their 105s and fired beehive rounds into them. There were bodies everywhere, from the firing pits clear into the woods."

The beehive round was designed to repel ground attacks. The cannon would be leveled parallel to the ground and aimed directly into the attackers. As soon as it cleared the muzzle, the shell casing would "banana-peel" back and eight thousand five hundred stainless steel darts flew out at three thousand feet per second in a sixty-five-degree killing field that would rip through any attackers and whatever else was in the way. They were first used in combat in Vietnam in 1966.

"There were gooks, pieces of gooks, and their weapons plastered to the trees as far as you could see into the woods. As we were flying in, those scattered beehive darts below us sparkled in the sun like diamonds. Large cargo nets were spread on the ground and the troops piled the bodies of dead VC onto the nets to be sling-loaded out by Chinooks. Someone had to climb on top of the pile and slip the net's doughnut onto the hook that was hanging from the belly of the Chinook. Then the load was lifted and flown deep into the forest and dropped into the jungle—net and all."

"I'll never forget that sight for the rest of my life," uttered the gunner.

The battle at LZ Grant was featured that night on AFVN TV.

Dyson still wanted to be a crew member, risking his life and limb to see what the hell went on out there in this war.

‖ ‖ ‖

Guard Duty

Dyson and Super Chicken were pulling guard duty on the perimeter in Bravo Company's sector along with SP4s Will Acheson and Ted Blunt, who, back in the World, was a cowboy from Wyoming. It was getting towards 21:00 when the guards changed watches. The four mechanics sat in a jeep behind the bunker they were to relieve. Light shone down from the half-moon and brilliant stars above. Music from the hootches drifted faintly with the breeze. There weren't any ships within hearing distance, a rarity for this place.

The men were in their field gear with steel pots on, weapons and ammo locked and loaded. Acheson was the driver, while Blunt—naturally—rode shotgun. Dyson and Soup were in the back. The smell of pot was everywhere. Ten minutes to go. Time for a pick-me-up.

Acheson lit up a small corn cob pipe (the PX sold hundreds of pipes) of the good stuff, a mixture of Cambodian Red and Mekong

Blonde. Dyson took a big hit and passed the bowl to Blunt, who took a turn and passed it over his shoulder to Soup. Soup looked into the glowing embers and toked up, then passed the pipe on back to its owner. Dyson lit a Camel. The guys were quiet, counting the minutes. Acheson started rolling joints for later.

"Why do you even bother rolling?" Soup asked.

"I can roll a joint with one hand on a rainy night in the back of a jeep going down a bumpy road and not get it wet or spill any."

"And he can, too," Blunt agreed.

"Hey," said Soup, "We're rolling," meaning the jeep was rolling.

"No, we're not," said Acheson.

"Yeah, we're rolling."

"No, we ain't," Acheson insisted. "The emergency brake is on," but he checked it anyway. Dyson looked at the jeep's tall antenna and lined it up with a distant light pole in order to see if the jeep was moving or not.

"Well," said Soup, "I know we're rolling."

"No, we ain't."

"Yes, we are."

"Fuck you guys," said Blunt, "I'll tell you if we're rolling or not." He swung his right leg outside the jeep and put his foot down on the ground.

"Well?"

After a pause, Blunt said, "I can't tell."

That was some good stuff.

MAY

Medic

Alpha and Bravo Companies had been working around the clock, mainly due to the enlisted men who knew the life-and-death importance of having the ships airborne and who volunteered for the extra duty. The enemy continued to barrage the camp with rockets and mortars day and night. A 2nd Airmobile Division Chinook company in Lai Khe had suffered a devastating stand-off rocket and mortar attack that destroyed eight out of their sixteen ships. It would be two weeks before the replacement ships would arrive.

Two hundred twenty days to go.

It seemed like ages ago that he left home. It seemed like ages ago that he was at Fort Eustis. And it certainly seemed like he'd been here for ages. Sometimes the days seemed to fly by while his days-to-go crept by at a snail's pace.

Sparse, the CO's driver, had flown home and been discharged. What he'd gone home to was anyone's guess—no fiancé, no money, no place to stay, no car. Dyson hadn't heard from Carol since the middle of April. Mom, God bless her, kept writing faithfully twice a week, page after page of gossip, local events, funny TV shows, and the news on TV. She said she worried a lot about him. He wrote to her and told snippets of how things were quiet and all they did was work on Hueys. He didn't dare tell her about being shelled by rockets and mortars, and that men right in camp getting killed and maimed.

Brady was asking for volunteers to fill and replace sandbags on bunkers and revetments damaged by the intense shelling. Dyson, Spook, Florida, and Riaz put their hands in the air, but the sergeant wouldn't have it. "Not you guys. We need you guys fixing the ships." And that was that.

After the midday break in the hootch, they were headed back to work. They all had, of course, a good buzz on. Dyson loved the sun, the heat, the music, working with the guys while mildly stoned. Someone, somewhere was playing the Lovin' Spoonful's "Do You Believe in Magic?"

"Incoming!" yelled Strickland. Everybody hit the dirt. They now knew Strickland could hear what no one else could—the last split second of a rocket's hissing flight. Then the blast, WHUMP! Some guys stayed down while others ran into bunkers. Seconds went by—

nothing. A minute—still nothing. People were yelling for the medics. Two minutes went by—*still* nothing. Behind the orderly room there was a flurry of activity as more people picked up the cry of "Medic!" Someone had gotten hit. A dozen guys surrounded a blackened and ruined jeep. The passenger seat took a direct hit by a 107mm rocket, *while* the jeep was moving. What little was left of the driver was now splayed in the dirt beside the vehicle. Why would anyone even yell for the medics? The right side of his body was blown away, his leg shredded, yellow bones of his hip and pelvis exposed, a gaping, blackened and bloody cavern in his torso, the splintered remains of his shoulder, and a pulverized beyond-all-recognition head.

"Am I really seeing this?" Dyson thought. He, or "it," didn't even look human. One solitary incoming 107mm rocket was launched from somewhere off in the woods and it landed in the front passenger seat. The driver was a door gunner in the gunship company down the flight line. He had less than thirty days until his ETS. His CO had taken him off flight status so he would have a better chance of making it home.

❘ ❘❘❘ ❘

Alpha Company had their own mess hall, orderly room, mail room, movie area, latrines, piss tubes, and shower room. Their water tower was the highest structure in camp, as high as the roof of the flight line hangar. It was made of railroad ties and perforated steel planking sections and supported a reconstructed tank six feet tall and twelve feet in diameter. It was painted silver, with a fuel-fired burner underneath to heat the water.

Dyson, Spook, and three other mechanics were working on another overworked and overdue-for-maintenance ship. It was almost time for the midday break—a little food, a little beer, a little music, and a little smoke. A shot rang out. It sounded like a round from an M16. It happened once in a while—someone accidentally fired a weapon, usually it was a .45 sidearm he was trying to clear of ammo. Then another shot. The mechanics ignored it and continued to work until someone yelled.

"Sniper! Sniper!"

Sniper? Where is he? Did he hit someone? No one knew anything as they sought cover. The shots were coming faster.

"Some guy in Alpha Company is on top of their water tower taking potshots." At this distance the guys couldn't see much, a little movement on the top was about all.

"Now they're saying this guy is pissed off about them not approving his hardship discharge." Which was entirely possible. Army pay for enlisted men was at poverty level. Guys with families could really be strapped, especially if the breadwinner got drafted. That alone could push a guy over the edge. Three more spaced-out shots echoed across the grounds. Ramirez joined them as they crouched behind the revetment wall.

"He's not trying to hit anybody. He doesn't even come close. He's just squeezing off shots for attention." Most everyone peered carefully over the sandbags. No movement was visible. But soon some guys emerged cautiously from hiding, only a few at a time, only exposing themselves just outside of their immediate cover. A couple more shots, but not in this direction. Now more and more men came out.

Finally, Horstall called everyone into the hangar which, thankfully, wasn't in the shooter's line of sight. "Everyone stay here until I find out what's going on." He headed over to Operations. It was hot and musty in the hangar. A few guys hung around the Lister bag drinking the tepid water. Horstall was back in ten minutes.

"All right, this is the story. Alpha Company CO Major Bentworth called a JAG at MACV and asked him if it was legal to shoot this guy Riley—the sniper. The JAG officer said no, you can't shoot him. They're sending a chaplain here. He will talk him down. Then Bentworth asked what to do if he can't talk him down. The JAG officer said we'd cross that bridge if we get to it. The chaplain is on his way here now." Another shot rang out, then another.

Brady appeared and told Horstall: "Sir, there are men working on the flight line."

Horstall looked out and sure enough. "Any of you want to go back to work?" Most said yes and they went back to work. Shattering the stillness, a single shot rang out. But soon someone was yelling, "All clear."

Word went around that Riley was only firing harmlessly at sandbags. The closest he got to anyone was twenty feet. Then word came around that Riley shot and killed himself.

When it was time to bring his body down, two lifers rolled his body off the water tower and let it smash on the ground below. It was the final insult to Riley.

▌▐▐▌

At a mandatory morning formation for Bravo Company on Monday, the men formed up in ranks and platoons. Lifers went up and down the company of two hundred men, inspecting uniforms, haircuts, and shaves. They were all called to attention and the formation was turned over to MAJ Brisco, Sliman's replacement. Someone farted, and giggles followed. Farts were always funny when in formation.

"I have to commend you men on your devotion to duty." Brisco was reading from notes. "Division and brigade both recognize and appreciate all the work this battalion and its companies are doing despite the shortages of ships and aviators. And I personally hold your efforts and long hours in high esteem." Brisco was on a list for promotion to lieutenant colonel. Bravo Company's excellent maintenance record would be to his credit. So, what's going to happen? Weekend passes for everyone?

Brisco turned the meeting over to 1SG Enrico, Peterson's replacement. "When you hear your name, yell 'Here' and form up in front of the Orderly Room . . . Akers . . ." After a few names were called, Dyson heard his name. When Enrico had gone through the alphabet, everyone else went back to work.

Horstall, as the OIC of Maintenance, was in command of the two ranks of men standing before him. "OK, at ease, men. Smoke if you want to." Was this going to end up being good or bad? "You guys have been selected to be on flight status." *Hot damn*, thought Dyson. "You have been recommended by me and Sergeant Brady because you have proved you can work long hours and under pressure. I'm not saying I've been spying on you guys, but I have. I like what I see. You're going to have hands-on training."

At last, I can fly, Dyson thought.

"First, you're going to have reorientation on the M60. We'll go from there to door gunner then to crew chief." He paused to let that sink in. "I'm sure you're aware of what flying out there every day is like. The battalion needs men that can double as mechanics and as crew at a minute's notice. We'll start tomorrow morning on M60 training." He looked at the twelve men. "I got faith in you guys. Back to work."

▌ ▌▌ ▌

The guys finished all their maintenance and repairs by 17:00 hours that day, a rarity, considering. There were no more writeups to work on. Right now, only two ships were actually being worked on. Unless an emergency came up, they might have a little more time off for a while. After showers and chow, it was time to relax. The officers drifted off to their club, the NCOs to theirs, and the guys to either the EM Club to watch tonight's movie, *The Graduate*, or they partied in groups around some music. Mister D didn't need to see a love story right now. He'd rather remain with his friends in his hootch, like most nights.

They sat in lawn chairs just outside a door to their sleeping quarters so they could hear the music and duck inside for quick hits. The sun had set, the clouds had lost their brilliant colors. Darkness descended quickly. Hopefully there would be no mortars or rockets, no one wounded or killed tonight. Strickland brought his chair over and sat down next to Dyson. Good. They would have no trouble hearing his warning if the gooks started another attack. Strickland smoked pot but not often.

After a while, he asked Mister D, "Why would you want to be

a crew chief?"

"You know, I want to see what's going on out there." Dyson took a long drag on a Camel. "I want to see the magnitude and the results of this huge military campaign we've had for so long. I don't want to go home and never have had a chance to see a part of, like, history, up close."

"Oh, you'll see some history up close, all right." Strickland had been in the 2nd Airmobile Division almost two years now. He was with them when the division was stationed up north. He was there for the Tet Offensive. That massive north-to-south attack on three hundred-odd LZs, camps, bases, villages, towns, and cities in '68 was the one that would go down in the history books. It was also the one in which he was shot through the arm. No one ever seems to mention how much a gunshot wound actually hurts. "You'll see things you'll never forget, that's for sure."

"Born on a Bayou" was playing, rockin' and mellow at the same time.

"What's the dumbest thing you've seen out there?"

"Oh, man." Strickland half-laughed. "There's so many of them. Let's see . . . from the air . . . one Loach pilot who couldn't tell Long Binh from Long Thong . . ."

Riaz chipped in, "How about the Chinook pilot who dragged a 105 cannon through the wire, over the berm and into LZ Barbara?"

"That was a good one. He just kept flying, too. But they were waiting for him back at Bearcat."

"Yeah, but crews fuck up, too," Strickland said. "Big thing is firing on friendlies—friendly fire. Happens a lot." It did, too. All kinds of guilty parties—jets, prop jobs, artillery, gunships, tanks. Panic, miscalculations, misinformation, frantic radio calls, wrong coordinates, garbled radio calls, on and on. Dyson made another commitment to himself, this one about friendly fire—not him, it wouldn't happen to him. What an awful thing to have to have live with. Many things here would be awful to live with.

Florida joined them. "Hey, guess what?" He was grinning.

"O'Grady wants to try smoking some." "Iron cock" O'Grady was a drinker, drunk almost every night. Months ago, he said he would never smoke pot. Wonder what changed his mind? Then again, hangovers in this heat are not pleasant.

"Where is he?"

"In the hootch."

"Let's go get O'Grady stoned." The guys piled into the hootch.

"Hey, Iron cock! You've never smoked?"

"No, man, never have."

"Wanna try? We'll turn you on. We won't fuck with you or anything like that. We'd just like you to try it with us. We'll walk you through it. Think of it like good booze." Good booze? Riaz had said the right thing. Everyone was sitting on footlockers and lawn chairs and a Sherlock Holmes-style pipe was passed around.

"You guys sure you won't fuck with me or anything like that, would you?" O'Grady was a little concerned, but knew he was among friends. They wholeheartedly assured him they wouldn't. Everyone was truly sincere about it. They just wanted him to try it.

"We would never fuck with you like that, Dan. Really." The guys seconded that.

"OK. I'm ready."

"Nothin' to it, believe me," said Riaz. "Here, sit here." When the bowl got to Riaz, he showed O'Grady how to take a hit nice and easy. O'Grady smoked cigarettes so inhaling was no problem—he didn't choke, cough, or hack on it. "Now let it out nice and slow." A long, long cloud of smoke went up in the air.

"Wow, man. Oh, man. That feels nice . . . really nice, man."

"Here, put this headset on," said Riaz. The Doors were doing "When the Music's Over" and at the end of the intro the guitar started wailing in his ears.

"OOOOOoooooooooooooohhhhhhhhh, man." Everyone grinned in agreement. "OOoooooo-aaaaahhh . . . far out." There was a new addition to the stoners in Maintenance. A good, strong addition.

I III I

Horstall and Brady assigned a few experienced door gunners and crew chiefs to orient the new group on the aircraft model M60. This machine gun did not have the pistol grip or the shoulder stock. It had a rear grip handle and trigger for each hand. There was an M60 of that type in each of four different bunkers. A crew member would take a few men into a bunker for training. Dyson's group went with SP4 Bob Anderson. He had on a CIB and Crew Member Wings. Bob had been out in the field when the Division was up north in the A Shau Valley, an area that was fought over again and again.

The weapon was on the sill pointing toward the woods. It rested on a bipod under the barrel (in a Huey, the gun was mounted on a post). It had a canvas brass-catcher bag on the right side to catch the spent shells and was fed from the left with belts of 7.62mm rounds out of a large metal ammo box on the deck—two-hundred-round belts were linked together. It had a spade grip for each hand and a fully exposed trigger in front of each grip, with a large ring-type sight. On a ship the gunners were seated in the aft end of the bench seat facing outward. It was a cramped area in the bunker, a lifeline was attached from the lower back of each gunner up to the ceiling.

"Each guy will get to use up a two-hundred-round belt," Anderson instructed. "You'll take short bursts and walk your tracers to a target. I'll have you stop, I'll break the belt apart, and you'll have to feed in a new belt. We'll do this about four times each."

The guys took their turns. After firing the last round on one belt, they'd open the pan, lay down the first round of the belt to be chambered, close the pan, and start firing. They learned to rapidly link two belts together. And to not bother to close one eye and aim down the barrel—simply watch the tracers and "walk" the rounds to the target.

"When the gun starts getting hot, it will probably malfunction somehow, and we will learn how to correct that." Anderson was right. M60s were known to stop firing because of a host of problems—

feeding, stripping the metal links, chambering, firing, extracting, ejecting, or a "stove-pipe," when an empty shell casing hung up in the breech. There was also the "run-away" M60 when the gun would continue firing without a gunner's finger on the trigger. The best thing to do then was to twist the belt apart where it was being fed into the receiver. Recognizing the problem was critical, correcting it vital. Some M60 gunners in the field carried spare parts. All of this in addition to an extra barrel and an insulated mitten to handle a hot barrel, along with four hundred to six hundred rounds of ammo, two canteens, an entrenching tool, steel pot, and all kinds of noise-making equipment out in the extreme heat and humidity.

It would be a full day of hands-on instruction, dead serious. When the guys broke for midday chow, no one stopped off at the hootch for a few tokes. The entire afternoon was spent in deadly earnest instruction and review of the gun's operation and maintenance. Some units had an SOP in which gunners had to ask for permission to fire—one of the inanest, chicken-shit ideas a few of the commanders came up with. But this unit didn't require that. "Fire at will" was understood.

Anderson answered dozens of questions from the guys. What about the chances of survival? OK, it was a dangerous job. All the crew members were in peril every time they went out. And, yes, the numbers of those wounded or killed was sobering.

"I heard the average life of a door gunner was thirty days."

"And then," said Anderson, "there are guys who spend their whole year on Hueys and go home."

"Yes, but if you're sitting . . ."

"It doesn't matter. It's just like here in camp. When your number's up, your number is up. On the flight line, in your hootch, driving a jeep"—that was a one-in-a-million hit, and it happened. When your name is "on the list," there's nothing you can do to remove it.

That night there was going to be a live Vietnamese band in the Bravo Company movie area, which sparked some excitement—a chance to blow off steam, get high or drunk or both, and maybe even see some legs and boobs. The band's roadies were setting up the equipment on the three-foot-tall stage. Dyson had never seen a Vietnamese band. Guys said they could be very good—sometimes.

After showers and chow, they brought along their folding lawn chairs. Much more comfortable than sitting on old rotor blades, some of which even had bullet holes in them. The guys were in Spook's area and a bowl was being passed around.

"Hey, O'Grady, want some?"

Down he came. He loved smoking pot now. "Maybe it can help me cut down on my drinking." They all agreed on that.

The movie area was crammed with Alpha and Bravo Companies' personnel—officers, NCOs, everybody. Even the chaplain was there, holding a beer. The rotor blade benches were full. Practically every available square foot of floor had a lawn chair in it. There must have been guys from other companies, but so what. The band's speakers and amps were set up: drums, guitars, a keyboard, and a microphone for a lead singer.

The band's name was on the drum set—Little Honey and the Cowboys. "Saigon Cowboys" was the jibe for draft-age men who should have been serving in the Vietnamese Army, in uniform and fighting for their country. Instead, there were thousands who hid out in the cities riding their motor bikes—like American cowboys riding horses—and snatching purses.

The Cowboys came out and played the intro to "Proud Mary" for a minute or so. Then the girls took the stage, and the guys went nuts. The lead singer wore a tiny, red, Suzie Wong dress showing plenty of legs and cleavage, the backup singers wore other sexy dresses. They shook and showed everything they had. The guys lost their minds. When the song ended, the lead singer said, "Hi, we're Little Honey and the Cowboys!" Everyone cheered. "And we are going to blow the doors off the place tonight." And she puffed out her lips as she emphasized "blow" in two distinct syllables—"bah-woe da dawz off."

They played some more Creedence Clearwater Revival, some Beatles, and then "We Gotta Get Out of This Place," one of the premiere songs of the entire war. The musicians were great. They swapped instruments and showcased their talent. Dyson was starting to see the Vietnamese as a culture of very able people—look how they waged war with the mightiest country in the world. His association with Tug and the hootch maids made him see they were "just like us." But the mindset of this godawful place put the GIs "above" the Vietnamese. How would you like to have a group of young horny guys ask your mom for a fuck?

Now they tried covering "The Letter," the Box Tops' top ten hit: "Give Me Ticket for Aeroplane." Those words lit a fire. The guys went nuts again. Dyson was getting tired of the whole scene. He couldn't get that excited about a song he didn't like—not psychedelic enough. Soon the band said its good-byes and the show was over. The persistent ringing in his ears became all too apparent again. It had just been drowned out temporarily by the music and the crowd. He thought of it as a good show by the band, a bad show by the crowd.

Back at the hootch, it was time for some mellow tunes and a "little help from my friends."

"Jeez," said Riaz, "those gooks could play." Gooks. It was funny about that term. It was a name the Vietnamese gave the French when they colonized Indochina, but over the years it got reversed and was used by the new occupiers to mean the Vietnamese. To GIs, though, it often meant the VC and NVA, the bad guys. "Dinks" had been borrowed from the Aussies, while the term "slope" was left over from World War II when Americans were fighting in the Pacific Theater.

The group of six settled back in their hootch and listened to Simon and Garfunkel while passing around a freshly lit bowl.

"Hey, Mister D," said Rector, "you looking for a good camera?"

"Yeah. Something I can take with me in flight."

"I got this here." Rector produced a Kowa 35mm he had bought months before in the PX. "It takes good pictures." He showed some he had stored in his locker. "You drop this Kodak film can in it to reload. I like using the film for color slides." But he advised caution. "If you've taken any pictures of the war—KIAs, WIAs—you'll lose them to the censors when you out-process to go home. Send the undeveloped film home to be developed there. That way, you'll have them to keep."

"How much?"

"Twenty. And here's a bipod. I set the camera on the bipod sometimes and take pictures of the sunsets. Use this lens cover faithfully when you're not taking pictures. Bring the camera with you on R&R."

R&R—rest and relaxation. Also known as I&I—intoxication and intercourse. Every GI could take seven days off and be flown on a free round trip to Tai Pei, Singapore, Manila, Bangkok, or Sydney, Australia. Hawaii was offered, also, but only for married men to visit their wives. Some went AWOL from there. Then there was leave granted to go home when you extended your tour for more than six months. Go home, come back, finish your extension for an early discharge. Or come back simply for the dope.

Friday, May 16—two hundred six days to go.

▌▌▌▌

Dyson finally got a letter from Carol. It had been almost a month. For a while, he would send a letter and get one back, write one, get one. That had stopped. Something was going on. Once again, a single page. "Fuck it." What's with her? He folded it and stuck in his pants' pocket. Not even worth reading twice.

On a sweltering afternoon, they were working in maintenance because there were a score of ships requiring work before they could fly again. The war in the three border provinces was grinding on. Spook, Dyson, and Riaz were with an FNG in Alpha Company, SP4 Ralph Gomez from New Mexico. He was on his six-month extension for an early out and had been in a Chinook company when the 2nd Airmobile Division was up north. He'd also been a crew member and was no stranger to maintenance. He was upbeat and he smelled like pot.

The four of them were overhauling the entire drivetrain. The aircraft commander on the last mission said there was too much play in the pedals. Other crews and ships were clustered around them. Horstall and Brisco were making their way down the flight line, sometimes stopping to talk with a crew, when Gomez asked, "Hey, who's that major over there?"

"That's Major Brisco, B Company CO."

"I don't believe this."

"You know that guy?"

"Yeah. When we were in Camp Evans, he was a CO up there. There was a big investigation going on about the black market and a lot of things he had signed for turned up missing, then BAM! he was reassigned and vanished."

"Amazing."

"Unbelievable."

"The Army takes care of its own."

Anderson appeared and chit-chatted with them for a bit. He told Dyson to stop by the supply room and pick up two sets of Nomex flight suits. Then he was to go to the armory and sign for a .45 sidearm.

"OK, I'll do it." He was one step closer to getting in the air.

At the supply room he asked for two pair of Nomex pants and shirts. The supply sergeant was Brent Penton from northern Maine. After basic training, he signed up for NCO School, passed, came out an SSG E6, and was assigned as a platoon sergeant in the infantry in Quang Tri. He was known to be jumpy and slept with a loaded .45 under his pillow. The guys in his hootch said he had nightmares.

"If you come back tomorrow afternoon, I'll have your name, rank, wings, and unit patch sewn on for you," Penton told Dyson.

"Yeah, thanks." They shook hands.

"Why do you want to fly?" Penton asked. Dyson had heard that Penton's platoon was patrolling near Camp Evans when the man in back of him stepped on a mine. Penton had unknowingly stepped over the mine. He knew about the "chances" in survival.

"I really want to see what goes on out there."

"I'll tell you. It's bad. Really bad."

"I know it's bad, but I want to help the guys out there if I can."

"You'll be helping, but it may cost you a limb or your life."

"That can happen around here."

"Yeah, it can. But you're really increasing your chances of getting hit. You may very well end up getting shot at much more often than guys out in the field. You could get shot at every day, depending on where you're flying. In a month, if you survive, you could have been shot at on more occasions than a guy humping it out in the field for a year. And that's a fact."

"Hey. We've been talking about this off and on since I've been here. You and me could get it right here in the supply room any second. But I can't live by 'what if this' and 'what if that.'"

"Fate."

"Fate. It's that simple," said Dyson. "Hey, I'll be back tomorrow."

"After 15:00 hours they should be done," said Penton. "See ya."

God, how many more people are going to ask, "Why do you want to fly?" It just now occurred to him this would be another thing he had to keep his mom from knowing about. He should tell his younger brother, though, but not in a letter addressed to their house. He didn't know what to write to Carol about anymore.

He entered the armory. It was one of the more heavily sandbagged bunkers. Next to it was the ammo bunker. They were both within the same revetment wall. It was like a little fortress within the camp. The Company armorer was Sergeant First Class Richard "Tricky Dicky" Lidecki—a lifer. He had been called in as a witness in the black-market investigation. It was rumored he was involved but no charges had been filed, yet.

"What can I do for you?" he said in a monotone from behind a waist-high counter.

"I need a .45 for a crew member."

"Did you ever qualify on one?"

"No, 'fraid not."

"Well, tomorrow morning, you and the other crew members in training will meet here at 08:00 hours and I'll qualify all you guys at once. Someone always forgets about this."

Qualification for the .45 sidearm. Another step closer to crew member. It seemed each step came at a snail's pace, right here in the very battalion that wants him to fly. They acted like they didn't want him. Hurry up and wait.

I III I

The Clap

A chronic malady in camp was "the clap," also known as "the drip"—venereal disease, VD. If your penis is dripping fluid, it was advisable to go on immediate sick call to the medics.

A raucous chorus of laughter erupted down the flight line.

"You gotta be shittin' me!"

"You'll never guess who went on sick call for the clap."

"I give up. Who?"

"Earlywhile." The big, fat, funky, mouth-breathing stupid, infantry washout. The one everybody rode about being "cherry." Now they were laughing in disbelief.

"Oh, man. He doesn't even know what a prostitute is."

"Ya know, he's supposed to go home in a couple weeks."

No one could leave the country with venereal disease. They had to remain under medical care until they were declared clean and cured.

"You know what he said? He said he got it off a hot towel at that massage parlor!"

The massage parlor was a room in the back of the barber shop where you could buy a massage-blowjob for ten dollars. Earlywhile maintained he wanted a massage only and got infected by his hot towel. Poor slob. Now he was going from being ignored and despised to ridiculed and despised.

By a twist of fate, the next day, O'Grady woke up with the drip. "Oh, fuck! FUCK!! Hey, what color is that stuff supposed to be?"

"If it doesn't look like cum or piss, you've got the clap," Spook prophesized. "And don't lie to yourself."

"Ah, Jesus, why me?"

"That's what you get for not wearing a rubber."

"I can't find any big enough, asshole." That may or may not have been true.

"Just follow Earlywhile to the medics and you'll be all right," said Riaz. He had the clap once, got three days of penicillin shots, and it was cleared up.

"Awhh, Jesus, look at this, Riaz."

"I don't want to look at that thing, Dan. You got the clap, believe me."

The guys didn't rag on O'Grady much, but when Earlywhile waddled through the company area on his way to and from the showers, they were unmerciful. He had sickly, fish-belly white skin, no body hair, a big gut, love handles, and thick government-issued, black-rimmed, Coke-bottle glasses that made his eyes nothing but a blur. He would never say a word.

▌▍▎▌

The big news around the company was that Earlywhile had gone through three days of penicillin shots and, after that, the three-day waiting period for the drip to stop. It hadn't. So, he was getting another three days of an increased dose of penicillin for another three-day waiting period. A large percentage of the cases would clear up after three days of shots. Not his. In some units, anyone getting the clap would get an Article 15 for disobeying Army regulation by not wearing a rubber. Earlywhile was due to go home next week.

O'Grady had gone through three days of shots and two days of the three-day waiting period, too. On the last day of waiting, he was in the EM Club drinking beer around 14:00 hours when Corelli, the medic, entered. He had personally given O'Grady the three doses of penicillin in the ass. Anyone entering the dispensary in the morning would see the men with VD facing the walls with their pants down and medics holding several syringes between their fingers and thumbs, going from GI to GI, first one shot, then another, and then the last—kind of an assembly line procedure. When Corelli's eyes got adjusted to the darkness of the club, he saw O'Grady.

"Hey, what the hell are you doing?" sounding like a high school shop teacher.

"Who, me?" O'Grady was the only customer in the club.

"Yeah, you! What the hell are you doing?"

"I'm off-duty 'cause I got the clap."

"I know that, asshole, but what the hell is that?" and Corelli pointed to his Hamm's.

"I can have this. I'm off-duty."

"No, you stupid shit! You're not supposed to drink beer when you're getting penicillin shots!" He was hot.

"Nobody told me that!"

"That's right, asshole, because there's a big sign in the dispensary telling you NOT to!" Things were starting to heat up between the two. The bartender, SP4 "Big Billy" Grains, was wondering what would happen next.

"Oh, bullshit! I didn't see no goddamn sign!"

"Come with me, you stupid asshole, and I'll show you!" They both went out into the bright sunlight of the company street to the dispensary, arguing all the way. Corelli led the way into the tent-draped bunker and into the room where the guys get their shots. "Now, look up there, asshole, and tell me what it says!"

"Oh, fuck," said O'Grady. Hanging eight feet above the area was a hand-painted, one-foot-tall, three-foot-long sign. Dan was no speed reader, but he saw the two words "NO" and "BEER." The rest was unimportant.

"OK, fuck-nut. You stop drinking beer now and come back tomorrow morning and we will start all over again. Got that?" Corelli was only looking after O'Grady's best interest. He really meant well, but what more compassion can you expect from a streetwise Wop from the Bronx. Even though, when he had been a combat medic he put the guys' care above all else.

O'Grady was almost out the door when Corelli yelled, "And keep that monster in your pants. I never saw such a sausage."

| |||

Dyson was again part of a mechanics crew. About half of the men chosen to be crew members had already been in flight, either as door gunners or crew chiefs, but he was still awaiting his first day of flight. It was OK since he was resigned to "hurry up and wait." He had heard from Carol once in April and once so far this month.

| |||

They were replacing the heavily damaged drivetrain on *078.* The ship had gone down in Tay Ninh and had to be sling-loaded back by a Chinook. Along came Horstall and two FNG CW2s. Both had to be younger than Dyson. "God. What a mess," said the captain. He explained to the pair of new pilots what happened to the ship, telling them it went down because of ground fire.

It did not go down because of ground fire. It had experienced mechanical difficulties and had a "hard landing." The pilots and crew were lucky to be alive. If a ship went down because of mechanical failure, it would often be termed "shot down." It looked much better for a commander to have a ship shot down than having it suffer mechanical trouble. The guys had heard this all before.

As he walked away, Horstall turned and said, "You're going up next week." He must have meant that for Dyson and another mechanic who had been chosen to crew. He just forgot his men's names.

One hundred ninety-two days to go.

| |||

Briefing

The deadliest year of all in Vietnam was 1968 when there were 16,899 deaths. May was the bloodiest month of 1968 when more than 2,000 soldiers were killed. This number only continued to increase because of the Tet Offensive through 1969. There was a total of 11,780 deaths in 1969.

Operation MONTGOMERY RENDEZVOUS, a search and destroy mission, was launched June 8 in the A Shau Valley by the 101st

Airborne Division.

In III Corps, the 11th Armored Cavalry began Operation KENTUCKY COUGAR in Binh Long and Tay Ninh Provinces and immediately sustained heavy casualties.

Time and again territories were fought over, "won," deserted, retaken by the enemy, then fought over again.

I III I

JUNE

It was the first Monday of the month. Mister D, Florida, and Super Chicken had just picked up their mail at the CONEX. Dyson got a letter from his mom. She typically wrote two- and three-page letters about everything under the sun. This time, he felt something small and hard through the envelope. He opened it and found an old St. Christopher medal. The patron saint of travelers far from home. It was the medal that was returned with the belongings of her brother Jerry, an Army captain killed in a jeep accident in Germany at the very end of World War II.

She wrote that St. Christopher had kept her brother safe on D-Day at Omaha Beach, through the fighting in Normandy, the Battle of the Bulge, and crossing the Rhine into Germany. "Bad things can happen to good people," his mom said. She believed that's the price we all pay for living in a world of sin and disease. She had not seen the medal in years and found it last week when looking through her family mementos. She insisted her son wear it to protect him. Knowing St. Christopher was watching over him made her feel better.

It was gold-colored, oval-shaped, one inch tall, a half inch wide. He took off its delicate chain, broke open his shorter dog tag chain and hung it on that one, sharing the medal with one of his dog tags. Officially, this made his ID tags "out of uniform," but it was hidden behind the dog tag. Like it was meant to be.

He wrote a letter that night, thanking her for it and telling her how peaceful and quiet it had been in their camp. Maybe other bases were getting hit, but not theirs, he told her. He didn't bother writing to Carol.

One hundred eighty-nine days to go.

I IIII

Enrico put the word out to the section chiefs and the motor pool to organize a small convoy of Bravo Company personnel and vehicles for a round trip from Long Thong to Biên Hòa. The convoy was to leave the next morning at 06:00 hours and return by 19:00. There would be one jeep for the OIC, two three-quarter-ton trucks, and two deuce and a halfs. There would be five drivers, one replacement driver, two men for each three-quarter ton, and three men for each deuce and a half. One M60 machine gunner was positioned on each vehicle. The others all had M16s.

The group would drive from Long Thong, through Long Binh, to Bien Hoa, make their drop-off, pick up their loads, and return the same way. MACV, USARV, and 2nd Airmobile Division regulations absolutely forbade anyone from stopping in the villages and towns between military installations; stopping and getting off their vehicles; or going off the specified route. Penalties were stiff: an Article 15 or court-martial, reduction in rank, heavy fines, and/or time in LBJ.

The convoy would be led by the OIC's jeep with SP4 Armando driving, Penton riding shotgun, and Papp in the back with a PRC25 radio. One of the drivers for the deuce and a half trucks would come from the motor pool, SP4 Zambini. In the cab with him would be the replacement driver for the convoy, SP4 Ruggles. Strickland would be the machine gunner with Dyson and Anderson, a company door gunner. They'd wear steel pots, flak jackets, bandoliers of ammo, canteens, and, in case they needed to call in close air-support, an assortment of different colored smoke grenades—yellow, purple, white, green. The gooks had them, too, and would throw them out during the fighting to create confusion. Everyone was glad Papp was the OIC. Dyson was glad he was riding with Strickland.

I IIII I

The Bravo Company convoy was ready to move out at 06:00 hours, all loaded up, fueled, outfitted, and manned.

"Got your sunglasses?" Strickland asked.

"Oh, yeah," said Mister D.

"Good, 'cuz you're gonna need 'em." He flashed Mister D and Anderson a box of Marlboro Greens. A lot less conspicuous than a big-ass smoking bowl.

"We have to worry about anything on the way?" asked Dyson.

"Nah," Strickland and Anderson pretty much agreed together, "We'll be fine. Be a nice trip." There were thousands of American GIs in the Long Binh-Bien Hoa-Saigon area—thousands of customers for prostitutes, dope pushers, and black marketeers who in turn coughed up most of their money in "taxes" to the Viet Cong war machine. It was an open secret where all that money went, but it didn't stop anybody from buying girls, dope and black-market goods. The VC would not dare kill the goose that lays the golden eggs.

Papp and Penton were walking around the vehicles, looking everything over. Drivers were ready, vehicles idling, and the men standing up in the truck beds, all facing forward. There were two pallets of unmarked crates on their truck to be dropped off in Bien Hoa.

"What's in those, Rick?" Mister D asked.

"No one knows," said Strickland. "And no one knows what we're picking up, either. Everyone just minds his own business and everything will be just fine. Just enjoy the ride."

A black-market run of some sort. Imagine getting killed or wounded on such a run. Wonder what the CO's letter home would say?

At 06:15 the convoy pulled out the main gate of Long Thong, right past the camp's dumping grounds. The OIC's jeep set the speed at forty mph and the vehicles proceeded to generate a swirling windstorm of red dust the whole journey. Dyson put on his aviator sunglasses and looked forward to a change of scenery, a welcome break from maintenance. It was a six-mile trip to Long Binh on one of South Vietnam's "highways." This one was like all the others in RVN—compacted laterite, a hard-ass red Southeast Asian clay-dirt that was hard as concrete, two lanes wide so the largest American trucks could pass each other. Garbage and litter ran alongside the road. Occasional motorbikes zipped past going the other way. This area was relatively flat with scrub forests, rice paddies, and a few villages. No stopping in the villages, no going off-route. This was Viet Cong territory.

The three friends were standing on the truck bed, leaning on the wood-frame bulkhead, weapons pointed outward. They looked battle-ready. Strickland lit up one of the menthol joints, and the guys shared it in the bright tropical sunlight. By the time they finished it, the pot was taking effect. Dyson looked past the roadside debris and grooved on the countryside. He knew some of these rice paddies had to be centuries old. And all these people wanted to do was live in the villages, grow rice, and be left alone. How simple.

Soon the sprawling little city of the Long Binh installation stretched before them. Mister D was struck by the sheer number of permanent buildings. Two- and three-story structures, rows of beautiful barracks, there were even blacktop roads. They were stopped at a main gate by a squad of MPs. A 2nd lieutenant conferred with Papp. They even yukked it up a bit. Papp got along with everyone. The MPs waved them into the camp. As their deuce and a half passed the MPs, he could see their highly starched and pressed jungle uniforms, their close shaves and haircuts, and their spit-shined jungle boots—stateside up the ass. They seemed to sneer at Papp's men as they passed.

Continuing through Long Binh, they passed the amphitheater where Bob Hope put on USO shows, an indoor movie theater, a huge PX, and a library. Sidewalks and civilian-looking people seemed to be everywhere. They stared at attractive women driving American automobiles. Officers' wives? Papp pointed to a big sign, "the Loon Foon Restaurant," then gave the guys a thumbs-up.

After the two-mile cruise through Long Binh, they got on the last leg of the journey in one of the most populated parts of South Vietnam, right where they had landed so many months ago. Hundreds of motorbikes were going in all directions. Some were outfitted for passenger service or carrying cargo, which added to the pandemonium. The exhaust was acrid and choking, the strongest fumes Dyson had ever encountered. The traffic seethed against itself. There was a zone where pedestrians tried side-stepping motor bikes, and a zone where oncoming and ongoing traffic attempted to merge, resulting in hundreds of near misses. Packed Lambretta minibuses and Vespas carrying one, two, or three Vietnamese traveled dangerously close alongside their little convoy, some of them inches from the wheels, the passengers not concerned at all.

"Ain't that a sight," said Strickland. Anderson just shook his head. Dyson was surprised they hadn't witnessed any accidents.

There were areas with sidewalks, no sidewalks, and traffic islands, alongside chaotic intersections melding vehicles and people—drivers, passengers, commuters, and pedestrians. Shops and cafes were located just feet from the bustling street and a frenzied tangle of humanity jostling shoulder to shoulder; an undulating mass coming and going as far as Mister D could see. Asians dressed in pants and shirts, black pajamas, shirtless, shorts only, Suzie Wong dresses. Saigon cowboys were everywhere, on the sidewalks, riding Lambrettas, nicely dressed, smoking, usually paired with a nice-looking young lady. There were clusters of beggars, some of them with deformities, reaching for a handout of anything, amid filth, stink, and squalor. They passed a passel of small children, orphans in dingy rags. The culture shock was overwhelming. Dyson realized he wasn't stoned anymore—he was down.

He hadn't brought his camera. But then again, he didn't know if he would want pictures of these scenes. To him the people were like Hieronymus Bosch characters set against a Salvador Dali landscape in a horrible nightmare. Five miles outside of town the convoy stopped at a gate to the Bien Hoa Air Force Base. It's where he had landed, but he didn't recognize anything. Jet fighters were constantly taking off and landing. Mission after mission, plane after plane, twenty-four hours a day, for bombing and more bombing.

Papp got out of the jeep and talked with the MPs manning the gate, going over some directions.

"I hope we can stop for some kind of lunch or something," said Strickland from the back.

"Shit," said Anderson. "I wish we could take another route home. That was like a zoo."

The guys lit up cigarettes and settled back to take in their surroundings. This was a city with many, many permanent buildings like Long Binh. It was filled with Army and Air Force personnel. There were civilians, but not to the extent of Long Binh. A commercial airliner climbed skywards at a rapid rate to reach the safety of the clouds for a bunch of guys going home.

One hundred eighty-seven days to go.

Still half an eternity.

The group entered the compound and headed toward the north side of Bien Hoa. The lead jeep pulled into a large parking area. Papp got out and guided each truck where to stop. Penton spoke with some of the convoy and then Papp came by their truck. "Strickland, you guys stay here on guard. We'll take a twenty-minute lunch at that stand over there, come back, and then you guys take a twenty-minute lunch. OK?"

"Yes, sir," and off went they for chow.

"You want to get a buzz on now?" asked Anderson.

"Why the hell not." Strickland and the guys passed around a Marlboro Green, smoking cigarettes at the same time.

"Wonder what the hell we're hauling here," said Anderson.

"Ya know," Strickland said, "you're better off not knowing. We got a day off, change of scenery, some smoke, some lunch."

"Wonder if Papp knows."

"Don't ask him. He wouldn't let you in on it even if he knew. The less anyone knows the better."

After a half hour, everyone had gotten a break and something to eat washed down with a quick cold beer at the roadside stand. They headed to their drop-off down a road with barn-sized buildings on either side. No one was around. The jeep had slowed down to a crawl until Papp spotted their destination. All came to a stop. Slowly a side door on the nearest building opened and two NCOs with sidearms came out, followed by three civilians, each cradling a CAR15, a cut down M16 that was used almost exclusively by SEALS and Special Forces. Wait . . . what's with the civilians carrying CAR15s? They snorted at the guys like they were shit. Fuck them.

The NCOs talked with Papp while the fuckheads slowly spread out and scanned the scene, CAR15s at the ready.

"You see anyone else around here?" asked Strickland. The place seemed deserted.

Everyone in the jeep started laughing. The NCOs and civilians went back inside and the two large garage doors opened. The four truck drivers were instructed to back into the warehouse, a deuce and a half and a three-quarter ton into each bay. The NCOs motioned them where to park. The big doors closed shut. Papp instructed his group to remain in their vehicles. The two deuce and a halfs were quickly unloaded by a forklift operator and the cargo was spirited to the darkened rear of the building out of sight. The forklifts came back loaded with pallets of unmarked boxes, all tightly banded shut. Each big truck held two pallets. The smaller trucks could only fit one small, but obviously heavy, pallet. The armed civilians paced around nervously, keeping an eye on everyone. Once the last truck was loaded, Papp and the two NCOs had a little conference. Again, they ended the talk with a burst of laughter. Papp called out, "OK, guys, get ready to follow me." The garage doors opened and the trucks fell in behind Papp for the trip back to Long Thong. It was 13:15 hours.

Their convoy meandered along a different route through the installation and out a different gate than they had come in. Papp was going another way back to Long Binh. This time it wasn't as congested as their trip coming in. This road was wider but cratered with potholes. Or were they bomb craters? It was a bumpy, jarring ride, and the pallets were bouncing up and down in the truck bed the whole time. They drove by acres and acres of shacks, lean-tos, tents, and even old cars and trucks that were used as house trailers. There were not a lot of villagers visible and hardly any traffic. The landscape was strewn with litter and trash. The gutters ran full and smelled like sewers. It seemed to be the dumping ground of everything that everyone discarded from someplace else. In 1969, there were one million displaced people in South Vietnam, an area the size of Florida.

The convoy crossed a bridge over a waterway and then they were back among the rice paddies. Almost a big relief. Strickland bent down behind the bulkhead to be out of the wind and lit a Marlboro Green. Mister D took a big hit and passed it to Anderson. The pot smoke processed through the menthol filter was intoxicating. The sunlight was beautiful, the paddies incredible. But riding in the open air continuingly eating red dust was wearisome. Still, he tried to groove on the nature around it all.

At 14:45 hours they pulled to a stop at a smaller entrance gate to Long Binh. The MPs descended on Papp's jeep. The lieutenant produced some papers from inside his flak jacket and handed them over. A MP captain scanned one page, then another, and then held them side by side, comparing something.

"What's goin' on?" Strickland wondered aloud. The captain motioned to Papp and they went into the guard shack. "Oh, man . . . LBJ is just down the road."

Two minutes went by. A jeep with another MP officer pulled up and he jumped out and went into the guard shack.

"Maybe we should get rid of the dope," said Anderson.

"Fuck a bunch of MPs," said Strickland. "Stay cool, man. It'll be all right." The whole group stepped back out into the sunlight. Papp said something and all the MPs started laughing. "See? I told you it'd be all right."

At last, they were motioned to pass through the gate and be on their way. On the return route through Long Binh, they passed a church that looked just like most churches back home—brick and mortar, beautiful stained-glass windows, a high steeple, and the cross.

They came to a sign that read "U.S. Army Long Binh Installation, Commanding Officer Barracks." Barracks? This place was a sleek, modern, stained-wood ranch house, the same as back in the World in any contemporary, affluent neighborhood. However, it sat in a six-acre lot, surrounded by rows and rows of coiled razor-wire implanted with Claymore mines every ten feet, dozens upon dozens of them in each row. There was a guard shack and gate at the entrance and a bunker in each corner of the lot. Gleaming air-conditioning units were perched on all the roofs. Your tax dollars at work.

After they were waved through the gate towards Long Thong and had driven out of the enclosure, Papp motioned for them all to slow to a halt. He got out of his jeep and spoke to everyone, truck by truck.

"Listen. When we are a few miles out, I am going to wave and point. When I do that, I want you to fire on the countryside where I'm pointing. You hear me? The countryside ONLY—NOT at any hootches or villages, NOT at any water buffalo, NOT at any civilians. You got me?"

"Yes, sir," they all responded in unison enthusiastically. This was going to be their daytime, traveling mad minute. Like a mad minute on the perimeter at night, but now from moving vehicles in daylight. Papp got back in the jeep and they continued.

"Let's do one," said Strickland and they passed around another Marlboro Green. On the home stretch to Long Thong, there were mostly just tiny peasant villages and rice paddies spaced out sporadically between acres of scrub forest, elephant grass, and low hills. After going by a second village, Papp waved, pointed, and motioned emphatically toward a low hillside. The group responded at once, letting loose with M60s and M16s for fifteen seconds. "Ya-hoo!" and that was the end of it.

Soon they were approaching the largest village they'd seen yet along the route. Even from their distant vantage point they could see two jeeps and a three-quarter-ton truck parked off the road—a very big no-no and against regulations. Papp's jeep slowed down and so did the convoy. They entered the village with hootches on each side of the road. In the small, unadorned town square, villagers were standing in groups. Some of the men and women wore black pajamas, some had straw conical hats, some had sandals made of rubber tire treads, others were barefoot. They all turned in unison and stared as the caravan drove slowly by. One man brandished a .30 caliber carbine. Was he a VC? Towering menacingly behind the diminutive Vietnamese were a half dozen, black American service members in worn jungle fatigues and two more in civilian clothes. They wore black GI-shoelace woven necklaces and crucifixes, non-uniform sunglasses, and sported big-ass Afros with the obligatory pick combs stuck in them. And, not the least, they were armed. Their jeep featured an M60 mounted on a post. None of them took their eyes off Papp's little convoy until it had disappeared down the road.

"I bet them are some of the blacks that are after control of the dope being sold here on post," said Anderson. "And they're probably pimps, too."

The guys had all been hearing rumors to that effect. The black soldiers wanted a piece of the action and would eventually run prices up from dirt cheap to outrageous. So far, surprisingly, other soul brothers acting like those blacks seemed to come and go, roaming wherever they wanted to. Were they supposed to be on duty somewhere? Were they AWOL? Dyson smoked every day, but he hadn't yet bought any himself. He just didn't need to. It was everywhere and everyone had some. One day his time to buy would come.

When the convoy was a mile outside Long Thong, Papp waved furiously and pointed again at a derelict old deuce and a half that had been probably left there by the ARVNs. Everyone let loose on it, blasting the cab, the wheels, and whatever else was left, all the while spewing up heaps of red dust.

They arrived at the gate into Long Thong where soldiers manned the gates, not MPs. After being waved into the compound they pulled over. Papp dismounted and gave each truck driver instructions. "Park it there and walk back to Bravo Company." He started to walk away when he caught himself and turned back. "Hey, remember I pointed to the Loon Foon Restaurant? I want to dream up a phony trip to Long Binh and we'll all go eat at the Loon Foon—best restaurant in Vietnam." That went over well with the guys. The lieutenant took care of his men. Then parked at a spot inside the gunship company area and everyone dismounted.

"Whew. I'm glad to be back," said Strickland.

When Mister D got to his hootch, he turned around to look again at their truck. It was gone.

I IIII

There was a mandatory formation on Monday at 06:00 hours. Most of the men had just gotten up, some had just finished work on the flight line, while others were still out at the flight line. Enrico was NCOIC.

"Listen up. First, everyone, everyone, and I mean everyone is to go all over this company, every square inch, and get rid of all FTA graffiti, you hear?"

A less than enthusiastic "Yes, Sergeant" came from the ranks.

"Second, a man in this company was Medevac'd to Camp Zama, Japan."

Whispers and low voices said it had to be Earlywhile. He had gone through three separate treatments with increased doses of penicillin. Unfortunately, that didn't work and he was way past his DEROS. He'd even received a shot of ciprofloxacin that, although it turned his big, white ass black and blue, it didn't clear it up either. They finally sent him to Camp Zama where they hoped they could find the right medicine that worked for him. Whatever he had was not just a simple case of the drip. Christ, O'Grady got over his in three days, with no beer—once he stopped.

"The Battalion Medical Officer, Captain Lopresti, wants to remind all of you to wear a rubber when you fuck these whores," Enrico recited. "And don't be fooled by these 'shot records' they have." Some of the girls actually had little books with records (genuine or not) attesting to their high degree of medical attention—ha, right. "OK. Get rid of the FTAs and wear a rubber. Everybody got that?"

"Yes, Sergeant," in unison.

"Dismissed!"

As they were filing out, Horstall called out a number of names, including Dyson's. "You guys go suit up and meet me at Operations in fifteen minutes."

When they arrived, Horstall wasn't there. They waited in the sun a while, then moved into the shady side of the Operations bunker. After a half hour the lieutenant appeared. "OK. Everybody here?"

"Molina, you're going to ride as door gunner on *081*. Go find it, the crew's waiting," and off Molina went. "Krysik, you're going to ride door gunner on *079*. Go, they're waiting." And off he went. "Dyson and Harvey, you guys are on standby. Wait at the standby shack. You will be needed if a ship or two have to return from their missions under emergency conditions. Got that?"

OK, so here they were waiting at the standby shack, sipping Cokes and smoking cigarettes. They would stay there until dismissed by Operations. Hurry up and wait.

One hundred-eighty-two days to go.

‖‖‖

It was Friday the thirteenth, 05:00 hours. Green, recently promoted from PFC to SP4 and made the permanent CQ, went through the barracks waking everybody. He entered their hootch and encountered O'Grady first off. Not surprisingly his huge cock was standing straight up in the air like the blue-ribbon cucumber at the state fair. "Gawd . . ." Green said, shaking his head. "OK, guys. Five hundred hours, five hundred hours, let's go, come on," he cajoled as he turned on the row of fluorescent lights. "Hey, Mister D. Suit up. You're going up today." Green was personable, witty, and just enthusiastic in general.

"You know, I keep getting suited up but never go anywhere."

"Well, today you are. You're on *085* leaving at 08:15. Be at Operations at 07:45. Got it?"

"Yeah. Thanks, man."

A small TV was on with the morning news. Someone was playing "Season of the Witch." Half the guys headed out for the mess hall. Floaty and Gator were on duty making morning chow. Dyson filled his tray with scrambled eggs (powdered today), hash browns, gravy, sausage links, OJ, and hot coffee to wash it all down. AFVN Radio was playing "Tis the Season." It was almost relaxing.

"Goin' up today, Mister D?" asked Grains. He ran the EM Club, and he was a good guy—a country boy, down to earth, and didn't talk a lot.

"That's what they say. Hear anything?"

"Taylor—SP5 Taylor, the Operations CP radioman—says you'll be on standby." There was a jungle grapevine telegraph that ran throughout the battalion between every section, so *everyone* knew *everything.*

Dyson stopped by the hootch for a toke. Not surprisingly, Spook, Riaz, and Super Chicken were doing the same thing. Maris was having his usual bowl of orange juice and pot, wolfing it down like it was Shredded Pot Cereal, the new Breakfast of Champions.

"Hey, looks like you might go up today."

"Maybe," and he took another toke.

"It's quiet out there right now," Spook said, "but that could change in any minute."

He could end up waiting all day at the standby shack. He loaded up with his Instamatic, two canteens of water, four candy bars, and his Camels and Zippo. To top it off he strapped on his .45 pistol— one full clip in the gun and an extra one in his web belt.

They all headed out to the flight line. Fourteen broken ships were being worked on. The Operations CP was an anthill of activity and radio messaging, all kept at an orderly level by Taylor—another unrecognized kingpin of this unit. His memory for tail numbers, call signs, and map coordinates, in addition to his coolness during emergencies, kept the missions humming. Dyson stuck his head into the CP and made eye contact with Taylor who, seeing he was standing by, gave him a thumbs up. Taylor had to be the calmest, most collected guy in the company. He was loved and respected by just about everyone.

At the standby shack, whose interior was like a pizza oven, were three other waiting crew members, Morgan, Naylor, and Dell.

"Hey! Glad you're here," said Dell, inspecting the names on the flight helmets lined up on a shelf.

Two warrant officers on standby, cradling their flight helmets under their arms like footballs, stopped by to touch base with the guys in the shack. Chief Warrant Officer Two Chase LaChappell, a seasoned Huey aircraft commander, and Warrant Officer One Jack Hendricks, fresh out of Division Orientation, stopped in for any updates to their status. Hendricks was a timid little guy and had a head like a house cat.

"We'll be at our Standby CP," said LaChappell. The officers had an air-conditioned bunker to wait in, not the oven-like shack where the enlisted men waited. And off they went.

"I hope we don't have to go up with Hendricks," someone said.

All that was needed now was for a ship to be pulled off its missions requiring a backup ship to take its place. The men on standby stood in the shade, smoked cigarettes, sipped water, listened to the music from nearby hootches, and walked back and forth to the Operations CP, which would be the first to know if a backup ship was needed. Dyson had paired up with Dell, a seasoned crew chief. He was on a six-month extension for his early out.

"Are you sure you want to fly?" he asked Dyson.

"Didn't you want to fly when you got here?" Answer a question with a question.

"Yeah, did. Every time I go up, I wonder if it's the last."

"Are you glad you fly?"

"Yeah, but I've had enough already." Strange. Guys that wanted to be crew members couldn't get the assignment, while some who were crew members kept trying to get out. "When the Division was up north, we flew out of Camp Evans. It was always hot up there. VC and NVA everywhere. We medevaced out of a hot LZ with wounded aboard. A green tracer zipped by my head, just missing my helmet, and hit the crew chief on the starboard side. I heard him cough on his mike."

"I know it's bad, man, but I want to see it."

"I wanted to see it, too. Now I see it in my dreams." Amen.

At 11:15 hours the Operations CP turned into a beehive of radio traffic and the high-pitched voices of frantic commanders in the field. 137th ASH Battalion ships had come under heavy fire while moving troops from Phuoc Vinh to a new landing zone near Nui Ba Den—Black Virgin Mountain. Three ships had minor damage but were still airborne. Another Huey was hit and had to set down at the nearest LZ. The last ship, from Charlie Company, suffered a hit in the tail rotor, spun out of control, crashed, and was burning out of control at that very moment. No word yet on survivors. Only one backup ship was needed to finish the missions.

LaChappell joined the guys at their shack. "OK, Dell, you'll be crew chief, and Naylor, you're the gunner." Then he addressed the remaining two. "I just can't have a new guy onboard today. It would be a bad move." He looked at Dyson "I am going to get you guys up when I see a decent mission sheet—promise."

▌▐▐▐▐▐

JoJo

For two days Dyson was needed in Maintenance. There was a sudden surge in ships that required repair. On Monday, June 16, he worked with PFC Janes, a FNG from Ohio, and Fredricks and Devaney replacing overhead rotors, a job requiring teamwork and vigilance. You had to keep your wits about you at all times. Although involved, replacing blades was a fairly routine job: positioning a portable overhead crane's hook over the center of a rotor blade, rigging two slings eight feet from each end, disconnecting the blade from the rotor head, and removing the freed blade to the scrap pile, then practically reversing the procedure for installing the new blade. The crew did not need an NCO breathing down their necks. Thankfully, the lifers always seemed to be glued to their air conditioners.

I IIII

On their midday break, Dyson and the guys saw a group of officers, including Bannon, the Battalion Commander, in the company street, so they took an alternate route. The detour passed by the Avionics hootch. In front of it was a strong and sturdy four-foot-square metal cage with a monkey in it named JoJo. Monkeys were common around camp, and this one had come to living exclusively on handouts like a tiny, human beggar. Some guys gave him food from the mess hall while others gave him candy or potato chips. Monkeys could be disgusting little guys. Besides picking and eating each other's lice, they shit and piss anywhere they want, and the males masturbate seemingly constantly. Sometimes JoJo would go ballistic in a wild rage for no known reason. He also liked to pick up a handful of his own shit and sling it at people through his cage wires. It was a good idea to keep your distance when walking around JoJo's cage.

At their hootch, wary eyes watched the group of officers while the guys got their buzz on. Ramirez opened his small ice chest and handed out cold Hamm's beer. For six months now, Mister D had been getting stoned daily on powerful pot. Everyone in their hootch smoked as did most of the enlisted men in the company and it was rumored Papp smoked, too. If the lifers caught them smoking in their hootch at noon, it wouldn't be a good thing. But the lifers and officers could drink at midday break and that was OK? Regardless, pilots drinking on duty was *always* a big mistake

"Well, I guess it's time." But no one moved for a while.

"I sure miss my hammock back home . . . laying in it and looking at the clouds."

"You'd need a nice big burger to go with it." They got up to go.

"No, man. How 'bout a nice cool, chicken-salad sandwich on fresh homemade bread? Then wash it all down with an ice-cold sweet tea!"

"I'd like a nice thick, chocolate milk shake, with real milk."

"What about the beach at sunset with a big fire and cold beer?" It went on and on until they reached the end of the company street.

Out of nowhere came a loud POP! and everyone jumped.

"Sounded like a .45."

It was hard to tell where it came from. .45 automatics were always going off, especially when someone was trying to clear his weapon. They watched the scrum of officers scurry off toward battalion HQ. An officer on each side of Bannon seemed to be fussing with his uniform, brushing off Bannon's uniform as they walked.

"Let's keep going," said Riaz. "Fuck them lifers."

It was after 14:30 hours. The group was removing an overhead rotor blade. Dyson was enjoying the sun, the work, and the smooth sound of Simon and Garfunkel floating from nearby. Suddenly, agitated rumblings resonated from a group working over near the hangar.

"What'd they shoot him for?" they heard someone say. The agitation seemed to be spreading out to the other groups of mechanics. Janes came over to their group.

"Do you know what them fucking lifers did?" he said. "They shot JoJo!"

Why shoot a defenseless monkey in a cage? The guys in Avionics took good care of JoJo. Putting all his faults aside, all the men loved him. When they gave him snacks, he became friendly, even well behaved. He never bit anybody and liked to be fed and petted at the same time. The guys had fun putting him on their shoulders for pictures to send back home.

Later that afternoon, it came out why one of the officers was ordered to shoot JoJo. It turned out that when the officers saw the cage, they just had to go and investigate. They were standing close to the cage when JoJo picked up a handful of his own crap and slung it through the wire. It got it all over Bannon's face and uniform. So, JoJo had to go, NOW!

I IIII

"Come on, guys, rise and shine. Riaz . . . Dyson . . . you awake? Come on, wake up." Green was rousing the men, on this day at 05:30 hours. "Come on, Dyson, you're going up today."

Mister D swung out of his bunk. "I've heard that before."

"No, man. You're going up. LaChappell has you on as gunner." He did say he would get Dyson aboard when they had a decent mission sheet. "You, Morgan, are crew chief for LaChappell and "Wobbly One" Fitzpatrick on *080*. Be down there at 06:30 hours."

"Understood. Thanks, Green."

Could this be it? Finally going up? This was the big rush he had heard about since Fort Eustis, the big rush to get pilots and crews for the Hueys. One of the guys' reel-to-reels was playing "Break on Through to the Other Side."

He gulped down his morning mess and made it down to the flight line at 06:20 hours. There were pilots and crews everywhere. LaChappell and Morgan were giving *080* a pre-flight inspection.

"Come on, Dyson," LaChappell said. "Let's go over this thing." He knew Dyson was a good mechanic and could spot almost anything that needed repair. Even though the ship had been released from maintenance, you never took anything for granted. Fitzpatrick, another warrant officer, joined them. They spent ten minutes going over the ship, its logbook, and the mission sheet. A mission sheet for the day was given to each ship. On it was a chronological list of individual missions. It could be Long Thong to Phuoc Vinh is the first mission, Phuoc Vinh to LZ Barbara the second mission, and so on, from start to finish. All the individual missions comprised the mission sheet.

"I know you're new," Fitzpatrick said. "Listen to everything we say. But what I say goes, understand?"

"Yes, sir."

It was time for Morgan and him to inspect their weapons, ammo, and gear. Dyson was on the starboard side behind the aircraft commander. He got into the seat against the rear bulkhead. A large metal box of M60 ammo was mounted to the deck, left of the mounting post for the M60. A selection of smoke grenades—yellow, purple, white, red, and green—hung on his right.

"OK, load up," said Morgan. He then seated the beginning of the belted brass ammunition into the breach—twelve hundred rounds, six two-hundred round belts.

Other crews and pilots were inspecting their ships, some were running up, a couple were taxiing for takeoff, a few had left already. Dyson and his crew put on their flight helmets and went through a commo (communications) check. LaChappell yelled, "CLEAR!" and started the engine. The ship lifted off, taxied to the runway, gained speed, and took off. They flew over the perimeter at seventy-five feet and kept climbing. Quickly. Long Thong was behind them. It didn't look so big now. "Gunners, test your weapons—short burst," said LaChappell. They aimed at the ground and fired a ten-round burst. They were ready.

The first destination was Long Binh where a satchel of correspondence would be waiting for them to take to Phuoc Vinh. Dozens of ships like theirs were in the air all over South Vietnam doing just this, running paperwork between installations. Forms, forms, and more forms every day. Imagine getting shot down and killed delivering worthless Army paperwork.

Dyson could hear radio talk between LaChappell and Long Binh. They would approach from the west, descend onto runway Four-Alpha, glide onto Alpha Sector, set down, and a satchel would be handed to them. LaChappell talked and flew them in and talked and flew them out smoothly. Now they were headed to Phuoc Vinh for drop-off. The ship climbed to five thousand feet, above small-arms fire. Dyson took in the countryside all around them. Towns, villages, and hamlets. Rice paddies, dikes, and dirt roads scarred by the bomb craters, new and old.

They were headed toward a swarm of people. On a stretch of railroad, an old locomotive, and the coal car behind it, had derailed and both plowed into the earth. The cowcatcher and steel wheels were buried deep in red-clay soil, but both cars remained upright. Dyson took out his Instamatic. There must have been five thousand Vietnamese laborers swarming over the wreck and the tracks, all wearing straw hats to shield themselves from the sun. They were arranged in dozens of lines with ropes or chains, all pulling in unison. Hundreds of men were digging the wheels out, carting and passing pails of soil by hand to be dumped and returned to the excavation empty and ready. Crews were putting wooden planks under the wheels of the coal car, while others gathered up the spilled coal. It was a moving mountain of people.

With their ship passing directly overhead, the level of organization and sheer manpower were impressive. There were teams of diggers, teams of riggers, teams of muscle to pull the locomotive out. Dyson took only six pictures and then secured the camera. The scene disappeared in a flash under the ship and was gone. His awe and respect for the Vietnamese rose. They weren't gooks, slopes, or dinks. They were an amazing people, capable of doing anything.

The aircraft flew over an expanse of scrub forest and jungle. It was sheer beauty from the air, but for grunts on the ground it was a bitch to traverse. With Phuoc Vinh in sight, the commander began their descent and flew at one hundred feet over the perimeter where a cluster of men were looking over bodies—remnants of last night's VC probe of the camp's defenses. LaChappell piloted the ship into the Division's compound as an officer waved them in and Fitzpatrick talked to the Operations CP. They never set down. Morgan tossed the satchel to the officer, who then put his hands out and shrugged his shoulders like there was something else. Operations had informed them there were supposed to be two satchels, not one. Somebody screwed up. Again.

So, it was back to get the second satchel that had been left in a jeep somewhere in Long Binh. Would heads roll for this one? What the hell. The weather was excellent, the scenery spectacular, and Mister D still had a good buzz on.

They flew over the derailment again. The coal car had been disconnected and pulled feet toward the tracks. Dyson took four quick pictures of the progress, this scene just one more permanently etched in his mind. The ingenuity, unity, and strength of the Vietnamese was inspiring. Why did so many GIs treat these people like shit? What else lay hidden here had he yet to discover?

The second satchel run mimicked the first. Dyson was enjoying every minute of it—the wind, the noise and power of the ship, the countryside. He could envision it as it was years ago, before occupation by foreigners. No craters, no defoliants, no sprawling military compounds surrounded by garbage dumps, no LZs despoiling the lush tropical terrain. A peaceful place where people could grow rice and be left alone. Not anymore.

Having dropped off the second satchel, they were headed for Lai Khe to take four FNGs over to 2nd Airmobile Division Field HQ, Phuoc Vinh, for assignment. Lai Khe was another base with aviation companies, and it was hit often by rocket and mortar fire. Consequently, it was also known as a Rocket City. The four men were on the flight line, waiting for the ship. LaChappell guided it to the pickup point and set down. Morgan motioned the FNGs on, pointing out their seats and where to put their gear. They wore brand-new fatigues and boots and looked confused and bewildered just like Dyson did not very long ago. One sat next to Dyson—a tough-looking kid with red hair. Morgan gave the pilots the OK and *080* was up and heading to Phuoc Vinh. These guys were going to be assigned to a unit in the 2nd Airmobile Division. Dyson hoped it wasn't infantry. All four of them looked like high school kids.

They dropped off the FNGs at Division HQ and headed back to Long Thong to remain on standby until they were needed or relieved by the next standby crew. Morgan talked into his mike to Dyson.

"Hey, gunner, we will fly along the marsh next to Long Thong. I'll tell you when to fire. Shoot at the water and get used to walking your tracers. I'll tell you when to cease fire. Got it?"

"Roger."

As they approached Long Thong and started their descent, he could see the marsh plainly—dead tree trunks, marsh grasses, and bodies of water. They got down to about two hundred feet. Morgan came on his mike.

"OK, open fire."

Dyson selected a wet area and opened fire, looking down range and above the barrel. The gun spat out smoke and tracers, rounds hitting the water and sending geysers in the air. He used disciplined short bursts and saw his tracers hitting right where the cap-and-ball rounds landed. Twenty rounds here, twenty rounds there, ten- or twelve-round bursts, another twenty-round burst there. He walked his rounds to targets like using the stream of a garden hose.

"Cease fire. Cease fire. Got the hang of it?"

"Yeah."

"You did good," said Morgan.

Now LaChappell swung around and approached the flight line while descending. In the Bravo Company area, a bunch of officers and lifers were standing with their attention focused on a hootch. For the benefit of ships and crews in the air, someone had spray-painted in big white letters about six feet high "FTA." The CO was wicked pissed.

▌▎▎▌

The pilots and crew of *080* were relieved of standby by another crew. It had been an uneventful afternoon of going over the ship and cleaning the M60s. Even when no one fired them, the M60s would pick up a lot of red dust, just like the crew and the entire ship. Back at his hootch, Dyson was greeted by the guys.

"Hey, how was your first day?" They handed him a Marlboro Green.

"Not bad. Not bad at all."

"There will be bad days, believe me," Rector said. "We haven't had to roll up somebody's mattress in a while. We're overdue."

"Not in this hootch," said Riaz. True. Other hootches had suffered losses and were rolling up mattresses and gathering all the KIAs' personal gear into duffel bags. A man would report for flight duty and never be seen again. A new mattress and an FNG would be brought in to replace him.

"What happens, happens."

When your name is on the list.

After showers and chow, the guys settled in for some talk, music, and smokes. Riaz produced a bottle of Jack Daniels, opened his ice chest, and offered cups with or without rocks.

"How 'bout you, Mister D? Want to celebrate your first day up?"

"Sure." He hadn't had any hard liquor since his leave home. It might be nice.

"Ice?" He took it neat instead, about four ounces of Jack. He and his brother had liked a little Jack Daniels once in a while. Riaz, Spook, Super Chicken, and O'Grady joined in a toast to Dyson's first day. They hoisted their cups. "Many more."

During the get-together some guys only smoked pot while the five others both smoked and drank. Spook and Soup drank very little, mostly smoked. Although O'Grady was feeling no pain, Riaz and Mister D were responsible for killing that bottle. After the first fiery swig or two, it went down a whole lot smoother. The hootch was beginning to tilt on an angle and some things appeared as double vision. The dizziness happened anytime Riaz and Mister D stood up. Oh, man. Smoking powerful pot and guzzling liquor was a bad combination. It wasn't the high he was used to. It was an unpleasant and disorienting drunk with the booze affecting the pot, the pot affecting the booze. It was almost oblivion, a state he would later come to know again and again. He needed to lie down. He rose unsteadily and had to lean on bunks and footlockers to get to his bunk.

"Oh, man. You need help, Dyson?"

"No, I'm fine." Yeah, right. Famous last words. He was staggering and unsteady. In the final four feet, he made what he thought was an uncontrolled dash for the mattress and crashed on his poncho liner. Fatigues and boots on, he was passed out. Unconscious.

By midnight, most of the company (the guys who worked day shifts) were asleep. A few hung outside their hootches, smoking and talking. Floodlights illuminated the work being done on some ships. Outgoing artillery boomed from the other side of camp. And then it started.

WHUMP! WHUMP! WHUMP-WHUMP-WHUMP! WHUMP! Mortars, coming in fast.

"Come on, man. Let's go."

As they ran out of their hootch, the mechanics yelled back at Dyson to get up and run. They all crammed into their bunker. And still the mortars were coming in. Now a gunship or two could be heard running up. Small-arms fire was coming from the western perimeter a thousand meters away.

"Dyson . . . you here? I don't see Dyson."

"I gotta get him," said Soup.

"Careful, man."

The mortars seemed to be targeting the flight line and hangar, but rounds were also falling into the Bravo Company area. Soup made his way back into the hootch to where Dyson lay passed out. He shook him violently.

"Dyson! Dyson! Wake up! Mortars, man. Mortars!"

"Fuck you, man. Leave me alone!"

"Come on, man." Soup pulled Dyson up. "Hurry!"

"I said fuck you." More mortars hit.

"Come on, man. Lean on me. Come on!"

"Leave me the fuck alone!" Dyson tore Soup's hands off him. Two louder mortars landed close by.

"OK, man. I'm leaving." Soup scurried back into the bunker. "He ain't coming."

"Oh, man."

WHUMP-WHUMP-WHUMP! WHUMP-WHUMP!

Who knows how many tubes in the woods were dumping their shells on the camp? The gunships were finally up and climbing for a little elevation. Right then the mortars stopped. Their mortar crews wanted nothing to do with gunships. Having sighted their targets on the ascent, the gunships laid down suppressive fire into the woods with rockets and miniguns.

After twenty minutes, someone was yelling "All clear." Men came out of their bunkers and were assessing the damage. Four mechanics' hootches suffered hits or close-by hits. An Avionics hootch took two direct hits and was destroyed. Rounds fell next to the hangar. The flight line and ships had been peppered mercilessly: four destroyed, four heavily damaged, and shrapnel holes in a dozen others.

Mister D was still passed out on his bunk. "Fuck that guy," said Soup. "I'll never help him again."

"No, man," said Riaz. "Don't be like that. He's drunk, that's all."

"Could happen to all of us." Spook shook Dyson's shoulder. "Hey, man. Mister D . . . you all right?"

"Aaaaawwwwhh . . . leave me alone. I'm sick."

"Come on, man. Want to get your boots off? Want to go to the latrine? I'll help you," Spook said.

"Nnnaaaahh . . . I just wanna lay here." So they left him alone.

Some guys stayed up all night, some slept with their boots on, some nodded out in their bunkers. Green came through at 05:30 hours waking everyone for work.

"Dyson. Dyson. Time to get up. No flight suit today." And Dyson slowly got up.

"He's up . . . he's up."

"Hey, you all right, Mister D?"

"Oh, man. I really feel like shit." He had his boots on the ground now. "Oh, crap." He staggered to the doorway, got behind the revetment wall, and threw up—twice—then came back in. "I feel much better now."

"Do you remember last night?"

"Uh . . . I remember going to bed."

"Yeah, what else? Remember anything else?" Dyson shook his head. "Remember the mortars?"

"I remember Soup telling me something. No, I don't remember no mortars."

"You passed out. We got hit. You stayed in here. Soup came in to get you in the bunker. Remember that?"

"Some of it . . . somebody shaking me."

"You told me to fuck off," said Soup. He wasn't as hostile now.

"I'm sorry, man. I'm really sorry." He swore he would not drink any more hard liquor. For the rest of the day, he learned what it was like to nurse a terrible hangover under the scorching tropical sun. It took two days to feel normal again.

▌▏▏▏▌

Dyson was assigned to ride as door gunner on *082* with Morgan, again, as crew chief, Papp as aircraft commander, and Berthal—he had never even seen Berthal before—as co-pilot. After his first flight as gunner, Dyson had worked in maintenance for the next ten days. He was glad he would be with Morgan and Papp.

This was going to be a good-sized mission in Tay Ninh Province, forty Hueys ferrying 2nd Airmobile Division troops of the 2/5 Infantry (everyone knew it as "the Second of the Fifth") to the jungle two miles north of Black Virgin Mountain.

The mountain, whose peak commanded everything in sight, was a strategic location for both sides. Known to U.S. personnel as "Indian Territory" for being an active Communist stomping ground, the Ho Chi Minh Trail was only a few kilometers west across the Cambodian border. It was full of roads and trails, hidden bunker complexes and tunnels. Americans were trespassers.

Another forty ships would transport the 2/7 Infantry ("the Second of the Seventh") from Phuoc Vinh to another jungle area just south of Minh Thanh. The plan was for these two units to move toward each other, make contact with hostile forces, and wipe them out—"search and destroy." Later in the war it would be called "search and avoid."

Things were bad in some rifle companies in the field. Not just in the 2nd Airmobile Division Infantry, but also with other infantry units all over the country. They were tired of losing men in ferocious battles when taking an area or a hill "of logistical importance" only to turn around, pull out, and abandon the area. "Hamburger Hill" was a case in point.

On May 20, after a dozen deadly assaults over 11 consecutive days, the U.S. military finally gained control of a 3,000-foot-tall mountain overlooking a remote valley. Hill 937-Dong Ap Bia ("Mountain of the Crouching Beast")-was the location of the first battle launched as part of *Operation APACHE SNOW*, a coordinated attack by the U.S. Army and ARVN against units of the North Vietnamese Army. The operation's goal: eradicate enemy forces in the A Shau Valley, including members of an elite regiment known as the "Pride of Ho Chi Minh."

When the U.S. abandoned Hamburger Hill only a few days after capturing it at a cost of more than 50 Americans killed and nearly 400 wounded, in addition to several helicopters shot, a firestorm of controversy erupted nationwide over what many viewed as a senseless loss of lives. It marked a turning point in America's involvement in the Vietnam War. The debate over Hamburger Hill reached the United States Congress, with severe criticism of military leadership and it is considered a watershed event of negative public opinion toward the Vietnam War. There were many other abandoned positions that were suddenly deemed months later to be strategic points that needed to be reconquered immediately, thereby requiring a new cadre of soldiers to sacrifice their lives in order to retake arbitrary geographical military locations. Now more and more troops were questioning their orders outright, with some even going so far as to defy them. Racial tensions magnified within the simmering caldron. In some units, it got to the point that when the shooting started, some whites shot at blacks, some blacks at whites, and some troops, both black and white, fired at their commanding officers. Dissention and a drastic decline in discipline and morale rapidly gave rise to fragging—using a fragmentation grenade to intentionally kill or maim unpopular NCOs and officers. The graffiti on buildings, tanks, and Quad 50s screamed "Kill for Peace," "Peace Through Superior Firepower," and "Kill Them All—Let God Sort Them Out."

Once Bravo and Alpha Company's ships were all present on the flight line, the crews finished their pre-flight inspections and word went out to man the ships.

"We'll be inserting troops," Papp said, looking directly at Morgan and Dyson. "They'll form up in the LZ so there will be no friendlies in the woods. We have the OK to use suppressive fire on the wood to keep their heads down if they're there. And it goes without saying, return any fire you receive." Everyone knew the NVA was in there somewhere.

At 07:00 hours, the lead Huey took off with Papp as the aircraft's commander. Two majors, Brisco and Bentworth, were the mission commanders for Alpha and Bravo Companies, respectively. The ships followed in one long line—like sheep to the slaughter. *082* was the tenth ship in line.

Jeez, this was really something. Dyson was glad he was a part of it. How could he spend a year over here and not be a part of something like this? He leaned out the starboard side and looked to the rear, but he could only see a few ships behind them as the line was not absolutely straight. As they climbed to five thousand feet, the country below seemed peaceful, except for the obscene, gaping bomb craters. Would they be under enemy fire? Would they get hit? Worse, would they get hit and go down? Would they crash and burn?

They followed the leader and descended into Phuoc Vinh. Peering ahead, he could see the main flight line crowded with clusters of troops and their gear all ready to board. The Hueys descended to ten feet, cruised and then set down easily next to each group of six soldiers. Crew chiefs motioned for the men to board on the port side and they moved with a rhythm like it was old hat. One grunt sat right next to Dyson. He turned and nodded to him. No response, just a cold stare. When all the men were loaded and ready, the Operations CP gave the go-ahead and the lead ship lifted off. The others followed. Dyson could feel a change in the ship's response and hear it strain under the weight of the biggest load he had ever flown with in a Huey. They flew north, then banked toward the west, slowly gaining altitude the whole time. He was impressed with the might of this little army in the sky. From his seat behind the gun, he could only see three troopers. No one made eye contact with him. They were sullen and separate. Perhaps they had premonitions.

The descent into the LZ a couple miles north of Nui Ba Den was rapid. "Eyes open," Papp said. They were going in and would scatter fifty feet from each other, set down, off load, and then take-the-fuck-off ASAP. The LZ was a four-acre lot smothered by elephant grass—eight-to-twelve-feet tall. The high winds from the prop washes flattened the grasses to four feet. When *082* set down, its troops off-loaded in a heartbeat. Morgan yelled "Clear!" into his headset and the ship shot upward. As the tall, turbulence-flattened grasses regained their height the troops disappeared. The land swallowed them up.

The ship swung in an arc until about two hundred-feet altitude and five hundred meters from the LZ, there was a loud WHACK! What in the hell was that? Morgan opened up with his M60 and yelled "Receiving fire!" The thunderclap they heard was a round that went through the skin of the ship. Morgan was spraying the area where he had seen a tracer come from but it quickly disappeared as they passed over it.

A couple of green tracers spat out of the trees on Dyson's side of the ship. He opened fire at the darkened area. Papp came on the intercom.

"What got hit?"

"Port side, past me, and through the roof," Morgan answered. Somehow the round had gone between the rotor blades while in their rotation. A lucky, lucky shot. Not only that, but a round had missed Morgan's head by less than a foot. His name wasn't on the list today.

082 was one of the ships ordered to remain in the area should they be needed. They would circle the LZ from two miles out while maintaining five thousand feet as other ships were in their own preplanned holding patterns. By now all forty of them had inserted troops in the LZ with two ships having reported receiving and returning fire. The NVA was there all right.

At 10:00 hours, *082* and a few other ships were ordered to return to Phuoc Vinh, refuel and remain on standby for their next mission. The radios were coming alive from the infantry units suddenly drawing resistance and fire to their north on the outskirts of Minh Thanh. They had made heavy contact with the NVA. The enemy was not only holed up safely in a bunker and tunnel complex, but it also had company-sized units attacking the 2/7 wherever they found them. The infantry was calling in artillery fire from outlaying LZs and close air support from gunships. A two-man Cobra gunship was shot down, bursting into flames and exploding, killing both officers.

As of midday, twelve other ships were on standby with them at Phuoc Vinh. Radio traffic and the soldier's informal "jungle telegraph" were relaying the high points of the battle. Some pilots and crew members hung around outside the Division Operations bunker listening to the radios. For over an hour, units were calling in map coordinates to U.S. artillery crews and marking targets with smoke grenades for the gunships and Marine jet fighters. Dyson and Morgan listened along with the other crews. A platoon from Alpha Company, 2/7 Infantry, was giving map coordinates to a 105mm Howitzer battery. Two other units were desperately requesting Medevacs. The platoon leader would give coordinates and the guns would "fire for effect." When the rounds were off target, he would call in another coordinate, and they would fire for effect again. Another impassioned plea for Medevacs. Then the platoon leader corrected the impact zone and the artillery unit fired again. After a pause on the comm line, the artillery unit tried contacting the platoon leader. They never answered.

The artillery had landed directly on their position. "Friendly fire."

The battle started suddenly and it ended suddenly. The NVA broke contact and melted away silently into the jungles and their tunnel complexes. While the 137th ASH was successfully landing Medevacs and supplies, *082* remained on standby. The 2/7 Infantry suffered thirty-two KIAs, while Alpha Company of the 137th lost two ships, one pilot, and two crew members.

One hundred-sixty-five days to go.

I IIl I

Two days after the battle was just another day in a seemingly endless task providing support to the 2/5 and 2/7 Infantries in their "hammer and anvil" maneuver to crush the NVA in War Zone D. The enemy had not been seen again. They hadn't been driven out; they were just staying underground.

This particular Sunday, Dyson and Morgan would be flying with E.B. Smith and Blaise Burke on *085*. Smith, a Chief Warrant Officer 2, was a seasoned Huey pilot on his second tour. Burke, a Wobbly One, was sent straight from his Division training-orientation. Smith was short and Burke was tall. Mutt and Jeff. Other crew members reported Smith was cool to fly with and Burke seemed very sharp. They would be on supply missions to the 2/5 and 2/7 units and were ready to help Medevac and evacuate troops as needed.

Dyson ate morning mess, went back to the hootch, strapped on his sidearm, stuck his camera in his chest pocket, and joined the guys for a morning toke on a Marlboro Green. Jim Morrison was singing "Crystal Ship." Morgan stepped into the hootch, took a hit and passed it on.

"Pretty quiet out there," he said, referring to the search-and-destroy mission.

"Hope it stays that way."

"You fuckin' know it won't," Riaz said. The NVA and VC always picked when and where to attack the Americans. Once again, they were just waiting for the right time and the right place.

It was time to go to work. Mister D lit a Camel, Morgan a Winston, and they headed out for the flight line. The tarmac was a bustle of activity. As they joined in with Smith and Burke on the pre-flight inspection, they went over the mission sheet, which was mostly resupply type stuff. Even though there hadn't been any contact since the battle, there were still numerous ground-fire reports. Most of them occurred when a ship either approached or left an LZ.

"You have my permission to fire," Smith told Morgan and Dyson. "But I will tell you when to use suppressive fire. Understood? Got it?"

"Yes, sir."

Ten minutes later they were aloft and taxiing down the runway for takeoff. The ship accelerated and began its ascent. At two hundred feet they were past the perimeter and over the forest on the west side of Long Thong.

Dyson looked straight down and got a glimpse of the forest floor. Suddenly he saw two Vietnamese on a bicycle below, one pedaling, the other sitting in front of him on the frame and holding two AK47s pointed up toward the ship. Both men were looking right at Dyson.

Jumpin' Jesus! Did anyone else see this? Here they were flying toward a big-ass-but-for-now-invisible NVA stronghold, and he spots two VC right here, only a couple miles from Long Thong. He grabbed the "on" switch hanging around his neck.

"Sir, I just spotted two VC on a bike!"

"OK, gunner. Will call Operations and report," said Smith oh-so-casually.

One hundred sixty-two days to go.

▌▐▐▐▌

Briefing

For the week of May 28 through June 3, 1969, two hundred forty-two Americans were killed in Vietnam. This was a period where the number of U.S. troops killed was also the average number killed during a week's combat, indicating an unarguable increase in KIAs. That brought the American death tally to thirty-six thousand by the end of June 1969.

| ||| |

JULY

More and more information on the 1968 My Lai massacre was reaching the troops in Vietnam. Not by AFVN TV or AFVN Radio or *Stars and Stripes*, the military newspaper, but by *Time, Newsweek,* and *Life* magazines mailed from home. The revelation was met with amazement about the number of civilians gunned down, but there didn't seem to be any outraged GIs. Vietnamese lives were deemed expendable, "Kill them all. Let God sort 'em out" was the widespread attitude. Some soldiers remained aloof about the atrocity as if the lives of innocent noncombatants were to be simply eradicated, known only to their relatives whose own lives could also be erased.

| ||| |

Stand Down

July 4 fell on a Friday. That morning Dyson stopped by the mailroom. Kosski had seen him coming and pulled his letter from a stack. It was from his mom, the second this week. Bless her heart, she wrote faithfully twice a week—town news, gossip, obituaries, anecdotes about friends and family, and what she read or saw on TV about the war. 'Are you sure you're OK?' she would ask in so many words. He hadn't heard from Carol since the middle of May. "I'll wait for you." Bullshit.

Since his first flight on June 18, Dyson had flown seven more sorties for a total of forty-eight hours. For every twenty hours spent in-flight, a crew member would be awarded an Air Medal. SP4 Jonas Franklin from Iowa, a clerk in Operations, kept track of everyone's hours—pilots, crew chiefs, gunners. There was a small group of pilots and crews who practically lived in those ships. Dyson's time was divided between performing maintenance and flying missions.

The enlisted men—maintenance and flight personnel—had

been putting in long, draining days keeping the ships up and flying. To celebrate the Fourth, boost morale, and express his gratitude, Bannon, the Battalion CO, ordered a stand-down for Alpha and Bravo Companies in Long Thong, and Charlie and Delta Companies over in Phuoc Vinh and Lai Khe. There would be a cookout with hamburgers, hotdogs, and cold beer, a time to just relax and get everyone's mind off the war for a brief time. It was scheduled for 17:00 hours with a movie after dark. The word went out: "No weapons allowed."

Some guys had volunteered to help Gator and Floaty build an outdoor grill between the mess hall and the showers. They filled a small utility trailer with ice and beer and were testing the cans of Hamm's and Pabst Blue Ribbon to make sure they were ice cold. Gator and Floaty made beef patties with chopped onions and seasoning, baked beans with onion and bacon, and great, cold, Southern-style potato salad with hard-boiled eggs, mustard, onions, and relish. The cooks made sure the meal for the guys was their best possible. They would also see to it that there was ample food later for the men still working and flying this evening. Kearny, the sorry-ass lifer in charge of the hootch maids, was there checking to make sure he got his share of all the free beer he felt was due him. Pops was nowhere to be seen and was probably off drunk somewhere—poor guy.

Men started drifting over to the grill around 16:40. Some of them had cleaned up a lot better than they had for many days. One guy even splashed on some Old Spice. The stand-down was open to everyone in Alpha and Bravo Companies of the 137th ASH Battalion.

By 17:30 hours, at least two hundred men had gathered. Everyone was asked to participate in saying Grace, led by the brigade chaplain, Captain Elias Castle, a towering son of a gun with a 1st Cavalry patch and a CIB he'd earned before he became a chaplain.

"Bless us, O Lord, and these . . ." It was the first prayer Dyson had heard since he was drafted fourteen months ago.

"OK," the chaplain called out, "let's dig in!"

One of the guys in the nearest hootch put on some music. First off was Janis Joplin, from *Live at the Fillmore*. Men brought lawn chairs, some sat on revetment walls. Officers, NCOs, and enlisted men partied together with the social lubrication of beer, liquor, and pot in the warm golden glow of the approaching twilight. Bannon went to the trailer and pulled out a Hamm's, so some of his fellow officers did the same. Only the highest-ranking men wore any hats at all, but only their soft baseball hats, another sign of relaxation. Some men wore OD T-shirts tucked in, some wore flip-flops with their uniform, some wore shorts and T-shirts. It was nice to be in such a casual atmosphere. The comradery was great. Crews shared flying stories, ex-grunts talked about their time in the field, a few guys told tales about home. Those who'd drunk more than their share of liquor easily identified themselves by their loud bluster and bravado. Jensen—the battalion NCOIC—walked around saying hello, but he would often revert true to form with a stage whisper in a guy's ear, "Get your hair cut first thing tomorrow" and "Your mustache is getting too long. Trim it." It was a decent low-key approach because he could have been a prick about it.

Belly laughs and ball-busting abounded. Soul brother Floaty and cracker "Georgia" Gator were the best of friends, insulting each other so all could hear.

"Your momma's ass is so big it's got a ZIP code."

"Oh, yeah? Well, your mom's so fat she can kick-start a B-52 with a broken foot."

"Your dad shoulda wore a rubber!"

A three-quarter-ton truck and a jeep pulled up on the company street. Seven black men got out of the vehicles and walked into the picnic. Four of them were in civvies, the other three had on partial uniforms. They all sported Afros; the three of them in partial, modified uniforms were huge—with pick combs stuck in their hair. They wore sunglasses. Everyone eyed them warily as they approached.

They helped themselves to the food and beer but talked only to each other. No one knew who they were. Could they be from Charlie or Delta Companies? Strickland and Dyson were both struck by the realization that these were the same Americans they saw in the village on their way back from Long Binh.

"Yeah, that's them." What the hell were these guys up to?

Brisco and Jensen walked over to the food line where three of the strangers had gone for seconds. "Hey, men. How ya doin'? I'm Sergeant Major Jensen of the 137th. Where are you guys from?"

The three just stared at both him and Brisco and were quickly joined by the other four.

"We're from Long Binh, man." Not even a hint of military courtesy.

"The 137th doesn't have anybody in Long Binh," said Jensen. Then, without even any pretext of courtesy, the men turned their backs and continued down the food line completely ignoring the two officers.

"Listen," said Brisco, "this food and beer is for men of the 137th. Are you men from the 137th?"

They kept moving down the chow line. Most of the guys couldn't hear what was said, but they saw what was going on. Jensen stepped in front of the first black soldier filling his paper plate. "OK, now. Stop. Stop. We let you men have something to eat and drink, but it's time for you to leave." He looked out over the camp and back at the uninvited guests. "It's getting dark. You need to get going back to Long Binh. You can't be out there after dark."

"Oh, we ain't worried about that, man," one of the soldiers said, and the rest of them chuckled.

Now all the men in Alpha and Bravo Companies were watching. Were these guys going to pull something? Why are they so cocky? Were they wearing .45s under their shirts?

Major Bentworth and Sergeant Hollingsworth came over and joined Brisco and Jensen. "All right," said Brisco, "I am ordering you men to leave here right now. Get in your vehicles and go. Now!"

"You sure you want us to leave?" said the biggest one, like he was talking to a kid down the block. He put a spoonful of beans in his mouth and chewed.

It was a staring contest. Guys were sidling slowly toward the intruders and looked like they were getting ready to throw them out, but that didn't seem to impress or concern them in the least.

"OK. We'll leave, man. We'll leave." And they all turned, put their paper plates down, and sauntered over to their truck and jeep. Without looking, one of them tossed his half-eaten burger back over his shoulder.

They took their time getting into their vehicles. The biggest one who had done all the talking rode shotgun in the jeep. They started their engines, gave the crowd one last glower, popped the clutches, and sped off, headed towards the gate to Long Binh. That remark by one of them that they weren't concerned about being on the road after dark was unsettling. Just who were these guys that could come and go as they pleased, didn't answer to anybody, and traveled around the countryside after dark?

I IIII

A news flash just in from the outside world: One of the Rolling Stones has died. Holy shit! Which one? Someone said he heard it was Mick Jagger. No, it was the drummer. Better not be Keith Richards. Oh, man. This is news. Half the guys were concerned, the other half not so much. Maybe they were Beatles' fans.

The movie was going to be *Cool Hand Luke*, a classic Dyson had seen twice already, once with Carol. He'd gladly watch it again, this time stoned. Fuck that little bitch. It was a right-on movie about a guy on a chain gang, a bit of a drunkard, resisting authority. A fitting subject for this place.

Back in the hootch, guys put on bug spray, opened cold beers, and gathered in Super Chicken's area for a tune or two from Deep Purple and some smoke. This batch was called Golden Triangle. The world's best pot, the connoisseurs said, not needing to be beefed up with hashish or chemicals. It was a golden color. Did it come down the Ho Chi Minh Trail? Did the drug money support the VC? Fuck it. Who cares if it did or not? Spook lit a corncob pipe and passed it.

"You guys saw that bunch in the village?" asked O'Grady.

"Yeah. Papp says it's the same bunch, too."

"We can't wear peace symbols, but they can wear that black shoe-lace-jewelry around their necks in protest of the white man's oppression." Since O'Grady started smoking pot, he would really open up sometimes.

"You know," Super Chicken said, "if they're only like twelve percent of the population, how come they want all the preferential treatment? Look at what you see around here, man."

"Why is it niggers like that can come and go anywhere?" Ramirez took a hit. "You know, they talk about discrimination and the white man's Army laws but look at them. We can't grow big hairdos like that, with pick-combs stuck in them yet!"

The racist comments startled Mister D, coming from this group of peaceful potheads. He was trying hard not to have any prejudices. There were only a handful of blacks in this aviation unit, but damn, no one gets to pick their unit, they're ordered to their unit.

"How can they get away with that shit?" asked Soup.

"Shit. The commanders are afraid of the sons of bitches," O'Grady hissed. "They're afraid they'll be nailed for discrimination."

"We gotta obey regulations. Why can't they?" This was starting to beat the purpose of getting stoned, talking like this.

"Hey, there's good ones and bad ones. Just like in any group."

"The worst people I know are white," said Spook.

"Hey. Forget about this shit," O'Grady said, taking a hit, "and think about this shit."

"Amen," said Soup, holding in the smoke.

Mister D lit a Camel. "Time to go." He grabbed his lawn chair. "Let's go watch Luke fuck with people."

There was a good turnout for the movie. Many had seen it before back home, but it was well worth watching over here. It should be like this every evening—cleaned up, full of good food and cold beer, in a good mood, and stoned. A bunch of the lifers had retreated to their clubs to drink. Papp and a few other officers stuck around along with a smattering of NCOs.

It was dark now. The movie area was filling up with the audience sitting on lawn chairs and on benches of old rotor blades, some of them pierced with bullet holes.

"I can't wait to see that broad washing the car again," said Hollis, a little country boy from Oklahoma. "I love it when she pushes her tits against the windows." He shoved his hand down into his pants like he was getting it ready to screw.

SP4 Bobby Lemmons from Alabama was the projectionist in a small, elevated plywood booth, kind of like a pay-phone booth, at the rear of the viewing area. At first the white painted movie screen showed a blank bright light. Then the opening credits rolled. The anticipation for the car wash scene was like that of a full house at the Saturday afternoon matinee overflowing with giddy, noisy kids waiting for the cartoons to begin, except these kids were high on beer and pot, and horny.

"I'd fuck a bush if I thought there was a snake in it," said Devaney.

Just when the big, busty blonde started washing her 1941 DeSoto with a big sponge and soapy water, the film stopped between two frames. Then it blistered, boiled and burned out right before their very eyes—nothing in front of them but white screen. The crowd erupted like sexually deprived wild men. Were they going to be denied the car wash scene? Were they going to castrate Lemmons?

"He's fixing it! He's fixing it!" someone yelled in defense of the projectionist.

Just then, Dyson got a glimpse of a small dark form just above the men who were seated twenty-five feet to his right. Someone yelled "Grenade!" Grenade? Here? And then BLAM! An orange flash was surrounded by hundreds of white sparks arcing all over and into the group of men. Two seconds later, BLAM! BLAM! It was the distinct explosions of M26 fragmentation grenades, along with two more orange flashes and white-hot shrapnel drilling into the crowd.

"MEDICS! MEDICS! Get the medics over here!" Six men were down and more were staggering around screaming from shrapnel wounds. That stuff is in a semi-molten state when it hits a person.

"Get 'em, guys! There they go!"

"Hey! Hey! Stop! Stop!" and a chase began.

A bunch of guys near the movie screen took off running. They tore after two shadows disappearing between bunkers and hootches. The shadows jumped into a waiting jeep that spun its wheels and sped off, vanishing into the east side of the camp toward a little-used access gate. In five seconds, they had barreled through the gate and out into the night. Gone.

A crowd gathered bent on helping their comrades. Medics rushed in and started to work. Now eight guys were down with at least five guys trying to help one. Other victims were able to walk to the dispensary on their own. Three grenades had been lobbed into the group of moviegoers.

"I saw this guy toss something. I thought was a baseball."

"Right after the first one went off, I saw two guys each lob something at the crowd. We started chasing them and they ran to a jeep that had a driver waiting for them."

Everyone said the same thing: It looked like they were wearing Afros, big Afros.

The medics pronounced two of the men dead. Six were carried to the dispensary. From there, four were taken to the flight line for Medevac to the 93rd Evac Hospital in Long Binh.

The grenades had landed about ten feet apart, three blast areas on the hard-packed soil, ripping into the nearest rotor-blade benches. There was blood and tissue marking where each man fell. Hundreds of pieces of shrapnel pierced the men or went harmlessly into the air. It was all over in four seconds.

At 23:20 hours, a Huey arrived from Long Binh. It had an investigative team from the Army's Criminal Investigation Department. They wore civilian clothes and sidearms. It was a "fragging" incident, but instead of sorry-ass lifers being maimed or killed, it had been a bunch of men enjoying a stand-down. Everyone knew that the black soldiers who had been asked to leave the scene earlier were the assailants. Papp told the CID about the blacks they had seen in the village and how these same men had been asked to leave the picnic. The investigators took pictures of the scene, of where the attackers were, their route of escape. They interviewed anyone who laid eyes on the attackers. By 05:00 hours, they were flying back to Long Binh.

Damn this place. No one is safe anywhere, anytime. How would the COs handle this clusterfuck? Tell their families they died in combat? List them as KIAs?

One hundred fifty-seven days to go.

I III I

Briefing

By the end of the war, records indicate there had been between nine thousand and ten thousand noncombat deaths of U.S. servicemen in Vietnam.

I III I

Chieu Hoi—Arms Up

In 1963, the U.S. military instituted the Chieu Hoi Program ("Arms Up" in Vietnamese) aimed at providing a way for NVA and VC soldiers to surrender peacefully. Hundreds of thousands of fliers and cards were dropped from the air all over South Vietnam encouraging the enemy troops to surrender by chanting "Chu hoi, chu hoi," with their hands in the air and no harm would come to them. Many field units received their surrender honorably, others did not. Some who surrendered were interrogated then disposed of—shot on the spot, thrown from helicopters. ARVN forces were notorious for their brutal treatment of Chieu Hois. When Asians fought Asians, to surrender or to be captured was to face torture before death. No quarter asked, none given.

I III I

"Wake up, Mister D . . . wake up. You're flying today." Green continued down the line of bunks with his wake-up call.

It's Sunday, Dyson realized, but it didn't matter here, and he swung out of his bunk. Just another day. There was some chuckling at the other end of the hootch. O'Grady was still sleeping with his enormous hard-on pointing skyward. Riaz was lighting a cigarette, before he even put his feet on the floor. Dyson threw on shorts and a T-shirt for chow and headed out.

"Wait up," said Soup. He and Spook joined up with Dyson.

A pall settled over the company after the fragging, a combination of shock, bitterness, bewilderment, and loss. The guys in the mess hall were quiet, no longer shouting out the usual good-hearted taunts. No one knew when they would have movies again. There was talk of having armed roving guards in camp, just to keep an eye on things.

Back at the hootch after chow, Dyson finished getting into his flight clothes, strapped on his sidearm, and locked up his wall locker. Maris was having his customary cereal concoction.

"Man, this batch tastes good! Bugs and all. You ought to try some," he said to Mister D.

"When I'm not flying," Mister D said, but he did share a Marlboro Green with Spook, Soup, Riaz, and Ramirez. AFVN Radio, like most mornings, was playing the Fifth Dimension's "The Age of Aquarius." They had learned that Brian Jones was the dead Rolling Stones member. Not Mick, thank God. The whole company was up, with lights on in every hootch. Guys were on the go in all directions. But it was definitely quieter than usual.

Dyson stuck his head into the Operations CP for a look at the board. He and Morgan were assigned to 082 again with Papp as aircraft commander and Cavecchio as co-pilot. Taylor gave him a big wave while relaying messages on the radio. The map showing ground fire was a bristling pincushion of hostile action—with a red-headed pin for each location. He walked down the flight line to 082 where the other three crew members were set to give it a pre-flight inspection. Papp had been concerned about the accuracy of the gauges but was relieved to see on the maintenance forms that they had been recalibrated. *082* was becoming Papp's ship, and Morgan and Dyson were his crew. Giovani Cavecchio, a WO1, was a short, stocky guy with the typical 'Bronx-Wop' attitude. He would fit right in with the rest of the company. He shook hands with Dyson.

"OK," said Papp, "we will be flying in and out of to LZs Dot, Dolly, Betty—you know how it goes—with changes as needed. Everyone, everywhere is reporting ground fire heading into or out of the LZs. You have my permission to fire."

"You're all set, Mister D," said Morgan. "Your seat is ready." What a jewel Morgan was to crew with. And Papp was a jewel of an aircraft commander. Confidence and expertise exuded from each one—the better chance of getting back alive.

"The first mission is flying way out to LZ Dolly to bring some VC suspects back to Phuoc Vinh for questioning," Papp said over the intercom as they were putting on their flight helmets and getting ready to run up. This type of mission was rare in the 137th ASH. Many Infantry units in the 2nd Airmobile Division had a policy and Company motto: "NO prisoners."

"Watch 'em close," Papp advised, "real close."

In a couple minutes, they were up and over the green line, climbing to five thousand feet. Beautiful countryside stretched in every direction—rice paddies, villages, woods, marshes, and elephant grass—sadly marred as always by bomb craters. But he never tired of looking at this landscape. All this land had been a peaceful kingdom long ago.

"Two minutes to touchdown," Cavecchio announced. Papp had given him control of the ship, part of the process of breaking him in on how things were done in the 137th.

This was the time to get ready for any ground fire. LZ Dolly was ahead of them, a bare, red-clay opening, a mass of bunkers, revetments, trenches, and mortar pits. It had a landing pad just big enough for two Hueys. Each ship would fly to Phuoc Vinh with two VC suspects. Their guard would be on deck so the crew wouldn't have to watch them.

A young, buck sergeant helped Morgan guide the suspects onboard. Rick Gerard was probably only twenty years old, but he had the countenance and weary eyes of someone who had already spent a lot of time in the field. The VC suspects were dressed in shorts only. Blindfolded, a stake ran across their backs through the crook of their elbows with their hands tied tightly in front of them. They each weighed less than ninety pounds, little guys. Had they been captured? Surrendered? Gerard pushed them down firmly to sit on the floor while he took a bench seat facing them. The first loaded Huey lifted off and *082* followed with their two VCs and guard. Both ships climbed for altitude and, surprisingly, they didn't attract any ground fire. At five thousand feet they leveled off for the flight to Phuoc Vinh.

It was a cloudless sky. At different distances in the airspace around him, Dyson could see other aircraft: Chinooks, goofy-looking Caribous, a trio of jet fighters going off somewhere on an "unofficial" bombing mission. Along a dusty road—a highway by Vietnam standards—a column of armored personnel carriers, tanks, and deuce and a halfs headed west, each vehicle churning up its own thick red dust storm.

The two prisoners sat cross-legged and motionless while Gerard stared at them point-blank. Were these the guys who could slip into camp undetected? Spring murderous ambushes? Set cunning booby traps? The scrawny pair showed no sign of stress. Their blindfolds hid any expressions they may have had. Dyson glanced at Gerard who stared back for a few seconds, then drew his extended thumb across his neck, the cutthroat sign. Innocent rice farmers? Laborers? Family men caught between the VC and Americans? What were their names? Why were they the ones taken into custody? Who knew what their stories were?

The ship to their port side was five hundred feet ahead. Suddenly, a figure appeared in silhouette just below the ship—one of its prisoners, trussed up just like the two aboard *082*. Just another freeze frame image burned indelibly into Dyson's brain. What a picture that would have been. Then the doomed man began his freefall, turning over and over, his mouth wide open as he screamed. He dropped like a rock and Dyson watched him go all the way down before losing sight of him against the forest's light and shadows. He was gone—swallowed up by the dense greenery.

Dyson grabbed the commo button hanging on his chest and asked Papp, "Did you see that?"

"Radio silence, please. Radio silence," the commander replied. Was this part of the mission? Papp and Cavecchio must have seen it. Was this the same fate that awaited their two prisoners? Dyson didn't know what to think or say. He didn't know how he should react if Gerard started throwing out his prisoners. He divided his time for the rest of the flight between watching the ship ahead of them and watching Gerard and the two Vietnamese passengers.

Following the lead ship, they made their descent into Phuoc Vinh and cruised to the Field Headquarters helipad. As soon as the other ship set down, the remaining prisoner was thrust out of the Huey and smashed onto the rock-hard dirt, powerless to put his arms out to cushion his fall. He looked like he was hurt. Gerard and Morgan guided their two off the ship without any abuse. Three NCOs from Army Intelligence approached *082* and took charge of the prisoners and Gerard. Both ships soon took off, separated, and continued their missions.

"Mail run," Papp announced over the radio.

The chaotic turn of events since Dyson arrived in-country was piling up in his mind. The common theme, "death at any time," was repeated hundreds of times a day to everyone, friend, or foe, civilian or combatant, anywhere, anytime. The fragging two nights ago followed by the man plunging to his death were just a couple more morose and unforgettable memories, joining the others amassing every day. What madness it all was.

I III I

The following Wednesday, July 9, was spent in the Maintenance hangar. Dyson felt like it was a break from seeing the war. He received another letter from his mom asking him to write a little more often—she knew they worked a lot as mechanics in a "nice, safe area" just like he wrote her. He hadn't heard from Carol since the middle of May. *I hope she's having a good time, the little bitch,* he thought. Thank God he could party every day with pot and music and almost forget what was going on around him. Almost.

Dyson made it a point to ask Jensen, the Bravo Company clerk, if he could come in after hours and use a typewriter to write letters home because it was so much faster than writing longhand.

"You can, man, but here's the thing. They really need a few more clerks around here—I've got thirty-five days to go, and Franklin in Operations is short, too. If they see you typing, you may be made a clerk whether you like it or not."

The thought of being stuck in the Orderly Room or Operations CP all day dealing with lifer assholes did not appeal to him at all.

"Well, OK, man," Mister D said, "thanks for the heads-up." He walked out and headed for his hootch.

He was approaching the drainage ditch that ran east-west through the company. It helped during the September monsoon, but now it was just a dry twelve-inch-deep trench to watch out for when walking at night. He thought he heard a distant voice yell, "Come in," but a split second later, WHUMP! It had been Strickland yelling "Incoming!"

Dyson dove into the ditch as the second and third mortars hit. WHUMP-WHUMP-WHUMP! WHUMP-WHUMP-WHUMP! They were coming in fast, close together. There was more than one mortar team out there in the woods. He couldn't see what was going on. He kept his head and body down as low as he could in the ditch. He was out in the open and parts of him were exposed at ground level. *Christ, don't stick your head up.* He tried to lie even flatter. It seemed his big-ass Zippo lighter was in the way between him and the ground. The rounds were getting louder and landing closer. WHUMP! WHUMP! WHUMP-WHUMP-WHUMP!

"Oh, God. Oh, God. God, please, God, please. God, Oh, God. Please, please, please, God, please." The explosions were hitting thirty feet away, getting much louder. Showers of hundreds of white-hot metal shrapnel arced out over him. "God, please, God. God, please, God." The impact zone seemed to be gradually moving away. Then two close ones, WHUMP! WHUMP! They were still coming in at an alarming rate. "Please, God."

Next the mortar teams began to walk their rounds toward the flight line and away from the company area. He picked his head up. Something told him to go now and he sprang up and dashed to the bunker.

"Where were you?" asked Spook, as Dyson tumbled into the relative safety of the hootch.

"Shit! I was between here and the Orderly Room."

"Oh, man."

"I was in that fuckin' ditch." Dyson was out of breath. He hadn't run that fast in a long time, certainly faster than for the previous attacks. By now the mortars had all but stopped. After five minutes there were three more explosions on the flight line and then nothing.

"Before we were so rudely interrupted," said Super Chicken, and he lit up his Sherlock Holmes pipe packed with Golden Triangle. Soup took a hit, then Spook took a hit, then O'Grady took a giant hit (naturally), then Mister D. "Man, this stuff tastes good." He felt himself going up already. He lit a Camel and noticed his Zippo had a dented side from when he dove into the ditch. Did he thank God for saving him? No. It was right back to the drugs. He didn't know it then but he had started a long journey down darkened roads. But for now, the smoke was salvation.

I III I

Kosski was sorting the mail in the company mailroom, a new CONEX that had replaced the container destroyed in the mortar attack. He spotted Dyson walking toward the flight line.

"Hey, D! Mister D! Over here!" Dyson joined him. "Here's a letter for ya." He was the first one in Bravo Company to get his mail. It hadn't even been sorted yet.

"Gracias," he said. It was from Carol. The envelope felt almost empty. He headed to the hootch to read it in private. Good letter or bad letter? Why the big gap in time writing to him? He had slacked off, too, in writing back. He just didn't know what to say anymore. He opened the letter. Single page, space at the top and bottom, twelve lines long. He glanced at the bottom first. No long lines of Xs and Os, no lipstick kiss on the paper. "Hi," it began. Hi?

Oh, how busy she's been. Her dad was sick, but he's OK now. She went to a party and everyone was there. They all say a big hello. She got a job at Sears in the Parkade Mall. That's all for now. Love, Carol. The "Love" looked awkward compared to the rest of her handwriting.

Let's face it. Anything we had between us is over now and saying it in plain simple terms hurt. Fuck her, that's it, it's over.

One hundred forty-six days to go.

▌▐▐▐▐

Anniversary

His dad had died July 18, 1967.

He graduated from basic training July 18, 1968. "Your Dad would have been so proud of you," his mom wrote at the time. Back then he didn't like his dad at all.

Today was Friday, July 18, 1969, and look where he was. He knew it was on his mom's mind, and he tried not to be superstitious about it. July 18 had never been a bad day before 1967, why should it be now? Some guys in the company were superstitious, especially those on flight crews. One guy always carried a rabbit's foot.

He lit a Camel. Maybe the dented Zippo was his good luck piece, or the St. Christopher medal. Maybe he just didn't realize God was watching over him. He didn't know what to think about God or praying because he was so burned out about the Catholic church with its mysterious teachings and a punishing God. But he wasn't an atheist, either. One guy said he used to be an atheist but quit because there were no holidays. An old joke, but here it was probably true.

The NVA and VC in Tay Ninh, Binh Long, and Phuoc Long provinces were meting out stiff resistance in holding their roads and tunnel complexes. Besides the Division's infantry units engaging them again and again, the area had been the target of B52 strikes with two thousand-pound, steel-tipped, delayed-action, bunker-busting bombs, and the enemy was *still* heavily entrenched. Agent Orange had been sprayed over acres and acres of vegetation reducing the landscape to ghastly-surreal, deformed dead trees. The enemy remained hard to find, but these North Vietnamese foes always found the Americans easily enough.

A platoon from the 2/5 Infantry was in trouble. It had been split into three tiny defensive islands of resistance, surrounded by NVA and VC in an ever-tightening grip. It had WIAs and KIAs, and only one of the three teams had a radio. The radio relayed the pilots' back and forth about a Huey being shot down, spinning out of control, crashing in the woods, black smoke billowing through the trees, the crew's fate unknown. The platoon leader in charge of all three was trying to identify the three isolated locations with landmarks and colored smoke to the circling Hueys, except one team had run out of smoke grenades. Those ships attempting to evacuate them came under a fierce hail of small-arms fire. One gunship had made a rocket run but it didn't seem to knock out any enemy positions.

Papp received the position of a group needing evacuation. There was no colored smoke to identify the precise place, just visible landmarks: two huge trees, one of them leaning. The ship was at one thousand feet and Papp was asking if the intended LZ was southwest or southeast of the two trees. It took two minutes of radioed reports to clarify the LZ was southwest.

Papp swung the ship in a wide arc, coming down to treetop level to escape the sight of enemy gunners surrounding the LZ. He had pulled this trick before. Sometimes it worked, sometimes it didn't.

"OK, guys," he said, "we're goin' in." This was it. Green tracers began seeking out *082* and its crew. Morgan and Dyson fired at the sources of the tracers. They couldn't see the enemy, just their position.

More hostile gunners were firing now, the foliage of the trees being the only thing between them and the ship. They arrived over the pickup point, the west end of a few acres of elephant grass. Enemy fire was getting heavier on the vulnerable ship as it slowed, almost to a stop, hovering in the humid air like a big fat bull's-eye. Morgan fired from the starboard side and Dyson sprayed one section of the tree line, then let loose towards another darkened place a hundred meters away from them, then he swept the entire area from the far left to far right. Tracers were flying in every direction, red tracers and green tracers. Those were only the visible rounds. Many more went crackling past like four-hundred-forty-volt hornets. There was one loud CRACK, then another as two rounds passed through the skin of their ship. "Oh, shit."

"Gunner," Papp was talking to him. "Gunner, watch for friendlies. Watch for friendlies," meaning watch what you're firing at and keep an eye out for the evacuees. Dyson and Morgan were pouring as much fire as they could on the gunners' locations. The prop wash flattened the tall grasses down to waist level, and three Americans appeared out of the ground cover. They were three-abreast, two troopers holding up the guy in the middle. Dyson kept on firing over their heads, to the left and the right. *Jesus, are we gonna make it out of here?*

The three were now forty feet from Dyson's side of the ship. They were losing their grip on the wounded man and were beginning to collapse themselves. Weak and exhausted, dehydrated, they sank to their knees. "I'm going," said Dyson into his mike. He undid his lifeline, peeled off his helmet and jumped out to go to their aid. If he didn't help them, they weren't going to make it. Tracers were zipping overhead. Dyson grabbed ahold of the middle man's bloody uniform and dragged him toward the ship. As he bent over to claw at the grunt's web-belt, his dog tags and St. Christopher medal were whipped out into the hurricane-force winds of the prop-wash. The blistering force of the downward wind made it almost impossible to stand.

"Get up! Get up! Goddammit, get up!" They struggled getting the wounded soldier to the edge of the cargo deck area.

Two of the troopers climbed aboard and began pulling the other one as Dyson pushed. He had his back against the threshold of the ship when he looked down range through the foliage to the darkened tree line. At about the length of a football field three NVA stepped into view. One laid down with an RPD machine gun while an assistant gunner lay next to him. Dyson could even see the green empty rations can attached to the gun to help feed the belt smoothly. The third man was preparing a shoulder-fired rocket-propelled grenade launcher. Tracers were crisscrossing all over the place. Although their ship was only visible through the dense grasses and trees to a couple of gunners, it seemed like dozens were shooting back at them.

Dyson had an unobstructed view of the enemy rocket launcher. Everything began to shift into slow motion enveloped by an almost peaceful silence. He could see the actuator handle of the RPD slam open and shut, open and shut, with empty shell casings slowly spinning out, and tracer trails frozen in the air. The grenadier with the RPG aimed right at them. Dyson was literally looking the enemy in the eye when he fired. RPGs do not have a lot of propellant and the NVA soldier had rushed to get the round off. The rocket was aimed too low and sank rapidly, exploding thirty feet from the port side. Dyson got a face full of soil and debris—he couldn't see and groped blindly for any handholds to pull himself aboard. He was conscious of being yanked violently into the ship, falling backward on an M16 and whacking the back of his head on the deck. There were two more loud CRACKs as rounds hit the ship.

"We're off!" Papp declared. Both troopers were firing their M16s at the locations of enemy gunners until *082* disappeared over the tree line headed to the field hospital in Phuoc Vinh. The wounded soldier lay across the deck, motionless. His two buddies were bent low over him and shouting at him, but he couldn't hear their words. He'd been shot twice in the torso and once in his right thigh. It happened hours ago, and he'd lost a lot of blood. Much of it was now dried and black. One trooper took off a towel from around his neck, bunched it up, and put it under the man's head.

With the water from his canteen, Dyson washed the dirt out of his eyes. His face was streaked with dirt, but he could see again. He put on his flight helmet.

"You OK, gunner?" asked Papp.

"Yes, sir. Thanks." Dyson couldn't believe he had jumped off the ship to help, but what else was there to do? Let the three men just sit there helpless? Wait for the grunts to finally drag themselves aboard?

At Phuoc Vinh teams of medics were waiting. The two troopers helped off-load the wounded grunt to the medics who gently put him on a gurney. As they got off, one of the troopers put his arm around Dyson's neck in a big hug.

"Thanks, man. Thanks," he said and the two grunts jumped off.

It was July 18.

One hundred forty-three days to go.

I I I I I

After reveille the next morning, Morgan stopped by Dyson's hootch.

"Hey, I got something for you," he said and handed Dyson a dog tag and a St. Christopher medal. Mister D took them and felt for his own dog tag chain. Only one chain and its dog tag were there. A piece of shrapnel from the RPG had gone through his second dog tag, snapped its small chain, and blew the ID tag and medal into 082.

"I found the gold medal on the deck against the starboard side. The tag was on the deck almost inside the cabin."

The dog tag had a hole like someone had driven a Bowie knife through it. When he was standing in the prop wash the tag had blown off him and into the air. That's when the RPG shrapnel pierced it.

Bullets and shrapnel don't care who they hit or where. Sometimes it's a one-in-a-million hit, and sometimes it's a one-in-a-million miss. Dyson's number just wasn't up, yet.

"I'm not supposed to tell anybody," Morgan said quietly, "Papp put you in for a DFC."

I III I

Dyson was scheduled for guard duty on Sunday. It would be a break from the routine, a chance to catch his breath. Before going on guard duty, there was always a guard-mount formation where the officer of the guard inspected the troops and passed on any special instructions. Tonight's officer of the guard was Captain Bullocks from Alpha Company. Alvin Bullocks was burly and short. He was also quick and agile. He looked like a bulldog, with curled little ears, big jowls, and a lower lip that stuck out a bit. The NCOIC that night was Sergeant Kearny.

The new routine was set in motion. Dyson, O'Grady, Blunt, and Devaney relieved the four men in Bunker 12 at 20:00 hours. Bunker 12 had a StarLight scope for night vision.

"Anything going on?" asked Blunt.

"Nah, not a damn thing." The four guards left.

Bunker 12 was twelve feet wide and eighteen feet deep. There were two folding cots for a pair of guys to nap on while the other two kept watch. No one was sleepy yet, so they took turns looking through the StarLight scope. The scope weighed six pounds and was filled with a fluid of some sort. It magnified starlight and the light given off by rotting vegetation. The field of vision was a yellowish-green color. Images were not crystal clear, but any movement could be plainly seen. It was a neat little item. Some nights, the guards would get a glimpse of a leopard on the prowl in the underbrush.

"Take a look out back," Devaney said. Blunt stuck his head out the back entry and looked around for any lifers. At night, officers would be in their club drinking, NCOs would be in their club drinking, and sometimes OICs and NCOICs of the guard would sneak back and have some drinks with them. Everyone knew Kearny would be holed up somewhere drinking. They just had to worry about Bullocks.

Blunt came back over. "All clear. Permission to fire up."

"Permission granted, motherfucker," so Blunt lit up a corncob pipe full of Cambodian Red and passed it around while the guards smoked tobacco cigarettes in a feeble attempt to help mask the smell. Everyone kept their glowing embers below the level of the sill on the front side so as not to provide a target for the gooks in the woods.

"Aaaahhhh . . . that's good." In a hootch nearby, Hendrix was wailing about the sky turning red and lighting up somebody's house on fire. The men paid the lyrics of "House Burning Down" no mind. Shit, they burned down houses and villages all the time.

After they were finished smoking, the four were content to just lean on the sill looking out. The moon was a waxing crescent, maybe twenty percent illuminated. They talked in low voices about the battles and missions in War Zone D, and rumors, rumors, and more rumors.

A big (and unofficial) topic was cross-border operations—crossing into Laos and Cambodia in "secret" military operations. It was not supposed to happen, but it did. Troops stationed four miles east of the Cambodian border would be airlifted and flown west for five minutes at one hundred knots. The math was simple. They were in Cambodia.

Blunt was the unofficial lookout behind the bunker, watching out for lifers. Then Devaney took his place and on it went.

"Hey, here comes Bulldog." Dyson lit a Camel. No one acted concerned. They were cool.

"Gentlemen." The captain entered the bunker. He sniffed three times and suspiciously eyed the men.

"Hello, sir."

"See anything?" he asked looking over at the scope. No one had seen anything. Bullocks had a bunch of information to relay about enemy activity. There were large and aggressive VC units within a four-mile radius of the camp. Observation posts in the woods reported heavy enemy activity during the last few nights. These units would target Long Binh, Long Thong, and Bearcat. That was news? Where had he been? "Division says they're planning an all-out attack on one of these bases." Really? It was a briefing, but it wasn't. Two guys talked with him. Two guys kept watch over the green line.

"You men need any Cokes or anything?" he asked. All declined. Bullocks turned to go out the back. "Oh, I almost forgot. Americans are on the moon." Then he walked away into the darkness.

The rest of that night Dyson, O'Grady, Blunt, and Devaney just stared at the moon, mesmerized. The perimeter didn't interest them at all. When he looked away, Dyson had the moon's image burned in his retina. The VC could have marched up to the green line in full parade-style in formation and he wouldn't have noticed at all.

One hundred forty-one days to go.

I IIII

Briefing

The American Red Cross provided aid to U.S. servicemembers as well as to Vietnamese refugees during the war. More than six hundred "Donut Dollies" served in Vietnam and throughout Southeast Asia for a salary of $4,800 a year. Not able to serve the donuts they were so well known for due to the tropical environment and usually remote locations they were now being called "recreational advisors." During the height of involvement in 1968, some 480 field directors, hospital personnel, and recreational advisors were sent to support the growing number of servicemembers at bases and hospitals. Five Red Cross staff members gave their lives, and many more were injured.

I IIII

Donut Dollies

"Hey, there's Donut Dollies in the hangar!" With that announcement, the mechanics in the flight line—who could— dropped whatever they were doing and rushed over to have coffee and donuts with the American women working for the Red Cross. The Donut Dollies were constantly being ferried to posts all over Vietnam. They came not only to camps like this one, the big bases; they even visited some LZs out in the boonies. Some were good-looking, some weren't. Some guys called them "Pastry Pigs."

Mister D went along with a bunch of the guys to the hangar and there they were—three women in light-colored, Red Cross dresses down to their knees. Some guys acted and talked like cock-hounds, stalking the women for a better look. For once, Dyson was glad there were lifers around to keep things somewhat decent.

The three Donut Dollies had name tags. Lucy, from Providence, Rhode Island, was very attractive and kind of classy. *She doesn't belong here*, Dyson thought. Chris, from Tulsa, Oklahoma, was like the girl next door—ponytail, freckles, and big, bright, cornflower blue eyes. Bertha (who names their kid Bertha?) was from Portland, Oregon. She looked like a Bertha.

Coffee and donuts were set out along a rotor blade on sawhorses. Dyson couldn't get through the crowd without having to shoulder someone aside, so he stayed put. The questions and comments were the usual high school-level mentality: "Oh, baby. What are you doing tonight?" and "Are you married?" and "What's a nice girl like you . . . ?" The guys were horned up beyond being civil. Dyson went back to work.

At 10:45 hours, a Medevac Huey was scheduled to fly the ladies out of Long Thong to their next stop. Dyson felt sorry for them. Later in the day, it got around camp that only two of them actually left. Bertha was still there. The rumors on the camp's "jungle telegraph" purported her brother was a Major League baseball player somewhere. She was being walked around by Bravo Company's first sergeant, Enrico, who, interestingly enough, had sleeping quarters in his own bunker, just like the other lifers who capitalized on their rank and privilege. Enlisted men acted as spies and were watching them to see what they were doing so they could surreptitiously broadcast their every step in what would be called in later years "real time." Bertha had frizzy salt-and-pepper hair, pale white skin, a Roman nose, a barrel-shaped torso with tiny boobs, a big ass, fat thighs, and skinny calves—much too skinny for that big body. *Enrico could do better than that*, Dyson thought, even over here.

The whole camp was watching to see when and how she was

going to leave before sunset as required. That didn't happen. At 23:00 hours, the spies reported she was staying with Enrico in his bunker—a big, blatant violation of Army regulations. Can this place get any more bizarre?

I III I

A mandatory formation was scheduled for the morning of Wednesday, July 23, for Alpha and Bravo Companies. There hadn't been one for a while because of the missions and heavy workload. Maybe something important was afoot.

"Wonder what this is about."

O'Grady piped up, "I know. I heard Brisco and Enrico talking in the mess hall."

"So, what is it?"

"You're gonna shit when you hear this one," said O'Grady. "Absolutely shit."

The companies were standing at attention when MAJ Brisco announced, "We are pleased to present an award for bravery to someone in Bravo Company." Murmurs and questions rumbled through the ranks of the 200 men.

"All right, at ease," some lifer said. "At ease, men."

"Staff Sergeant Thomas Kearny," Brisco said, "front and center!"

Kearny? For what? Has he ever even been out of the company area? How the hell did he earn anything, never mind an award for bravery? The grumbling sounded hostile and resentful.

"At ease!" the platoon sergeants were calling. "At ease!"

Kearny appeared and marched up to the major, did a right face, and saluted him. "Staff Sergeant Thomas Kearny reports, sir." Brisco returned the salute.

"Here we go." O'Grady knew what was coming.

"On the night of February 3, 1969, Alpha and Bravo Companies, 137th Assault Support Helicopter Battalion, 2nd Airmobile Division, Vietnam, came under heavy enemy mortar and rocket bombardment . . ."

"You gotta be shittin' me."

"Which attack was that?"

"I think it was when the Avionics hootch was hit."

". . . during which time the barracks areas, mess hall, orderly room, mail room, and company street received numerous hits from mortar rounds and rockets . . ."

"Yeah, I remember that."

"I do, too, but I don't remember seeing Kearny around." Kearny wasn't even present when he was on duty, never mind when something like that happens. He was a slacker of the highest degree.

". . . realized there were casualties . . ."

"I realize this is bullshit, that's what I realize."

". . . guiding the dazed and confused men to their bunkers . . ."

Now the rumbling became outright vocal objections and guffaws. "Oh, bullshit!" and "Dazed and confused!" and "Never happened!" and "Did anybody ever see him there? Anybody?" No one could say they did, suspecting instead that he had been cringing someplace in a bunker.

Kearny stood at attention, staring straight ahead without eye contact. This was his award and he was going to get it. Undeterred, Brisco carried on with the citation.

". . . was instrumental in organizing medical aid for the wounded, comforting the wounded . . ."

It was like a scene out of Kafka. A citation describing something that did not happen. Who wrote this bullshit script? Who the hell put him in for a medal?

". . . without any regard for his own personal . . ." and it kept on going. ". . . awarded the Bronze Star for Bravery."

Brisco pinned the Bronze Star on Kearny's left chest pocket. They saluted each other. Then Brisco made a monumental faux pas.

"Let's have a big hand for Sergeant Kearny." The NCOs and officers gave a round of applause, but just a handful of enlisted men offered a sorry smattering of cheers. Kearny stood there, proud as a peacock, beaming from ear to ear with his rotten teeth.

At last, Brisco said, "Companies. Dismissed."

Phony and false award citations given to undeserving lifers were the norm during this war, a disgraceful practice that devalued the real purpose and recognition for awards and decorations.

I III I

Second Airmobile Division, along with all other Divisions, mimeographed and distributed a weekly casualty report of all Division personnel killed in action. Each KIA was listed—name, rank, serial number, MOS, date of death, cause of death, and location. A sample line:

DOE, John E., SGT E5, US 55555555, 11B20, 10 July 69, GSW, Tay Ninh Province. (11B20 is Infantry, GSW is gunshot wound—there were always many gunshot wounds.)

SMITH, John F., SP4, US 66666666, 11B20, 10 July 69, FW, Tay Ninh Province. (FW is fragmentation wound—there were many listings of those wounds as well.)

Man after man, line after line, page after page, week after week, month after month.

One hundred thirty-eight days to go.

I III I

On Saturday, July 26, not one, but two American civilian women were seen walking around Long Thong. One was Bertha, Enrico's personal Donut Dolly, and a slender brunette about forty years old. Bertha being shacked up in the 1st sergeant's bunker was an open secret; strictly forbidden by both Army and Red Cross regulations. The brunette was seen accompanying Joseph Styner, a crusty old warrant officer pilot who had flown every kind of Army helicopter imaginable dating back to the Korean War. Everyone called Styner "The Creeper" because he would creep up and appear suddenly next to anyone, anywhere, and then disappear.

A small house trailer was tucked away between the motor pool and some unused barracks. For a long time, no one knew how it got there; it just suddenly appeared. As it turned out, The Creeper bought the trailer from a Vietnamese farmer from the village of Long Thong and had it dropped off next to the motor pool. The brunette turned out to be his wife. Styner had rendezvoused with her in Hawaii during his R&R and they flew back on a commercial airline. Just how she got into the country was not known. And now the husband and wife were living in the little house trailer.

It was just another dumbfounding example of blatantly flouting the regulations and getting away with it. Brisco and Bannon, the Battalion commander, both knew of the unauthorized living arrangements—the entire camp knew about them. The Donut Dolly was one thing, but an American civilian wife living on post? What if she got killed in camp by enemy rocket fire? How the fuck would that be handled?

▮ ▮▮▮

Enemy weapons caches were found all over Vietnam. Many of them included guns and ammunition made in Communist countries as well as materiel made in the U.S.A. The serial numbers on the American-made weapons—M1s, Thompson .45 caliber submachine guns, Iver-Johnson .30 carbines—revealed they had been issued to U.S. forces during the Korean War. Captured in Korea by the Red Chinese, they were stored and distributed years later along the Ho Chi Minh Trail to South Vietnam.

Captured American-made weapons were prized as war souvenirs by just about everyone stationed in Southeast Asia. Enlisted men ran into unending difficulties trying to take one home legally. Lifers didn't have any problems at all.

▮ ▮▮▮

That Saturday evening, a crew chief, SP5 Donald McCarthy, from Kansas City, walked into the mess hall after flying all day. He was in his flight uniform and carried an American M1 Garand rifle that had been found in a hidden VC weapons cache. He had traded something for it with a grunt. It hung over his shoulder by its sling as he went down the chow line and chose a seat with some friends. He set the M1 against the wall and began eating.

Minutes later, Enrico and Brisco entered the mess hall to eat. The Major and First Sergeant took their mess to the cadre dining area, separate from the enlisted men's area. Enrico caught sight of the M1 and came back out, walked straight to the M1 and slung it over his shoulder. "First Sergeant," said McCarthy, "that's my weapon, 1st Sergeant," using all manner of military courtesy.

"Having this weapon is against regulations, McCarthy."

McCarthy rose. "So is shacking up with a woman on post, First Sergeant." Everyone was dead silent, looking at Enrico for his next move.

"At ease, McCarthy. At ease!" Enrico yelled. No EM was going to talk to him like that.

"1st Sergeant, you're going to take that M1 for yourself, aren't you?"

"I said at ease, McCarthy!"

Now Brisco strode into the fray and motioned for Enrico to give him the weapon. "I loved this weapon when I came into the service," the Major said. M1 Garands are great weapons, sought after by shooters and collectors all over. "McCarthy, I'm going to keep this for you while you go through the proper channels to take this weapon home. Fair enough?" Everyone knew enlisted men went through hassle after hassle of red tape and delays in order to take a war trophy home—lifers, no problem.

"All right, sir. But I would like to take it down to the green line and shoot it a couple times."

"OK," Brisco told McCarthy. "Carry on," he said to everybody. Everyone continued with their meals. Brisco had appeased the enlisted man and ignored the officer's co-habitation arrangement.

Blind eyes. Two sets of rules.

I IIII

AUGUST

The last few days of July had been very hot—unbearably so, even by Southeast Asian standards. The first of August brought no relief. Temperatures on the Long Thong flight line topped one hundred ten degrees. But as brutal as it was in camp, it was even hotter out in the field for the men of the 2/5 and 2/7 Infantry, soon to be joined by the 1/9 and 2/12 Infantry. The entire area of the Tay Ninh, Binh Long, Phuoc Long, Long Khanh, Binh Duong and Bien Hoa provinces was a heavily bunkered and tunneled complex of entrenched and battle-hardened NVA and VC units. They remained resupplied and reinforced by the never-ending convoys coming down the Ho Chi Minh trail onto the three major "highways," each with its own network of side roads and tertiary trails sprouting out like tentacles into the countryside, villages, and towns.

The VC would watch the Americans broil and bake for days as they slogged their way through the forests and jungles, sapped by heat and humidity, man-eating insects, and venomous snakes. Then the enemy would spring their ambushes with surprising volumes of heavy coordinated fire. Ferocious company- and battalion-sized battles lasting one, two, maybe three days ensued over terrain that really didn't have a name, only coordinates on a tattered field map. If by some wild chance, one of these obscure battles for some unknown reason happened to be mentioned in the press, the figures reported would always include so many more of the enemy killed than Americans—body counts. The omnipresent, all-so-terribly important body counts were the inflated statistical figures that proved the Americans were winning the war.

Along with the disturbing number of fatalities and casualties in the field units, the numbers of killed and wounded in the aviation units supporting those ground troops were also mounting. Pilots and crew members' lives were lost at an alarming rate in War Zone D. But the powers that be acted more concerned about the total number of helicopters lost—the number of lives lost seemed an afterthought.

||||||

In 1966, the First Infantry Division, proudly known as "The Big Red One" and "The Bloody First," built the camp called Bearcat, on Route 15, about 16 kilometers southeast of Bien Hoa. Bearcat took its name from its Special Forces radio call sign.

Besides American units, there were 5,000 Black Panther Royal Thailand Army soldiers in their own camp-within-a-camp and a few thousand Australian/New Zealand troops who were also in their own camp-within-a-camp. They did it that way because they had both determined the perimeter around Bearcat was too long for them to man adequately. In order to provide a more "homier" look to their camp, the Thais had their perimeter decorated with VC and NVA heads that they had taken as trophies while out in the field. The ANZAC troops maintained a more disciplined appearance.

The Aussies had repulsed several Viet Cong units in a big battle in the zone, which was also the First Infantry's Area of Operation. Together they fought to clear out the VC—and then both were pulled out to other places.

The 2nd Airmobile Division had to move from Quang Trị over to War Zone D and start the process all over again. Territories were taken, then abandoned, reclaimed by the Communists and fought over again . . . and again. It made no sense.

On Saturday, August 2, Morgan and Dyson crewed *082* with Papp and a brand-new warrant officer, WO1 Levi Simko from Chicago. Simko had a constant air of bewilderment about him, his brow permanently wrinkled, like he was analyzing everything. Maybe it was extreme culture shock, but Simko was clearly intelligent. Meanwhile, Morgan and Dyson were always glad Papp was their pilot, and Papp was glad the duo was his crew.

Ship *082* had spent the day flying a host of missions—supply, resupply, sling-loading a huge, rubber waterbag under the ship out to an LZ near the border, transporting FNGs to Phuoc Vinh, and flying a lucky grunt, whose time of service was up, over to Long Binh for out-processing. At 17:20 hours, they set down in LZ Dolly to transport one 2/5 Infantry KIA to Graves Registration at Phuoc Vinh. The two waiting litter bearers lifted the KIA up off the ground and slid the entire load feet first, crosswise onto the ship's deck. The young infantryman wasn't in a body bag—"there weren't any." What, no goddamn body bags in the entire camp? You gotta be shittin' me.

Morgan yelled, "Clear," and they lifted off. The guy's head was on the port side—Dyson's side—facing up. There was a large wound on his left cheek and the eyeball was missing. His fatigues were blackened and stiff from the massive amount of dried blood covering them, obscuring the nametag sewn above the pocket of his shirt. Plastered to his wounds and fatigues were dirt, pebbles, and bits and pieces of vegetation, just like he was a piece of rubbish. Couldn't the medics at least have put bandages over his wounds? He had died hours ago. What was his name? Where did he come from? Did he have a wife and kids? What about his parents? How will his CO's letter home attempt to smooth over his death . . . "killed instantly . . . did not suffer . . . fighting for democracy . . . ?" He must have been the fiftieth KIA Dyson had ridden with so far, but the first one without a body bag. Unimpeded by the horrific spectacle within, the ship sailed along smoothly like it was nothing but another trip over the lush green countryside.

It was twilight. The clouds were bright yellow, orange, and deep red. The sun was resting on the distant hills and forests, but it was sinking fast like it does all over the tropics, creating a sudden transition to darkness. This is so beautiful, he thought.

Dyson looked over again at the passenger. His head had been jostled, his face—what was left of it—had turned and was now seemingly focused on Dyson. How the fuck could that happen? This guy had rigor mortis. It wasn't *that* windy in here. Still, he looked at the dead man staring back at him with only his right eye, as if he still had some spark of life left, and right now it seemed like he was glaring intently at Dyson. Although the eye typically becomes hazed in death, the blue of his iris was so bright it shined fiercely through.

Phuoc Vinh was in sight. "Two minutes to touchdown. Look alive, guys," said Papp as he began their descent. "He's gonna be off-loaded from your side, Chief," he told Morgan. They received no incoming hostile fire, followed the flight line at ten feet off the deck and headed right over to Graves Registration where one man stood, arms raised, to wave them in. Papp set the ship down and an SP4 trotted over to the starboard side. Morgan started to get up to help, but the soldier shook his head and waved Morgan off. Grabbing the litter handles and ducking, he walked backwards, sliding the litter and the body feet-first off the deck causing the back of the head and shoulders to smack down onto the rock-hard red clay.

Morgan came unglued. "What the fuck you doin'? You fuckin' asshole motherfucker!" His howl could be heard above the roar of the ship's engine and rotors. He pointed his M60 at the SP4 who quickly dropped his end of the litter and froze. "I'll kill you, you motherfucker," Morgan screamed, but not over his mike. The SP4 was petrified as he looked down the barrel of a locked and loaded machine gun. His lower lip and chin quivered. Slowly, he raised his hands like he was being held up for his money. Dyson really thought Morgan was going to open fire any second.

"At ease, Chief. At ease!" Papp was yelling over his mike. "Let it go.

Let . . . it . . . go."

Morgan's face was beet-red with rage. He was far beyond pissed at the SP4 for being a sorry-ass REMF and for man-handling the infantryman's body like it was nothing but a piece of trash. Morgan took his hands off the weapon and sat back, giving the SP4 the finger while never letting up on his tirade. Papp lifted off, cruised to the flight line and made a beeline for Long Thong. It took the entire length of the flight for Morgan to regain his composure.

One more face to add to the nightmares.

One hundred twenty-eight days to go.

I III I

It was another hot Sunday morning. "Hey, Mister D!" yelled Kosski. "Hey!"

Dyson joined the mail clerk in front of the Orderly Room and asked, "Want to get stoned?"

"In a little bit. Give me a hand first. Top wants me to put some more asphalt sealer on the roof of the Orderly Room." Kosski had parked a jeep next to the back wall of the Orderly Room so they could climb up from the vehicle and boost themselves onto the corrugated metal roof. Kosski went up first. Dyson handed him two one-gallon cans of asphalt sealer, some rags, and a few wooden paint-mixing sticks. Then he boosted himself up onto the roof.

Shit! The roof was way too hot to kneel on. They squatted like baseball catchers to do their work. The metal seams ran parallel to each other four feet apart. They started with the first one and worked their way from the front of the Orderly Room over to the rear where the jeep was parked. They gobbed the tar onto a seam, spread it over the old gobs and waddled onto the next. It was broiling hot up there, with no breeze. While squatting almost shoulder-to-shoulder, they suddenly were aware they were not alone—they felt a presence behind them. They turned slowly and came face to face with Styner—The Creeper. How in the hell did he get up on a metal roof without them hearing him?

"This thing leaks, you know," said Styner. He had an office in the Orderly Room bunker below.

"Yes, sir. We know. Top showed me where the leaks were."

Styner's face was just a blank stare. Believe it or not, this man was a legend in aviation circles. He flew helicopters in two wars and had medals up his ass. The guys turned back and continued with their patching job. They finished one area, stood up to move along and turned. Styner was gone. The Creeper was gone. How did he do that? He hadn't made any noise on the metal roof.

"They don't call him The Creeper for nothing."

"Jesus. That's spooky."

"Yeah. And he creeps all around the company at night."

I I I I I

The following day, Dyson was scheduled for maintenance—a welcome break. The morning routine started after waking—get dressed, clean up a little, mess hall, back to the hootch for eye-openers. O'Grady was ready first today with the pot and called the guys down to his area. Ramirez had his tape player going—Simon and Garfunkel with "Feelin' Groovy," nice and mellow to start the morning right. O'Grady let the guys know that when he bought this pot earlier from Han, the water truck driver, the usual ten-dollar bag was now suddenly thirty dollars.

"Yeah," said Riaz, "I paid forty dollars for this," and showed a big dark chunk of Cambodian hash. The word going around camp was a new group had taken control over the drugs sold on the bases, and the new group was not Vietnamese.

Dyson took a big hit and was passing the bowl off when he looked outside and saw Papp motioning for him to come out. Papp had caught Dyson—and the rest of them—in the act. Oh, shit, he thought. Sheepishly he stepped out of the hootch and walked a few steps to Papp.

"Don't worry about it. I'm not here to bust anybody." Dyson lit a Camel. "I pulled some strings. You, me, Strickland and Morgan are going to Long Binh and eat at the Loon Foon Restaurant."

"But I'm scheduled for . . ."

"No. Captain Horstall is letting you guys off for the day. The lifers do this all the time. Don't worry about it. Just put on a complete clean uniform along with your .45 and we'll all leave here around ten." He used civilian time and was talking to the guys like they were buddies, not enlisted men.

At 10:00 hours, they were ready and got in a jeep. Morgan and Strickland had their M16s and ammo, Papp and Dyson wore their .45s.

Morgan was driving, with Papp riding shotgun, and the other two in the back. Everyone brought a canteen of water and stashed them between the two rear seats. They were waved through the north gate for the six-mile ride to Long Binh. There were almost no American vehicles along the way and they encountered just a few Vietnamese drivers. It was going to be a hot and cloudless day. The only drawback was the choking red dust that erupted from the road. By the time they arrived, they would need shower and clean clothes, but that's just the way it was—no shower, no clean clothes. At twenty-five to thirty miles per hour, the six-mile trip took about twenty minutes.

They approached an eastern gate at Long Binh manned by MPs. Morgan slowed down to stop but the MPs recognized Papp from his previous trips and waved them through—no salutes, they knew each other.

"The Loon Foon doesn't open until noon so we can ride around for a while. Want to go to the PX?"

They were like little kids before Christmas anxious to go window-shopping at the stores on Main Street. Papp gave Morgan directions to the PX. The parking area had a lot of military vehicles and a few American cars—a '65 gold GTO, a maroon Plymouth station wagon, a '62 white Pontiac convertible, a black '65 Chevy Impala, a yellow Rambler convertible.

The PX was huge. They checked their weapons with a clerk. Looking around, Dyson thought he was back in the States. This store had a camera section—not just a few on a shelf, but a whole section with a clerk. There were racks of men's clothes, sports jackets and business suits, white shirts, and ties. And women shopping everywhere—blondes, brunettes, even a redhead with a beehive hairdo. Were they government employees who worked somewhere nearby? Officers' wives? Was all of this necessary in a war zone? Where did the approval and the money come from? It was mind-boggling. Dyson picked up film for his Instamatic and 35mm cameras. He also bought two pair of aviator flight sunglasses; the only ones authorized by the military to be worn with Army uniforms.

At 12:20 hours, they drove to the Loon Foon. Doing the best they could with what they had, they tried to swat the red dust off their clothes and baseball caps and then went straight to the men's room to wash up. It was sparkling clean with gleaming white ceramic tile and porcelain. An Asian hostess greeted them when they walked out.

"Meesta Papp. Nice to see you again." She smiled and flashed a solid gold front tooth, probably her family's fortune, while escorting them to a table in a secluded corner. Military and civilian diners were seated at the tables. He took it for granted that the couples there were husbands and wives. While a few men were in uniform, most were in civvies. Two hostesses brought them steaming hot washcloths to wipe their faces and hands. The towels got grimy instantly and the guys continued wiping with new towels until they finally stayed clean. The group all ordered a beer while they read over the menus.

"We'll order a la carte," Papp said. "Much bigger servings. Try the South China Sea shrimp. They're huge." And they were—as big as Maine chicken lobsters. There were rice dishes, sweet and sour pork, and delicious crispy egg rolls with golden, paper-thin pastry dough. Just about every dish came with a hot ceramic cup of Vietnamese-style sake. And the cold beer kept flowing. This was heaven on earth.

The hostesses were very pretty, little, Asian ladies. Dyson couldn't tell if they were Korean, Japanese or what. They couldn't have been nicer. The men concentrated on the enormous meals set out before them on sparkling dishes, each entree wonderfully prepared and presented.

"This is so great. Thank you so much for bringing us," said Morgan. The men unanimously seconded his thanks.

They knew Papp was due to DEROS and ETS in September.

"Oh, man. We hate to see you go, sir."

"Let's drop the 'sir' for the rest of the trip," he said.

"Are you going to fly the whole time until you go?" In some units, short-timer pilots and crew members were taken off flight status their last thirty days in-country to help them increase their chances of making it back home alive.

"Well, actually," Papp wiped his mouth, "I've had my last flight."
Really? "And I'm going home tomorrow." The guys were visibly
shaken.

"I thought your DEROS is next month."

"I've got prostate cancer," Papp said.

I III I

That evening, after they had gotten back from the Loon Foon,
Papp just disappeared. Many guys wanted to say good-bye to him, but
he was gone already. Even though he had managed to give everybody
the slip, he had spent his last day with friends.

Morgan and Dyson asked Kosski, the mail clerk, for Papp's
home address. "No, man," said Kosski, "I can't give it to you. Besides
regulations, he made me promise I wouldn't give it out." If Papp had
asked Dyson and Morgan to keep a secret, they would, too. They
hunted down Jensen, the company clerk, and he said, "Nope. I can't
do it." Papp was gone. Someone so special was gone from their group.

I III I

On August 8, the 101st Division launched *Operation CAROLINA
BLASTER*, a search and destroy mission into the A Shau Valley—
again.

I III I

During the war, thousands of Army enlisted men signed up to
become helicopter pilots. It was a two-part course—starting with
classes at Fort Rucker, Alabama, and then in-flight training at Fort
Wolters, Texas. Upon graduation the pilots had a six-year obligation
to the Army. However, a small contingency of student pilots went
all the way through training and quit just before graduation. They
learned to fly without the six-year hitch and planned to be civilian
pilots when they got out. Most of these men were sent to Vietnam,
some directly to infantry units, others to an aviation company. One
of them was PFC Donnie Rhinehardt from Maine. He landed in

Bravo Company in Long Thong.

The night of August 8 found Dyson and all the guys passing around a bong with one big hit of Cambodian Red allowed per man. One was all you needed. At 22:00 hours they were in the hootch listening to Iron Butterfly when Rhinehardt stepped in.

"Can I join you guys?"

"All are welcome here, friend," said Riaz, "'cept lifers."

"I'm no lifer, believe me. I'm Donnie." Hands were shaken all around.

"You smoke?" asked Soup.

"Sure do." Riaz handed Donnie the loaded bong, someone lit it, and Donnie drew it in up through the bubbling water. After the usual amount of time the average smoker would have inhaled a maximum hit, he kept on going and going until the ember burned out.

"Goddamn!" said Riaz appreciatively. "That was a big one!"

"Hey," said Spook, "why don't we call him Iron Lung?" Donnie was blowing the smoke out in a long, slow exhale.

"Yeah. Then we would have Iron Lung and "Iron cock" O'Grady!" Riaz had a big smile.

"Are you the new guy that went to flight school?" asked Soup.

"Yeah, that's me."

"How was it?" asked Mister D.

"Well, in the beginning I wanted to pilot. We went through all the classroom and mechanical stuff at Fort Rucker, and that was a just lot of bullshit."

"Bullshit like . . . what?" asked Soup.

"The uniforms, the inspections, the barracks, PT, and close order drill, and all that other petty bullshit just seemed to be more important than the real schooling. Then there were gaps between some classes starting and . . ." *Just like at Fort Eustis*, Mister D thought. "And when we got to flight school, it came out that we hadn't had enough training in some of the more critical areas."

Can't even coordinate two schools, he thought.

Robbie caught himself rambling. "Anyway, a lot of trainee pilots got killed during training at Wolters. Especially in formations and in night flight. A lot of trainees. Two trainees killed one week, four the next, and it wouldn't even get reported to the papers or TV. I started slacking off so I would get disqualified near the end, but then I had a close call on a night flight and I said, 'I've had enough.' Somebody else's miscalculation almost got me killed."

"What happens when someone quits?" asked Riaz. Everyone knew the Army has ways of fucking over people who don't comply.

"First, they take you in for an interview. I thought they were going to beat me up." Now, a Marlboro Green was being passed around. "There were about twelve of us that wanted out. I was about number ten in the group to quit. They put us on details and KP every day to get us to change our minds. For three weeks they kept it up. Some guys went back to in-flight classes. I got orders for ten days' leave and then had to report over here. Man, that Green is good."

He'd never had a menthol-flavored, factory-rolled joint.

▌▐▐▐▌

Early in the war there were actual helicopter companies whose sole mission was Medevac. They were identified with a red cross on a white background. The dreamers in power thought, "No one would ever fire on a Medevac ship picking up wounded combatants." They were so wrong. The dreamers also thought Medevac ships did not need to be armed. They were wrong again. As the war escalated on both sides, small Medevac companies were overwhelmed trying to reach all the wounded quickly, so non-Medevac ships had to step into those missions. The big, easily identified international Red Cross symbol on a helicopter was an open invitation for every Communist gunner to draw a bead on. The Medevac missions were flown by armed Hueys, sometimes Chinooks, all without any Red Cross symbols. Many times, the larger Chinooks had to go in where smaller Hueys normally went and perform the same missions. The term "Medevac" was redesignated "Dust Off." Dust offs were absorbed into the daily missions of every active helicopter unit.

I IIII

Now that Papp was gone, Morgan and Mister D were cast back into the entire pool of crew members in Alpha and Bravo Companies, rarely getting to crew together again. The hundreds of missions of the 137th ASH dragged on and on, day after day. It had become long tedious work, and Dyson remembered all the times he had been asked "Why would you want to fly?" But still, there was a sense of accomplishment and of helping the guys in the field.

The Maintenance and Operations sections were putting the word out that in June and July three Hueys from different divisions had crashed, killing two officers and four crew members. The causes were unknown but surviving pilots reported the same scenarios: They were loaded near, at, or over capacity, were accelerating, climbing, and banking when the ships suddenly lost power and dropped out of the sky. Here again was the malfunction they had first heard about months ago. MACV and USARV had failed to find the deadly problem. No one could reproduce the malfunction in test flights.

On Saturday, August 9, Dyson and Morgan got a chance to crew together again when they were scheduled to join Sheckly and Cavecchio on *088*. Lieutenant Ben Sheckly had flown missions for ten months and was a skillful aircraft commander. Giovani Cavecchio was going to be promoted to CW2 shortly for the simple reason he had earned it. Each one wouldn't hesitate to volunteer when the need arose. Morgan felt comfortable with both in the crew.

088 spent the day flying in and out of the cluster of LZs in the Division's AO, from Long Thong to Phuoc Vinh to transport supplies, hot chow, water to three LZs, over to Bien Hoa to pick up FNGs and transport them to Phuoc Vinh, stop to refuel, then more supplies from Phuoc Vinh out to LZs. One Medevac received fire going in and out of the LZ to 93rd Evac Hospital, Long Binh, and again after refueling at a fuel depot named Castle Pad in Long Binh. At 17:40 hours a radio message from Operations to *088*, *083*, *075*, and *090* requested they extract a recon platoon and take them to LZ

Dot. The extraction was in a hot area, but the recon unit said there was no enemy in the immediate vicinity. As the ships headed for the extraction, those ships not involved in the actual removal of men would provide covering fire if needed.

When they arrived at the location, *075* had already taken out six men from the recon platoon. They had received and returned fire a thousand yards from the pickup point, so the enemy was now in the area. The platoon leader radioed *088* where to find the next six men and to look for the yellow smoke. Once spotting it, Sheckly guided the ship to the pickup point as two recon squad members showed themselves. Sheckly set the ship down as four more troops appeared from the brush. Three men piled onto the starboard side and three onto the port side. Green tracers started buzzing by the ship from two directions, but not from real close by. Both of *088's* gunners laid down a hail of lead toward the sources of the ground fire. Dyson could feel the strain of the ship as it lifted off the ground and tilted forward. Now there seemed to be four different positions of enemy fire. The guys in the recon unit began firing their M16s. There were dozens of tracers. Sheckly gained altitude and headed for the tree line.

Here they were, thought Dyson, and maybe some of the crew did too, with conditions very similar to those of the mysterious engine stalls. They were at max capacity, accelerating, climbing, and banking for the tree line—the four requirements for the engine stall. Everyone was shooting, but whether they hit anybody was anyone's guess. "Go! Go! Go!" someone was yelling into the intercom system. Dyson fired at a dark spot in the forest where fire was coming from. Finally, they ascended over the tree line and disappeared from the gunners' view. The shooting stopped.

In the intercom system, one of the pilots made a high-pitched Three Stooges noise. That's kinda strange, thought Dyson.

Then the other one answered with a Three Stooges laugh, "Nyuk-nyuk-nyuk." Dyson had never heard anything like that over the system on any ship—ever. In fact, Operations and other authorities forbade any fooling around on the radios. Sometimes the intercom in the ship was monitored, sometimes not. They maintained a heading for LZ Dot, only minutes away.

Sheckly guided the ship down onto the LZ landing pad for the six troopers to jump off. One of them leaned forward and yelled right in Dyson's ear, "You lucky fucking REMF!" and jumped. Wait, didn't we just rescue these guys? Sheckly lifted the ship off and they headed for Long Thong, hopefully for the end of today's missions.

It was a routine approach and descent, following the flight line down to where a ground crew member waved their ship in. It settled on the tarmac. Sheckly shut the engine down and the rotors gradually stopped. Morgan and Dyson undid their harnesses and stepped off to stretch. Sheckly and Cavecchio climbed out of the ship. They were both drunk.

One hundred twenty-one days to go.

I IIII I

At the morning formation on Tuesday, August 12, Enrico read off a dozen or so names, including Dyson's, to fall out and form up by the Orderly Room. The sergeant's girlfriend, Bertha, dressed in her Red Cross uniform and hat, was riding a bicycle around the company area. She was so unattractive not even one horny guy bothered to look at her.

"OK, you men," Enrico announced, "have been chosen for a three-day in-country R&R in Vung Tau. Be ready at 08:00 hours tomorrow." Wow! Three days in Vung Tau. Guys who'd been there raved about it. Bars, hotels, room service, a beach, and nice-looking whores with shot records.

Morgan, O'Grady, and Super Chicken were also in a group of crew members and mechanics selected to go. It was a huge morale booster. As they headed for the flight line, Bertha was riding toward the mess hall when the bike's front wheel suddenly pinched a rock from underneath and she took a spill onto the hard, red dirt. She was all tangled up with her Red Cross dress up to her hips exposing her fat cottage cheese white thighs and skinny calves. Those men who were scattered around the company area laughed out loud. Enrico ran to help her, and everyone else became invisible. Although he looked tough, he was in no shape to run the length of the company area in the heat and humidity. When he reached under her armpits and heaved, he couldn't pick up the portly Donut Dolly. Bertha had to pretty much extricate herself from the bike and get up on her own, dusty and all scraped-up.

Chivalry was long dead in Long Thong.

I III I

Dyson was trying to process the war he was witnessing. What was happening before his eyes, he realized, was brief and fleeting, but those things were going on all over the country all the time, all day, all night. He felt like he was in the rear row of an empty movie theater watching a review of all the bad shit going down. On the outside he looked OK, but inside he was filled with turmoil and grief. It was said the chaplain was always available to talk to, but rarely did anyone go to see him. A few guys actually went to regular church services every Sunday morning. Most kept emotions locked up inside themselves. Perhaps the R&R in Vung Tau would do Mister D good.

I III I

Vung Tau

At 08:30 hours, Wednesday, August 13, the men were flown by two Bravo Company Hueys to Vung Tau on the coast. Regulations required the men to be in uniform with their weapons, then to report to the In-Country R&R Center to sign in and surrender their weapons. While they changed into civilian clothes, they were shown a list of hotels that were approved for check-in, then told in no uncertain terms: "Do not do anything to get arrested by the MPs in town. You will be taken into custody and jailed, and your Company will be notified. Be further advised not to possess or use marijuana or any other drugs." Each man was issued a pass and warned: "Carry it with you at all times and do not lose it."

Guys in Bravo Company told them the two best places were the Villa Hotel and the Riviera Hotel. Both had dining rooms, bars, room service, and very sexy-looking prostitutes who just so happened to also have up-to-date shot records. The Villa had two double rooms available, so the four friends checked in there. It was an old three-story stucco and brick building with a red ceramic-tile roof. They had traveled light and carried their own bags up to the rooms while being harried by two bellhops wanting tips. Morgan and Dyson chose a room and quickly blocked one of the bellhops from entering.

"My name is Than. You need something, I be here, anything, I be here, water, ice, girls, I be here . . ." They closed the door in his face.

The room had twelve-foot ceilings, a red tile floor, stucco walls, two double beds, big rattan chairs, and ceiling-height French doors opening onto a private patio. There was also a long, folding room divider for privacy.

"Look, D," said Morgan, "we can sit out here and drink." It was beautiful, looking out over the town of Vung Tau, the coastline and the blue-blue waters of the South China Sea. They could almost forget where they were. "We can buy a bottle of Jack Daniels or something and just relax right here." That appealed to Mister D, rather than sitting downstairs inside the darkened bar.

Morgan opened the door to their room, saw their room servant in the hall, "Hey, Than!"

"Yes, boss. Yes. Than here. What you need?"

"A bottle of Jack Daniels, real glasses, and lots of ice."

"OK, I get. I get for you. Fifteen dollah for bottle, ice, and glass." And off he went.

In no time, the two men on the patio were at ease in the rattan chairs, an open bottle of Jack Daniels, and a bucket of ice. They lounged in the spotty shade of huge palm trees, looking down the avenue in a quiet and peaceful city.

"Listen . . ." said Morgan. A minute went by. "You don't hear any artillery or choppers."

Amazing.

"I think the Jack is watered down," Morgan refreshed his glass. "But who cares . . ."

Almost on cue, a Huey flew overhead. They saw how people in the street looked up at the noisy ship. Away from here no one would even pay any attention to it. Dyson was again conscious of the ringing in his ears.

"Your ears ring, Morgan?"

"They have for months now. Everyone gets it, I guess."

Dyson remembered he vowed to himself not to drink any more hard liquor, but, hey, this is R&R. He refilled his glass.

"I haven't even seen a glass since I got here," he said. They sat in silence for a while. "Ya know, I sincerely thought you was gonna blow that SP4 in Phuoc Vinh off the face of the earth."

"Ya know, I can't even remember all of it. I remember that guy's head slamming down on the dirt, pulling the gun up and yelling something, I don't know what. I was just so pissed and it happened so fast. No warning—just WHAM! I was going to help him get the litter off the ship and he just waved me off." Morgan took a gulp of the whiskey. "I guess I was so pissed I blacked out or something."

"Who knows how long you'd be in LBJ over that."

"They send anyone with more than six months to Leavenworth, like maybe the lieutenant from the My Lai massacre."

"That's when you'd wonder if that was all worth it."

"Glad I didn't."

The two friends toasted with a clink of their glasses. Four hours later they finished their bottle and got ready for some chow—or here it was dinner. O'Grady and Super Chicken came in for a brief visit and they all walked downstairs to the dining room.

A gorgeous, well-shaped and classy hostess showed them to a table for four next to a courtyard. Here they were, all dressed in civvies, nice and clean, in an elegant dining room on the seacoast. Hard to believe. They ordered beers and examined the menu. When the hostess brought ice-cold bottles of Budweiser, she recommended they order a la carte, "Much more food and cheaper, too."

GIs dined at the other tables in pairs, foursomes, and bigger groups. There was the usual trash talk to the pretty waitresses, a lot of it about boom-boom. "Five dollah? Ten dollah? Fifteen dollah stand on head." The words "fuck" and "blowjob" flew everywhere. Why would guys behave like that? Is it just because they're "guys" and they're expected to act that way?

Each man had his own pretty waitress, to be tipped, of course. What did it matter, this was R&R. They ate jumbo shrimp, sweet and sour this, that, and the other thing, fried rice, all kinds of meat and vegetable dishes, and crunchy, delicious egg rolls washed down with ice cold beers. Desert was four rounds of Jack Daniels.

By now it was after 20:00 hours and time to move to the bar. There must have been thirty GIs in the place. Waitresses and prostitutes fawned over every man. His group sat at a table and were immediately set upon by six smiling women in Suzie Wong dresses—very low cut, very short and slit up the side. "My name's Betty. What's yours?" Really? Betty? There was also Bonnie, Laura, Cathy, and a bunch of other All-American names.

A rather attractive whore latched on to Dyson. "I'm Barb. I like you. Like you very much." Her dress pinched her boobs over the top. He hadn't seen any naked boobs since he'd been in country. OK, time to start talking here.

"I'm glad you do," Mister D said.

The others were overjoyed to be the only object of these women's attention. Their hands were all over the men, suggesting this and that, and probably looking for wallets, too. Then one of them, Betty, happened to grab O'Grady's cock. *Oh, I was waiting for this*, Mister D thought. Her mouth opened wide in disbelief and she started talking rapidly in Vietnamese to her cohorts. A couple others reached over to explore it, too, and they all began to smile and talk even more excitedly. There was talk of "numbah one" and "numbah ten"—"number one" the best, "number ten" the worst. It was a genuine event of interest in the barroom. Other working ladies sauntered over to get their hands on his huge, new, love muscle.

A momma-san bustled over. Probably a VC financial officer of some sort, but definitely in charge of the women. She felt it, tried to remain nonchalant, then smiled despite herself. The bantering and debates went on for a while: Who would handle it? Who wanted to try it? How much? Could O'Grady himself pick his girl? The momma-san picked four girls out and O'Grady ended up choosing one with long black hair for a fair price. Good, now that's settled.

The whole time, Dyson and Barb continued talking. "You buy me Saigon tea?" Saigon tea was a very weak but expensive drink for the girls that, when bought by the GI, signaled that he would rent her for a duration. When the drink arrived, the momma-san chatted with Barb. Barb produced a worn shot record from her purse. Her boss went through the little pages showing multicolored seals and dates stamped all over them.

"Very good," the mamma-san told Mister D. "Her shot record up to date. She can go with you. One hour. Forty dollah. Pay me." Forty dollars? On Long Thong it was five or ten. But then again, this was R&R and the girls are much prettier—they even smell good. He gave her forty bucks.

What the hell, he thought, and bought her another Saigon tea. Barb said she was from Da Lat, in the Central Highlands. She left home for the city life like thousands of young Vietnamese and hadn't seen or heard from her parents in years. A couple times, she coughed. Could she have contracted TB like many Vietnamese? It was contagious, they had received warnings about that. At 22:00 hours, the momma-san said they could go upstairs now.

This scene was repeated hundreds of times in Vung Tau every night. Wherever GIs bought drugs and black-market goods, or paid a prostitute, the money went directly to the enemy war effort. From the generals on down, the American men all wanted to get laid. Here in Vung Tau and other cities, beautiful half French-half Vietnamese call girls cost the high-ranking officers and NCOs hundreds of dollars a night. It all tied in with the drug traffic, the black market, the corruption, and the big stinking mess. The war had transformed an entire nation into black marketeers, drug dealers, pot growers, smugglers, thieves, pickpockets, prostitutes, shoe shiners, orphans, widows, hootch maids, corrupt government officials, and Viet Cong guerillas. Yet, somehow the rice farmers kept on growing rice while the war dragged on around them. South Vietnam grew more rice than North Vietnam, Laos, and Cambodia put together. Some people believed that the war was over that very rice bowl.

Than, who knew everything that was going on in the hotel, was angry that guys had bought girls in the barroom instead of going through him. "Maybe next time," Mister D said as he and Barb entered the room. He locked the door (Morgan had his own key) and put up the seven-foot-tall, ten-foot-long room divider. They had one hour, maybe less now.

"I like you, Mister D." She had caught his nickname in the bar. He stripped naked and got on the bed—tan arms and head, pale white otherwise, easy to see the pattern in the dark. Barb slipped out of her Suzie Wong dress and panties. She looked like someone's thirteen-year-old little sister. Her dress had made her look much more buxom. He wasn't as aroused as he had been downstairs. She started giving him a hand job. She was really examining him for signs of VD. He wasn't getting hard. "Wait . . . I help," she said and brought her face down to his cock and took it in her mouth.

One part of him wanted the whole works, the other part wanted her to pack up and go. He toughed it out. He was getting hard. "OK, now." They switched positions. God, she looks too young. I'm screwing someone's little sister. He penetrated her but could feel himself going soft, so he picked up the pace, faster and faster and finally he got his rocks off. It was a soft and unfulfilling climax. He bet she felt nothing either.

"OK, I'm done. You can go now." Shit. He never even thought about a rubber. Well, she had her shot record up to date, right?

She didn't say a word. She got up and dressed while he put on a pair of OD boxer shorts. He opened the door for her and came face to face with Morgan and his date.

"That was fast," his friend said.

I III I

Briefing

On August 18, the 5th Special Forces began a reconnaissance in force named Operation BULL RUN along the northern border of Tay Ninh Province and Cambodia. There never were any fences, walls or no man's land designating the Laotian or Cambodian borders—only an invisible line running through the mountains and jungles. Everybody crossed the international boundaries daily.

I III I

Between the trips to the Loon Foon and Vung Tau, Dyson had enjoyed a real break in the routine. By Wednesday, August 20, he had flown one day and pulled maintenance for two days. He was tired.

After chow, he set up his 35mm camera on a tripod and pointed it toward the sunset, another red and orange spectacle. He needed to get some sunset pictures before the monsoon came in September. He took six pictures until the horizon got dark.

Tonight the guys were smoking and listening to *The White Album*—"Happiness Is a Warm Gun." What would this place be like without the music they had? Without the smoke? "While My Guitar Gently Weeps" was on now. The guys took turns with the headset in order to listen to the song undisturbed. That way the others could talk over the music. O'Grady was holding court with his bar room tale about the whores in Vung Tau examining his cock.

Rector was crew chief on *084* yesterday when they flew a hairy dust-off mission with three wounded. Smith was the aircraft commander. They didn't receive fire on the way in, but all hell broke loose when they lifted off. A green tracer came so close it took the swivel-hinge off the sun visor on his flight helmet. Said he was still stoned from that morning's eye-opener and it looked like the tracer was traveling in slow motion. Dyson had seen slow motion tracers, too.

"I could see it come out of the trees, man." He was gesturing.

"And I'm thinking, 'Is this the one? Is this the one that's gonna get me?' And WHAP! The thing took my swivel off!" Granted, it was a close one. Red tracers, good guys. Green tracers, bad guys.

"The millisecond and the millimeter," said Spook.

"If my head was that much to the left, if that gunner had fired a little more to his right, if Smith had lifted off a split second later . . . ?"

"That much sooner and that much closer." Spook demonstrated it.

"Fate," whispered Rector.

"Karma," said O'Grady.

"Karma Sutra," said Florida.

"Karma Sutra?" said Maris. "Karma Sutra's got nothing to do with it! Karma, for sure, but not Karma Sutra, man."

"Why? What's Karma Sutra?" asked Florida.

"It's Kama Sutra," Maris took a hit off a Marlboro Green, "It's this ancient Indian text from the Hindu's holy book, like their Bible, man, and it shows all these different ways to fuck, man. How to fuck. There's even sculptures, man, statues in a temple over there, man, in India, man, that show dozens, man, dozens of ways to fuck."

"Well, I'll be goddamned."

"Yep . . . how to fuck, man . . . how to fuck."

Would anybody even remember this in the morning? Regardless, Dyson remembered seeing pictures from a late 1800s copy of the text when he was stumbling through college—you don't forget pictures like that.

"I flew with that Smith-pilot-character once," said Riaz. "I think he was stoned."

Around 22:00 hours, Mister D decided he had enough smoke and talk. "Night, guys," and he went to his hootch and got in his bunk. His mind was full of all kinds of things—the missions, the shelling, Carol, the wounded, parties back home, the dead, the ground fire . . . He dozed off hoping he could dream about home.

Some dreams he'd not remember, others would stay with him forever, recurring over the years. Tonight, they were crewing a Huey. The members remained anonymous behind their sun visors.

Red, green, blue, yellow, orange, purple tracers zipped through the air. Below treetop level the skids tore through the foliage. He and the crew chief sprang into the companionway to the pilots' cabin.

"Up! Up! Get us out of here!" someone was yelling. Now there were six grunts on the ship. They were screaming and getting shot. The pilots turned and stared at them through their visors that masked their identities. Tracers crisscrossed from every imaginable direction, and not just the usual red and green colors, but neon blue, yellow, and purple tracers coming from the trees, the elephant grasses, even the sky. The pilots slowly turned back to working their controls, pedals and sticks, seemingly uninterested in the intense enemy fire. "Jesus Christ, man, move it!"

Slowly the ship rose. He looked back and saw the grunts getting hit—flinching, jerking, screaming. Then the ship cleared above the tree line, but the main rotor was going way too slow, he could see each blade slowing down like a ceiling fan. At two hundred feet, the ship nosed downward into a dive. The impact site came into view, a clearing loaded with bamboo punji stakes—hundreds of them. Sticking up through the soil the warheads of live mortars and rockets, just waiting detonation by the ship speeding toward them. He felt the air rushing on his face and through his helmet, propwash roaring in his ears. Then he spotted VC gunners hiding in the foliage, giggling and grinning under their straw hats. The points of the sharpened bamboo were only inches from the plexiglass bubble. "Aaaarrrrrrgggggghhhhhh!!!"

"Wake up! Dyson, wake up, man." It was Spook, shaking him. He tried to get up. "It's OK. It's OK. You're dreaming again."

No one else seemed to be awake, just him and Spook. He rubbed his face with his hands. Man, that was real. So real. He only catnapped until reveille.

One hundred nine days to go.

At morning formation, Brisco's announcement was short. "CID

has arrested and taken into custody four black men stationed at Bien Hoa for their roles in the fragging at the 137th ASH stand-down." The military police criminal investigators had come back to Long Thong to re-interview witnesses to the attack twice. While the enlisted men at the scene and those who chased the attackers could give only vague descriptions, some of the NCOs and officers provided detailed facial and uniform descriptions. The four suspects had no airtight alibis as to where they were that night. One of them was arrested on duty, the other three where they lived over a shop in the town of Long Bien. But there was talk that the CID was pressured to close the case ASAP and may not have arrested all of the real attackers.

I IIII I

In the past three months, the 137th ASH had lost more pilots and crews than ever before. Battalion also lost men who worked on the ships in Long Thong. To date, no one from Dyson's hootch had been killed. Other hootches had already experienced packing up some of their fallen comrades' personal gear.

When the rain came, there would be times, even entire days, when flight would be impossible. The monsoons would hinder the Communists, flooding tunnels and bunkers and making the Ho Chi Minh Trail and other routes a quagmire and morass, but it didn't stop them. U.S. forces also had to suffer sodden roads, installations, FSBs and LZs, and slogging through swollen rivers, streams, and swamps. A grunt's unbearable life in the field got even worse during the monsoons. There was no escape from the rains, mud, slime, leeches, cold nights, insect bites, cuts from razor sharp grasses and vines that became infected in oozing sores of puss, and never having a change of clean, dry uniforms, or boots for days and weeks at a time.

The 2nd Airmobile Division Engineers worked on the Battalion areas in Long Thong, digging better drainage ditches and making raised wooden sidewalks. The men traded their hot, humid, sunny workdays for cooler and very wet conditions when it would start raining the same time every day.

I IIII

Mechanical Trouble

As August dragged on, Communist activity in the five provinces never let up. It was constant. Missions for the 137th ASH started before sunup and ran well after sundown many days. It didn't seem to matter. Dyson and everyone else pulled long hours either working in Maintenance or on a mission with flight providing only changes of scenery. As far as danger went, you were either a target on the ground or a target in the sky. The VC activity had increased immeasurably. Alpha and Bravo Companies ships received fire coming and going from Long Thong. Gunships prowled above the woods surrounding the camp to force the enemy's heads down.

Morgan and Mister D were on *091* with LaChappell (which was good) and a relatively green WO1, Stewart Phillips (which could be dicey). Phillips had been quarterback for Tulane University but he flunked out of school. They had spent the day flying to LZs and in and out of Phuoc Vinh. On one trip heading into the Division Field Headquarters, they were instructed to move in a wide circle around the camp until a rocket and mortar attack stopped. It was the first time Dyson saw from the air mortar and rocket rounds hit a camp. After the "all clear" (how does anyone know it's "all clear"?) they carried on as if nothing happened.

At 14:25 hours, LaChappell radioed Operations that he had a slow response in both pairs of the ship's pedals. Taylor from Operations told him to come back to Long Thong immediately. "Roger, return to base. *091* out." It didn't seem like an emergency. The ship didn't seem to be experiencing any trouble in flight.

Three miles from Long Thong LaChappell reported a vibration in the pedals. Something was getting worse. Now Dyson and Morgan could feel the vibration. The ship was on a steady keel but gradually losing altitude. Then came the message crews hate to hear: "Setting down . . . setting down at 487-324 (map coordinates, two miles east of Long Thong) . . . repeat . . . setting down at 487-324 . . . *091*, out."

LaChappell was descending onto a partial clearing of downed trees, an uneven landing surface, but clear for the rotors. He couldn't set down exactly where he wanted because of the poor response in the controls, resulting with one skid on a fallen tree trunk, the other on the ground. The aircraft was positioned on a side-to-side slant with the cabin pointing up on an incline. The port side—Dyson's side—was upward. The pilots shut the ship down. Morgan took off his flight helmet.

"D," he said urgently, "pull your 60 off, grab the ammo, and let's get away from the ship. Every gook within seven miles seen us go down." This was the same general area where Dyson had seen the two VC on a bike weeks ago. The pilots quickly disembarked with their M16s and all of them merged into the foliage. The pilots were listening to Morgan, not Morgan listening to them. "Let's make for over there." He pointed to the far edge of the clearing. Army Engineers had cut down the trees with chainsaws two years ago for an LZ, but later plans changed the LZ's location to somewhere else. The field was a maze of dead tree trunks overgrown with vines, saplings, and bamboo.

They stepped over the logs and through underbrush to a spot where two trees were cut down with their trunks almost parallel to each other, six feet apart, two feet off the ground. Some brush growing around the little position afforded good concealment.

"You watch that way," said Morgan, indicating the eastern part of the field, "and I'll watch this way." They got down between the logs, put the muzzles of their M60s on each log and peered over the edge. They had no radio. How long would it take only two miles from camp? Are the VC here? Would they wait for rescue ships to come in, then open fire? Or just try to capture or kill the crew and burn the ship? His mind was racing. "Quiet," Morgan whispered.

Five minutes went by and there were no sounds of rescue ships, only birds calling warnings. "Fuck," said Dyson. This was his first time in the woods, like a grunt. It was around a hundred degrees and humid like a nursery greenhouse. His Nomex flight suit was soaked with sweat. Shit, no wonder the grunts wear towels around their necks. Soon the birds stopped chirping. If a leopard was in the area the birds would be squawking and scolding. It was dead quiet.

Fifty feet from the pilot's cabin, a man wearing a black pajama top and carrying an AK47 rose up into view. He stood motionless, studying the ship, the clearing, and then the route the men took across the clearing. Dyson imagined an American Indian, mentally tracking the crew's spoors through the logs and vegetation. He had to know the crew was right here, somewhere, in this direction. The VC took a few steps over the logs and two more appeared behind him on each side. One had an AK47, the other an all-black ChiCom 9mm submachine gun. The VC with the ChiCom was smaller—a woman for Christ's sake. Then the three stopped and stared out over the clearing. These guerrillas aren't here to talk. Dyson saw movement behind them—more VC. Was the crew surrounded already? He heard the warning in his head: "Do not get caught by the VC. They will torture you to death." He'd heard stories of bamboo under fingernails, hanging by the wrists tied behind the back, evisceration. Use your .45, one shot in your head if you have to, but whatever you do, do not get captured.

Of all times, a "fuck-you" lizard hidden in the maze of logs let go with his infamous taunt as the VC advanced. Dyson moved the muzzle slightly, keeping it trained on the lead man. The lizard's "Fuck you . . . fuck you . . . fuck you" call was getting weaker and weaker as the lizard ran out of air. Don't let the gooks get any closer.

This is it, he thought, and with both eyes open looking down the barrel he drew a bead on the lead VC's belly. He pulled on the twin triggers and let loose. The first round hit the VC in the stomach. Things started happening in slow motion and it was as if he was thinking in complete sentences as he fired. The rounds drilled their way up through the VC's chest, his neck. Then a tracer blew out the back of his head. The closest of the other two were frozen in the lag time between surprise and reacting, their eyes wide open. Dyson was conscious of, and pictured in his mind's eye, the gun's operational process—the belt feeding into the left side, stripping the links off, chambering the round, the firing pin hitting the percussion cap, the round firing, the round exiting the barrel, the empty shell casing extracting, the link and the shell casing ejecting from the breech, and the next round. It played through his brain just like in the class training materials at Fort Eustis. He was reduced to tunnel vision and saw only the targets while his peripheral vision was a swirling red-orange mass, as if he was looking at the sun through his closed eyelids. He swept the muzzle from left to right and right to left, first blasting the man through his torso, then the woman through her stomach and shoulder with another tracer as she collapsed. LaChappell and Phillips laid down fire with their M16s. Five tracers, Dyson thought, plenty left to go. He swept his fire back and forth where he had seen movement before. The swirling mass turned a brighter red and orange, and he was conscious of only his M60's targets, as if in a trance, all the while receiving fire from unseen VC in the woods. The incoming rounds and splinters of wood-shrapnel whizzed past his head. Bullets crackled by like invisible four-hundred-forty-volt hornets.

"Dyson! Dyson!" Morgan was shaking him, causing his normal vision to return. "Under the logs! UNDER the logs! They're creeping up on us!" The warning "They crawl like snakes" echoed in his mind. He pulled the gun off his log and now sprayed underneath the tree trunks. All this time he had been unaware of the actions of his three crewmates furiously firing their weapons.

The VC stopped shooting first, then the four of them stopped. Above the ringing in his ears, he started hearing Hueys. Two Bravo Company ships circled overhead while pouring fire all through the tree line without receiving any in return. Morgan gradually stood up. Nothing happened. He waved to the ships and crew members waved back.

"D, let's go see." They hefted their M60s and plodded their way over the logs. Bullet creases and broken branches were everywhere on the downed trees from the hundreds of rounds fired by the VC and crew. Firing at the VC Dyson had riddled 091 with about fifty bullet holes. Then they reached the spot where Dyson killed the three gooks.

They were gone. In the face of intense automatic weapons fire, the bodies had been dragged off by their comrades and only their blood trails remained. An eyeball hung by an optic nerve from a branch.

It was Friday, August 22.

▌ ▌ ▌ ▌

He had become more conscious of his feelings lately, or was it the lack of feelings? Was he getting callous and numb seeing all the gore of war? Didn't he care anymore or had he become just plain used to it? His flight helmet visor hid his true feelings from others. But then again, maybe he wasn't showing any or maybe he didn't have any. Numb apathy or numb empathy or numb sympathy? He couldn't even explain to himself how he felt at night when in bed trying to get to sleep after smoking mind-numbing pot, trying his best to sleep without bad dreams. When he got to Bravo Company, getting stoned at night and falling asleep was wonderful, enjoyable. Now he would nod off for a while and then his active thoughts dominated. Memories and dreams seemed indistinguishable, blending into each other. His dream typically took place in the hootch—hard to tell fact from reality. He had to force himself to write his mom and brother—now to both in the same letter. He and Carol stopped writing long ago. He didn't miss her now. He wasn't sure if he missed his mom and brother or not. He justified his negative feelings by convincing himself he "deserved to feel like this, after all, look at all that has happened." Dyson had entered his own dark zone. Didn't the other guys feel like him inside? Nobody ever talked about their feelings. Men don't do that stuff.

Today was Sunday, August 24, and there were church services in a little bunker-chapel-tent over in Alpha Company. "All welcome," the sign said. Some men even went to Long Binh for services every

Sunday. He just wasn't with it. He remembered the Division chaplain, Captain Thomas ("Doubting Thomas," they called him), saying a few words at a ceremony for an Alpha Company pilot who was killed, " . . . and he's with Jesus now."

Some guy in the back of the crowd said, "Oh, for Christ's sake! He's not with fucking Jesus. He's fucking dead!" No one spoke up to chastise him. Not even the chaplain.

God, or no God. If God exists, why does he let this go on? Questions and scenes constantly going through his mind, on duty or off. Would he be able to leave this stuff here, forget about it, carry it home then forget it, or never let it go? He was not at peace with himself, at least not over here. He would feel better when he got out of this place, he thought.

I III I

"Hey, you going to fly today, or are you going to stay in bed?" asked Spook.

"OK, Mom, I'm getting up."

"Well, have breakfast then, you big motherfucker." Spook put a big smoking bowl in Dyson's face. He took it. Maris was already having his mess kit bowl of pot. Mister D would stick with the powdered eggs and the rest of the grub in the mess hall. He'd seen too many bugs and such in some of the pot—tiny insects crawling in and out of the buds. But then, so what? He smoked the pot, bugs, and all.

One hundred five days to go—one, zero, five.

I III I

SEPTEMBER

Dyson, Florida, Spook, and Super Chicken had put in a long two days in Maintenance. The 137th ASH ships were showing the wear and tear of constant use and abuse. The guys had spent those days on engine and drivetrain write-ups. For the first time, there were not enough ships for the missions. It was that simple. They had a little breathing room.

As soon as they left the flight line, they very distinctly heard Janis Joplin singing "Piece O' My Heart." "Where's that coming from?"

"You're not going to believe this, but it's Lambert down in Avionics," said Spook. That hootch was way down at the end of the Bravo Company area, next to the perimeter and its bunkers. SP5 Burton Lambert was an electronics and sound equipment genius. He could troubleshoot and repair anything the Avionics guys needed, and he put together his own sound system with a huge volume and speaker setup. Nobody else's stereo systems had that stupendous volume. The whole camp could hear it.

"Watch . . . someone will tell him to turn it down."

"Man, that is something." A minute later, the volume was cut down.

"The lifers in the NCO Club complain and tell him every time. They say it drowns out their country-western crap," said Spook. "Fuck those assholes. Tammy Wynette, Charley Pride, Patsy Cline . . . Christ."

"We'll go down there sometime and see if Lambert will do 'Purple Haze' or something."

Coming toward them was a WO1 whom Dyson and Super Chicken had never seen before. He was an FNG in Alpha Company. "See this guy?" Spook said under his breath. "He was at Woodstock, man." They had all heard about Woodstock and wished they had been there. They didn't have a lot of details, but knew it was the first of its kind ever—peace, love, and dope. "His name's Beyers." WO1s are the lowest ranking officers to rate a salute. Some NCOs wouldn't salute them and got away with it.

"I gotta ask him," said Soup, and saluted, "'S'cuse me, sir?" They all stopped.

"Yeah?" The warrant officer returned the salute.

"We heard you was at Woodstock, sir."

"Yeah, I was there."

"What was it like, sir?"

"Just a bunch of dirty hippies." He exhaled heavily. "A lot of dirty hippies."

I IIII

On Tuesday, September 2, Dyson, Morgan, Devaney, and SP4 Randy James were working on a ship at the end of the flight line, sixty feet from a bunker on the perimeter and less than a hundred feet from the Avionics hootches. They could smell the guards in the bunker smoking the good stuff. This ship, *086*, had no fuel in it and was isolated from the other ships, so the guys took a smoke break. Mister D lit a Camel with his hefty Zippo.

"Man," said Morgan, "that thing sounds like cocking a .45 when you open it." Dyson nodded . . . it certainly did sound like a .45. There was next to no breeze. Their smoke drifted up lazily in the sun.

They were startled by a mortar round landing way over in the northern part of camp. Then some more came in. Small-arms fire broke out on the northern perimeter.

"I hear AKs," said Morgan. The AK47 had a sound that was distinct from American firearms.

A few mortars fell in the 137th—closer this time. When small-arms fire started on the east side of the camp the sirens signaled "attack." It was time to seek cover.

"Hey, the bunker," said James. They all trotted into the nearest bunker on the perimeter, surprising the guards inside. "Hey."

The bunker's landline rang and a guard answered it. The small-arms fire on the two sections of the perimeter was increasing.

"Yes, sir. Yes, sir. Roger, out." The guard spoke to the guys, "Says it's a probe. The gooks are probing the camp."

A probe. Not an all-out attack, but a daylight "exercise" by the enemy to watch and see how a position like Long Thong will defend itself from ground attack. They would exchange fire with the defenders in broad daylight to observe where they were weakest or had gaps in the defenses. Often the VC and NVA didn't even bother to show themselves but instead just sent in rocket and mortars. But a probe was still combat. People got killed and wounded.

Dozens of green tracers were streaming out of the woods in their sector. The guards returned fire. The four friends just sat down on the two folding cots and stayed out of the way. The bunkers on both sides of them were firing.

"See anything?"

"Nope," said one of the guards firing twenty-round bursts from a M60. A few AK rounds were hitting their bunker, loudly smacking into the sandbags.

Out of the blue the opening bars of "Sympathy for the Devil" blasted from Lambert's stereo. "Pleased to meet you . . ." and the chorus, "Ho-hooo . . . ho-hooo . . . ho-hooo."

"Oh, man," said Soup. "Let's light up," putting a match to a Marlboro Green.

The exchange of casual gunfire continued. Then Lambert *really* turned it up. "Hope you guess my name . . . ho-hooo." Guys began shouting their own call and response while shooting, "Ho-hooo . . . ho-hooo . . ." "And what's puzzling you is the nature of my game . . . Ho-hooo . . . ho-hooo." Is this crazy, or what?

"I rode a tank, held a general's rank . . . Ho-hooo . . . ho-hooo . . ." Now the bunkers increased the amount of fire, some shooting between their "Ho-hooo's."

God, this was a gas. Before long the fire from the woods ceased, but the guys kept shooting and singing.

"Cease fire! Cease fire!" But a few short bursts and single shots rang out until Jagger's vocals faded out. Someone waited an entire ten seconds before firing off one last round. He wanted to get the last word in. The guys lit cigarettes in case an officer of the guard came by—like he couldn't smell pot.

"That was wild."

"Wonder what the gooks thought."

"Oh, man. Imagine if the Stones heard about this."

"You couldn't dream this stuff up."

"That could never happen again."

But while everyone was exhilarated, a mortar had hit the northern part of camp and killed a cook. Life and death in Long Thong.

Ninety-four days—a "two-digit-midget" with less than a hundred days to go.

I III I

Since their return from the whores in Vung Tau, Dyson would check himself first thing every morning for the drip. He had not used the highly recommended rubber and was a little worried. At 05:00 hours on Friday, September 5, Green rallied all the men out of their bunks. Dyson could feel something, turned away from everybody and looked. A brownish, unhealthy-looking, semen-like fluid was drooling from his dick. Shit, he thought, and that fucking whore even had her shot record up to date. That dirty, little, junior high school bitch from Da Lat. Damn it all.

That morning he went on sick call, which meant he would be off flight status until his drip cleared up. He walked to the dispensary and entered the bunker-hootch-tent-chicken-coop that served as the medical facility of the 137th ASH. Dyson told the medic that he had a drip.

"Let's see," SP5 Galveston ordered. "Yep, you got it."

"What do I have?"

"You got the clap." Medics were famous for their lackadaisical attitudes. "Clap is all you have to know." Galveston told Dyson to hang loose until they had everyone together for their penicillin shots—in the ass. Other men were filing in with various complaints and ongoing treatments.

"You six guys line up, you three here, and you three here. OK, face the wall and drop your trousers." Now the medics outfitted themselves with penicillin-loaded syringes and sterile needle attachments. "Here we go." Dyson received a full dose in the left buttock and another full dose in the right buttock. Galveston put a new needle on, gave him half a dose in the left cheek, put another new needle on and gave him his final half dose on the right side. No needle was ever used twice—not even on the same patient. Dyson noticed one guy's ass was black and blue from, it would appear, a significant number of shots.

Galveston gave each man his treatment plan. "Dyson, you from New York?" Darren Galveston was from the City.

"No, man. Connecticut."

"Oh. You sound like you're from NYC, or maybe it's Boston, a Boston accent. Anyway, you're getting two more days of shots just like today. We'll wait three days after that. If you're still dripping after three days, there will be three more days of increased penicillin. Do not drink beer, at all, not even one beer. Understand? OK, all of you, do NOT drink beer at all. Understand?" Some muttered weak responses saying they understood. "You guys here for your first day, we give your names to your CO, and he will start an Article 15 for not wearing a rubber, remember?" Article 15s were punishable with fines, reduction in rank, and/or extra duty. But so what?

As it turned out the COs of both Alpha and Bravo Companies were way too busy with keeping the ships up in the air to be bothered with the back-and-forth bullshit of the Article 15s. Dyson lucked out.

Ninety-one days to go.

‖ ‖ ‖

At the beginning of Dyson's tour, only a few guys in Bravo Company shot up with heroin. There was Medina, in his hootch, who was hardly ever around except when it was time to crash. He shot up with two other SP4 buddies, Norman Blevins and Reggie Grouse, from other hootches. A couple times. Dyson had watched Medina and one or two of the others shoot up and then lie back in their heroin-induced high. The heroin around these parts was 95 percent pure China White, originally just $2 for enough to fill a little box of Rosebud wooden matches. Now, because of the new people in control of the drug trade in these parts, it cost ten times more. But that hadn't stopped anyone from using as much or as often. In fact, as the price rose, so did the number of heroin users in the 137th ASH Battalion. There was a rippling undercurrent in the men, a level of consciousness about the creeping epidemic of hard drug use. The number of addicts in Alpha and Bravo Companies had soared to about sixty. And it was exploding all over South Vietnam.

I III I

Dyson got a clean bill of health. Everyone wondered what ever happened to Earlywhile after he got to Camp Zama in Japan for advanced treatment of what he had "caught off a hot towel in the massage parlor." The medics would not tell the men if it was gonorrhea, trichomonas-something or chlamydia. You just had the clap and that was that. He remembered Groucho Marx singing, "Oh Lydia, Oh Lydia, you gave men chlamydia . . ."

I III I

On Wednesday, September 10, Morgan and Dyson were assigned on *094* with Lieutenant Don Reynolds as aircraft commander and CW2 Anton Pillars, an FNG to Bravo Company. Reynolds was a seasoned Huey pilot on his third tour with one year piloting a gunship company up north. Pillars was an up-and-coming pilot in his own right, known for his cool head and precision maneuvers in tight spots. Morgan and Dyson had confidence in them, and both pilots knew the two friends were a good crew to fly with.

They spent a long morning and half the afternoon ferrying troops and supplies, mail, and hot meals from mess halls out to the grunts. There was a stop to refuel at Castle Pad in Long Binh. Then one flight took them almost to the border of Cambodia. Division was beefing up the forwardmost LZs and camps with supply and personnel in readiness for the monsoon and limited flying weather. Everyone was bracing for the rains.

This leg of the mission, the ship was seven miles from Long Thong. They had deposited six grunts from their own 2/5 Infantry into the woods. The aircraft was empty on the trip to pick up four FNGs. As they were making their descent, they flew over acres and acres of rice paddies and scattered clusters of hootches. Reynolds spotted something. He radioed to Operations he was going to circle a location for enemy activity and was granted permission. He was descending while maintaining a circle's arc. To Morgan and Dyson, he said, "Check out three personnel on the dike approaching the village, three on the dike."

They were down to three hundred feet, skimming over the dikes and ponds of the paddies. Bunches of men and women were working in the water, the backbreaking toil of rice growers, still being done just like it was centuries ago. Ahead of them, Dyson could see three men on a dike heading for the village. One man followed two others carrying a bundle of bamboo between them on their shoulders. Reynolds stayed at three hundred feet and circled them at a distance of one hundred yards. First one man, then the others waved at the ship and continued walking.

"Check out their bundle," Reynolds said over the intercom. Was that something hidden in the bundle of bamboo? Reynolds maintained cruising until the ship was in the rear, now at a distance of one-hundred feet. Then he changed direction and began circling again. "Get ready," he said to the gunners.

The ship stopped over the dike between the men and the village, pivoted ninety degrees and hovered, pointed right at the men. They stopped. It all fit. There was bamboo growing all over among the hootches, along parts of surrounding dikes, and on the unworkable plots of land. Why did they have to carry a bundle of bamboo where there was already bamboo? Dyson and Morgan brought their muzzles up toward the men, and with that the three men reacted.

They may have rehearsed this or not, but in unison, the two forward men dropped the bundle and all three drew out AK47s. At that instant Morgan and Dyson opened up. So did the three VC.

While divots of hard-packed soil and geysers of water spiked into the air, Dyson heard loud thunderclaps as a few AK rounds hit the ship. Three AKs pouring lead at their ship was no trivial matter. Reynolds kept the nose of the ship down and gained elevation. Dyson kept pouring his tracers into the killing zone. The men were in the open without any cover. First one fell and then the other two. The shooting stopped. "Stay alert. Stay alert." Reynolds slowly guided the ship towards the quarry and their contraband. One man was lying on the ground on his back and picked his arm up to shield his face. The two gunners each poured one good-sized burst across them all. It was over.

The bundle had been a crude crate stacked with what appeared to be RPGs and RPG rounds. There were also a half dozen weapons that may have been SKS assault rifles.

Reynolds' previous experience had told him something wasn't right the minute he spotted the three Vietnamese carrying their load. He now radioed in. Operations told him to proceed with the missions, other people would be sent to investigate the scene. That was OK with Dyson. He didn't want to be on the ground facing the Viet Cong again.

Eighty-six days to go.

||||||

Around about the same time, in a gunship Company in the 2nd Airmobile Division, a Huey with rockets, miniguns, and M60s was flying in Phuoc Long Province when the crew spotted five men chopping down trees bordering on some rice paddies. The ship came down for a closer look. Two of the woodchoppers waved as the ship cruised past. As the workers continued what they were doing, the pilot decided to investigate and descended to fifty feet, hovered and turned the nose of the ship pointing toward the workers, about two hundred feet away. The ship remained in a hover. The woodchoppers stopped working and eyed the ship. They were talking between themselves. The crew studied the men who stared back at the ship for a few minutes. They were looking down the barrels of two miniguns, two M60 machine guns, the warheads of thirty-six pecker-head rockets and the four gunship crew members glaring at them. The ship gently swayed at the hover.

The men bolted. The pilots let loose with rocket and minigun fire. It was over in five seconds. An Intelligence officer flown to the scene later found five dead villagers and no weapons or any proof they were Viet Cong. What would anyone else do in that same condition, faced with a fully armed gunship hovering at the ready for minutes in a staring contest? What could the five civilians have done to convince the crew they were not the enemy?

I III I

"I'd rather have a sister in a whorehouse than a brother that's a REMF," said Dell, an SP5 and crew chief.

"Where the hell did you hear that?" asked Riaz.

"Some grunt we evacuated had it on his helmet."

"I didn't know we were so well-liked."

I III I

Lo and behold. A letter from Carol. Surprised she even remembered. Today's the twelfth of September . . . haven't heard from her in, like, two months . . . "I'll never let you go." Should he open it or not? It felt like another single-page job. He opened it and scanned for important words, not bothering to read each one.

". . . in a long time . . . hard to tell you . . . friend Peter Warren . . . his baby . . . around Thanksgiving . . ." Thanksgiving. He pictured a calendar in his mind. That meant they screwed like in February. Jesus, she sure didn't wait long. Good ol' Peter. But it takes two to tango.

"Just fine," he thought. "I hope they'll be very happy—bitch."

Eighty-four days to go.

OD

Bravo Company—and all the other units in South Vietnam for that matter—had rampant alcohol and drug addiction. Officers and NCOs drank endlessly in their clubs at night, enlisted men were split between alcohol and drugs, and the heroin epidemic was really skyrocketing. Things seemed to have had a lid on them until the junkies began showing up unable to function on duty. Whereas drinking and smoking pot had existed side by side for years, heroin was now rocking the boat. As usual, it was ignored in the beginning, but then it was impossible to avoid the sheer numbers of users and their abysmal job performance on duty.

Medina had been using ever since Dyson met him. He usually disappeared in the evening to hang with the other shooters. The lifers in their clubs drinking, the potheads in their hootches smoking, and the heroin addicts shooting up in their favorite haunts. In some units, when lifers tried to stop all drug usage, fraggings by the enlisted men put a stop to their efforts. So far, the only fragging in Dyson's unit had been at the Battalion stand-down.

On Friday night, September 12, the guys were smoking and listening to *The White Album,* one of the best albums ever during this war. There were the blasts of out-going artillery from the north end of camp, overriding the music that drifted from other hootches. The guys were startled by a good-sized black spider that sped through their listening area in a flash. "Yeoow!" It disappeared and a few guys chuckled. With the rains, they could look forward to rats, snakes, scorpions, and spiders along with an assortment of big bugs in their bunkers, hootches, and shithouses, all looking for dry places to hole up.

SP4 Blunt came dashing in yelling, "OD! OD!"

"What! What!" O'Dayle said. "What do you want?"

"You gotta come. Sommerfield's ODing."

O'Dayle had a reputation for knowing just what to do with heroin overdoses. He had worked in his hometown hospital emergency room as an aide. The Army in its infinite wisdom made him an aircraft mechanic.

The guys turned down the music and a few of them hustled along with OD to a nearby hootch. Sommerfield was on the dusty floor on his back shaking all over, in a seizure. He was foaming at the mouth. "Oh, man, here's OD. Can you do something?" Blunt pleaded.

OD dropped to his knees next to Sommerfield's torso. Even the casual uninformed observer could see the lines of needle tracks and the hardened veins in his arms. OD started going over him.

"Jesus Christ! How long's he been like this?"

"I don't know. Ten, fifteen minutes."

Sommerfield was white as a ghost, accentuating his bluish lips. His pupils looked like two tiny buckshot in the snow. Gasping for breath he began choking on his vomit.

"Up! Up! Sit him up!" The guys sat him up on the floor. "Sommerfield! Sommerfield! Look at me, man. Look at me."

But his eyes couldn't focus. When he threw up again, everyone assisting him tried unsuccessfully to avoid getting puke on them. His air passage might have been cleared but he was still struggling to breathe.

"Let's take him to the mess hall. Come on!" And without a litter, four guys picked Sommerfield up and lugged him the fifty yards to the mess hall. "Get Floaty or Gator," someone screamed.

Floaty came running up as they approached the rear of the bunkered building. There was a chest freezer in the back of the kitchen.

"Can you open the freezer?" Floaty quickly reached up on a rafter where the key was kept and unlocked the eight-foot-long field freezer.

"Get the medics!" and someone took off. The guys put Sommerfield on the floor. "Clear a space for him! Come on! Clear it out!" Boxes of frosted frozen foods were tossed onto the counters. OD kept trying to get a response from Sommerfield.

"Oh, man, I don't know." He was shaking the man's head side to side and opening one eyelid then the other. "OK, put him in! Put him in!" Once Sommerfield was laid out in the freezer on top of some boxes, OD told the guys to put the other packages on top of him to snap his senses back on line. Not once did he show any signs of consciousness. Galveston, the dispensary medic, arrived with a stethoscope.

"Oh shit!" He tried to hear a heartbeat on Sommerfield's chest. "Pull the plug out! I can't hear." Someone yanked the plug and the noise from the freezer's compressor stopped. Galveston listened, then moved up to the jugular vein, and back to the chest. He felt his wrists, then his neck. "He's dead."

No one questioned the medic. They knew Galveston was a great medic. He had saved a bunch of lives. If he said Sommerfield was dead, he was dead.

"Can some of you guys carry him to the dispensary? I'll get him ready." Galveston left with the men taking Sommerfield away. Floaty and OD put the food and freezer back together.

There had been other overdoses in the 137th ASH, but this was the first fatality. That night, even after the whole camp heard about Sommerfield, his buddies who were hooked on heroin shot up, with the exact same stash Sommerfield had used. Death or not, H is always calling, telling everyone that a little bit is nice, but more is even nicer.

▌▐▐▌

A few nights later, after another long, long day of heavy repairs, Dyson, Spook, and Super Chicken were invited to hang out at the Maintenance hootch. It was between the hangar and the perimeter and isolated from the others. These guys had built a supercool bunker as an addition to the end of the hootch. It had two entrances, a seven-foot ceiling, four-foot fluorescent lights hanging from the ceiling, and two speakers connected to a reel-to-reel tape recorder. Spirit was playing "I Got a Line on You."

Someone had spray-painted the plastic shield over the lights yellow, which gave the room a rich golden glow. There were bench seats along the walls and three folding lawn chairs. It was a smoking room. They were welcomed by eight other mechanics. There were still a few seats available. Of those eight mechanics, Dyson recognized four heroin users—Albion and Broze, both SP4s, and a couple of PFCs, Williams and Ulrich, an FNG who hadn't wasted any time getting in with the heroin shooters.

There was talk of how cool the room was, how the two outside entrances were inside the revetment that ran around the entire hootch, and, after a quick look outside, how there was room for about six lawn chairs on the roof. It was really a piece of work. A big bowl of Cambodian Red was passed around. Only two of the shooters took a hit. There was more talk of Woodstock now that people knew more about it and of the antiwar protests at home, plus the usual rapping about crazy shit when they were kids, and on and on in the haze of smoke and tunes.

While the conversations continued, the four took out their works and stashes. They laid out four dubious-looking syringes, the two mess kit spoons, a belt, a sixteen-inch-long surgical rubber tube, a Coca-Cola can filled with water, and two Rosebud matchboxes packed with 95 percent pure China White heroin. Each box that used to cost two dollars now cost twenty because of the new control over the drug traffic in this area. But the new cost did not deter anyone from buying the dope.

They prepared for one guy at a time to shoot up. Albion tied his arm off with the belt. Water was drawn into a syringe. A bit of the white powder was cooked in a spoon with a lighter under it. When it liquified, it was drawn into the syringe to mix with the water. Albion pushed the needle into his vein, hurriedly withdrew it, released the belt and sank back into his lawn chair.

"Aahhhhh . . . oooooo . . . mmmmaaaaannnn . . ." and he was off. The effects of heroin shot into the veins comes on fast and hard, with instant euphoria and an all-enveloping warmth. Nothing like it, they said. Didn't any of these guys remember what just happened to Sommerfield?

Another hit was being cooked in a spoon. Ulrich took Albion's syringe, wiped it on his pant leg, passed the flame from his lighter under it, then wiped the black soot off on a dusty cotton ball. *You're shittin' me*, Mister D thought. Broze had tied himself off with the rubber tube. Ulrich drew the water, then the drug, up the syringe, and handed it to Broze.

"Wanna try some?" Ulrich asked the visitors as Broze drifted into his dreamland.

No thanks. This smoke was good enough for them. They watched Ulrich and Williams shoot up and fall out of reality. The four were zonked out. Each looked like he was in heaven. But Mister D could see they didn't look so good otherwise. He liked to keep himself showered and shaved. They were unshowered and unshaved. They looked pale and kept their long sleeves down even during the heat of the day.

All the known heroin users in the Company were being dropped from flight status. "I'll never shoot that stuff in my veins," Dyson told himself.

❙❙❙❙❙

The Army had lied to them about smoking pot: "One hit and you're hooked for life." That was blowing smoke right out of *Reefer Madness*. Cases of hepatitis C were rare and, back then, not even attributed to dirty needles. Nobody knew the danger of exposure to the new toxic chemicals introduced during their daily lives in Vietnam. Agent Orange didn't just stay confined in the countryside where it was sprayed as a defoliant. It became airborne and waterborne, contaminated wells and rice paddies, got into the lungs and the food chain, and carried blood diseases (some not even named yet) that resulted from constant contact with human blood, from handling the dead and wounded, and from airborne blood cells in the helicopter prop wash that infiltrated the crews' lungs and livers. Many Vietnamese had TB, which was highly contagious in social and sexual intercourse with American GIs. Vietnam was a deadly place.

A frantic mechanic poked his head in the entrance. "OD in here?

Know where OD or Galveston is?" Another overdose.

Eighty-three days to go.

▌▐▐▐▌

Visiting

The next time he and Morgan flew was Tuesday, September 16. They were assigned to *087* with Cavecchio, who had been recently promoted to CW2, as aircraft commander and WO1 Ken Gesso, a native of Portland, Oregon. Cavecchio had matured into a savvy and cool-headed commander. "Tiny" Gesso was so small that people wondered how he made the height and weight requirements for pilot, but he was a quick learner and adapted well to life in the war zone.

087 had been airborne a couple of hours and was empty on its way to ferry some troops when Cavecchio reported increasing vibration to Operations. He sensed it first and after about twenty minutes the crew could notice it too. Dyson could feel it through his boots and when he grabbed the handgrips of his M60. Operations told the commander to set down at the closest LZ that had a helipad, LZ Dolly, which would be expecting them. As they approached Dolly, Dyson could see people in the camp getting away from the landing pad, making their way into bunkers and behind revetments. They scurried like ants. That's reassuring, he thought.

By now, the vibration was too much to fly with and they landed with no time to spare. The plan was Operations would send out a team of mechanics to see if they could fix it. If not, the ship would be sling-loaded out under a Chinook. For the time being, the crew would stay with the ship inside the camp.

Platoons from 2/5 Infantry, 2nd Airmobile Division, were coming out of the field accompanied by armored personnel carriers. They were going to have a stand-down right on the perimeter with cold beer, grilled hot dogs, and burgers. They had been out in the field for nine days.

There was a Delta Company, 2/5 Control Point near the helipad.

It was a beefy bunker with a hand-painted sign over the main entrance, "Delta Company, the Headhunters, No Prisoners." Warm and friendly. "Headhunter" was their radio call sign and "No Prisoners" was their motto. An infantry 1st lieutenant welcomed the four crew members. "No salutes," he said in advance. This guy was wild. He had a big soup-strainer mustache and wore root-beer-colored trip glasses. "You guys are welcome to join the guys on the perimeter for the picnic." He called it a picnic instead of a stand-down.

The officers stayed together talking while Morgan and Mister D made their way to the gathering on the green line. Four armored personnel carriers had formed a semicircle against the perimeter berm and faced the woods. The cooks had a barbeque grill going, and a small utility trailer was filled with ice and cans of beer—Hamm's and Pabst. It was a picnic under the blazing Asian sun. Some of the guys were friendly, some not.

"Hey, REMFs," someone said.

"Yeah, we're REMFs," Morgan said.

"Hey, just kiddin'. I'm Joker. That's Paladin. He's Matt Dillon. Meet Cochise." The nicknames kept coming, hands were shaken, and the smell of pot wafted through the air. Dyson could see some guys wearing long hair—too long for Long Thong and other bases. There were guys with necklaces with peace symbols and medallions of all sorts. Two guys wore what looked like necklaces made from pieces of bacon. But they were actually human ears, cut off dead NVA and VC. At least Dyson hoped they were dead. As he and Morgan scanned the surrounding scenery, they saw that some of the steel fence posts holding the razor wire around the camp had skulls on them and a few had heads in various stages of decomposition.

Two more APCs came out of the woods. Passing by the stand-down, one had a body hanging on the side of the vehicle. It was an Asian man in bloody khakis, and he was over six feet tall—too tall for Southeast Asians.

"He has to be Chinese," Joker told Morgan and Dyson. "The Division's Intelligence Unit is flying out here to see this guy."

"Army Intelligence," one guy scoffed, "there's an oxymoron for you."

A while later, they were having a hot dog and a Hamm's. Joker and two other grunts joined up with them at the ass end of an opened APC.

"Never seen the inside of these," said Morgan.

"They're death traps," said one grunt. "They make too much noise. One mine can kill everyone on board."

"There's next to no armor on the bottom. They need some steel plate down there or something," said Joker.

There was shoptalk among the men—shoptalk for grunts. Everyone just blended in nicely. Some guys in the field had real respect and gratitude for flight crews, more than a few owing their lives to them. Others figured a REMF was a REMF, and that was that—they were all no good. A lot of the grunts looked like they were still in high school or maybe twenty; no one looked over twenty-five. A half dozen or so black guys were scattered in the gathering. It seemed to be a unit where everyone got along.

"Dessert," someone said as a beautiful hand-sculpted meerschaum pipe was passed around, full of kick-ass Golden Triangle pot. When the pipe heated up, it turned from white to a golden brown. Classy.

"Don't worry about that shit." Joker had spotted Dyson looking around warily. "The lifers are in their bunker." Morgan said they would stick around a while, maybe even for the night. Around 14:30 hours, he, Mister D, Joker, and Cochise were sitting in the little shade provided by an APC, facing the woods.

"It's cool. We're safe," said Cochise. Over the no-man's land of wire, trip flares, and mines were the woods one hundred yards away—typical of LZs of the 2nd Airmobile Division.

Joker pulled something out of his pocket wrapped in a piece of green towel. He unrolled it and produced a dark gummy ball, plastered with lint.

"Wanna do some O?" Opium, pure opium.

"Is it cool?" asked Mister D.

"Shit, yeah, it's cool," said Cochise. "The CO smokes O." Just then a captain walked briskly up to the beer trailer. Guys nodded to him and said "Hello, sir." No salutes anywhere. This was Captain Anthony Braun, the commanding officer of Delta Company. He had on a black Stetson with cavalry officer's ropes on the brim, trip glasses, no shirt, and a web belt with holster and .45. He was muscular and had lines of scars on his shoulders and back. He looked like he had been whipped.

"Good job out there, guys. Good job," and off he went. He was referring to the previous nine days when the Company searched for a bunker complex built by the local Viet Cong. After three days of looking almost microscopically through the dense vegetation, with the help of a former VC, they found a camouflaged four-inch-wide bamboo vent pipe for a tunnel below. Then they located an entrance and Company tunnel rats went in after the enemy to stir things up. They didn't encounter or kill any VC but they came upon an enormous weapons cache: AK47s, 7.62mm RPD light machine guns, RPGs, anti-tank mines, ammunition, hundreds of mortar rounds. It had to put the hurt on some VC unit. For a while, anyway. The Division commander had flown out to see it.

Someone produced what the guys called their "Super Bowl" made for smoking opium—a piece of bamboo three sections long with a bowl from a briarwood pipe improvised onto the stem. Joker broke the gumball into smaller pieces for easier lighting, put the pipe to his mouth, and Cochise used his lighter until Joker's puffing produced some glowing embers. He passed it to Cochise who took his hit, and he passed it on to Dyson.

"You don't need a big hit."

Mister D took a decent-sized hit. He passed the pipe to Morgan and set back to keep the smoke in his lungs. He felt himself slipping into a very heavy stone. Fleeting scenes of nineteenth century opium dens in story books came to mind.

The power of the sun went from oppressive heat to a rich, warm sensual glow. The blood in his veins coursed through his body and became one with the sap flowing upward in the trees, up their trunks, into every branch and leaf. The same force was now coursing through all the wildlife in the woods, through the insects, snakes, birds, and monkeys, all circulating from the heartbeat while the veins themselves were undulating in time with the pulse. He was one living thing joining other living things. He thought of nothing else but the path of life going through him and all else. A totality of the here and now. He could see it—a life force of unity, moving in a phantasm of sunlit yellows, oranges, magentas, and violets. Nothing man-made or civilized existed. He was on the outside of time itself, looking into the universe. Time wasn't here, it was there.

A coolness settled in, the sunlight waned, all living things went their separate ways. Almost the whole unit of men had left. He and Morgan were there, sitting against the APC. He had been tripping for five hours.

"Guess what," said Morgan. "The crew ain't going to be back until morning. But we got a place to sleep."

They were up now, walking into the camp with Joker motioning them to a hootch. Dyson would never forget this stone. Cochise gave him a pair of Ho Chi Minh tire-tread sandals. They were taken off a dead VC. Dyson wondered what kind of story they held.

Eighty days to go.

▍▎▍▍▍

Dyson and SP5 Ernie Dell, a crew chief, were assigned to *093* with Sheckly as aircraft commander and Smith as co-pilot-navigator. It was Thursday, September 25. Cloudy skies had moved into South Vietnam ahead of the monsoon. Yesterday was half clouds and sun, today all clouds and no sun. The first rains would arrive on Friday afternoon, and then they would start and stop at the same time every day all season long. Crews would get wet every day from then on, no way around it.

093 had put in a full day of carrying troops, supplies, hot meals, mail, FNGs, and a couple of Medevacs to Long Binh. One guy died on the way. It was 19:45 hours, almost dark, and they were under the cloud cover. They were headed to Long Thong. He was thinking of the opium experience. He could still feel the drug's effects.

"Climbing to five thousand," said Sheckly over the intercom. As they entered the cloud cover, the mists poured through the ship, his first taste of flying in monsoon season. Not only was Dyson getting wet, but it was also freezing cold. It took a few minutes for the ship to rise above the clouds. Suddenly it was like daylight. Astounding. He forgot all about being soaking wet and cold.

This night was the full moon. There it was, big as a basketball, the biggest and brightest one he had ever seen. Stars and stars and *more* stars, constellations, and the Milky Way in a brilliance and magnitude like never before. Only light years separated him and the stars. The spectacular illumination shown down on the top of the cloud cover, a white and silver stainless-steel blanket. Not a single ship sailed in sight, no running lights anywhere. The sound of their engine was like blasphemy defiling the panorama. Starry, starry night. This was heavy, and he wasn't even stoned. He would remember this forever, and years later look at the cloudy night skies and know what was on the other side.

"Descending to two thousand feet." The words jerked him out of his reverie.

Goodbye, he said to the heavens. The ship entered the clouds and he got soaked again.

Seventy-one days to go.

I III I

Friday at 14:15 hours, it started raining on Long Thong.
Seventy days to go.

I III I

About this time the 25th Infantry Division launched *Operation CLIFF DWELLER* in Tay Ninh Province with Nui Ba Den Mountain the main target. The mountain had been fought over and then deserted by the 1st Cavalry Division and 4th Infantry Division after suffering heavy casualties. Take the territory, then pull out—the war of attrition.

I IIII

OCTOBER

The blazing sun and sweltering humidity were replaced with cloudy, cooler, damp weather. The ground was either pond-sized puddles of mud or laced with wooden sidewalks that the engineers had laid down, some already submerged. In the perforated steel-planked airfield, water and mud oozed up through the metal tracks. Canvases and tenting were draped and suspended over the ships being worked on. Everyone tried to perform their specific tasks before the afternoon's onset of rain.

It rained hard, like someone turned on a spigot. When the wind picked up, it came down almost horizontally. It blasted through the bug screens on hootches, floors became a muddy mess. Snakes, rats, and other detestable critters invaded the camp, seeking dry places, like shithouses, bunkers, and up in the rafters of hootches.

On the night of Thursday, October 2, Dyson and Dell were walking back to the Company area after a day of flying when they approached a six-man shithouse. They were wet, tired, and hungry.

"Ya know," said Dell, "I gotta shit."

"Well, I ain't gonna go in and watch ya, man." Mister D stayed outside while Dell entered the darkened crapper. There was partial clearing in the sky, some stars out. He lit a Camel.

Halfway through his cigarette, POW! POW! POW! What the fuck! Muzzles flashes seared through the clapboards of the shitter. Dyson drew his sidearm.

POW! POW! POW! POW! Dell had unloaded the entire clip from his .45. The door slammed open and he hopped out holding his pants up with one hand and his weapon in the other.

"Fuckin' snake, man. Big fuckin' snake." Now a few of the stoners came over as others came out of hootches.

"What's going on?" Someone had a flashlight and into the shitter they went, along with a couple weapons.

"There it is!" In the half barrel underneath Dell's seat was a big dead snake with brown banding on it.

"Cobra," someone confirmed. "A dead cobra."

"As soon as that thing touched my ass, I knew it was a fuckin' snake." He was damned lucky he didn't get bit.

Snakes were in shitters all over. They loved wallowing in the warm human shit.

I I I I I

Things slowed down, somewhat, with the monsoon. Guys consigned themselves to being wet for most of the day: at work, in the air, in the hootches. When incoming rocket and mortar attacks hit Long Thong, everyone sprinted into bunkers engulfed with muddy floors, puddles, and leaky roofs. No more sitting on the ground.

Warnings were repeated to guards on the perimeter that sappers loved the cover that rain provided by muting any little noises they might make, in addition to giving the defenders a false sense of security. The enemy never went away. They were always there. It was they who always chose the time and the place.

I I I I I

Long Thong

On Friday, October 3, Dyson, Florida, Scooby, and Molina were scheduled for perimeter guard duty on the Bravo sector, closest to the woods. The rain was steady but light. The four wore ponchos and carried M16s with bandoliers of ammo. They relieved the men in Bunker 4 at 20:00 hours. The floor was muck. The roof was dripping constantly. An M60 was resting on the sandbags of the firing port, aimed at the woods. It was difficult to sit or relax anywhere in the bunker. This time, the officer of the guard was Lieutenant Reynolds who did not put up with anyone slacking off on guard duty.

At 20:15 hours he entered their bunker. "Dyson. Miami. And . . . you are who . . . ?

"Scott, sir," said Scooby.

"OK. Here's what's going on. There is VC activity in the area tonight. Forward outposts report movement all over the place north, east, and south of here. So be on your toes. I mean it."

"Understood."

Reynolds looked at the cots. "If I had it my way, all these cots would be taken out of the bunkers."

"Sir, they're soaking wet," said Scooby.

"Remember what I said. And no smoking pot. I catch anyone smoking pot, I'm gonna have them court-martialed. The hell with Article 15. Court-martial." He left. Yeah, right, tell a pot smoker over here not to smoke pot.

"Fuck him," said Molina. "We can smoke if someone keeps watch." By now, the guys were smoking pot all the time. In the morning before work, at work, at lunch break, before evening chow, and every night up until sack time. It's how they functioned, how they lived, how they coped. A couple of Marlboro Greens kept the four of them stoned for a few hours. The light rain continued. Two men at a time would crouch down to smoke cigarettes out of sight from the no-man's land. The guys would take turns manning the M60.

Reynolds kept popping in, at 21:00 hours, 21:30, 21:50, 22:20, 22:40, 22:50. No one knew when he would be there next. Sometimes he never said a word. There always seemed to be an air of disdain from the officers toward enlisted men. Then again, maybe the lieutenant was just pissed it was so fucking wet and he wasn't at the club drinking with the other officers.

Around 00:00 hours, midnight, the northern sector reported movement. In the south sector, a trip flare went off and bunkers opened up, but nothing could be seen. It was putting people on edge. The guys in Bunker 4 kept quiet and watched their field of fire through the rain.

At 01:20 hours, Florida said he heard something. They all listened—nothing.

Everything changed in the blink of an eye. In front of them to the right, in the field of fire of the next bunker, a brilliant flash lit up an amazing scene. Like a still photograph, a trip flare shot skyward and illuminated the figure of a skinny little gook as he turned away from them. He wore only black shorts. His wet body was gleaming, his mouth was wide open in shock. At his feet were two men crawling on their hands and knees while two others' hands held open the razor wire enough to crawl through. They were reversing their route and going out the same path they made in the wire just before one of them set off a trip flare they failed to neutralize. The standing man knew he was dead.

There was a heartbeat's delay between recognition and firing. Then, all at once, every single bunker on the sector opened up. Molina unleashed the M60 at the three VC who were enveloped in a hail of tracers, muddy divots, and water spitting high up into the air. A fusillade came from the woods to their front. Mortar teams in camp launched four parachute-illumination flares to light up the perimeter, bathing it in an eerie pale orange light. Bullets smacked into the sandbags of their bunker. A green tracer blasted past their heads and buried itself in the back wall. This was not a probe. It was a ground attack.

Figures could be seen out in no-man's land, running and firing, hitting the dirt, popping up and shooting, a rough line of them halfway across the open field. Shape-shifting shadows moved along the ground as the parachute flares sank and dimmed. These damn VC were coming in standing up! Enemy gunners in the woods laid down uninterrupted fire at the bunkers while their comrades advanced. They were crawling through paths in the wire that had now been blown open by the sappers. The advancing VC started launching RPGs. One bunker to their east took a pretty bad hit, but the men in it resumed their fire. An RPG slammed into the right side of Bunker

4, but the sandbags absorbed it. Some Claymore mines were set off, but many had been neutralized by the sappers. Sometimes sappers would turn them around so they pointed back at a position, but then this could screw them up, too, because they never knew *when* the mine would be set off.

The attackers were gaining ground, getting closer. Murderous fire from both sides continued raking positions. Dozens of men facing each other blasted away with automatic weapons. There appeared to be three distinct VC fire teams: one in the tree line and two advancing. They seemed to be at the last row of razor wire before the bunkers. Another RPG slammed into Bunker 4, just under the firing port.

"Don't stop! Don't stop! Shoot! Shoot! Jesus, this is bad."

"Keep firing! Keep it up!"

"We got 'em! We got 'em!"

"Fuck you, damn gooks, cocksuckers!" The guys were getting mad. It's what men do to defend themselves. Kill or be killed. Get mad. Let them know it. Yell at them.

Two ammo bearers entered the bunker with more M16 bandoliers and cans of M60 belts.

"Gooks! Gooks! Fuckin' gooks in camp!" one of them yelled. Fuck! The two joined right in. One of them had a 40mm grenade launcher. He put one round at a time right into where the firing was coming from, lobbing grenades in as if he was tossing horseshoes.

Dyson looked outside. The second ammo bearer went with him.

"Jesus!" Bullets crackled past them like high voltage hornets. "Keep down!"

"Medic! MEDIC!" Dyson couldn't imagine being a medic in this shit.

Red and green tracers came from every direction. There was a firefight going on in the Bravo Company area. Guys behind the hootch revetments poured fire at a place near the Operations bunker, where VC figures were visible. Dyson and the ammo bearer unloaded two clips each at them but lost the targets in muzzle flashes.

As a new flare illuminated the sky, Dyson stared momentarily to watch the men in Bunkers 5 and 6 shooting gooks off the top of each other's bunker. Even though five or six attackers were either climbing onto or already on top of the bunkers while returning fire, they were still getting the worst of it.

"Die! Die, you fuckin' gooks!"

As one VC tried to ignite a satchel charge, he was cut down by one of the bunker's guards with his .45. Now the VC and the guards pitched hand grenades at each other. Dyson could see VC stick grenades spinning end over end before exploding, so he fired at the positions they came from. With grenade after grenade being thrown, he thought it looked like the snowball fights they had as kids. At last, the noise died down. There were no more definite targets to fire on. Suppressive fire from the camp dwindled to nothing.

Within the space of five minutes, the VC were cleared off the bunkers, while dozens were left lying in no-man's land and between the perimeter berm and the camp buildings. The firefight in the Bravo Company area broke the back of the attack. The VC failed to capture and destroy the Operations Bunker and the Control Point. The sappers were wiped out. No more fire was coming from no-man's land, and the firing from the woods had stopped. All he could hear was the high-pitched ringing in his ears. Otherwise, it was deathly quiet.

After an uneasy hour guys went around making sure the VC were dead by using single shots or short bursts into enemy bodies. Others were kicking their bodies and removing their weapons as war trophies. Just feet from Dyson and the ammo bearer a young sapper lay next to their bunker. He wore shorts, no sandals. He was struggling for air and bleeding from wounds in his shoulder, chest and legs. He looked from one American soldier to the other. He wanted help, he wanted to go home, he wanted to see his family again. The ammo bearer bent down and looked him right in the eye. The gasping sapper raised his hand.

"Here, breathe this." The ammo bearer shot him twice in the

face point-blank with his .45. The back of his head blew off into the muck.

"Don't let your guard down. Don't think it's over," Reynolds said as he came out of Bunker 3 and walked their way. "You guys stay alert. They're still out there. Everybody OK over here?" He went in the bunker and came back out. "Good. Good job. Stay alert." He continued to Bunker 5.

Dyson was still breathing hard. He sat down on a low wall of sandbags and lit a Camel. His heart was pounding in his chest like he had just run a hundred-yard dash.

"Man, I thought this was it."

"Yeah, t'was hairy, all right," the ammo bearer said.

Two Hueys started run up procedures for Medevac flights to Long Binh with the wounded. So far, two guards in this sector were KIA, as well as three more men in the Bravo Company area. He hadn't heard any names yet. He had just seen a dying man who wanted help murdered right in front of him. He really didn't feel anything one way or the other. Is numb an emotion?

Blue cordite smoke hung in the air, like an early morning mist over the fields back home. Dead VC were strewn in the sloppy-ass muck and rain. Blood and mud. Little streams trickled from one pond to another. Everyone's boots made sucking noises when they slogged through the detritus. Guys grabbed VC weapons, slinging them over their shoulders or carrying them in out-stretched arms. (A few would hang on to the enemy weapons for trophies, keeping them hidden. Getting them home would be a miracle.) The bodies were dragged off to a point behind each bunker and two three-quarter ton trucks soon were making their way from bunker to bunker. Enemy KIAs were unceremoniously thrown into the truck beds. The enemy dead in no-man's land along the perimeter would have to wait for now. The mortar crews saw to it that at least two parachute flares hung in the air at all times to illuminate the area. The scene was surreal.

Reynolds and some ammo bearers were soon going to the bunkers telling the guards to get inside the bunkers because there was going to be a "mad minute"—a full minute of continuous fire from everyone on the perimeter whether there were VC out there or not. Dyson went inside to join the guys. It was no drier in there than it was outside.

They locked and loaded and waited for the shooting to start. This tactic served to break up any VC still out there preparing for a counterattack, or those dragging their dead back to the woods. Mad minutes were SOP all over the country. The VC were probably long gone. Who knows? They were like ghosts.

An M60 down the line started, then everyone followed suit. The guys raked no-man's land and the woods. A minute later, the shooting stopped. It was over.

I III I

Around 03:00 hours, Molina came back in from the shithouse with a look of disgust.

"You know that crazy, little hillbilly Barnett?" Some of the guys did. "He cut the head off of one of them!"

"Where is it?"

"Reynolds made him throw it in a three-quarter ton with the rest of the gooks."

I III I

Two days later, the details of the battle of Long Thong came out. The north and south sectors as well as Bravo Company's all came under attack within minutes of each other. The VC had a main force element in the woods waiting to receive word where the camp's defenses had been breached. They breached the southern sector first (next to Bravo's sector) and dozens of them poured in bent on only one purpose: overrunning the camp. Bravo's sector was breached just as their main element charged the camp. Practically all 137th ASH personnel in the barracks had been armed and met the advancing VC, stopping them only a short distance from the perimeter. VC swarmed over the berm while the guards in the bunkers kept them from gaining entry. Dead VC were piled up around each bunker. The battle line was the perimeter berm itself. The furthest point in camp the VC reached was the Operations Bunker, which they held for just a matter of minutes. They managed to destroy four ships on the flight line and damaged six more, but they had to do it under withering fire.

A crisscrossing search of the camp found no living VC. At daylight, the dead had been piled onto a spread-out cargo net awaiting pickup by an inbound Chinook. Barnett, the fucked-up hillbilly, volunteered to climb up and stand on the pile of gooks to loop the net's doughnut onto the hook attached to the belly of the ship. Later, the entire load, cargo net and all, were dumped somewhere out in the green forests. A standard 2nd Airmobile way of getting rid of piles of enemy bodies.

One VC body stunned everyone. It was Han, their water-truck driver, the friendly guy who brought in smoke and whores for the guys and knew the camp like the back of his hand. Driver by day, VC at night.

A total of eleven men from various companies were KIA, seven men were Medevac'd to Long Binh, twelve were treated for minor wounds at the 137th ASH dispensary. One of the men in Bravo Company who died was SP4 Toohany, the Electric Indian. Lifers spitefully said he was drunk. So what if he was drunk? Dyson would always have a bittersweet memory of him saying, "White women talk too much."

▌▐▐▐▌

The next time he was scheduled to fly was Tuesday, October 7. Of course, it was cloudy. There was no getting around being totally soaked. Sometimes he would pull on his poncho, put his harness and flight helmet on over it and make sure his lifeline was secured to the ship. Often that got too warm and off it came. He cut one to ribbons one time to get it off without removing his harness. Company morale seemed to sag beneath the unrelenting rains. The monsoon put everyone in a melancholy mood. They still smoked and listened to music every night, but a good many guys were lost in their own thoughts, and no one talked about it.

He and Morgan were on *095* with Cavecchio and George Wallace, a FNG Wobbly One. Wallace said the name had gotten him in trouble a few times. Cavecchio was pushing as hard as he could to get the most missions done before the rain started in the afternoon, but some of the missions were on a timetable.

Dyson could look down through the treetops and see water on the forest floors and the red dirt roads of the villages. Farmers kept working the rice paddies like they had for centuries. Very few Vietnamese would even look up at them or wave. Whenever someone looked upward at a ship, their upturned face looked just like an orange pumpkin among the vines—even in the woods, it's a dead giveaway.

They had descended to a thousand feet when they were flying parallel to a local road on the port side (Dyson's side) running through acres of rice paddies. He looked ahead and could see a gathering of villagers. During the few seconds of their passing, he saw about twenty villagers standing in a rough semicircle staring down at five people lying in the water with their heads and shoulders on the dike. They had on bloody blindfolds and their hands appeared to be tied behind their backs. No one looked up as they sped past. Some of them looked as if they were grieving.

What was that? VC executions? He had just seen five people who were apparently murdered and it didn't faze him. What if he was back home and saw five neighbors who had been murdered? What was happening to him?

Fifty-nine days to go.

▌▐▐▐ ▌

"Dyson." It was Enrico, calling him as he walked to the flight line. He stopped and turned. In a nearby hootch, someone was playing "Love the One You're With"—loud.

"Yeah, Top?"

"Dyson, this is a Red Cross Inquiry," the sergeant showed him a typewritten form sent to Bravo Company. "Write your mom, son. She hasn't heard from you in almost four weeks."

God, what was wrong with him? This wasn't the first time the Red Cross had to inquire about a guy for not writing home, where someone was worried to death about someone who was perfectly fine. Sort of.

▌▏▌▌▌

Water Buffalo

Dyson was scheduled to fly Friday, October 10, his first time with SP5 Melvin Naylor, from the north woods of Maine, as crew chief. The aircraft commander for *089* that day was CW2 Burton Bethesda, a New Yorker with a master's degree. "Tiny" Gesso was co-pilot. One thing, though, he heard Naylor was an asshole.

The mission sheet for *089* was a busy one. After dropping off supplies to a new LZ in Phuoc Long, the ship headed for Phuoc Vinh and was making its descent three miles from the camp. Men and women were working in the paddies, and there was an occasional water buffalo. A water buffalo was like a tractor to a Vietnamese farmer. It took years of backbreaking labor to save up enough money to purchase just one. They were an organic John Deere for cultivation, hauling heavy loads, pulling tree stumps. Not only did they plow the fields, but they also fertilized them as well.

The paddies appeared peaceful, and for a period of minutes it seemed like there was no war at all. At an altitude of five hundred feet within sight of Phuoc Vinh, Naylor opened up with his M60. With a quick glimpse over his left shoulder, Dyson saw the crew chief's first burst was fired toward his front right side. He was sweeping the muzzle to his left when it disappeared from Dyson's view around the bulkhead that separated them. Naylor continued firing—three bursts of about twenty rounds each—until whatever "it" was passed out of range.

"Yeeehhaaaawww!" Naylor screamed over the mike.

No words from the pilots, nothing to fire at on this side. He must have just felt like blowing up some geysers in the paddies. Weapons were often test-fired at the beginning of the missions, but this was midafternoon. Most crew chiefs, like Morgan and Dell, would warn the crew they were going to fire, but not Naylor and a few others. Some pilots put up with that. Some didn't.

It wasn't until hours later back at Long Thong when they were done with the ship and leaving the flight line that Naylor told Dyson he shot a water buffalo, real close to a bunch of farmers.

"A water buffalo," repeated Dyson.

"Yeah, man. I love shootin' buffaloes."

Callous disregard for people's lives, safety, and property. Just shoot the damn animal they depend on to make a hardscrabble living out of the dirt. And we want these people to love and respect us for trying to save their country. Naylor glanced at Dyson out of the corner of his eye.

"You don't seem impressed." He sounded puzzled.

"I ain't." Dyson kept walking.

"Hey, there's a guy over in Alpha Company they call the Water Buffalo King. He's shot maybe twenty or so. I want to beat him out."

"Good for you." God, what a dick. Dyson was going to try not to fly with Naylor anymore.

Fifty-six days to go.

| ||| |

Many things had changed around Bravo Company. Some of the best guys weren't around anymore. Of course, there was Lieutenant Papp whom no one had heard from concerning his cancer. Toohany, the Electric Indian, was KIA. Rick Strickland, he of the "incoming" warnings, went home. So did Mechanics Blunt and Devaney, both back to the mountains of Wyoming. And these guys also went back to the World: "Big Billy" Grains, who ran the EM Club; O'Donahue, the full-blooded Irishman who became a naturalized citizen; "Stinky" Rivers, the permanent shit-burner; "OD" O'Dayle; Ramirez, who lit up a Salem cigarette in his first waking minute; and O'Grady, the man with the world's biggest cock. When he walked through the Company area to the showers the morning before he flew out, someone yelled, "Hey, "Iron Cock!" One last time!" So O'Grady pulled out his legendary phallus for one final display amid cheers and good-byes. Gee, whatta guy. One good crew chief, Dell, left too. Thank God, Morgan was still here.

FNGs replaced all of them, *but it just wasn't the same.* It was like they left and took the heart of Bravo Company with them, starting a darker chapter in Dyson's final months in Vietnam. After evening chow, guys gathered in the hootch around the music and smoked. Most of the FNGs fit right in, but the stalwarts were just about all gone, their personalities and antics sorely missed. Very few who went home ever wrote.

Another thing was the increase in guys shooting heroin. They went from a half dozen in the Company to at least thirty percent. Just in his hootch alone it was Spook, Florida, R.J. Gray, and Riaz. The first fatal overdose was Sommerfield. Then in Dyson's hootch Medina OD'd but was alive when he was Medevac'd. Like all the most serious cases, Medina simply disappeared. Whether he died or not was never known. Now during evenings there would be one group smoking pot with music, one group shooting heroin that didn't need music, and one group just disappeared for a few hours.

Such was his mindset when on Sunday, October 12, he and Morgan were scheduled on *085* with Reynolds and Cavecchio. Reynolds had told Taylor in Operations he wanted to fly with Cavecchio, Morgan, and Dyson whenever possible—Taylor would make it happen. It was great when crew members knew they could depend on each other.

The 137th ASH was part of a large 2nd Airmobile Division operation to entrap and destroy a known Viet Cong brigade in Phuoc Long province. This brigade was led by a cadre of battle-hardened veterans of the French occupation twenty years before. They got rid of the French and they were going to get rid of the Americans, too. It was a formidable, crack unit notorious for brutality, torture, and life-and-death domination over the province. Villagers disobeying their rules were executed. Death for the guilty party, death for the entire family. Usually, the guilty party had to watch his family murdered one by one, and then he was executed.

The plan was to have elements of the 2/5, 2/12, and 1/8 Infantry Brigades of the 2nd Airmobile deploy by helicopter in a circle four miles across. Joining the infantry would be companies from the mechanized units with forty APCs, ten big M48 Patton tanks, and twelve light recon M24 Chaffees. Any kind of heavy vehicle got stuck in the red muck of the monsoon. Also on hand were the Aerial Rocket Artillery gunship companies and artillery batteries.

"No monsoon rains are going to keep us from trapping and annihilating the Viet Cong in Phuoc Long," Brigadier General Roland R. Richards, the 2nd Airmobile Division commander, vowed—while he stayed dry in Long Binh.

At dawn that Sunday, every available ship was up in the air and all other standby ships and their crews would be at Phuoc Vinh. Troops and equipment were ferried from Phuoc Vinh and scattered LZs to locations comprising the encirclement. *085* on-loaded troops at Phuoc Vinh and delivered them to their new LZ. Then it was back to Phuoc Vinh and repeat, four times. The mood of just about all the grunts being moved around was somber to say the least, anticipating weeks in the field, days and nights of rain, and enemy contact almost guaranteed. On the fifth trip from Phuoc Vinh, *085* carried new body bags—a stack of factory-folded and banded heavy-duty black rubberized fabric, 36 inches by 90 inches, ready for use. Unzip heavy-duty zipper, insert remains, zip up tight.

By the time the rains started at 14:20 hours, almost all units and equipment were in place and digging in for the night. Only one sector of the encirclement experienced any contact. So far, so good. The last two missions for *085* were flying hot meals to a Company of the 2/5 and carrying mail and various supplies. Then it was back to Long Thong for the night.

"Same thing tomorrow, gentlemen," said Reynolds.

I III I

Just as the lieutenant said, Monday the thirteenth was going to be the same. Superstitious people surface everywhere, and flight companies have their share of guys who do not like flying on the thirteenth of any month, no matter what day it falls on. It weighed a little on Dyson's mind, along with all the other baggage of the war. But he was on the same ship with the same crew and felt safer with them than any other crew members and pilots. You're going to make it home, he kept telling himself.

Today was the second day of the Division's big search and destroy mission. All units would begin their advance, closing in. Word was there would be missions of picking up troops in the field and leapfrogging them around to strategic locations. There were to be no gaps through which the VC could escape—above ground, anyway.

The rains had filled many of the tunnels and bunkers, but the NVA and the VC did not have to go deep to hide. They were the masters of camouflage and concealment. They were invisible when they wanted to be.

As planned, some units were already entering rice farming villages. These places were known to support the VC with men and women soldiers, money, and rice. They were pro-VC whether they wanted to be or not. The units began their systematic search for tunnels, bunkers, and caches. Any excavation under a floor of a hootch meant it would be burned down or leveled by APC or tank. The villagers were caught between two brutal forces. Appeasing one side brought the wrath of the other.

Meanwhile, *085* continued transporting troops and supplies— many, many short hops—as did the other 137th ASH ships. At 11:45 hours the radios exploded with reports of hostile fire in the northwestern section of the 2/5. A village they approached opened up on the troops and ships. Immediately, there were American casualties. One ground unit was requesting Aerial Rocket Artillery gunships on the outskirts of the village. An Alpha Company ship was hit and landed on its side on a dike. The VC fled before the ARA got there and the crew of the ship was rescued.

Now it was back to Phuoc Vinh for fuel, noon chow, and standby. After setting down, Reynolds and Cavecchio went to the officers' mess hall (which was pretty impressive for a forward area) and Morgan and Dyson went to their enlisted men's mess hall, a roomy wood-frame, heavily bunkered, tent-top, chicken coop-type affair with a leaky roof. Other gunners and crew chiefs were there along with a permanent party. Surprisingly, the hot chicken noodle soup was top of the line, and the ham-on-white-bread sandwiches were fresh. Plus, the milk was cold and the coffee hot. The crews from Alpha and Bravo Companies mixed and ate.

Morgan and Dyson sat down at a long table. The guy across from Dyson was leaving big black fingerprints on his white bread sandwich. What did it matter? He was eating it black marks and all.

"Name's Roccoco," just like on his uniform. They shook hands.

"You guys can have seconds! Seconds!" a cook announced. Dyson couldn't believe his eyes. It was a cook from his Company mess hall in Fort Eustis. They recognized each other at once. Here was a guy he knew from the States, light years away. It was a little boost to his morale, and then it was over.

As they left the mess hall, they passed a lifer SSG telling the crews. "You guys can hang out in the EM Club," the sergeant said, "but no beer, ya hear?"

Since Phuoc Vinh was Field Headquarters for the Division, wooden walkways above the puddles made getting around much easier. And there it was, a sign above said, "Welcome to the Long Branch Saloon. Enlisted Men Only. Lifers Keep Out." How do they get away with that?

It sure reminded them of the Old West—everyone with sidearms, loud music, and tons of smoke. Tons of tobacco smoke, that is, but with a hint of Golden Triangle pot. Morgan and Dyson started scouting for sources. A puff or two now would be great.

Arthur Brown was belting out, "I Am the God of Hell Fire!" It was a party. Who knew if they would be alive later tonight?

"That guy looks like his eyes are welded shut. Let's sit there," Morgan said. Bingo.

"Hey, man," said the red-eyed guy, "have a seat. Name's Lizard." They shook and said their names. Four other guys were at that table. One of them was telling a story.

"Why they call you Lizard?"

"'Cause of my last name. Lazzaro." It was all in good humor, like being peace-loving hippies back home. Mister D couldn't wait to let his hair get long, maybe even grow a beard. There was raucous laughter, loud spacey talk, rambling stories, rock music, and pot. Fuck the war. Forget the war. It was just outside the door.

The storyteller went silent. "Oh, man, what were we talking about?" Everyone laughed.

"Here, man," said Lizard, and he had a factory-rolled joint going. Dyson took a hit, passed it, exhaled, and lit a Camel. Everyone was smoking something.

"I've heard stories how they make these things, man," Lizard said, admiring the factory-perfect marijuana cigarette. "They blow out the tobacco from each tube with a bicycle pump and then use the pump to suck back in the pot." One guy imitated the job raising his arm up and down.

"Out with the bad, in with the good."

They were stoned. Morgan and Dyson knew Reynolds didn't like pot smokers, so they took it slow. A sergeant from Operations came in, unphased by the smoke.

"OK, we need the crews from ships *044, 046, 050,* and *051.* Down to the flight line, gentlemen." Those ships were from the 139th ASH, not theirs, the 137th.

Eight crew members got up. "Back to the war . . ."

"Peace, man." The peace symbol was thrown, two fingers like a "V" with the palm-side out. Churchill's "V" in WWII was with the palm facing in, meaning Victory.

"Peace."

"Be safe, man."

"Safe return."

"We'll have a seat for you." And off they went.

"God watch over you."

"God? What the fuck's God got to do with us?" Whoa.

"Yeah, man, you're right. What's God got to do with us?" That kind of talk made Dyson uneasy. He didn't want to go to hell, but he did wonder where God was.

Morgan said in Mister D's ear, "Even I can only take so much hippie-talk, man."

"Me, too. Wanna go?"

"Yeah, let's go sit on the ship." They said their good-byes.

It was a relief to get out in the air, and the relative quiet of the damn muddy camp. The mechanics and crews and pilots were conferring about the ships and the missions. As they passed by it seemed some of the pilots had been drinking. They were glassy-eyed, unsteady. Morgan and Dyson reached *085*, checked things out, and put on their ponchos expecting to get rained on. Reynolds and Cavecchio caught up to them.

"Get ready. We'll be flying home for the night."

There were enough ships operating and on standby around Phuoc Vinh. It was important for eight ships from Bravo Company to get back to Long Thong for service and repairs, with ships and crews ready for flight by 06:00 hours. They landed around 14:20 hours. The rain had just started. Thank God for small favors.

I IIII

After they returned to Bravo Company area, Dyson shed his clothes down to his underwear, wrapped up some clean dry underwear and socks in a dry towel, and put on his poncho, steel pot, and dry boots. This is how guys went to and from the shower in the monsoon. Everyone had to get those wet clothes and socks off, shower (or take a quick helmet bath), rub salve where needed, and hope not to get infections.

Once cleaned up, they had evening chow, then back to the hootch. He was tired—tired of this whole place, the mindset, the slaughter, dead civilians, displaced people, the frustration, and the loneliness that can come while living in a Company of a couple hundred men. He could sure use a good laugh if there was one.

I III I

A few of his good friends were gone now from the hootch. OD was replaced by Phil Wiggins, the private first class who was a bookworm. Ramirez's bunk belonged to another PFC named Roland Glotz, drafted because he couldn't prove he was the sole support of his mother. SP4 Roberto Hernandez replaced "Iron Cock" O'Grady, but he didn't have a big love muscle like O'Grady. Maris, the pot-cereal eater, was replaced by PFC Gary Parleki, a chain smoker from Boston. And Medina, who OD'd and was Medevac'd, was replaced by SP5 Tim Collins, drafted the month he graduated from college. Spook, Miami, Riaz, and Gray were heroin users. Kranicki, Super Chicken, and Rector were the only old potheads left. Dyson joined them in Rector's area for music and smoke. It didn't seem the same.

"Can we join you guys?" Glotz and Parleki had walked over.

"Sure can." Room was made for them to sit. Music and Marlboro Greens were passed around.

Fifty-three days to go.

I III I

The next morning, October 14, the Hueys and crews were ready to lift off at 06:00 hours. A little *deja vu*—same ships, same crews, same pilots. Crews were at the ships, either seated inside or standing next to them. 06:10 hours and no word to lift off. 06:20 hours and word spread there were changes in today's missions. Here we go again—some of the brass, in their offices, want to make changes. What an organization. It was 06:30 hours. There was hot coffee in the standby shack.

"What's the thing they say sometimes? Hurry . . . something."

"Hurry up and wait."

"Yeah, that's it. Hurry up and wait, man."

Really, what are they waiting for?

Finally, at almost 07:00 hours the word was out. Each ship had changes in their mission's sheet. Couldn't these have been done when the ships were in the air? Bravo and Alpha Company ships lifted off, cruised down the runway and gained altitude to three thousand feet, the bottom of the cloud cover. They started going their separate ways in groups. *085* headed to Phuoc Vinh, pickup resupply, and drop it off to a Company of the *2/8* that spent a quiet night next to a hamlet in VC country. They were part of a four-Huey formation for the day, and Reynolds was the group commander as well as the commander on his aircraft. He was going to be a captain soon.

The four ships set down at Phuoc Vinh, piled on supplies, and headed for their drop-off point with C Company, *2/8*. About two miles from touchdown, the C Company commander, code name Comanche Six, radioed they were under attack by VC of unknown strength, and to approach the drop-off point from the south, hopefully away from the enemy contact.

The ships under Reynolds' command changed course and approached the LZ and village from the south. Ahead they couldn't see anyone yet, just red tracers, then some green ones. The VC were there. They were flying over scrub forest and then dikes and rice paddies. Normally workers would be seen in the paddies, but there were none now. The Company LZ area with three APCs was in sight. Gunners in the APCs were pouring fire onto the east side of the village. Green tracers began pouring out toward the APCs. The lay of the land, ground clutter, and the APCs' coverage afforded protection for the helicopters while they dropped off resupplies. The ships didn't seem to be immediate danger.

When *085* lifted off, Reynolds swung back to the south and the three others followed, away from the fire. Still, no one could be seen working the rice paddies. Reynolds was advised about a group of civilians a thousand yards north on a dike moving away from the village. Comanche Six requested aerial reconnaissance to determine if they were friendly or VC. That meant flying close enough to eyeball them and invite getting shot at.

"Roger, Comanche Six. *085* will give a visual, over."

The four ships spread out. *085* and *087* swung out and around a milewide circle and spotted the tight civilian group on a dike walking away from the village. These villagers had been through American searches before and would rather be gone when they arrived to avoid the interrogation by Company "intelligence officers," the shoving, taunts, insults, separations of family members, even sexual assault by the grunts. Everyone got squirrely in those situations, both sides, fearful Vietnamese, edgy Americans.

Reynolds and *087* circled counterclockwise, two hundred feet above, an eighth of a mile out. Dyson's port side faced the civilians, a mixed group of about forty, many holding onto each other. He could see bright sky-blue tops on some of the women, conical straw hats, and black pajamas. Women carried small children either papoose-style or on their hips. The older kids walked. The men in the group were dressed like rice farmers—"farmer by day, fighter at night," hide in plain sight. Some had bundles. Personal belongings? Hidden weapons? They were all staying so close together, not spreading along the road at all. Now he could see many walking with difficulty, shuffling and jostling. Why were they packed together so tight?

"Closer look," was all Reynolds said in the mike. The two ships tightened the circle.

Then on the radio, "Be advised, *085*, there is VC in that bunch . . . VC."

Were those people tied together? Dyson could see something like ropes joining some people together. Then in an instant that made him tighten his grip on the twin triggers, there was a flurry of activity in the group. People separated as far as their ropes permitted, some just knelt down, many were screaming, and all of a sudden AK47s and other weapons were brought out and up and firing. Dyson and the VC looked directly at each other. And just like when he was a mechanic and saw the three men blown up by a mortar round, time slowed down so he could think in complete sentences between every round as he opened fire on the VC amid the villagers.

"I've heard about this—hiding in hostages . . ." he told himself between the first and second round, "Little pumpkin faces . . . we're the bad guys." He could feel and picture the jerky mechanical operation of the gun, live shells going in, spent shells coming out. Between the second and third, "If we don't shoot . . . we're dead," between the third and fourth, "There are no winners . . ." and his murderous fire just spat out of both his and the other ship's M60s in a steady stream, dozens of rounds pouring into the entire group sending chunks of flesh, gore, muck, and water geysers high up into the air.

"How many VC? Four? Five?" The two gunners remained right on target for fifteen seconds or so until no one was left standing or firing. Just a fucked-up pile of civilians. Dyson doubted if anyone was left alive.

"Going in for a visual. Stay alert." Reynolds closed to a point twenty-five feet above the group. There they were—men, women, and children, and three weapons visible. They were definitely all tied together. And God, was this fucked up. The fusillade had torn apart the people—hostages and guerilla fighters alike. Gaping torso wounds, massive head wounds, limbs off, bloody clothes, expressions of agony and terror on their faces. The carnage was in its own lake of blood. Nobody moved, all dead. Half of them were kids. What did they do to deserve this? Take that pile of gooks, count them all as enemy KIAs, and inflate that number by ten. That's the way it's done.

"Good job, boys," said Reynolds in the mike. Good job? Boys? Is he even remotely a humanitarian or Christian? Does he have any compassion, sympathy, or empathy to what just happened? Is this how we get?

It had been a long Tuesday. He was tempted to just shed his clothes and do a quick whore's cleanup, eat, get stoned, and turn in. No, he thought, I am not going to start looking like the heroin users and other bums we got around here. He planned the gamut. Shit, shower, shave, clean clothes, eat, then get stoned, and go to sleep.

Floaty and Gator had made Salisbury steak and gravy, mashed potatoes, and canned, pale green string beans, served with home-made muffins and apple pie. They had the best two damn cooks in the entire Division. There was always time for a heartfelt handshake with the cooks when going down the chow line. There were some pretty miserable chow lines in a whole lot of camps. Floaty was going home soon.

"Love you guys," said Mister D leaving the mess hall.

"Love you, too, D."

Back at the hootch, Kranicki, and Super Chicken motioned for him to join them as they dug *The White Album*.

"Hey, D. Bet you're tired."

"Yeah, but I'd rather be out there. Oh, I don't know. It all sucks." He sat down on a footlocker. Now the two FNGs, Glotz and Wiggins, joined them. They'd been introduced to the dynamite pot that was everywhere. They accepted it with open arms, just like Dyson had. He could feel himself going up with the first big hit. The best joints with a menthol kicker, he loved them, the Marlboro Greens.

"Hey," Super Chicken asked, "you hear anything on your DFC?" Papp had put him in for a Distinguished Flying Cross for leaving the ship and helping bring the wounded infantryman on board on July 18. That ominous date—Dad died July 18, 1967, he graduated from basic July 18, 1968, and it was one of his worst days in Vietnam, July 18, 1969. What would next year bring?

The question took him by surprise. He hadn't given it a thought for months. "Nope, not a thing." Now he wondered a bit. But it was beginning to mean less and less as the madness dragged on.

Spook, Miami, and two other heroin users, Ulrich and Broze, came in, sat down and set up in Spook's area next to the five smokers.

The two groups weren't unfriendly to each other, but there was a coolness between the heroin users and the others who smoked or drank, or both. The four newcomers got a bowl of pot going to start them off.

George Harrison was wailing about his gently weeping guitar. It was raining. The 105mm Howitzers on the north side started firing a few H&I rounds—harassment and interdiction—into the woods. A pair of Hueys were coming in late. Now the four heroin freaks prepared to shoot up. They were ready to cook with their spoons. Wiggins' eyes bugged out when he saw what was going on. What was the percentage of users? 40 percent? 50 percent? Those guys were getting so bad the mechanics and everyone else had to pick up their slack in maintenance. Some were absolutely worthless.

Spook, Miami, and Dyson used to be good friends, but there was the distance between them now. Spook and Dyson happened to lock eyes.

"Wanna try it?" he asked Mister D.

D looked at Soup who shook his head no. D shook "no" also.

"O . . . K . . ." said Spook, "Wanna try smokin' it? Just a little?"

Still D shook his head. He didn't want to start slipping downward. He saw the heroin users barred from flight status, he saw the ODs, he remembered Sommerfield, and he pitied the way these guys looked so wasted. He didn't like a lot of the lifers and pilots, but he didn't want to get on their shit list either.

Two guys tied off their veins while the other two cooked their works, then shot themselves up and released the rubber hoses. They fell back into instant euphoria—like Dyson did on opium with the grunts. Then the other two shot up and drifted off. The four were gone. They would be out of it for hours. Wiggins just stared. He would write home about this.

During their wandering conversations, it turned out Wiggins and Glotz were OK guys, good additions to the hootch. Wiggins was sharp and said he had a bachelor's degree in something. They weren't dummies, yet they wanted to know how to get on flight status.

After *The White Album* and *Live at the Fillmore,* it was time for the mechanics and Mister D to turn in. It was 22:20 hours. One quick piss and he hit his bunk.

He closed his eyes and soon the sound of the surf breaking and the salt air enveloped him . . . They were on the five-mile-long beach on Block Island, during the summer . . . everyone was scattered along the length of the beach . . . Linda and Sherry were there . . . Dutch and Bobo . . . it seemed like they were still in high school . . . but everyone else was Vietnamese . . . what's going on? . . . this group of sunbathers Vietnamese . . . those swimmers Vietnamese . . . he and the two girls neared a small Vietnamese boy playing in the white water up to his knees . . . the kid gave them a look like he had received many times from those people . . . they said "Hi" . . . the boy bent down putting his hands into the surf and pulled up an AK, snapped the bolt, aimed at them and screamed, "You die, GI!"

Fifty-two days to go.

▌▐▐▐▌

China White

Another Bravo Company member who would be missed was Green, the permanent CQ who knew where every man worked, knew where every man bunked, knew who would be flying. He had tons of knowledge that kept the Company on time schedules. Dyson never heard he was going to go home; he was just gone. But Green had spent time breaking in a new man for the job, Armand Gershon, a Spec. E4 from Georgia. Everyone started calling him "the Bird," because he looked like a bird—a stork or an egret or something.

So, when Gershon woke him up on October 15, Dyson didn't recognize him right away and didn't know where he was or what day it was. The dreams last night still had his mind messed up.

"Dyson? Dyson, right?"

"Yeah. Am I flying today?"

The Bird looked at his notes, "No. Maintenance."

"You SURE I'm not flying today?"

"Ah, yeah. Maintenance. Says so here," meaning his notes.

"Let's see," and the Bird's notes were some of the sorriest, scrawled, and scattered lists with scribbled, second grade printing that included cross outs and arrows and names jammed in between names. "Jesus."

"No, I mean it. You're in Maintenance today, believe me."

"O . . . K . . ." and he started dressing. Hope he's right.

He was sitting on his footlocker lacing up his boots in the low light of the hootch when he looked at the floor across the aisle to something on the floor. That was Gray's area. Gray had shot heroin last night and was still out in his bunk. In one deft move, Mister D snatched the object off the floor, faced into his own wall locker, and looked at it. All rolled up in a cigarette-pack cellophane wrapper were about two small bowls of China White heroin. The wheels started spinning. He would smoke it, not shoot it, the first opportunity he had. Dyson tucked it out of sight in a fatigue shirt hanging in his locker and went to morning chow. Morgan came down the chow line and sat with him. Morgan was in regular fatigues, no flight suit.

"You're not flying either?" Dyson asked.

"Reynolds told Taylor to give us a day off. Then he asked Brady to give us a day off from Maintenance. So we have a day off in company. We can't go anywhere or do anything, but we have the day off. I feel like getting drunk."

That happened once in a while; guys would get a day off. This was going to give him the time to do the stuff he found. He knew what he was going to do, and who to ask—Florida.

"I don't feel like getting drunk and hung over. I just may read all day."

"Suit yourself, buddy."

Florida was at the hootch, slowly getting ready to go to work. They had been good buddies until Florida started shooting up and hanging with another crowd.

"Florida, how goes it?"

"Oh, you know . . ." He really looked like shit—not like he used to. "What's up?"

"Someone gave me a little China White. For a first timer, ya know."

"You don't want to shoot it, do you?" D shook his head. "Well, smoking it is a hassle. Just snort it. Same thing."

"How much do I snort?"

"Got it on you?"

"No," he lied. The stash he found could have been Florida's, he didn't know. "I hid it."

Florida took a pencil and mapped it out on a pin-up of Barbie Benton on his wall locker. "'Bout this long, that wide. Roll up a straw of some sort and snort it up all at once. POW! Takes about ten seconds to hit you."

"Thanks, man."

"You know," Florida said, "I've snorted it, smoked it, and shot it. Snorting and smoking will get you there, but shooting it . . . Wow, man, wow! Much more intense, man. Much more." Mister D started to walk away. "Oh, you won't be able to do much for a while. Best to plan ahead so you don't attract attention."

By 08:15 hours there was no one else in the hootch. The hootch maids would not be around until 10:00 hours. He made a little sign "DAY OFF," put it on his footlocker in plain sight, and made it appear he would be reading—*Playboy*—and napping under his mosquito net. He prepared the stash on the latest issue of the magazine, according to Florida's description. He made a straw by rolling up a five-dollar MPC, looked around, exhaled heavily a couple times, and sucked it up all in one snort. It was sweet and sour at the same time. Then he lay down in his bunk with the mosquito net obscuring him from view.

"I can feel it . . ." Warmth and light, even though it was damp and cloudy. "Oh, man, I bet I could go to work like this." An increase in strength and confidence. "No. Better stay out of sight." A lot of positive feelings. Happiness. Mellow contentment. The inside of the hootch beautiful for once. "Can't explain it. Just beautiful. There's nothing bad around here."

Two hootch maids entered to start work. "Oh, my God," he thought, "they're beautiful," even though these two were mama-sans in their forties and certainly no beauty queens, with aged-lined faces, leathered skin, arthritic hands, and red gums and black teeth from chewing beetle-nut.

"Who you?" one asked.

"Dyson, Mister D."

"I never see you. You gone all time."

He lay there, lost in his thoughts, letting the drug take him wherever, then realized he was descending into feeling just wonderfully warm. "I bet I could go to work on the flight line. Better not. Someone might see. I'm gonna get up and walk." He put his boots on and looked out into the company area. It seemed really odd being off, not flying, not working in maintenance. It wasn't going to rain for a few hours. A walk would do him good. He made sure he was in full uniform with baseball hat, sunglasses and lit a Camel. "Man, that feels good."

The Company area was easy to navigate on the wooden walkways, though ponds and puddles covered some of them. The entire camp was either pools of water or deep, copper-colored mud. Wheel ruts on the roads were like canals running every which way. He gave vehicles a wide berth so as not to get splashed. He walked to the mail room where Kosski was sorting mail.

"Hey, Ron."

"D. Come on in." He entered the CONEX and sat in a folding chair. "I heard you was off today. Let me finish here and we'll take a little ride around camp." That sounded good. Now he had his sunglasses off and Kosski asked, "You fucked up?" He nodded "yes." Kosski finished sorting and grabbed a mailbag. "I have to pick up a bunch of these and then put them on a ship to Long Binh." Kosski locked up the CONEX and they got in a jeep.

The sun was trying to burn through the clouds. Kosski drove slowly through ponds and puddles, over an occasional rock in the muck, and headed to the far side of camp to pick up outgoing mail.

They made a couple stops and then rounded a bend.

"I always light one up here." He lit a Marlboro Green and passed it to his friend in this deserted part of camp.

That menthol felt exceptionally good. He still had that sense of being mellow, happy, safe, warm, confident. "I snorted a little China White this morning."

"Oh, man." Kosski took another hit. "You can get 'drain bamage' from that stuff."

Drain bamage? That was funny, and a dire warning. Drain bamage.

They finished the Marlboro Green, lit cigarettes, and talked while they picked up the mailbags.

"I ain't doing that stuff. Pot's good enough for me."

"We smoked some O out at an LZ Dolly last month."

"Now THAT is what I like to do. Smoke some O. That's as heavy as I like to get."

"It was something else, all right."

"Which do you like better. Smoking O or snorting H?"

"O. Smoking opium, for sure." He took a drag on his Camel.

"Good. Stay away from the H, Mister D. Stay away from the H."

"I know I should."

"I mean it, man. You know what's been happening in our company. Look at all the overdoses. I heard at Battalion that they are going to start giving guys piss tests before they DEROS, and if they show up dirty with H, they ain't going home right away." Kosski had said the magic words.

"Really?"

"Yes. Piss tests."

"I'm glad you told me that, old buddy. I ain't doing that H no more."

"I get some O when I want some, and I'll turn you on to that. Just don't do no more H. You know, we get this ass-kicking opium and heroin over here cheap, I mean dirt cheap. You're going to be paying hundreds of times more for it home, and it isn't even going to be ten percent as strong as this stuff. Then they wonder why they have guys going home that run into a $1,000 per day habit."

"That's cool, Ron. Thanks."

They arrived at the flight line with all the mail bound for Long Binh. "Now what ship did they say? Was it *086*? Or *068*? *066*?" Drain bamage. They both started laughing.

Fifty-one days to go.

▌▐▐ ▌

On Friday, October 17, Morgan, Mister D, Reynolds, and Cavecchio were on *085* again. The level of confidence in this crew was reassuring, a relief from some of the worry. The pilots trusted the two crew members, and they trusted the two pilots. On his way to the flight line at 05:30 hours Dyson stuck his head into the Operations bunker and threw a peace sign at Taylor. Taylor motioned for him to wait, then came over and said, "When you get back tonight, I want to talk to you."

"Yeah, sure. I'll look you up, man. What's it about?"

"Can't tell you here. Tonight, OK?"

"For sure, man."

▌▐▐ ▌

At 06:20 hours *085* and five other Bravo Company ships picked up supply at Phuoc Vinh and headed for a new Fire Support Base two miles east of the Cambodian border and three miles west of Loc Ninh—"Indian Territory," NVA stomping grounds. Reynolds was their aircraft commander and Brisco mission commander of the six ships. Besides internal cargo, three ships also had a load slung underneath for drop-off. The new FSB and three others were to be artillery batteries of 105mm, 155mm and it was rumored a couple 175mm canons, all aimed over the border. It was a hub of activity with Army Engineers bulldozing berms around the camps and firing pits for each artillery piece. The base they were to supply was called FSB Lucy. It was the closest one to the border. The entire area was the Fish Hook Region and the Parrots Beak—after shapes outlined on the border maps. No one had to tell anybody it was alive with thousands of NVA—thousands.

As usual for October, there was a low cloud cover at two thousand feet. Some low areas below were shrouded in fog, ideal for Communist gunners. Contact had been made throughout the area, all NVA. Ships being fired on and hit by .51 caliber anti-aircraft machine guns.

FSB Lucy came into view. The ships with external loads were first, one at a time. *091* went in, set the load down, then the ship set down, off-loaded, and lifted off. Dyson could see three 105mm Howitzers being set up and the second ship, *094*, approaching the drop-off point. Then an explosion went off between a howitzer and the berm. What the fuck? Then another one right on the FSB. The Huey had punched its load about fifty feet above ground when a third explosion detonated right under it. The ship was blown onto its side and dropped to the ground, blades smacking and bending until they hit solid earth, burst into a fire ball then blew up in an orange and black cauldron of burning fuel and smoke. More explosions on the FSB. These were no little rockets and mortars. They were artillery rounds coming from across the border in Cambodia. The Bravo Company crew and ship was lost, all hands. No one on earth could ever have survived that fireball.

The explosions continued every two to four seconds. The ships were advised to gain altitude, then leveled off under the cloud cover and made a wide circle. All they could do was watch the FSB getting hammered. These were Communist artillery rounds from several canons, much more powerful than the usual bombardments. At least fifty rounds were pulverizing the FSB. The shelling petered out. Had they fired the last one? What remained was an area of deep red mud with so many craters that they often overlapped each other. Bunkers, revetments, the perimeter berm, and some perimeter bunkers were in shambles. No one could be seen yet. How many guys did we lose this time?

There was no radio contact from Lucy. *091* had unloaded, so it went in for a closer look. After cruising over the base three times, the ship set down. Guys started coming up out of the remains of bunkers. Some were already clearing away collapsed sandbag-walls to find anyone inside. It would a miracle anyone to have survived that bombardment. The pilot of one of the Hueys took it on himself to set down in camp in order to Medevac. Six men were quickly loaded aboard. A second ship landed for a Medevac as more and more grunts came out of their shelters and dug for survivors.

The NVA forward observers had to have coordinated the whole thing, calling in the artillery at the right time and sending back the results. The NVA also shelled two other local FSBs in the same manner, but without the deadly results at Lucy. What made it amazing was there were no ground attacks after the shelling stopped. It was strictly heavy artillery from across the border.

Plans were hastily changed. Brisco was ordered to bring the Bravo Company ships back to Phuoc Vinh for short-hop missions, Medevac, and standby. When the afternoon downpour came, it was back to Long Thong. The wind, prop wash, and driving rain soaked the two crew members. The pilots stayed drier but not completely. Radio transmissions were garbled and broken up.

It wasn't too long after they shut down for the night that word came out on the flight line who was lost when *094* was blown out of the sky—LaChappell, Berthal, Anderson, and Harvey. Dyson made his way to Operations to see Taylor. He was still there, on duty. The guy was a dedicated son of a bitch who showed up early and stayed late, even popping in later at night.

"Hey, you too busy to get high?"

Taylor was officially off duty and joined his friend. "OK. Let's walk." After putting some distance between them and Operations he asked D, "How many hours you got for Air Medals?"

"Oh, shit, I don't know. About a hundred fifty hours?"

"You got like 200 or so. Listen, I have to give some of those hours to a couple lifers, man."

At this point, Dyson was not surprised. He earned an Air Medal every twenty hours in flight. He was getting out of the Army anyway. Some Air Medals would be OK with him. What difference did it make?

"They're ordering me to give a list of lifers Air Medals. So, I'm asking some guys like you if I can move some of your hours to them. We're changing the books."

"Ah, who told you to . . ."

"I can't tell you man . . . but it was Brisco." Brisco, reassigned here because of a black-market investigation up north. "I can't mess with the figures of ship numbers, but I can take hours from guys like you and give them to lifers." Lifers. "Brisco said he'd sign any sheet I give him. I'm sorry, man."

"Hey, I don't care," he said convincingly. "We get about one Air Medal every four or five days around here."

"That's why you're one of the guys I'm asking. I still got to talk to a few more guys with a lot of hours . . . Fuck this place."

"Who you giving hours to?" Taylor named a couple sorry motherfuckers that never saw the inside of a Huey in the air. Typical, so typical.

"Have you heard anything about your DFC?"

"Nope. Not a word, from anybody." Taylor looked more upset than Mister D. "I'm getting out anyway."

"Yeah, but a DFC, man. A Distinguished Flying Cross!"

Would it mean anything? Ever? It had gotten commonplace for officers to get DFCs and Silver Stars for leading troops in battle . . . from a ship up in the air above the battle. Majors, Lieutenant Colonels, and full-bird Colonels in crisp starched uniforms, watching with binoculars, calling in orders, and maybe disgusted things on the ground weren't going right.

Forty-nine days to go.

I IIII I

Tonight was Floaty's going-away party. He was leaving the next day and would be discharged from the Army. Floaty and Gator made damn sure the men had the best-prepared meals with what they had to work with. They said sometimes Broyer would pull strings, when he was drinking, of course, and get some of the real meat, real vegetables, and other surprises to help the two cooks do their job. Guess Pops wasn't as worthless as a lot of people thought. The alcoholic sergeant would get a lot of the credit from the lifers, but everyone knew who the real cooks were.

The party was at the smoking bunker the guys in Maintenance had made attached to their hootch. There were snacks, cold beer, music and, of course, smoke. Floaty wasn't the only soul brother there as other blacks came over from Alpha and Bravo Companies. Stories and jokes were told, there was a toast to the guys lost this past year, and an announcement was made about a surprise for Floaty—a "whore" had been smuggled in.

"Floaty," said Kosski, "we have a special going-away present for you—and here she comes!" Everyone cheered. It was one of the short guys in Alpha Company all dressed up and made up like a Suzy Wong "ten-dollars-clothes-off" Saigon prostitute. "She" and Floaty danced as the guys sang "Fortunate Son," the Creedence Clearwater Revival anthem about the privileged sons not having to serve. Bottles of Jack Daniels and J&B Scotch were shared and chugged. Marlboro Greens were everywhere and bongs were passed specifically for big, complete individual hits only. The number of guys whose lung-filling hit could take in the entire bong-load was growing.

"OK," Conley announced, "we have a special award for you, Floaty. Please come over here." Floaty joined him and was feeling no pain with the liquor and smoke. He was wearing a baseball cap with a major's leaf on it and holding a Budweiser. "Floaty. In special recognition for all the fantastic meals you—and Gator—made for us, for coming through time and time again, under fire, under harsh working conditions, under the heat of the tropical sun and the fury of the monsoon rains, we present you with this company's highest award," and it was held up so everyone could see, "the Purple Shaft with the Razor-Wire Cluster."

It was truly a piece of work: a polished wood pedestal about four inches square mounted with a one-foot-high, two-inch aluminum tube cut at a 45-degree angle on top. The tube was painted purple, and near the top gold-painted razor wire was bound around the tube several times like the Crown of Thorns. "Here you go. You earned it." Everybody gave him a standing ovation.

"Oh, God, thank you guys, thank you so much." The men hugged him and shook his hand.

"Hey, Mister D, I'm gonna miss you." He gave him a big hug.

"I'm gonna miss you, too, Floaty."

"I probably won't write," said Floaty.

"I probably won't, either. But I'll always remember you."

"And I'll always remember you."

If every night was like this, there would be no reason to seek a heroin high—maybe. His dark thoughts were gone—temporarily.

I IIII I

Gravy Run

It was Sunday, October 19, an easy day with only a few missions for the 137th ASH. Twelve ships flew out on missions, twelve were on standby. Dyson and Morgan would fly on *083* with Cavecchio and Phillips to Vung Tau, the in-country R&R center where he got the clap. Their mission was to pick up an internal load, unidentified, and off-load it at Division HQ, Phuoc Vinh. A gravy run.

The four crew members were going over a pre-flight inspection of the ship, as always, and reviewing the maintenance and repair records. It was evident that quality and production control was suffering from the slow and inferior work of addict-mechanics. Heroin's insidious infiltration was skyrocketing all over Vietnam, and absenteeism, carelessness, apathy, inability, and erroneous entries had steadily made their way into an array of responsibilities, all of which were quite evident in Maintenance. It was always a bit unnerving to climb aboard an airship wondering if the necessary repairs had been done right.

Though the crew and ship were ready at 08:00 hours, they

couldn't leave until word came from Vung Tau that the load was ready and waiting. Wait. There was no estimate of how long that would be. At first the four of them hung around the ship. Then the pilots drifted to the Operations bunker while Dyson and Morgan headed to the standby shack. Somebody had made a sign with Snuffy Smith, a hillbilly in a popular comic strip, welcoming crews to the shack. A few other chiefs and gunners on standby were already there.

"They're probably going to wait for it to start raining," said a seasoned crew chief. A seemingly clairvoyant comment on the way the missions would go today. Dyson lit a Camel. He had been smoking more than a pack a day. Morgan said he had been smoking since he was twelve, Salem menthol.

They had been waiting for so long that the EM Club in Bravo Company opened for midday break. "Anybody want any pop?" And one gunner left to bring back a bunch of cold sodas. There were too many lifers around to light up a Marlboro Green. Dyson was thinking back to the high he got on his day off just as Cavecchio stepped in.

"Let's go." On their way to the ship, he said Vung Tau radioed and wanted to know what the holdup was—so typical of Army communication. Apparently, this load was of some importance to somebody and now they were late.

The ship was up against the three-thousand-foot ceiling of cloud cover. Everything below was dark red mud, deep green vegetation, or the mirror-silver of water. When it was like this, the skies were crowded with aircraft, many were being held below three thousand feet, sometimes lower. Rice paddies filled most of the land all the way to Vung Tau. He wondered if that little whore that gave him the clap was still working there.

Images flashed through his mind like they were on a slide projector: *094* blowing out of the sky and bursting into flame; the VC sappers surprised by the trip flare; the annihilation of helpless villagers tied to each other; the ammo bearer shooting the wounded man in the face; the VC walking up to the downed Bravo Company Huey; bodies in the rice paddies . . . Who knows what was going on at home? Did anybody even care that they were over here?

"Vung Tau in sight," Cavecchio said over the mike. There it was; the town and the joint-military base—Army, Navy and Marines. Airstrips ran in several directions. All kinds of aircraft. Rows of fixed wing of all sizes along with Hueys and Chinooks. It was one of the most peaceful areas in South Vietnam; even out-going artillery was rare. Some guys stationed there went downtown after work. A few even lived off-post among the civilians and VC. The VC were everywhere. Let the GIs spend their MPC on drugs, booze and whores—that money went right into the enemy's coffers.

Cavecchio was following directions over the radio. He brought the ship down and made an approach like they were in a Cessna, cruising down a runway, low-level to another flight line, waved in by a wing-walker, setting the ship down and cutting the engine. A three-quarter-ton truck swung onto the flight line and backed up to their ship. The driver, a sergeant and the passenger, a lieutenant, got out. The sergeant dropped the tailgate. The lieutenant seemed to be in a snit. He ignored Morgan and Dyson and talked only to Cavecchio. There were four plywood crates strapped in metal banding and four smaller wooden crates nailed shut. The smaller boxes were stenciled "FRAGILE" in red.

Morgan and Dyson stacked the larger crates two high, side by side in the center of the cargo area and tied them down. The smaller ones were centered, put on the webbed seats and strapped in. No way to know what was in them. Maybe the smaller ones were liquor, or they could even be a new weapons system to be tested in the field. Or was it a big-time black-market, graft, or bribe?

"Do not off-load these crates until Major Brisco says so." Brisco, of black-market-investigation-reassignment fame, their commanding officer.

"Yes, sir. Major Brisco only," Cavecchio assured the surly lieutenant.

Cavecchio and Phillips ran the ship up, lifted off, cruised down the flight line, and were directed to continue to the end of a runway, hovering at ten feet until told to take off. They were about seventy-five feet from the towering tree line that formed a barrier of palms and taller alatus and retusus trees. With its tail pointed toward the woods, *083* hung hovered there awaiting their takeoff command, being told there was an incoming aircraft on approach.

Above the engine and prop wash noise and the muffling of their flight helmets came the unmistakable roar of aircraft engines. Dyson and Morgan looked to their rear just as a goofy-looking, dark gray, two-engine Caribou cargo plane appeared over the tree line two-hundred feet away. There was only enough time for Morgan to yell "CARIBOU!" before everything was drowned out by the thunder of the aircraft bearing down on them.

Once again time slowed down for Dyson. He could see into the cockpit as two pilots, with white flight helmets, peered over their controls and dashboard. They were wide-eyed at the sight of the unexpected Huey, knowing a blast of displaced air was coming. Dyson could see the individual rivets on the aircraft's skin. The impact of the Caribou hit their ship like a hurricane blowing downward. Phillips desperately fought for lift to keep the ship from slamming violently into the ground. Instead, what he managed was to be blown downward in a teeth-rattling, hard set-down—BOOM! Then came the brutal bounce back up. During those seconds Phillips grappled to keep the ship level and stay in control as the turbulence vanished. All this within a span of four or five seconds.

Dyson wondered to himself what kind of mechanical damage happened. The ship should be set down and inspected.

"OK, *083*," said the tower casually, like nothing had happened, "You're cleared to take off. Have a nice trip." OK? Nice trip? Jesus! Did that shit happen all the time? Dyson wondered if the surly lieutenant had seen the whole thing, but neither he nor the truck was in sight.

That was a close one—another close one. Cavecchio, and maybe Phillips, also, had saved all their asses. What if they'd had some green Wobbly One for this "gravy run?" What if they had been a few feet higher, or the Caribou was a few feet lower? They could have been blown out of the sky like *094* and incinerated. There can be only so many close calls before the end comes. Dyson was afraid to admit it was his guardian angel or God that was saving his ass in all those close calls.

▌▐▐▐▌

Brisco was waiting for them in Phuoc Vinh. He took delivery of the goods along with two lifers and a three-quarter-ton truck. When the truck was loaded, Brisco told Cavecchio and Phillips that he had specifically requested that they fly this mission and thanked them for the good job, ignoring the two crew members. And this was the guy who signed and forwarded Dyson's recommendation for the DFC— or did he?

During these times of flight at higher altitudes, going from place to place, with nothing pressing going on, his mind drifted into a quasi-conscious state of thoughts and images bordering on dreams. Pictures paraded in front of his eyes. It seemed like light years ago he was home, and he was on a seemingly endless Odyssey farther and farther from that place. This land and what was happening here were surreal. Did other guys in the Company feel the same way? Did Morgan?

It was good to get back to Long Thong while dry. The rain wouldn't start for another hour—set your watch by it. When he entered the hootch, everyone was huddled at the other end. They were all quiet. One of them motioned him over.

"What's going on?"

"Florida, man. Florida OD'd and died, man," said Rector. "And Spook OD'd and was Medevac'd."

"Yeah," said Glotz, "they both came back here at lunch time and did some up before going back to work. It didn't go well." They had shot up with some of the guys present like they often did—but this time they either did more than usual or the China White was more powerful."

"The lifers do anything?" Mister D wondered.

"No, not really. We got all of Florida's stuff all rolled up," said

Super Chicken. It was all so matter of fact. Someone dies, his stuff is rolled up in one of these sorry three-inch mattresses, sent somewhere and an FNG comes in. They would have to wait for word on Spook—dead or alive if they heard anything at all.

Of the original four shooters in the hootch, Gray and Riaz were left, and they had been joined by Parleki and Kranicki. As the surge in heroin use in Bravo Company continued to increase, mechanics like Dyson and the other stoners were trying to fill the gaps in their flight hours. The lifers didn't want the shooters in flight status. Between the overdoses and rumors of piss tests before going home, Dyson swore he was not going to shoot up. "Twenty times better than snorting" was calling him.

The rain came. Dyson, Super Chicken, and Rector put on their ponchos and trekked over to the mess hall. Gator had made breaded fried chicken, gravy, mashed potatoes, green peas, biscuits, and apple pie.

"That's Southern-style fried chicken there, guys, Southern-style." The company was lucky Gator was still there, for now. Good food can do so much for morale. Gator was not going home without a party for him—and an award.

"If I had known we were going to have this fried chicken, I would have smoked a joint."

The guys walked on the raised, wooden walkways through the company area. On someone's sound system, the Animals were singing "It's My Life." Standing in the rain were two of the dogs that lived in camp. The bitch had a male mounted on her back with his penis stuck inside her, one of his rear legs over her hindquarter, the other three on the ground. He was facing east, she north, both shivering in the rain. Even the dogs were miserable over here.

Three guys got closer and thought they could help separate them, but they decided it was going to be painful for both dogs when they howled and growled to leave them alone. Then Barnette, the little hillbilly that cut the head off a dead VC, came over.

"Nah, leave 'em alone. It's OK. Let nature do it. They'll free themselves. I seen it before." Him being a hillbilly, they took his word for it and left the pitiful dogs alone.

The hootch was changing too fast. Two shooters gone; four shooters and six stoners present. Wiggins and Glotz fell right in with the smokers, so far. Tonight, the shooters were at one end of the hootch, and the stoners were in Super Chicken's area. Music was drifting through the company area as a light rain was falling. Then, POW! POW! Two pistol shots rang out. The guys looked out through their mesh screening and out the doorways.

When someone would screw up trying to clear his .45 it would only be the sound of the one round that was in the chamber—not two shots.

The "jungle telegraph" passed word through the hootches—a lifer had shot the two dogs, "to put them out of their misery." No. It was because he wanted to shoot something, damn asshole lifer. Just like when they shot JoJo the monkey.

"Shit," said Soup, "they would have freed themselves up."

No one and nothing was safe around here.

Forty-seven days to go.

▌▐▐▌

93rd Evac Hospital

There was a marked increase in NVA operations in the five provinces. Contact spiked Monday at Tay Ninh. On Tuesday a battle raged in Phuoc Long. A slew of missions had been scheduled for the 137th ASH for Wednesday, October 22. Alpha and Bravo Companies had all available ships on mission or on standby, which was at Long Thong and Phuoc Vinh. Troops from the 2/5 and 2/8 Infantry were to be inserted at three LZs in Binh Long and work northward. Contact with the NVA was guaranteed.

Dyson and Morgan would crew for Cavecchio and Wallace on 092. Wallace, a Wobbly One who'd joined Bravo Company a month ago, was showing great promise and hadn't made any mistakes— yet. He would make the sign of the cross, pray for a bit, and then cross himself again before getting on a ship. Officially Wallace was requesting duty as a chaplain. As they all were boarding *092*, Cavecchio caught Morgan's eye and said something to him and Mister D.

"I heard something in Operations I wasn't supposed to hear, you guys. It's gonna be bad."

At 06:00 hours, the ships lifted off to pick up the troops and insert them in Binh Long, six men per ship. Some ships would ferry supplies to the landing sites. The grunts were waiting for them at Phuoc Vinh, groups of six with their gear, lined up along the flight line. A line of ships would come in, set down, they would on-load, and then continue following the first ship to the landing zone.

This group of guys was a war-weary, seen-it-all, fatalistic, and aloof bunch. Where many rifle companies were strict with military appearance—full uniform, shave, haircut—these guys were the "screw you," "don't fuck with me" grunts seen in every war. Their skin showed the wear and tear of living in the jungle—sores, scratches, scars, and premature aging on their grimy faces. Many knew to light cigarettes *before* they entered the prop wash. Crew members rarely had to show them where to sit. Figuring out weight distribution and load balancing were routine for these infantrymen. Some sat in the webbed benches, some on the floor, and some on the door sill with their legs hanging out, like on the tailgate of a pickup truck, ready for the jump six-to-ten feet to the ground. They had peace symbols on necklaces and helmets, long hair, big mustaches, and stubble beards. The guy next to Dyson skipped his boots and socks for just a pair of Ho Chi Minh sandals. He stared straight ahead with his legs hanging out. One young scruffy staff sergeant spat his tobacco juice right on the deck and gave Dyson a "fuck you" look. The others just ignored the crew. So be it.

Everyone could feel the ship descending. They were coming up on a two-acre lot of elephant grass where three ships were off-loading troops. There was no enemy fire. The ships lifted off empty and their trio was next. *092* and two others landed and off-loaded troops. They jumped off and were swallowed up by the elephant grass. Still no hostile fire. They lifted off and gained altitude while making a wide arc back to Phuoc Vinh. Dyson watched as the next three Hueys set down in the landing zone. There was an explosion between two of the ships, then in rapid succession a burst of mortars rained down on the landing zone. WHUMP! WHUMP-WHUMP-WHUMP! He could hear them above the racket of the ship and his flight helmet—it was literally raining mortars. One round landed next to *095*, burst the fuel tank, then a fire ball engulfed it. *094* took a direct hit, and one of its rotor blades was blown off and cartwheeled, as another entire crew was immolated in a ball of fire. The third ship had already lifted off when it was hit in midair and burst into flames before slamming to the ground. Twelve crew members and three ships gone. Each downed Huey was pouring a cloud of black smoke into the sky. The NVA had encircled the LZ and had zeroed-in on every square foot of that landing zone with mortars. The omen from Cavecchio.

Who knows how long the NVA had this LZ and others nearby sighted in? All of them had been nothing more than traps. Green tracers raked the LZ from three different directions, and the infantrymen formed their defense. The radios crackled with requests for close air support and medics. The mission commander advised that the gunships would be there in two minutes and to hold on. All ships were to maintain high and wide circles until needed.

The ground troops marked their locations with three yellow smoke grenades, dropped at their feet. One Cobra gunship and one Huey "Hog" gunship swooped in and unleashed at least fifty rockets, dozens of rounds of 40mm grenades, plus electric Gatling guns and M60 fire. Many of their rockets were the "peckerhead" type (2.75-inch rockets, white with a purple head) loaded with flechettes—tiny circular saw blades made of stamped metal, thousands of them. A peckerhead would detonate in a purple explosion. "Purple Haze," it was called. The pilots and gunners aimed close to the grunts because the NVA were so close, raking swaths in the tree lines with surreal firepower that was amazing to watch. Then they were needed at another LZ and off they went.

Company commanders and platoon leaders made frantic appeals for Medevacs to pick up "many wounded." As two Hueys were setting down, enemy rounds kept coming from the woods that the gunships had just strafed. It was only small, scattered small-arms fire compared to a few minutes ago, but still a big threat. Door gunners on circling ships were providing effective return fire. Dyson watched as the wounded were loaded. It seemed everyone in the LZ was bandaged, walking or not, with the wounded aiding each other. When their ship set down, a medic jumped onto the deck and helped with seating some and laying down others as grunts lifted them aboard. There were blood-red field dressings shrouded over heads and faces, tourniquets wrapped around limbs, and gashes plastered over with mud, pebbles, and grasses. The medic worked on a sucking chest wound, then moved on to a serious head wound. He had a grunt with numerous wounds hold one of his own veins in his teeth, like a rubber tube, to staunch the blood flow.

092 was outbound for the 93rd Evac Hospital at Long Binh. There were other Evac Hospitals in RVN, all doing the same, going twenty-fours a day, seven days a week. This trip to the 93rd was exactly like a previous trip there. That's the same head wound on the same guy lying in the same place on the deck. The same right leg blown off below the knee of the guy slumped over on the web seat. The same sucking chest wound the same medic couldn't close. The same bloody steel pot that doesn't seem to belong to anybody.

I'll bet there's blood on my face, he thought, and wiped his hand across his face. It came out bloody. How did I know that would be bloody?

Dreams, memories, and images were getting harder and harder to tell apart. At least he thought he knew he was on this ship and not back in his bunk dreaming. Once again blood was being pushed along the filthy gray anti-slip aluminum deck, propelled along by the winds and prop wash, from front to rear, under their boots and into the seams and joints of the ship, gradually turning from shades of red to black.

Nobody knew back then that exposure to other people's blood, either directly on the skin or inhaling airborne blood cells, would later be the cause of serious diseases of the liver and the immune system.

By midafternoon, *092* had returned to Long Thong. It had been a day of three Medevac missions to Long Binh. Earlier this past year, he would have been viscerally shaken by this catastrophic episode. Right now, his mind was a constant blur of his conscious and subconscious perception. As he stepped off the ship for the last time, he thought he needed a few double-headers of Jack Daniels after this shit. Morgan called out to him.

"Hey, D, come over here." Dyson walked around the nose of the ship to Morgan's crew station. "Wanna see somethin' funny? Look at that." He pointed under his gunner's seat. There was a standing jungle boot with the bloody stump of somebody's foot, a splintered yellow bone protruding up a couple inches, broken like a tree branch. Morgan picked it up and carried it nonchalantly to the dispensary. Let them take it to Graves Registration. Maybe they can piece together who it belongs to. Maybe the guy who lost it is still alive in the 93rd Evac.

Forty-four more days.

I IIII

One day the following week, two FNGs were assigned to Maintenance and placed in Dyson's hootch. Bob Barnes had left the mountains of Idaho while Lee Cappachio was straight off the streets of Manhattan. Both were SP4s who extended their tours for six months. They transferred from the 2/5 Infantry to Bravo Company and were going to be door gunners. They had CIBs and knew all too well what life in the field was like.

Super Chicken made sure to show them around the company and took them to evening chow. They were comfortably at home in their new hootch by the time Dyson showered, dressed, and ate. When he returned, the Marlboro Greens were being passed around while Morrison belted out "Backdoor Man." He went over to Soup's area to meet the new men. They were so grateful to get out of the field. Naturally, both of them had been airlifted by 137th ASH ships a few times. "Its crazy out there, man," said Cappachio. "Makes no sense whatsoever."

"It's crazy here, and everywhere, man," Dyson said. An image of the foot in the boot was fresh in his mind.

"On my last day in the field," Barnes said, "a fire team brought in this little old man they found in the woods. He had an antique rifle, bolt action with those goal-post rear sights and two dead monkeys he had shot. Right?" He took a big hit of the menthol Marlboro. "Anyway, the CO and an interpreter ask the old guy a few questions, and he's shaking his head 'No, no, no.'" This old man was nothing more than a peasant trying to bring home some meat, and apparently, he had used up all his ammo. "A big threat, right? Well, the CO said, in so many words, 'Get rid of him.'" Barnes got quiet and looked to the floor.

After a bit, Cappachio lifted his head, swallowed, and said, "So some guys kinda 'volunteered' for the job. They take him down to this stream, or river, and they make him stand on this rock in the water and one guy gives him a short burst and the water just takes him away . . . He was no VC, man. Not a VC."

Songs by The Doors were being played in their hootch as well as the hootch next door in a competition for volume. What was there about their music that meshed with the war? The mood, the tone, the lyrics, and the psychedelic sound of the keyboards, drums and Krieger's guitar. Songs of death, sin, sex, revolution, the other side, and war. The Doors had it all.

"So then," Barnes said, "every time we went out, we had to bring back a body count, and every time the platoon leader reports five enemy KIAs—five. And it wasn't five. It wasn't even one. This platoon reports five, the Company reports twelve, Battalion takes that and adds twenty, and Brigade doubles it, and good ol' 2nd Division doubles that. Yeah, we're making progress, all right!"

"When's it gonna stop? 'Light at the end of the tunnel.' Bullshit."

"Let's talk about something else."

I III I

Halloween. Dyson received two letters, one from his brother and one from his mom. Oh, man. He knew he hadn't been writing even once every two weeks. Both letters felt small through the envelopes. When he got to a semi-private spot, he opened his brother's first.

He skimmed it. "Not much longer . . . Mom worried sick . . . doesn't sleep . . . few drinks . . . started smoking again . . . news on TV . . . try to be more positive in your letters to her . . ."

Now he opened and read his mom's. "News been terrible . . . worried to death . . . sick to my stomach . . . please . . . more often . . . my son . . ."

Guilty. I am so guilty.

That night after chow, before the music and the smoke started, he wrote a heartfelt letter to each one, begging forgiveness. To his mom, he whitewashed the whole scene, blaming the workload, guard duty, and KP but reminded her it's not much longer now. To his brother, he wrote exactly what had been going on, but not about his mental state. He couldn't go there.

Thirty-six days to go.

I III I

NOVEMBER

In a surprising turn of events, or maybe just a typical SNAFU in Army Administration, within the space of a week thirty FNGs arrived in Alpha and Bravo Companies. Many of them had an aviation MOS, some had been in the infantry, others had previous tours in RVN. It was like getting a Christmas present early. The FNGs were a much-needed boost to the labor force—maintenance and flight especially.

Some hootches had to absorb two more men, two more bunks,

and two more wall lockers. Every man had to move a little and give a little to squeeze them in. It was crowded with men and crammed with furnishings. The two SP5s coming into their hootch were Tim Maynard from Ohio and John Robertson from Colorado. Maynard was on his second tour as a Huey mechanic. Robertson spent some time in an aviation battalion in the states. Both had a couple years in college but never graduated.

On Monday, November 3, there was a mandatory formation at 06:30 hours. With no wooden walkways in the formation area, everyone had to stand in water or mud. They were shuffling along, lazily forming up by platoons, talking and smoking.

"Maybe you'll get your DFC today," Soup said to Mister D.

"Fuck it," he said, "it don't mean nothin' . . ."

He couldn't get excited about it after seeing lifers get Bronze Stars for not being there, Purple Hearts for tripping and falling, Air Medals when they didn't fly, and commanders getting Silver Stars for leading troops in battle, from a helicopter. The awards system had been defiled, along with duty, honor, country, democracy, patriotism, apple pie, the flag, the girl next door. Girls like Carol? Oh, fuck her, man.

After Enrico—of Donut Dolly fame—called them to attention, the sergeant turned the formation over to the CO, MAJ Brisco, of black marketeering fame. And they will retire with big pensions for this shit.

"Stand at ease," said Brisco. "It has come to our attention that there is heroin addiction in Bravo Company." It's been going on for months. Where's he been? "As you know we have had several fatal overdoses and many other nearly fatal overdoses. We are aware of men under the influence of heroin not being able to perform their duties," Hey, don't forget the lifers under the influence of booze. "Beginning now, we advise all you heroin users to stop using." Tell an addict to just quit, right now. "We will be looking for those of you under the influence. We will be looking for needle tracks, syringes, cookers, and any amounts of heroin." Amazing he never brought up pot. "Depending on the circumstances, users will face an Article 15 or court-martial, and a less-than-desirable discharge from the Army." A long, loud, juicy fart was heard by the entire company. Snickers, sniggering, then hearty laughter. Farts were always funny when it was supposed to be quiet.

"At ease! At ease!" the lifers yelled.

After the guys composed themselves, Brisco continued. "I encourage the Section Chiefs, the Platoon Sergeants, and the Barracks Sergeants . . ." Barracks Sergeants? Since when have we had Barracks Sergeants? "to confront heroin users and give them the choices to stop using or face the consequences." This guy has no clue. How can men with such little common sense and so little a grasp on reality earn positions of such responsibility?

Now there was a brief staring contest between Brisco and the men. Undoubtedly, some men in the company thought Brisco was a prime candidate for a fragging. How would it go down? Roll a grenade or two into his hootch? Put some C-4 plastic explosive in his light switch? Watch for him to go to the shitter? Brisco had nothing but contempt for his enlisted men. The feeling was mutual.

The company formation was dismissed. The guys walked back to the hootch. "Fuck that guy. Let's have a Marlboro Green." They shared a joint while getting ready for work. Riaz, Gray, and Kranicki got their works together and shot up. So much for the threats. Bravo Company business as usual.

For the mechanics it was another day of pulling inspections and making repairs. Dyson was working with Fredericks, Ernie Dell, and Ralph Gomez replacing overhead and tail rotor blades. Everyone was trying to get as much done before the rain started. The ship they were working on was at the very end of the flight line.

"Anyone looking?" asked Dell.

"Why, no, there isn't." Dell handed D a small smoking bowl of Golden Red.

"Always good to have a little break," Fredericks said.

A jeep appeared at the far end and was slowly driving toward them with the driver and four dogs aboard.

"Hey," said Gomez, "that's Major Isaac Hines." Damn Gomez knew everybody. "He's from the 140th ASH Battalion. Chinooks. Wish he was our CO."

Hines pulled the jeep up to a stop. "Is that you, Gomez?"

"Yes, sir, it's me."

The major got out of the jeep and the dogs did, too, milling around the guys, wanting to be petted. Hines was tall, like six-foot-five, needed a haircut and his ears stuck out. He had on a rumpled and faded soft cap. "Anyone got a cigarette?" He had some sort of Southern accent.

The guys whipped out their Winstons and Salems and Dyson his Camels. "My favorite. Thanks." He took a Camel and lit it. He and Gomez chit-chatted, then he and the dogs got back in the jeep and took off.

"He told me he's assigned here in the 137th someplace," said Gomez.

At 15:50 hours, the guys were closing the last ship they had to work on before the rain. They gathered their tools and headed for the hangar. Something was abuzz with the men there who were gathered and talking in small groups. "Hey, what's going on?"

"Wanna hear something wild?" said Smirk. "Brisco is gone, man. Gone!" This was damn good news. The asshole prick—more concerned with making money than the missions or the welfare of the men—gone.

"Is there a new CO yet?"

"Yeah, his name is Hines." This is great—a new CO and more qualified FNGs.

Thirty-three days to go.

▌▐▐▐▌

Brisco leaving was a big boost for everyone. No one, not even Jensen the Company clerk, knew if he was reassigned (again) or went home. He just vanished. A few guys said they saw pairs of men in

civilian clothes and sidearms lurking around the 137th area at night—
CID investigators. Enrico, Brisco's collaborator, was still around and
the grapevine said he wasn't talking about it. Hines was a hands-on,
get-the-job-done, treat-everyone-like-a-man officer and was on a
list to be a lieutenant colonel. His main mission was to keep the men
and the ships up in the air. Everywhere he went his dogs went with
him. The big anti-heroin campaign folded—for now.

▌▐▐▐▐

Brady

On Wednesday, November 5, Dyson and Morgan were assigned
to *094* with Cavecchio and Burke. The previous incarnation of *094*
crashed and burned at an LZ under NVA artillery bombardment in
October. Dyson saw it happen. This was a new Huey designated *094*.
Something is destroyed, it is replaced. Someone dies, he is replaced.
Today Hines was the mission commander, as he would be quite a
few times more, out there with his men. He was not at all like the
spit-and-polish prick Brisco who ran things from the safety of the
Operations Center.

Another helicopter assault was planned between Loc Ninh
and the Cambodian border. There was more and more talk lately
among grunts and the crews about just where the border was. No
signs marked that international boundary, no fences, no painted line,
just map coordinates. Infantry would get picked up by Hueys three
miles from the border, fly at 100 knots for five minutes and then
set down. By marking the time it took and their speed, they easily
determined they'd flown much, much further than three miles. They
were inside Cambodia, end of story. Not only would they be inserted
in Cambodia, but they also had to be picked up in Cambodia.

Nobody knew it at the time, but Nixon and Kissinger had a top-
secret program to have electronic grid squares of South Vietnam
moved due west so many miles into Cambodia and Laos. When
bombers had the grid squares and map locations in their sights, they
thought they were bombing South Vietnam when, in fact, they were

bombing Cambodia and Laos. They only problem was they swore about fifteen hundred people to top secrecy to do this, and not all of them kept their mouths shut. Did they truly believe no one would divulge the horrendous secrecy and deception? The noncombatant civilians in those areas were the innocent victims of nothing less than a brutal, illegal, non-stop bombing campaign.

"Brace yourselves, guys," Cavecchio said when the pilots and crew were inspecting 094 before liftoff.

Alpha and Bravo Companies were in the air at 06:00 hours. This time, 094 was one of the last ships to lift off. Dyson always mused about how a large formation of Hueys in the distance looked like a swarm of mosquitoes. The number of 137th ASH ships in today's assault totaled thirty or more. Prior to the troop landings, artillery and jets were going to shell and bomb the area, but massive bunkers and deep tunnels always sheltered the enemy.

Their ship was to pick up 2nd Airmobile Division troops in Phuoc Vinh and insert them at a landing zone between Loc Ninh and the border to the west in the nebulous area with the invisible line that was either South Vietnam or Cambodia. Since the monsoon season started, many of the grunts seemed even more dejected than before. When the sunny weather went away, it took something with it. Living out there was no picnic, and the rains made it worse. The flight to the landing site was one of the more morose transports Dyson could remember. The six grunts ignored the crew. Everyone was in his own personal world.

The ships began their descent. The troops stirred as they always did during these last couple minutes as they got ready to jump. Dyson and Morgan prepared themselves for enemy fire. The ships ahead of them, three at a time, were setting down, off-loading troops, and lifting off—no hostile fire. Nothing ever happened on the early morning assaults, he told himself.

Their trio of ships entered the landing zone next. Dyson could see U.S. troops here and there, mostly where the elephant grass met the woods. The foliage had swallowed the rest of them. As they neared the exact point, the prop washes from the ships swirled the tall grasses. When they were all hovering about six feet off the ground the troops jumped. That's when the shooting started. He could see the change in facial expressions as the men jumped into the LZ under fire.

All the tracers were coming from Dyson's rear, nothing toward him from his front. Morgan was laying down fire as Cavecchio accelerated and gained altitude as soon as rounds began piercing their ship. There was still nothing for him to shoot at. WHACK! WHACK-WHACK! WHACK! like thunderclaps above the engine noise and roar of the rotors, rounds were driving into and through the ship like molten green spears. He could see them coming from a dark area in the trees and laid down a stream of return fire. Suddenly the ship faltered and jerked before it recovered on its climb out of there. He continued shooting at his only visual target until they were over the tree line as they continued their ascent. He looked down and couldn't see anything of the landing zone—no ships, no tracers, nothing.

The radio reported the hostile fire. All three of the 137th's landing sites had come under fire. Once again, the enemy knew exactly where the ships could land and had them bracketed and surrounded within mortar range.

Burke's voice in the intercom said, "We've lost the AC. Say again, lost the AC." Cavecchio? Cavecchio had gotten shot. He looked forward into the cabin and could see Burke at the controls with blood splattered inside the plexiglass. "Gunner, check the chief, please. Check the chief."

Dyson unclipped himself from the lifeline, crouched down, and shuffled along the bulkhead. Morgan was slumped forward in his web seat. Dyson pulled him up by the collar and flak jacket to seat him upright. Jagged pieces of his flight visor framed his bloody face and throat. He had been shot in the face and neck. Dyson's left hand was on the nape of Morgan's neck. It felt sticky. He pulled it back and it was dripping with blood and brain matter. His friend was dead. No coming back. He didn't feel shock or anger or grief. He realized all he felt was disappointment. Just how callous had he become? His strongest and most dependable friend just died. What's wrong with me?

Again, Burke said, "Gunner, check . . ."

"One KIA here," was all he could say.

"One KIA in the cabin," said Burke. Then he radioed Operations. "094 returning to base with two KIAs, two KIAs. 094 out."

His biggest shock yet—Cavecchio and Morgan, at the same time. Fuck this place. He had to look in the cabin. Stooping through the companionway, he saw Cavecchio in his seat and that Burke had pushed his feet away from the pedals. He was facing skyward, still in his flight helmet. Every plexiglass panel of the cabin had bullet holes through it. Lucky Burke appeared not to be wounded. Cavecchio had multiple wounds. Dyson went back and reattached himself to his seat. He was numb. No negative feelings at all. Just numb.

A crowd awaited them when they landed at Long Thong. The men descended on their ship as Burke was shutting it down. Officers went to the cabin to retrieve Cavecchio. Enlisted men retrieved Morgan. Dyson joined them on Morgan's side of the ship. He was carefully set on a litter like he was still alive. As the group carried him around the rear of the ship, they saw Brady inspecting Dyson's M60 with the pan up and looking into the brass catcher.

"What the fuck are you looking at?" demanded Dyson.

Brady closed the pan with a snap and said, "I wanted to see if you returned fire."

In a second, Dyson slammed into Brady football-style and started pummeling him on the ground.

"You motherfuckin' chickenshit lifer!" He rained heavy blows on Brady's face and head. This was one of the guys who was getting an Air Medal by claiming someone else's flying time.

"D! D! For Christ's sake . . ." Four guys got the two up and separated. It took a while for Dyson to stop throwing punches, but he was still hot. He had been out of control—rage, adrenaline pumping, heart rate up, heavy breathing. Brady was a bloody mess with most likely a broken nose.

CPT Horstall, the Maintenance OIC, walked up to the group. "Sir," Brady said, "I want this man court-martialed." He wiped bloody mucous off his face. After all, an SP4 had just assaulted a sergeant first class.

"That's up to Major Hines, Sergeant." Horstall half-smiled at Dyson. He knew what happened, and Brady deserved all of that and more. "I want you to go to the dispensary, Sergeant, and see if your nose is broken."

"Yes, sir," Brady walked away, desperate to get out of there.

"Watch that motherfucker get a Purple Heart." Everyone knew what the game was around here. Christ, Dyson was wearing a .45. He could have easily shot Brady. Dyson looked at his left hand, the one he had cradled Morgan's head on, and there was his friend's blood and brain matter dried on his palm, wrist, and sleeve. He'd have to scrub it off.

I III I

The afternoon rains seemed to finally cool off Mister D. Word had spread all over Alpha and Bravo Companies about Brady getting his ass beat. He had a broken nose and a black eye. He was lying low in the NCO Club, getting drunk, telling everyone he tripped backward over the lip of a PSP panel; otherwise, he would have pummeled Dyson in a fair fight. "Then go get him, Brady!" one lifer said, but Brady stayed put.

Dyson didn't respond much to the praise he got for decking Brady. If he had assaulted a sergeant in the states, he would have been in the brig awaiting court-martial. Small comfort. Now they were back in the hootch for the evening.

Super Chicken put on a reel of one of his jam tapes. No one knew what song was coming next, just like an FM radio station back home, but without the DJ.

"This tape is kind of mellow," he informed the guys and started out with Simon and Garfunkel.

The newer members of the hootch wanted to be crew chiefs

and gunners and looked up to Mister D. He was not only a crew member, but he had kicked an E7's butt. And here they were smoking Golden Triangle dope with this guy! For the FNGs it made the high all the better. The talk drifted from the war to back home to the demonstrations and back to the war. Wiggins, the bookworm, had seen Janis Joplin and Big Brother and the Holding Company at the Fillmore and talked about how the joints and the wine bottles were passed freely down the rows of seats. The smoke in the air was so thick "you could cut it with a knife."

"Things are different now in the States," Maynard said. "You can smell it in the streets."

"Yeah, and there are hitchhikers, man, when you pick them up, they don't even know where they're going," said Glotz. "Some nice broads hitchhike like that, man. And a lot of them don't wear bras anymore either." That reminded Mister D that Carol, that little slut, was due this month.

The shooters were in their own area. Riaz, Gray, Parleki, and Kranicki had finished passing a bong around—who knows what was in it. They'd been listening to the music for a while when it was time to get their gimmick together.

He remembered his first opium high at the LZ stand-down. He recalled snorting the little bit of China White on his day off. And he remembered Florida saying how shooting it was "ten . . . twenty times better." But Florida OD'd, and now Morgan was dead, too.

Dyson was unintentionally facing them when they took out their stash and implements. He had watched the process time and time again. A couple guys would cook the dope on a spoon while another tied off and waited. When the syringe was ready the shooter would take it, fire it into his vein, then untie the belt and sink into oblivion.

When one syringe was ready to go, Kranicki looked over at D and held up the needle like toasting a drink. It was a few seconds before D shook his head "no."

Thirty-one days to go.

|||||

By 23:30 hours, everyone was in their bunks, only shadows beneath their mosquito netting. Dyson was more mentally than physically fatigued. He finally drifted off, and his sleep bordered on being at rest with his eyes closed or seemingly open to the horrific scenes that played out before him. In his most recent nightmares, which could easily have happened at any time during the night, a figure bent down and peered at him. He couldn't tell if that was really someone who stopped in front of his bunk and bent down over him, or if it was just a dream.

"Dyson, Dyson. It's time to get up, man." Just inches from his face on the outside of the netting was a crew chief—complete with flight suit, a .45, flak jacket, and a flight helmet with the visor shot all to pieces showing a bloody pulp for a face. It was Morgan. "Come on, man . . ."

|||||

He had been having nightmares and bad dreams most nights for about a month. Up to now he would have both good and bad dreams the same night, before that were typically nights of good dreams, with maybe one or two nightmares a week. Almost all his dreams—good and bad—were about the war. He could no longer escape into peaceful sleep. Even the little bit of security he enjoyed when flying with Morgan and Cavecchio was gone. When his dad died, he didn't feel anything, but at the funeral he broke down and cried because he wasn't sorry. Now he felt the loss of someone and it hurt.

Thirty days to go.

|||||

Short

Everyone in his hootch knew he had only thirty days left. It was right there in plain sight on his wall locker, the daily countdown calendar. Dyson was up and about when Super Chicken came over to him.

"Hey, I got something for you." He handed him a short-timer stick. It was a fifteen-inch mahogany stick about an inch in diameter, finished and rubbed smooth, with a live 7.56mm M60 round pointing out from each of the ends, quite tastefully done.

"Wow, Soup," Mister D said. "Is that cool or what!"

"Thought you'd like it."

"Thanks, man. You're a good friend."

Carrying a short-timer's stick was "out of uniform" and against regulations, but it was overlooked in the 137th ASH. When he entered the mess hall for morning chow, he announced, "Short!" to a chorus of cheers, guffaws, table-pounding and applauds.

There was a work formation at 06:30 hours. He attended with the short timer stick under his arm. Three guys there had their sticks, too. Headcounts were taken, all men accounted for. As Dyson headed back to the hootch, Jensen told him that the major wanted to see him in his office right now.

"Hope it's not a court-martial," said SP5 Maynard.

He and Jensen entered the orderly room. "Wait here," the clerk said. He went in to tell the CO that Dyson was here. When he came back out, he said, "OK, report to Major Hines," meaning march in there and use the military routine.

Dyson marched into the CO's office, stopped in front of his desk and saluted.

"Sir, Specialist Dyson reports, sir!" Hines returned the salute and told him to stand at ease.

"Do you know why I sent for you, Dyson?" Hines still had all the bearings of a man from the Ozarks with backwoods knowledge, a sense of patriotism, and an all-out commitment to the mission and his men. Gomez had said Hines put the welfare of his men above all else.

"I believe you are going to tell me, sir, that I am going to be court-martialed, sir."

"No, Dyson, no court-martial, no Article 15. Horstall told me all about you giving that REMF Brady (He called Brady a REMF!) a whuppin'. Wished I'd a'seen it. Have a seat." The major gestured to the chair facing his desk.

What a relief, but now what? "Thank you, sir. I thought I was . . ."

"Well, look, Dyson, you and a whole bunch of other guys keep the ships in the air and crew those ships. That's what we're all about . . . Are your ears ringin'?"

That caught him by surprise. "Yes, sir. For some time now."

"You've got hearing loss for life, believe me. All you guys that fly will have it, believe me. It's no little thing, and it's going to cause you problems in the future . . ."

"It's constant, sir."

"Oh, I know. I got the same thing. I also know about the flight hours being taken from crewmen like you and the others and given to Brady and that bunch of REMF assholes. I also know you were put in for the DFC. It went forward a long time ago. It's still up there in channels. You think somebody's working on it every day and they're not. I hope it comes back before you go home next month. Also, that Purple Heart for a mortar attack some time ago. Which brings me to another thing. I am taking you short timer crew members, putting you in Maintenance, and will use you guys only if we have no one else that can crew. We are getting even more FNGs here soon. And we can't have those heroin addicts on flight status. I'm letting those guys weed themselves out. In my mind, I don't want to do anything about the pot smoking if I don't do anything about all the drinking around here, either."

"Well, sir, I don't know quite what to say."

"I want to see you guys get home in one piece, like you deserve. This whole damn war is being run all wrong . . . This whole talk was just between you and me, see?"

"Yes, sir. Understood."

"OK, glad we spoke. It's hard to get to know everybody, but you guys make the Company's work stand out. Don't think nobody notices. I notice. OK?"

Dyson stood up and saluted. "Thanks so much, sir. I mean it." Major Hines returned the salute.

"Dismissed." Then, as Dyson was leaving, "Oh, hey . . ."

"Yes, sir?"

"You got one of them Camels? I'm out."

‖ ‖‖ ‖

Kosski, the mail clerk, was another good friend in the company. Guys would be able to stop by the mail room and ask if they had mail. For those who couldn't stop by, Kosski would hunt them down and give them their letters and packages, even when crews came off the ships at night.

Dyson's mom was still writing twice a week, sometimes with a few words from his brother. He would write home once a week. He hoped his present state of mind wasn't showing. His talk with Hines, or Hines' talk with him, was encouraging, but the death and maiming persisted. Like an ice-cold abyss in his heart or soul, or psyche—he didn't know if he had a soul anymore.

Kosski looked up Dyson after evening chow. "Hey. Package for you." He fished around in his fatigue pockets until he produced a cardboard Rosebud matchbox, made in Ohio.

It certainly hadn't come through the mail. Dyson slid it open—something to smoke, copper-colored chunks of something.

"It's real opium-laced Cambodian Red hashish," Kosski said. "Rare as hen's teeth."

"Oh, man . . ." Dyson examined the contents. The smell was intoxicating. Someone had scribbled on the cover, "Do Not Operate Heavy Equipment."

"This is as heavy as we have to go. I love smoking this stuff. It's like religious," Kosski mused. "There's enough there for about two weeks . . . sparingly."

Mister D believed him. Right now, he wasn't feeling quite as bad, but he wasn't trying to get to sleep, either. Too much of it came back at night.

"Let's just do two hits each," said Kosski. "That's all. Then join the other guys and hardly smoke any at all with them, alright?"

"Just two hits," D agreed, "and just a little with them." He nodded down to the area where the smokers were getting ready for the evening ritual. Kosski produced a little brass pipe with a screen in the bowl, broke up some of the opium-laced hash, tenderly arranged it on the screen, and lit it with a lighter. Then he passed it to D for one carefully drawn hit. They held it in, then a long, smoky exhale. Whew. Kosski relit the bowl, took a second hit, and then D took his second. They could feel themselves slipping into a heavy mellow fogginess.

"Oh, man."

Down the way, the smokers were listening to Iron Butterfly, sitting on bunks, footlockers, and lawn chairs.

"Remember," said Kosski, "just a little will do ya," parodying a contemporary Brylcreem hair gel advertisement.

They walked over to join the other guys, passing the shooters in the middle of the hootch. Shooters and smokers staying separate. They sat down in Super Chicken's area in the smoking section. Marlboro Greens were making their way around. Dyson and Kosski both took one light hit. Of all things, Wiggins, who seemed to have read all the classics and tons of textbooks, Glotz, and Super Chicken were talking about the afterlife. What could have brought that on?

"Did you ever wonder what death is like? After death, are we able to watch what is happening? Or do we just forget everything and journey on forever? Do we have any consciousness at all?"

"My whole family and me believe in spirits, man. Our old Ohio farmhouse was built in the 1820s. There were spirits in it. We all heard them. They would say things even in broad daylight. Believe it or not, late afternoon was like prime time, man! One would call a name. We didn't know if it was 'Mommy-Mommy' or 'Minnie-Minnie.' Then we found out that Minnie Dortmunder was born in the house in the 1850s."

"Amazing, man."

"Then there was the rapping. If we were downstairs, someone would rap on the floor over our heads. When we would be in the basement, same thing. I put my hand against the bottom of the floor over us and it felt like a hammer hitting the floorboards. We ran up the steps and no one was around. No one."

"Did they ever get . . . ah, scary?"

"Nope. They were never evil or malicious or anything like that."

"Ever see any of them?"

"Never. But other people in town who also had old houses had spirits, too. One of them said the spirit or spirits would start showing themselves to my little sister when she started puberty. Sure enough, that's when it happened. When she was in junior high, she had one of her friends over for the night. They were sleeping in her room when noises woke them up. In front of them was an old lady with both hands shaking the coat rack next to the door. The girls held hands and walked right by her to get out of the room. And she just disappeared before anyone else could see her, but everyone in the house had heard the coat rack shaking."

"Well, my family moved to Pennsylvania when I was a kid. We lived on an old, Amish horse farm. The house was made of brick and the front porch had two front doors placed side by side. Place was fucking haunted big time, man. Footsteps going through walls and shit, man. Scared the living shit out of me and my old lady. Neighbor came by and asked why we blocked off a door on the inside with a cupboard. Told us both doors must be clear so good spirits can come in and bad spirits can leave."

"And what happened?"

"We moved it aside and never had another problem."

"There has to be something to the afterlife, man. Has to be."

"Yeah, well, that don't make me feel better about dying, or getting killed over here."

"Who the fuck wants to be blown the fuck up with your guts hanging out and go that way? Does how you die or get killed choose the type of afterlife you have?"

"If I die over here does my spirit stay in this place or go home?"

"Do all the guys that get zapped—Charlie, NVA, VC, us, rice farmers—have the same afterlife? Does a violent death doom us to something horrible for eternity?"

Dyson and Kosski didn't do any of the talking. They just listened. Dyson was glad this Doors album didn't have "Unknown Soldier" on it.

"What do you think about the afterlife after seeing what goes on out there?" an FNG who wanted to be a crew member asked Dyson. At least he was a little realistic about his question. Dyson thought of the one-ness he had felt with all the life around him when they had smoked opium at the LZ with the grunts. Right now, he and Kosski were on an intense stone of their own.

"I believe there is a life force out there, but I don't know how my afterlife—if I even have an afterlife—will fit into all this." He did not want to be part of this conversation right now, having to dig into death and suffering, the images and the dreams, the waste, and the futility. It had to stop, both in his mind and in reality.

Simultaneously, and without any word or signal, Kosski and D got up and went down to D's area. It was almost midnight and the rain had stopped.

"Let's get some air." They stepped outside.

"They kind of dampened my stone."

"Lots of times people think I'm listening, but I'm not. I can put myself elsewhere, like in a big psychedelic, phantasmagoric, inter-galactic rock concert in the stars with five million stoned hippies for an audience."

Now they had Dyson worried about an afterlife.

I IIII I

Later that night, it must have been at 02:00 hours or so, he finally fell asleep. The opium-hash helped, but he was still sleeping-waking, dozing, sleeping-waking, dozing. Lying on his back, he picked his head up when something moved in the central aisle. A big dog? It came into full view. It was a big, black cat, big as a Doberman, skulking and slinking down the aisle. Jesus. Dyson shifted slightly in his bunk and the steel springs creaked. The cat looked right at him and leapt out of sight. Did he just see that?

Someone started yelling.

"Leopard! Leopard! Leopard in camp!"

"There! Over there!" Bases all over Vietnam had experienced uninvited wild animals—leopards, monkeys, cobras, and other snakes, and a Marine base had found unmistakable tiger pug marks in camp.

This time he wasn't dreaming.

I III I

It was Monday, November 10. There were twelve damaged ships on the flight line and in the shops and hangar. Crews on each worked far into the night. FNGs were arriving every week. New UH-1s were being delivered, one and two at a time, with old ships set aside for salvaging parts. Ships replacing ships, men replacing men.

Clouds hid the moon and stars. Work lights powered by gasoline generators powered the necessary illumination for work. Large puddles and small ponds filled in the low areas of the flight line. A few of the ships had wooden walkways and pallets around them for the mechanics to stand on. The whop-whop-whop of Hueys could be heard in the air, near and far. Music was coming from the hootches. Rock over here, country over there, soul from another spot.

Dyson, Maynard, Gomez, and SP4 Carl Holgerson were in on the flight line with one of the older ships that had a dozen or so write ups. A hundred feet away, Dyson saw an FNG carrying a tech manual toward a ship in the maintenance area. In the next millisecond, an orange flash like a ten-foot-wide, ten-foot-tall curtain backlit the black silhouette of the FNG and his tech manual hanging in the air. The guy was two feet off the ground, head and shoulders pointing down. His legs were gone at mid-thigh, ending in nothing but shreds and rags. His arms were almost straight out. The bulk of the manual was spread wide open with dozens of pages suspended by the blast. The man and the book were there for an indelible millisecond while Dyson itemized what he saw.

I III I

That was the only round to come in. Once again, he had looked right at someone the instant he got zapped. Did this happen to any of the other guys? Did they have to witness the split second someone else was killed? Was it ESP, a skill, or a curse? What purpose did it serve? Man, just one time was more than enough.

As Dyson approached his hootch after 02:30 hours, guys were passing around a bottle of Jack.

"D! Want some?" He said no, he was going to try to sleep.

"This'll help."

No, it won't, he thought, and waved goodnight.

Tired as he was, sleep wouldn't come. By 04:00 he was outside on the sandbags, smoking a Camel. Guys were working under the lights. He stepped back inside and crawled under the mosquito net. From there he could see Blevins and Grouse cooking up some White. As far as he knew, those two had never been outside Long Thong to see the war raging and dragging on. But maybe just what happened in camp was enough for them. Did anything block out the madness?

I III I

Word was put out that all available ships and crews were to be up in the air or on standby Wednesday, November 12. Another aggressive sweep and destroy mission in Binh Long Province. Again, the war of attrition, take an area, then move out. The assignments of ships, crews, and pilots were circulated Tuesday evening. Dyson and Robano were assigned to *096* with aircraft commander CW2 Eaton Lewiston, a Crimson Tide football player in Bravo Company two months now. FNG WO1 Roy Stone from Alabama, fresh out of 137th ASH Battalion Orientation, was scheduled for his very first flight. Great. Something else to think about when trying to get to sleep Tuesday night.

Super Chicken caught up with Dyson when they finished evening chow. "Hey, where's you short-timer stick?" Shit. He had forgotten all about carrying it to chow. He had forgotten about getting short, forgotten to write his mom, forgotten what day it was.

"Shit, Soup. I just didn't notice it when I left the hootch." Soup made him go get the coveted stick.

"It's OK, man. Wish I was short."

Maybe he could turn in early. Maybe he could get to sleep. Maybe he could stay asleep. To think that when he came over here, he wanted so badly to be a crew member. Now look at him. If he had stayed in Maintenance and in camp all the time, how would he have been today? Who can say? What if? What the fuck?

Twenty-five days to go.

▌▐▐▐▐

He was wide awake at 04:30 hours when the CQ came through waking everyone. He must have slept for a total of one hour all night. Doze, wake, doze, wake.

"Big mission today," said the CQ. They're all big when your life is on the line.

Alpha and Bravo Companies were up and rolling. Music started blaring around the camp. Super Chicken put on *The White Album*—good for all times. Trying to cheer himself up, D carried his short timer stick into the mess hall.

"Short!" he yelled when he entered. Other short timers were there, too, and they let him know it.

"Short!"

"Short-short!"

"Short-ER, motherfucker! Ten days!" That is short, but he was a crew member, too, and might not make it. Were they showing everyone they were not concerned, or not afraid of any mission? FNGs wanted like hell to be crew members. A couple offered him a chair at their table. Dyson made like he didn't see that.

Back at the hootch, he joined Super Chicken for a toke or two of Golden Triangle. "My mom sent a big goody package," said Soup. "Look at this stuff—cheeses, sausages, cashews, almonds, chocolates, cookies. We'll dig into this stuff tonight."

"Looks good, man."

Soup expected his friend home tonight, which bolstered him. They finished a small bowl of the dynamite pot.

"See you later." Dyson went out the door and smoked a Camel on his way to *096*, his ship for the day, a new replacement. It arrived a month ago, but already some of the plexiglass in the cabin and skin on the fuselage had to be replaced because of bullet holes.

Robano, the crew chief, and WO1 Stone were there already, going over the ship. "First time together," and they all shook hands. Stone was athletic-looking and didn't seem nervous at all. CW2 Lewiston joined them.

"Nice to meet you guys," he said to Robano and Dyson. "I've heard you're good crew members." He shook hands with them. "You have my permission to fire whenever you need to." He had been out there forty times now, Dyson knew. The four of them went over everything on the ship: inside, outside, rotors, maintenance forms, nose to stern. Nothing deficient.

More than half of the 137th's ships ferried troops that morning to scattered landing sites in Binh Long. The remaining aircraft, *096* and seven others, were on standby in Phuoc Vinh or in the immediate vicinity. Medevacs were to be priority. Now all there was to do was wait. Operations in Phuoc Vinh told the men they could leave their ships but remain on the flight line and use the standby shacks—the nice one for officers, the dinky one for crews. Robano and Dyson walked to their standby shack just to stretch their legs and shoot the shit with other crews.

"Just like taxis waiting at the airport," said a chief named Argento. "Name's Tony." They shook hands.

"I'm D. He's Robano."

"Robbie," said Robano.

Most of these guys were from Alpha Company. D had never seen them before. They all had the look of weariness, physical and mental. Everyone had witnessed everything out there. Everyone knew that when your number's up, it's up. If not today, tomorrow, maybe. These were guys living on borrowed time, himself included. Worry increased the closer one got to going home. Standby for eternity, which is a long, long time.

D and Robbie locked eyes. Pot, someone's smoking pot right here. One of the guys had passed Tony a factory-rolled joint and he hit on it. He passed it to D. What the hell, he took a big hit. Robano was next. He could feel himself slipping into a stone. No one seemed to be looking. No one seemed to care. He lit a Camel.

Word spread around that a ship was returning to Phuoc Vinh shot up and losing power and control. Everyone looked to the west, where the missions were. A Huey could be heard off in the distance and it didn't sound normal. It grew louder. Then it was at the tree line, trailing gray and black smoke. Its skids sliced through some treetops. With that the pilot immediately tried to set it down but the ship was turned toward the port side and came down hard in no-man's land. As the volume and thickness of the smoke increased, the engine was shut down, and the crew—out of sight from the shack—scrambled to get out and away from the ship. Seconds later the fuel caught fire and the ship disappeared in a hellish fireball. That was close. The crew was lucky.

"Next!" Gallows humor. But really, who *would* be next?

Several pairs of pilots motioned over to their crews as they walked toward their ships. Dyson and Robano caught up to Lewiston and Stone.

"It's bad out there, right now," Lewiston said in a low voice. "So get ready." Brace yourself. The short timers were flying today because the 137th needed them, like Hines said. "We're going. Prepare to lift off."

‖‖

Binh Long

Within five minutes 096 and four other ships from the 137th were heading toward western Binh Long. The 2/5 and 1/8 Infantry were fighting it out with entrenched North Vietnamese major units—thick and heavy, bloody and deadly. Operations advised them the NVA had American colored smoke grenades to confuse chopper pilots trying to identify their landing sites. As soon as an American would throw a red smoke grenade to identify a landing site, NVA would throw their red grenades to disorient the pilots. It was very effective in the heat of battle, with the urgency of getting the wounded out and resupply in. This mission was going downhill all the time.

In just over ten minutes, their group was circling the battle below. To the west a plume of black smoke rose out of the forest where a Huey had gone down and was burning. Two ships were circling that area. To the north came a larger and blacker cloud from another crash landing.

"Be ready for Medevac," warned Lewiston and they began to descend. Lewiston didn't have to worry about smoke grenades since he'd received a landmark for a reference point.

When they had descended to an altitude of two hundred feet, rounds began smacking into the ship. Dyson couldn't see any sources of fire, but Robano was blasting away at something. Since friendlies were everywhere, he couldn't just lay down suppressive fire at random. At one hundred feet, Dyson could see tracers coming their way from a tree line. He opened up. They were shooting directly at him, the gunner who was answering their fire and defending the ship. Rounds crackled past his head. Three smacked into the bulkhead behind him. This was personal now. An NVA stepped out into view to get off a better shot. They both were shooting at an individual enemy—each other. Dyson laid out a continuous forty-round burst snipping off branches and sending up divots of earth until the enemy gunner fell down and out of sight. Enemy fire was coming from three areas. He could hear yelling in the intercom but couldn't make out what was being said. Jesus.

"Gotta get these guys off us," he hissed.

He fired over the tops of the tall grasses in the landing zone.

Lewiston set the ship down amid a chaotic bunch of grunts firing outward into the surrounding trees and grasses. A kneeling platoon leader was yelling into the mic of a PR-25 radio connected to a bloody radio operator sprawled on the ground. The three severely wounded ready for Medevac were thrown like potato sacks onto the deck and two bloodied and bandaged walking wounded were helped up and shoved onto the web seats. As soon as Lewiston lifted off, Dyson and Robano resumed return fire over the tall grasses. Liftoff and ascent seemed so pitifully slow when under heavy fire like this.

Now coming from seemingly everywhere, rounds smacked into the ship at an alarming rate.

"Jesus! Jesus! Jesus, help us. Jesus, help us, Jesus . . ."

They gotta hit something anytime now. Don't run out of ammo now! He remembered linking belts together in the large magazine under his gun. Come on, keep going!

White smoke escaping from the engine compartment was trailing the ship as they climbed up over the tree line. The shooting stopped.

"We're hit! We're hit!" growled Robano into his mic.

Get some distance between us and them, Dyson thought. The three wounded men lying on the deck were motionless. The other two wounded could only turn their heads from time to time wondering what was happening. One made the sign of the cross, moving his lips in prayer.

Lewiston saw the white smoke in his rear-view mirror, then black smoke started streaming out as well. "Heading to LZ Dolly." Dolly was the nearest "safe" spot to put down—if they could make it there.

This is a bad one. Are we going to die in these woods? Am I going to die in a fireball? Am I going to be pinned in the wreckage so the NVA or VC find us alive? VC will torture you to death. If NVA capture you, no one will ever hear from you again, or you could become a POW. Three equally shitty outcomes.

The ship was gradually dropping to treetop level while the trail of smoke expanded. Every gook within five miles in every direction could see where the ship was going down. Now Lewiston was just above the trees. "LZ in sight. LZ in sight." Thank Christ. The engine was losing power at an alarming rate.

Dyson caught sight of a Cobra gunship coming up quick to his rear on the port side, the pilot in front and the gunner behind him under the plexiglass canopy. The Cobra was catching up to them. Dyson held up two fingers in the peace symbol. The pilot waved back. Dyson looked ahead and saw the camp. Everybody there looked like ants running away from them, scrambling into bunkers and trenches for protection. That's a bad sign. The ship was nearing the tree line at the border of no-man's land for LZ Dolly.

"Hard set-down. Brace yourselves. We're going down . . ." Lewiston's voice trailed off. There was excited talk between him and Stone but Dyson couldn't make out what was being said. Over the clearing they sank to fifty feet, the tail sagged and the ship banked a few degrees, dropped like a rock, crushed the skids against the ship's belly and snapped the tail section away from the smoking engine compartment. The concussion bounced everyone a foot into the air. Without the tail rotor the remaining cabin spun violently twice, ejecting three WIAs out of the ship. The entire crew and the two walking-wounded were still strapped in, feeling every bone-jarring collision with the ground. The ship lifted one more time, spinning again until a rotor blade smacked into a tree trunk, stopping the whole mess.

"We fuckin' made it!" yelled Robano. Dyson undid his harness and freed the wounded man seated beside him while Robano did the same with his. Stone and Lewiston undid themselves, opened their doors and jumped out. With two guys holding up each wounded man they walked as fast as they could before any fuel ignited. There were only a few gallons left when it caught fire, no big fireball this time.

Grunts from LZ Dolly quickly came out to help with three "mules" (four-wheel-drive trucks, rated for half-ton loads) to carry the wounded. The Cobra continued to circle overhead, providing them with cover as the ship burned, sending up a cloud of thick, black smoke.

They were lucky. They were lucky they made it out of the trees; they were lucky a tree trunk stopped the rotor blades when it did; they were lucky they were not carrying a full tank of Av-Gas; they were lucky they had Lewiston and Stone to handle the ship; they were lucky they went down miles from where they were hit.

The three wounded thrown from the ship were not so lucky. Two were dead, the other was in bad, bad shape. A Medevac dusted off the surviving WIAs to Long Binh.

The officers and crew walked with some grunts into LZ Dolly. It was 14:45 hours. The officers were whisked away to the Control Point. D and Robano were invited by some friendly troops to a hootch that was "party central" in LZ Dolly.

"Who wants a cold beer?" Cans of Hamm's were passed around from an overloaded ice chest. A wild-looking guy wearing only shorts put on a tape that started with Iron Butterfly pounding out the legendary "In-A-Gadda-Da-Vida."

"Man, you guys were lucky, man . . . lucky," said a red tan SP4 named Janner as he lit up a classy briar bowl packed with coppery-colored pot. Another guy, called Soda, took a Winchester pump shotgun out of his wall locker, and slammed open the breech.

"I thought we was dead after the tail rotor broke off," Robano said.

"They told us a ship in trouble was coming in. A lot of those don't end well, man," said Janner, shaking his head. He took a big hit, then got the shotgun. He put the pipe stem into the open breech and chambered it into the barrel. Soda put the muzzle of the gun in his mouth while Janner put his mouth over the smoking bowl and blew. A huge volume of smoke poured into Soda's lungs on the receiving end of the barrel. He exhaled an intoxicating blue cloud that packed enough punch to stone every hippie at a small rock concert and grinned, "Shotgun, baby!"

"I saw all you guys running like ants for the bunkers," said D. His turn on the muzzle came and he easily inhaled the massive amount of smoke without choking. All these guys were experienced smokers.

"Yeah, but you made it, man . . . You made it."

"D here only has twenty-four days," Robano announced.

"I got ten," said PFC Dannon.

"I got five, motherfucker," bragged a SP4.

"They try to keep us off missions when we have under thirty days," said D, "but today they needed us."

"They don't do that around here. We stay in the field right up until the end . . . the very end." Then Soda took a big toke. This bowl still had a lot of pot left to burn.

"We had guys out there in goddam firefights on their last day. Big battles, even. Then priority-one is to get them on the chopper home. Nobody goes past DEROS."

"How 'bout the big fights trying to recover some guy's body . . . That's fucked up, man."

"I don't know what to think about that, man. What if that was your . . .

"Hey, ya know what? I bet you guys get shot at more often than we do," observed one thoughtful grunt. "I bet you anything you do . . ."

"Well, it's pretty damn often. I'll tell ya that," said Robbie.

"Imagine being the last guy to die over here? What a fucked-up thing that would be . . . Or, what a fucked-up thing that WILL be," said Dannon.

"But, when your number's up, your number's up."

"Exactly, man, exactly."

"You almost bought the farm today. I might buy the farm tomorrow."

"You can't let it worry you to death, man. We all stand an equal chance getting killed, and we all stand an equal chance going home. Don't matter if you're a badass or a whimp cocksucker . . . It's all fate . . . fate . . . that's all."

A different bunch of guys, but the same topic again. They may not all admit it, but everyone thinks about death over here. His own or somebody else's.

The group killed an hour like this talking about the absurdity and futility of it all, with no debates or argument. Each one a grain of sand in the desert, sometimes in the bright sunlight, sometimes in the black of night, and sometimes blown by the wind without any choice in where they're going—on the surface or buried forever.

A Huey could be heard now. It turned out to be their ride back to Long Thong, in the pouring rain. The four crew members were passengers for once, sitting on the web seats like grunts. He didn't see who the pilots were, but he knew the gunner and crew chief from Bravo Company. There was a very low cloud cover and they flew at only one thousand feet. A whirlwind of rain whipped and swirled through the open cargo area. The crew and passengers got soaked to the skin. The pilots sitting up front in these circumstances get wet gradually.

Peasants still worked the rice paddies like nothing was going on, like they had for centuries. Rain or no rain, war or no war. Dyson still thought the country was beautiful, like some ancient kingdom. It's what was happening in Vietnam that was ugly.

▌▐▐▐▌

Jack

Dyson had somehow missed Gator's going-away party. Now the mess hall was run by a cast of characters who didn't care anything about the food, the men, or anything else. On this night, they chose to serve grease-con-carne: Sloppy Joes with the meat sauce accessible by ladle under three inches of red grease. Greasy trays and greasy utensils were the new normal. Many guys said they had the shits from all the grease. Contributing to the problem, on Monday mornings troops were given M11 pills, the designation for the large, orange, anti-malaria pill CP (chloraquine-primaquine) that produced diarrhea within a couple hours. The Army steadfastly maintained the booster did not act as a laxative, but the lines at the latrines every

Monday said the opposite.

Malaria was a constant problem, and the medical staff did their best to prevent it or at least keep it at bay. In addition to the orange CP pills, U.S. troops were given dapsone, small, white, anti-malarial pills (the "whites" in the phrase "two whites and a yellow") daily, hence the nickname "the daily, daily." They were used in the Central Highlands in conjunction with CP pills to counter *falciparum*-resistant strains of mosquitos. Allegedly distributed to prevent malaria, the real purpose of the medication was to prevent leprosy. Every man was required to sleep under a mosquito net.

When he got back to his hootch, there was something on his bunk—a new fifth of Jack Daniels. Scribbled on a piece of cardboard the note said, "Thought you might need this. (signed) A Friend." Something clicked—or snapped—inside him. It might do him good to get drunk for a change. He took it down to Super Chicken's area.

"Hey, Soup. You get this for me?"

Soup earnestly said, no, and D believed him.

"Want to have a belt, or two?"

"Aww, man, I hate that stuff."

"What? Jack?"

"No. Hard liquor, period. I love beer, but wine and liquor, uh-uh."

Their evening started in the usual way: setting up by someone's tape player, then digging the music and smoking. Wiggins was always a good contributor in the conversations. He could start something, elaborate, and put in his own opinions, which were usually logical and well thought out.

"I'm going to remember that," D often said when he heard something from Wiggins while smoking with the guys. But he'd always forget it, like everyone else did. Tonight, he was going to drink, without the pot. Mixing hard liquor and smoke simply made him sick. He would use some beer for wash.

Talk started with the crash, but D changed the topic after a bit. Then it was about the big demonstrations back home. It was obvious everybody wanted the war to end—and soon. Who knows how many guys burned their draft card? Rock bands performed at massive protests. Leaders like Andy Stapp and Abbie Hoffman captured the spotlight. Stapp was popular with many GIs because he had been court-martialed twice for his opposition to the war, Hoffman because he co-founded the International Party-political movement known as the Yippies and was also a leading proponent of the "Flower Power" movement.

He drank right out of the bottle. The first belt burned his throat, not a good sign. But each belt, with a swig of beer, got easier. After twenty minutes he was OK with it, taking a swig and a little chaser every five minutes or so. In the background, the eerie harmonies of Procol Harum were murmuring about vestal virgins visiting the coast. Although the words didn't relate to anything in the song, it was a kick-ass line regardless. The wandering, trippy lyrics suited him just fine. After forty-five minutes or so, he was on his way.

Creedence came on doing "Senator's Son," and the volume was cranked up. That song always got the guys going. He was getting more wired. Fuck this stupid war. Fuck that damn slut, Carol. Fuck carrying KIAs to Graves Registration. Fuck taking WIAs to the 93rd. He was heating up inside. He could hear the conversation, but he wasn't part of it. Fuck the stupid body counts. What's with us giving lifers like Brady our flying time? A Purple Heart for tripping over something, a Silver Star for flying over a battle? How 'bout another big nip of Jack . . .

"D . . . D . . . D!" said Soup.

"Yeah, what, man." Dyson looked at his surroundings. The hootch was tilting on its axis, like the floor in a carnival funhouse. "I'm half-done then, ain't I? And fuck, the world, man . . . fffuuuck the world." He guzzled the Jack again. The booze piling up with the grease-con-carne. "Where's zhat fuckin' Brady-muzzerfucker? Where's zhe, huh?" Slouched in his lawn chair, Dyson was now a downer on the gathering . . . belligerent and drooling.

"Hey, D, man, don't you think you had enough? You gotta . . ."

"Don't tell me . . . Soup . . . don't tell me how s'much ta drink, man . . . want some?" Soup had never seen his friend like this, it was trouble brewing. "Want some before I . . . go? Huh, man . . . want some?"

"No, man. I don't like the stuff. Where you going anyway? It's fucking wet and muddy out there. Stay here with us, man."

"OK, man. I'm stayin' dry in here . . ."

Soup knew about drinking. He knew what blackouts were. His dad and mom were both stoned-ass alcoholics. He let himself get drafted just to get away from home. Big mistake, but that's what he did.

By 22:30 hours, Dyson had drunk more than three-quarters of the bottle. "I'm . . . I think . . . I'ma gonna go to bed, man . . . bed . . . sleep, maybe . . . ya see, I don't sleep much anymore, man . . . too much goin' . . . too much . . ."

He managed to stand up but almost fell, reeling, looking like he would fall, but he made it over to his bunk. He pawed the mosquito netting open and crashed onto the bed, seemingly unconscious. After twenty minutes the lights were out and everyone else was asleep.

Around midnight, he sat up. Where is everybody? Something's not right. He set the bottle on the window ledge, took his .45 out of the holster, took two loaded clips from his web gear, picked up the bottle and staggered outside. He inserted one loaded clip, chambered a round, drank all the remaining Jack, then laid the empty bottle on a sandbagged wall. "Fuck it . . . it's gone, man . . . gone." An entire fifth in less than four hours.

The cloud cover blocked out the night sky. He knew what was on the other side of the clouds—a sea of white and silver cloud tops, billions of stars, and a basketball-sized moon. But he was down in this place.

"I'm tired of living in this dump . . . like chicken coops . . . mud . . . rats . . . snakes." And tomorrow? "KIAs . . . WIAs . . . MIAs? I'll be there, motherfucker . . ." Was that a gook? Did a VC duck into that bunker? He shuffled along the wooden walkway to the bunker.

Bringing up his .45, he peered into the darkness. "Hey, VC . . . VC
. . . *chieu hoi* . . . *chieu hoi*, motherfucker. Won't come out, huh . . ."

He pointed the gun into the bunker. POW! the orange muzzle
flash illuminated the inside of the empty structure and sent a dozen
good-sized rats scrambling. Men began yelling, "Who the fuck's
shooting? What the fuck's going on?"

"Fuck that gook." He fired two more into the bunker. POW-
POW! "And fuck this place!" He shot the weapon the air POW! "And
fuck them stupid fuckin' missions." POW! "And fuck them stupid
fuckin' lifers, man," POW! POW! The clip was empty.

Guys were on the walkways, peering out of hootches, some
had M16s. The CQ was shining a flashlight in his direction. Dyson
pushed the magazine release and the empty clip fell into the mud. He
loaded his second full clip and hit the slide release, chambering the
first round.

"D! D! Dyson! What're shootin' at, man?"

"Oh, fuck you, man!" He shot into a big puddle, sending up a
geyser. "Fuck this place!" POW! POW! "Fuck those Silver Star lifers!"
POW! "Fuck them stupid cock-suckin' missions!" POW! "And fuck—
and I mean FUCK—them stupid fuckin' assholes running this war!"
POW! POW!

Now he was out of ammo. "Geeze, Dyson. What the hell you
doing, man?"

"He's in a bad way," Soup told the spectators. Dyson was
struggling to stay upright, swaying then leaning against a revetment,
drooling in strings onto his chest. Soup went over to his friend and
took his empty .45.

Horstall and other lifers were at the scene now. "Jesus, Dyson,
what the hell are you doing? What the hell you shooting at?"

Soup had D's right arm over his shoulders. "He's just really
drunk, sir. He hasn't had any hard liquor for months now and it just
hit him hard."

Horstall asked if anyone was hit. Witnesses said he only shot
into the sandbags, earth, and sky. No one had seen him fire the first

three shots into the empty bunker, which could have killed someone. Some guys often slept in bunkers for peace of mind.

It was quite a crowd in a mismatch of uniforms. Some guys wore just shorts, some with boots and shorts, some with flip-flops, a helmet here and there. Many figured there were VC in the camp when the shooting started and had weapons ready.

Dyson's eyes were bleary. He was slobbering and leaning on Soup. "Well, there's no sense talking to him now," said Horstall. "Trone," he said to Soup, "you got his .45? OK, take him back to the hootch, let him pass out, or sleep, and watch him. That's your job, Trone, until you're relieved. Understood?"

"Yes, sir."

▌▐▐ ▌

Dyson had a hell of a time getting up on Thursday, November 13. He was still half drunk and had the worst hangover of his life. He knew he would have to stand before somebody like the CO soon. The guys in the hootch didn't ride him about last night, but there was bound to be an asshole or two who would say something this morning so he avoided the mess hall.

Everyone in Bravo Company knew who was shooting last night. He wasn't the first and he wouldn't be the last to go off like that in camp. There had been far more serious incidents when someone lost it for one reason or another. Even Long Thong had its own water tower sniper a few months ago.

At 06:30 hours he stood in the work formation with the rest of the company. Robano, Soup, Rector, and Wiggins made it a point to stand around him in formation. Topics of the formation were changes to the duty roster, an upcoming Division inspection, aircraft availability, a new tech manual, and volunteers for permanent shit burning and guard duty. After they were dismissed, everyone either headed to work or the hootches for eye-openers.

Then one asshole yelled, "Hey, it's Boom-Boom Dyson!" It was a mechanic named Adams.

Loud enough for Adams to hear, Soup said, "It's Asshole Adams." They kept walking.

Again, Adams said, "Hey, Boom-Boom, out of ammo?"

Dyson turned and said, "You know, I'm glad you said that, Adams, because every time I take a leak, I grab your fuckin' mother by the neck, and when I'm done, I give her head a good shake." A few guys laughed.

They started toward each other, but some men stepped between them. They all knew Dyson could kick his ass easily. "Adams, shut the fuck up. You ain't shit and you know it."

While the rest of the hootch went to work, Dyson stayed behind for his appointment with the CO. He didn't dare smoke dope, though he could have used some. He sat on his bunk and lit a Camel. He watched one of those big spiders roaming around the floor along the wall, hunting cockroaches before disappearing into Soup's area. Hueys could be heard all around. Then he heard a Chinook, so he decided to have a look. There to the east about a mile away a Chinook at two thousand feet was heading toward Long Binh. Sling-loaded underneath was a Huey that had crashed, its overhead rotors had been removed for transport. Just another reminder of what was out there.

It was time to go. He checked his uniform and boots, lit another Camel and headed to the orderly room. He doused the cigarette in a red butt can and entered the Company Clerk's office.

"Hey, Dyson," said Jensen, like he was surprised. "Hang on." He went into the CO's office. After a half minute he came back and said, "Report to the CO." Here we go. This could be serious. Long Binh Jail? Now he felt sick to his stomach.

He marched into the office, stopped in front of the desk, saluted and said, "Sir, Specialist Dyson reports as ordered, sir."

Major Hines studied him for a bit, then returned the salute. "At ease, Dyson." He stood at ease and looked at the CO. "What happened last night?"

"I let the Jack Daniels get the best of me, sir. And I screwed up, sir."

Hines let out a big heavy exhale. "Sit down, Gary." Gary? Very unusual in the Army world of last names only. "Smoke, if you want to." Dyson lit up. "This is serious," Hines said, "but it's not . . . not with me. I've seen it every tour I've had over here."

"Well, sir, . . . I . . . "

"Relax, OK? What was bothering you so much you had to drink like that and go off?"

"It's not one thing, sir. It's the whole damn scene, sir. The killing, the maiming, the waste of life . . . the waste of our guys' lives . . ." He stifled tearing up.

"You Catholic?"

"Yes, sir, but I haven't gone to church in a few years." Why go to church? Why does God let the killing go on?

"That was a close one yesterday," meaning the crash of 096.

"I'm glad Lewiston was piloting, sir, and Stone."

"Well, he's no Cavecchio, but he's learning. I know I told you short-timer guys about not flying your last thirty days, but the numbers are just not there. Like yesterday, we had to provide so many ships and crews. You, and other short timers included."

"Well, we expect that, sir, and I expect to go up again before I go home, sir."

Hines put out his last cigarette. "Can I have one of them Camels? I promise; I'll buy my own. Thank you." He lit up. "Some people around here want me to court-martial you, but it would be a general court-martial." Meaning that a general would hear it, most likely the Division Commander. "But that wouldn't happen until after Christmas, and maybe New Year's. That's after you've gone home. So, I'm going to tell everyone that I haven't made up my mind yet, and we're considering another form of punishment. I'm gonna stall on the paperwork and find all kinds of things wrong with it. I've learned all kinds of tricks to get around the Army's way of doing things . . . How many days you got left?"

"Twenty-three, sir."

"Wow. Well, the numbers are the thing and I need you guys. Saturday, we have another big commitment. I hope we can get enough ships out of Maintenance to make it. Guys like you are indispensable because you are both mechanics and crews. And you guys are going home, or worse, faster than qualified guys are coming in. But Operations knows who you short timers are and when you're to be used in Maintenance. Taylor . . . look at Taylor. He's only a SP5 and he is one of the most indispensable guys we have. I'm gonna miss a lot of you guys, Gary, and I'm trying my best to let you go home alive." This man was from the Ozarks—he had a lot of good common sense and saw things as they really were. Why couldn't all commanding officers be like this man Hines?

"I understand, sir, and I don't have any problem with that."

"So, what did you have a problem with last night?"

"I had too much Jack Daniels—too much, too fast. To tell you the truth, sir, I can only remember a couple of, like, snapshots of last night. A scene here and a scene there. If I had to write down everything that happened or everything I did, I couldn't do it."

"Oh, boy. Well, good thing you didn't shoot anyone or it would be a whole different ball game, Gary." He used his first name again.

"I realize that, sir."

"OK. If anyone asks you what's going on with this, you say you honestly don't know because I am weighing a couple different options. Captain Horstall's statement is going to be written by him and me, and we're going to word things very carefully. And we are going to take our time, blaming the workload around here and the missions, OK?"

"Yes, sir. Thank you very much, sir."

"OK. You're one of the more respected enlisted men around here, you and about fifteen other guys, respected by the pilots and maintenance personnel. So, keep up the good work," then he grinned and said, "and stay off the damn Jack, OK?"

"Yes, sir." He stood and saluted.

Hines returned the salute. "Very good. Dismissed."

As he turned to leave Hines said, "Oh, hey, you got another Camel?"

"Here, sir, there's three left. I got another pack."

In some men's eyes, he had made an asshole out of himself last night. To other guys, he was cool, blasting away with his .45. Although out of the woods, he was back on the treadmill to the meat grinder. He was still hung over and would be all day.

I III I

All the mechanics worked throughout Friday night to have all the ships ready in the morning, November 15, for another big insertion of troops in Tay Ninh Province. Every man available was working on ships or flying on them. Only four from Alpha and Bravo Companies were unflyable and grounded. Liftoff from Long Thong started at 06:00 hours. To Dyson, there was always something stirring about seeing so many Hueys takeoff. Just what it was he could never describe. Good and bad vibes all at once.

Dyson and Robano were assigned to *088*. Hines was the aircraft commander and the Alpha Company mission commander. Smith was co-pilot. Hines told Taylor in Operations that this was the crew he wanted. It was comforting to hear Hines' laconic voice on the intercom. He was always so laid-back and confident, the Ozarks in him.

The first part of the mission was picking up troops in Phuoc Vinh and ferrying them into Tay Ninh to an area within sight of Nui Ba Din—Black Virgin Mountain, an enemy stronghold. The name Tay Ninh was always associated with thousands of NVA troops, and hundreds of local Viet Cong—tunnels, bunkers, ambushes, main force contact.

As in some other insertion operations, those LZ areas were first bombed and strafed by fighter/bombers and worked over by artillery. How successful that strategy was always depended on how well dug in the enemy was. The gooks went deep below ground during the bombing and shelling, only to spring out of their cover and concealment when it was over. This tactic was repeated year in and year out in every province over the same previously contested areas. *And here we are again,* he thought.

At Phuoc Vinh, it was always the same choreography: a row of ships flying in, setting down in a row, each ship on-loading six troops with gear, lifting off in a row, and taking off in a row. This bunch of grunts was four old-timers with faded uniforms and equipment, and two FNGs with new uniforms and worn equipment. The old guys, who averaged an age of 21 years old, were blank and showed no emotion whatsoever. The FNGs were wide-eyed scared. The vets were grungy and wore necklaces of beads, chains, and peace symbols. The grim features on the hardened faces of the older guys on Dyson's port side showed a depth of fear, deprivation, and weariness well past their young ages. These guys were quite used to sitting on the edge of the deck with their legs hanging out of the ship. One was a fierce-looking guy with a pockmarked face, red hair, and a long red mustache, like a biker. He had a tattered ace of spades in his helmet band and a crude tattoo on his hand between his thumb and forefinger, like it was done with a ballpoint pen, either in prison or juvenile detention. Dyson always liked that no one could tell where he was looking from behind his sun visor.

"Landing zone in sight. Landing zone in sight," said Smith on the headsets. Everyone braced themselves. The first wave of ships off-loaded and lifted off incident-free. Now their wave was going in. What was the enemy strategy today, he wondered? As they descended, they watched the treetops come up to meet them. There were Bravo Company ships loaded with troops on each side of them. Dyson was watching for muzzle flashes and tracers from hiding places. He glanced at the redheaded trooper, and once again, time seemed to stop. It looked like a big green spear had come straight up from the trees to the grunt, struck him in the face, and exited at a forty-five-degree angle through the top of his steel pot. Then the spearhead mushroomed, splaying out into a viscous red and pink cloud. The man's face reminded him of pictures of test pilots on rocket-sleds with their faces buffeted by two hundred-mile-an-hour winds, blasting their mouths open, expanding, and deforming their cheeks. That's a big fucking round he surmised. And it was. It came from an NVA .51 caliber anti-aircraft machine gun. The rest of the rounds followed in real time. The trap was sprung.

Dyson and all gunners on the other ships opened up on the sources of ground fire. Some grunts on the ships were also returning fire. Hines was on the radio telling the other ships to abort this landing and climb out. The .51 caliber they had flown over was concentrating on the port side of *093*. While he was firing at the ground positions, Dyson could see *093* raked by tracers which appeared larger and slower than the incoming small-arms fire. There was turmoil among the troops and crew in its passenger area. The aluminum skin over the engine compartment and on top of the aircraft was shredding where rounds had gone through, with some rounds hitting the overhead blades. As thick black smoke billowed from the engine, the tail rotor assembly fragmented. The gunner on that ship looked directly at Dyson and held up two fingers in the peace symbol as *093* nosed down. It fell like a ton of bricks, hit the ground, and exploded, launching a black and orange mushroom cloud like an atomic bomb. All on board were engulfed in the inferno. Six troops, two pilots, two crew members—gone. Ten KIAs, ten letters home, ten coffins, ten funerals, ten families decimated, and ten FNGs to replace them.

On the radio, Operations, the troops on the ground, and the pilots were all at once requesting help and giving situation reports. *088* had taken a few rounds but two of the sister ships in this wave were limping out with their load of troops and groundfire damage. Robano told the pilots via intercom that there was one KIA aboard. The troops needed to be set down somewhere and the wounded flown out. Hines and Operations went back and forth. Right now, the ships were circling wide, maintaining altitude at the cloud ceiling of three thousand feet. The troops already inserted had moved to a defensive position away from the landing site and a fierce and all-out pitched battle was now raging showing dozens of green and red tracers, and explosions from hand grenades and RPGs.

A Cobra gunship and two Huey Hog gunships began tearing up

the woods surrounding the original positions, making passes north and south, then east and west. When they were done ten minutes later, Hines received instructions to bring in the second wave and off-load the troops. Thanks to the gunships, the second wave was able to go in, set down, off-load, and get out of there almost unscathed. Minutes later, the third and final wave was also able to insert troops and leave without encountering much resistance. The ships with WIAs and KIAs were directed to fly to Lai Khe to off-load and refuel.

Dyson looked down at the dead redheaded guy. What was that crude tattoo supposed to be? One of his buddies had draped an OD green towel over his head and helmet. The blood stained the green cloth black and the whole mess leaked onto the deck, as happened dozens of times before. They dropped his body off in Lai Khe, took on fuel, and flew back to join the operation, ferrying troops, resupply, a Medevac to the 193rd in Long Binh, and then back to Long Thong for the night.

❙ ❙❙❙ ❙

Surprise

That one day, the 137th ASH lost seven pilots, nine crew members, and five ships. The gunship company in Long Thong lost two pilots, three crew members and two ships. *093* had crashed and burned with two pilots, two crew members, and six grunts, all burned beyond recognition. A recovery team from the 137th retrieved all the bodies out of and around the ship, bagged them, and took them to Graves Registration at Phuoc Vinh. *093* will be replaced by a new ship and FNGs will replace the men lost. It never stops.

That evening, after another deplorable dinner of mystery meat, dehydrated potatoes, pale green beans, stale white bread, and warm milk, only Soup, Mister D, Wiggins, and Rector were in the hootch. Mister D was in his lawn chair facing the south door of the hootch and the entryway through the sandbagged wall of the revetment. "Back in the USSR" on Soup's tape was just starting when there was the roar like a low-level jet fighter. He looked at the doorway and time in a split second stopped. There was a live white pecker-head rocket entering their hootch doorway, with its tail fins out, the rocket hung suspended a fraction of an inch off the concrete floor. He was able to think in full sentences. "That thing is loaded with flechettes. If that thing goes off, we're fucked." Now there was an ear-splitting-hissing SWOOSH! He never knew those rockets made so much noise. At twenty-three hundred feet per second, it skidded almost the entire length of the hootch and out the other door—the warhead never touching the floor. Gaining a little altitude, it hit the bulldozed berm of the perimeter, and detonated in the purple explosion the peckerheads were famous for.

"JESUS!! HOLY FUCK! Did that just happen? Was I seeing things?"

"What the fuck was that!"

"Did you see that!?" Everyone was incredulous of what just happened.

There was a tell-tale white skid mark tracing the rocket's path onto the floor and out the door.

Mechanics working on the flight line had seen it leave the gunship—maybe a hundred meters away from the hootch. Guys in the company area saw the rocket fly in one door and out the other, then hitting the berm and exploding. A crowd came to see the trail on the floor for themselves. And there it was—the guilty gunship way down the flight line surrounded by some attending mechanics who were no less dumbstruck.

One of the mechanics had been loading a rocket pod on the side of a ship pointed directly at the mechanics' hootch—it had to point somewhere, right? When he inserted the rocket into its individual tube, a static electric spark from his hand ignited the rocket's fuel, sending the peckerhead right through their hootch. The new mechanic said he saw the blue spark snap between his hand and the two terminals on the rear of the rocket. A freak, freak accident, even though the ship had been properly grounded.

If that thing had been an inch lower it would have killed four guys listening to the Beatles.

Just another night in Long Thong.

Twenty-one days to go.

| ||| |

For the next two days, Dyson spent his time in Maintenance. More new guys were being selected as crew chiefs and gunners, which was a godsend. Time was really dragging as he became shorter and more bad memories piled up. Thrown into the thought process was the fact Carol was having her baby around now, "about Thanksgiving," she'd written. Would she write and tell him how it went? He wished she'd write so he could spitefully not open the envelope and write on it "Return to sender."

On Monday night, November 17, after another disgusting evening chow, one of the shooters stopped by his area.

"Hey, D."

"Hey, Gray. How's it going?"

"Look. I know you've been turned off by the heroin scene around here, and I think I know one of the reasons why."

This was interesting. D wasn't sure what to make of it. He noticed the needle tracks on Gray's forearms, and he didn't try to hide them.

"I wanted to show you a couple things here. I have gotten away from shooting that China White everyone around here buys and I started getting this much better stuff from one of the day laborers. They call it White Dragon. It's heroin, all right, but it's much cleaner than China White. When I cook it, it cooks much cleaner with none of that brown and black slag that forms on China White."

This guy's a heroin salesman, a connoisseur of dope, pushing a cleaner and safer lethal drug.

"And here's the best part," and he unrolled a scrap of OD green towel. "I got these sterile, disposable needles from a medic who sells all kinds of this stuff. Open the wrapper, fill the syringe, use it, throw it away—no sharing. I've been doing this by myself and it is a much safer ball game. It's a better, cleaner, safer high . . . Want to try some?" Gray had used dirty needles, but now he's using sterile needles.

Dyson looked at the shiny, gleaming syringes in their clear cellophane wrappers. Sterile needles and cleaner heroin, he thought. At last, he said, "No, man. The opium and the opium-hash highs are high enough for me."

"D . . . When I shoot this stuff, I can leave all this behind me. I mean I'm gone, gone from here, man . . . A heavy, sexual warmth . . . in a trip out of here, man."

"Nah. Thanks anyway."

"OK . . . But I'm always around if you change your mind." And off he went.

Tempting. Just think—a better and safer way to shoot heroin.

Nineteen days to go.

I IIII I

Details of the 1968 massacre of hundreds of men, women, and children in the village of My Lai finally came out and spread all over South Vietnam and the world. *Stars and Stripes* reported on it extensively as did AFVN TV and Radio. A lot of GIs absolutely hated the Vietnamese. Opinions and news blown all out of reality were everywhere, distorting events leading to the massacre and the numbers of villagers gunned down. Many guys had seen the deaths of a civilian or two here and there, a dozen or so there, maybe, or a village here and a village there. People were shot on the spot. Entire villages were wiped off the face of the earth by U.S. artillery and bombs. That was a hard fact. Hundreds of stories were always circulating by GI "eyewitnesses" about murders, tortures, gang rapes, mutilations and massacres.

"Happens all the time."

"Ever hear of Binh Son and *Operation DOSER?*"

"When we flew over, there must have been fifty-sixty-or-so villagers lying dead. Kids, women, old men."

"You wouldn't believe how many bodies were in those rice paddies."

"Somebody fired a shot, and everyone just started shooting."

"You know how squirrely everyone gets when you enter a village."

"You could hear this baby crying and crying and crying. Then there was a shot and the kid weren't crying anymore."

"While this was going on, five guys from the platoon had this young babe in a hootch, and they were pouring the cock to her, man. And I don't know what they did with her when they were done, man."

"You couldn't stop them. Once the shooting started that was it."

"One asshole went around cutting ears off these people."

"You shoulda' seen the gold teeth he pulled from them people."

"The CO said, 'Leave 'em there. Let the pigs eat 'em. That's an order.'"

"Let's say fifteen villagers equals thirty VC. That sounds good. Thirty VC KIA."

"If you don't want nightmares, man, don't go over there. It's really bad."

But this story was different. A US Army rifle commander's company rounded up villagers, herded them into groups, and then systematically murdered them. We are the guys in the white hats. We aren't supposed to be doing this shit.

Dead civilians are part of every war.

I IIII

On Thursday, November 20, three Bravo Company ships were assigned to transport troops and supplies all day between LZ Zorro and two supply depots in Phuoc Vinh and Lai Khe. LZ Zorro was a sorry-ass outpost in Binh Long Province, hacked out of a swamp in the woods back in July. The bulldozers clearing the campsite and building the berm around the perimeter were constantly mired down in the soft earth. It should have been sited on higher ground. It had a very narrow no-man's land around it with the woods dangerously close. Everyone bitched about the location but no one would move it. It was one of the premier, manned, hellhole LZs in South Vietnam.

Taylor told Dyson and Robano that Hines wanted them on this gravy mission to try to keep them out of harm's way for a day. They were assigned to a brand-new ship—*102*—with Sheckly and Simko, flying men and materials as needed and directed by LZ Zorro's Operation Center. The two sister ships were *099* and *097*.

"You won't know where you're going from one minute to the next," Taylor told them. "So just sit back and enjoy the ride." Mister D and Robano had heard all that shit before.

Before Dyson left the hootch that morning, he'd given himself two big hits of that dynamite copper-colored hash. He was stoned when Sheckly lifted off and began their first mission for the day. *102* set down in Phuoc Vinh and took on two bales of new jungle fatigues, two Vietnamese tailors with their sewing machines, and three Vietnamese barbers. This was easily one of the strangest loads he had ever seen. As they approached LZ Zorro he could see concrete pads had recently been poured in anticipation of new buildings. Grunts and engineers were constructing bunkers, walls, and revetments. The ship set down on a new landing pad, off-loaded the uniforms, tailors, and barbers. *102* was directed to remain on the landing pad until given the go-ahead. This was while two Chinooks came in with sling loads under each ship carrying plywood, metal roofing, wooden trusses, and perforated steel planking. After they set down their loads and departed, *102* headed toward Lai Khe. Zorro was the busiest little LZ he had ever seen.

The three Bravo Company Hueys spent the day flying between the three camps hauling troops, mess hall equipment, ammo, Lister bags, anything and everything related to building up LZ Zorro. Around 14:00 hours, *102* approached for the fourth time and the transformation in the LZ was amazing. Barrack walls were up and sheet metal roofing was being installed. Large bunkers were ready for a CP, supply, ammo dump, and Operations. New wooden sidewalks ran every which way. There were wooden latrines and a mess hall.

When Sheckly got to the landing pad he was told to shut the ship down and take a break. It felt good to get out and stretch. Then the reason for the break became clear.

F-4 Phantom jets from the nuclear-powered USS Princeton aircraft carrier were going to literally move the woodline back away from the LZ. The jets used the bomb-and-burn technique. The first Phantom came in low, dropped two napalm canisters onto the tree line and turned the woods into an orange and black firestorm. Exactly three seconds later the next jet followed and dropped two five hundred-pound bombs into the inferno, sending the burning napalm even farther out into the trees and forest. Within a half-hour the woods had been bombed, burned, and moved back a full two hundred yards, a much wider no-man's land.

The crew was watching the bombing when an infantry captain began small talk with Sheckly and Simko. Robano and Dyson were within earshot. Sheckly asked the captain what was with the big push to get this LZ all built up.

"We got company coming tomorrow," the captain said. Sheckly asked if it was the Inspector General. "No, it's a presidential fact-finding team . . . There's a TV crew with them so we have to be ready."

Whatever you do, don't let them see how it really is.

At 16:30 hours, Sheckly set the ship down in Long Thong after an uneventful day. Not once did the crew fire weapons and there had been no emergencies. On the way past the Operations bunker, Taylor informed Robano and Dyson they would be flying tomorrow with Major Hines on another gravy run. They wouldn't have to lift off from Long Thong until 10:00 hours. It sounded OK.

As Dyson entered the hootch he could tell something was up. Everyone turned and looked at him.

"You hear what happened?" one asked.

"Ah, no. I didn't hear anything."

"Gray. He OD'd at noontime. They couldn't save him," said Soup.

So much for that safer, cleaner way to shoot up, with the better stuff and the sterile needles. It surprised Dyson only momentarily.

They all end up like that. The other shooters, Riaz and Gary Parleki, were there but remained mum. They were gathering up all Gray's personal stuff. What do they say this time in the letter home? He was KIA? He had an accident. He was a heroin addict and overdosed?

"Ya know, he wasn't a bad guy. We had a good time smoking with him."

"I always liked him."

"Yeah, but he couldn't do his job anymore. He'd work a little and disappear, come back for a while, go get some more." He was a true addict.

Dyson washed up and walked to the mess hall. This evening it was skinny, red hotdogs on stale buns, pork and beans, crusty potato salad that no one dared to eat, chocolate cake with a thin white frosting, and, again, warm milk. *I hope I don't have to eat this shit much longer*, he thought.

After chow, he secretively took a couple of hits from his stash of hashish, immediately got stoned, then joined the others over in Soup's area. He asked where they found Gray.

"Well, he didn't show up for work after noon mess, so Horstall went looking for him. He didn't find him in the hootch, but he looked in the bunker and found him frothing at the mouth. He got some guys and rushed him up to the medics, but they said it was way too late. He was gone."

"One of the medics said that's seven fatal ODs this month for Bravo Company and nine for Alpha Company." Riaz and Parleki were not in the hootch now. They were probably shooting up somewhere else.

The talk continued until around 23:00 hours when everyone turned in. Dyson stripped down to his shorts, pulled back the mosquito netting, and lifted the blanket to get in bed, exposing something that was under the covers, rolled up in green cloth. He unrolled it and dumped it onto the bunk. It was a packaged sterile needle, a packaged sterile syringe, a mess-kit spoon, and a little stash of pure white heroin, with a note. "Here, friend, have some on me." It had to be from Gray. Was it his going away present? Did he intentionally OD?

Sixteen days to go.

▌▏▏▏▌

At 09:30 hours the next morning, Dyson and Robano were giving *103* a pre-flight inspection when a jeep dropped off Hines and Smith. All together they went over the maintenance forms and the ship's logbook, comparing the work that was done to the records. Robano and Dyson checked out their weapons, ammo, and gear. Hines called them together on one side of the ship to inform them about the mission.

"We are going to pick up five Red Cross personnel in Long Binh and fly them to the DP Camp in Phuoc Tuy, near the coast," Hines said, referring to the site for Displaced Persons. "We'll remain there while they inspect the camp. When they're done, we'll fly 'em back to Long Binh. We'll make a dogleg or two in the flight so we come into the camp from the southwest and take the same route back to Long Binh. Any questions?" Nope, seemed simple enough.

It was a short hop from Long Thong to Long Binh where they set down near the USARV HQ. Of the five Red Cross civilians, two were women. All were in their forties and fifties. They were dressed in colorful summer clothes. Two had cameras around their necks, three carried valises. They boarded *103* and strapped themselves in. Hines climbed steadily to three thousand feet at the cloud cover and began the circuitous route to the DP camp. The passengers craned their necks looking out this side, then that side. After twenty-five minutes, the camp came into view and the ship descended to the landing pad outside the main gate. Hines shut the ship down. The passengers off-loaded and were met by a gaggle of Vietnamese civilians shaking hands and talking excitedly.

The camp comprised six acres enclosed by an eight-foot chain-link fence with a guard tower on each corner. ARVN soldiers manned APCs, jeeps, and scattered bunkers. There were also ARVN

MPs, whom the Americans called "White Mice" because of their uniform of white shirts and white hats. The facility had rows of neat, tidy barracks, latrines, and a plywood movie screen. It was teeming with Vietnamese men, women, and children in clean clothes. The Red Cross inspectors were hustled inside the gate to start their inspections.

"Well," said Hines, "we'll just have to wait until they're done—probably most of the day."

They were the only American troops at the camp. There was no one to bullshit with but themselves. Plus, there was always some animosity, mutual distrust, and the low regard American forces had toward all ARVNs. About half the ARVNs were doing what they were famous for—sleeping. Around 14:30 hours a jeep drove up to the gate and was waved to a stop by the ARVN MPs. The driver was an Army sergeant first class and riding shotgun was a major. Their civilian male passenger in the rear seat got out and was let into the camp. The jeep drove over to their ship and stopped. This Major Thompson walked up to Major Hines.

"I thought that was you, Donnie," Thompson said. The two men shook hands and chatted. Then they strolled away from the group to talk privately for a few minutes.

"OK, Tommy, thanks for telling us," said Hines. Thompson got in the jeep with his driver and they drove off. "OK, guys, the Red Cross people are going to stay here tonight, and we're going back to Long Thong. But I want to tell you that we will take a little spin northeast and fly over the big camp—the real DP camp. This little camp here is to show the Red Cross and the world that the Vietnamese government is treating displaced civilians with the greatest of care . . . so they can keep receiving American aid."

They were soon aloft at one thousand feet and headed northeast. In only three minutes the camp came into sight, the one the Red Cross was not supposed to see. It was a sorry, broken-down mass of humanity, a squalid shantytown made up of acres of lean-tos and tents, old cars and trucks and trailers, and crude shacks made of sign boards, scrap metal, and bamboo. Muddy walkways spanned ponds of rainwater. What seemed to be canals served as open sewers. Multicolored garbage and debris peppered the exposed ground. It was worse than any Vietnamese village or town he had ever seen. Idle villagers milled about everywhere with no sign of security personnel. When people heard the chopper, they looked toward it and started waving and running, thinking it was going to drop some aid packages or something. When the ship got closer to the camp the stench of raw human waste and garbage swept inside. Hines banked sharply toward Long Thong. That was *really* how the Vietnamese government treated displaced people. In 1969, there were one million DPs in South Vietnam. There were "fake" and "real" LZs, and "fake" and "real" DP camps, and "fake" and "real" who-knows-what-the-fuck-else, all under the guise of guiding a war-torn nation toward democracy, a nation like a rudderless ship, stuck on autopilot, lost in the fog of war.

Fifteen days to go.

‖ ‖ ‖

It was all over Bravo Company that Hines had gone to the mess hall and assembled the cooks for a pep talk. He ordered them to stand at attention while he dressed all of them up and down about the deplorable meals they were serving. It was Monday, November 24, and all the turkey, stuffing, and fixings were being delivered today, tomorrow, and Wednesday in time for Thanksgiving Thursday. Missions were to be scaled back all over South Vietnam for the holiday. "A word to the wise . . . Do not screw up this dinner." Half the cooks looked like it might have sunk in; the other half showed no emotion. Floaty and Gator were just memories now.

Dyson was done for the day at 14:00 hours after pulling his shift in Maintenance. He had cleaned up, changed, and was in his area by himself. The gift left in his bunk was right there in front of him. Why hadn't he thrown it away or given it to one of the shooters? It was calling him. He couldn't fathom his emotions anymore. During daylight when he was busy, it was the thought process going over and over the wasted lives and futility, frustration, and impending doom. At night, the picture show always took over. Some scenarios were like they had happened. Others, during the netherworld of drowsiness, restless sleep, and nightmares, were not as they really happened. A couple times he dreamt he could see Gray just standing in the shadows, watching. And last night he traveled back to the company standdown when black drug dealers fragged the guys watching the movie—only this time the grenades were as big as footballs, just hanging in the air, ready to explode any second.

In her latest letters, his mom was so looking forward to him coming home, she couldn't wait. He wondered what he was going to be like when he got home. Could he revert to his good old self, like he was before he was drafted? He knew he would be dragging his demons home with him.

▌▐▐▌

Sunshine Super Man (or Super Chicken?)

"Hey, D, I got something for you." Super Chicken stepped into his area and opened his hand. He held a little orange pill the size of a saccharine tablet. "Acid, man, some fine acid. Orange Sunshine, really big back in the states."

"Acid . . . How do you know its acid? That could be anything . . . rat poison even."

"No, man, it's good. We bought a bunch of it. This one pill is enough for four people to trip their asses off. Everyone who's done it said it was dynamite. No one got sick or anything. They're raving about it."

Still, Dyson was hesitant about taking something he questioned the real ingredients of or the results. Yet, he smoked dope he didn't know the origin or content of, and he was holding onto some heroin he didn't know the purity of either.

"I'm going to cut this little thing in four quarters, one quarter each. I'll take a little tiny quarter and you take a little tiny quarter. I'll be right there with you."

"Can you maintain on it? Like go to work?"

"Oh, no, man. No, no, no. We need like to drop it like around three in the afternoon (some guys always used civilian time regardless) so by the next morning we'll be down enough to go to work. You'll still be grooving, but OK to work." He paused. "Should be, anyway."

"It's around three now," Dyson grinned.

"All right! You're going to love this, man." He took out a Gillette Blue Blade razor blade and split the saccharine-size tablet into quarters. The inside was a lighter color than the outside. It looked so small, could this really get him off? "Let's put some tunes on," and they went to Soup's area.

Wiggins and Rector came by. They all sat around getting comfortable as Soup put on a jam tape. He gave each guy a quarter tab. "Put it on your tongue and just let it melt, man." The other guys had done it before. D was the only newcomer to LSD. Rector lit up a Marlboro Green, took a hit, and passed it on. The clockwork-like afternoon monsoon started pouring on the metal roof.

"OK, man, let's make a pact we don't start fucking with each other. OK?" All agreed in unison.

A visitor—a big, black shepherd-mix from the Avionics hootch—walked in from the rain and shook himself off. "Come here, boy, come here." The dog sat down amongst the guys and loved the petting and attention he was getting. Twenty minutes later, D noticed the vertical lines of lockers, studs, doorways, and window frames gently pulsating upward.

"Anybody seeing anything?"

"Yeah, man, I'm getting off." Their surroundings were being enveloped in a warm glow of gold and orange. The pulsating swelled, keeping time with the music.

"Oh, man, here we go," grinned Wiggins.

D looked at the big, furry, friendly dog, except now it was starting to appear a little mean and threatening. He sloughed it off and listened to the music and the beat in sync with the pulsations. He looked over again and stared as the dog's shoulders and chest grew muscular, his eyes became slits, and his teeth turned to fangs. D felt uncomfortable and tried to direct his attention elsewhere. He could tell the other guys were experiencing their own hallucinations. He looked at the shepherd again. It had turned outright evil-looking—a devil dog from a nightmare. "What's with the dog, man?"

Soup, who was closest to it, said the canine was OK. But Rector said, "Jesus Christ, he's a damn werewolf!" Now the dog had turned into something sinister. "Get him out of here!" Soup slapped the dog's rear and it trotted out the door into the rain.

The tripping was heavier now, the talk spacey. How much time had gone by was anybody's guess. The scenes inside and outside the hootch were bathed in the same light. It was hard to tell if it was day or night. Was that Simon and Garfunkel or Creedence Clearwater? People drifted through the hootch. Did they walk or float? Were they male or female? Were they even real? Are we attracting attention to ourselves?

"Oh, no, man. I ain't going to the mess hall like this, man."

Dyson looked at his watch. It was just after five. He looked around and promptly forgot what time it was. He looked down again and it read eight o'clock. Three hours had gone by. He and Soup caught each other's eye. They both looked at the rotating tape reels.

"Soup, do you see what I see?" A roller coaster of written music on floating ribbons of staffs, notes, and signs weaved through the air.

"I see written music, man." Communal hallucination number two.

Mister D would only steal quick glances at the others. He didn't want them turning into zombies or werewolves, so he tried concentrating on the music. It sounded like Melanie singing "In-A-Gadda-Da-Vida." She didn't sing that, did she? Someone came in, walked through the hootch, looked at the group, and started laughing like hell. He left and came back with two more guys. They looked and sounded like jackasses when they laughed. D looked at his watch. It was just after two. Two what? A.M.? P.M.? Did his watch run backwards? Was he supposed to be at work now? Oh, man. This is heavy.

"Hey, Wiggins," one of the visitors said, "you got a razor blade on your tongue, man."

These guys obviously knew about LSD trips. Wiggins slowly stuck his finger in his mouth and gingerly explored this way and that while the apparently straight guys laughed hysterically. Shit! Now Dyson could feel a razor blade on *his* tongue—a Gillette double-edged Blue Blade. But he wasn't going to fall prey to those practical jokers. He glanced at the other trippers and their eyes said they were feeling it, too.

He drifted off into his own realm. He didn't know what he was listening to. Was it a grand piano or Jimi Hendrix? Who's here? Is it still daylight? Was that the rain on the metal roof or a drum solo? He was feeling pleasantly warm, like being out in the sunlight. He decided he wasn't going to get involved in the spaced-out chatter. The intruders were gone—good. Finally, *The White Album* came on, familiar territory to him. Joints were passed around but he waved them off. Everything was bathed in yellow, gold, and orange half-light, all vibrating in a soothing rhythm. It reminded him of the opium high, the pulsing of his blood joining the pulsing of the sap flowing in the trees. It was really very nice, wonderful, he loved it. He was one with the universe. He started thinking that the trip could go from real cool to really bad, if he let it. He could sense something bad "over there" in his brain, but he would stay "here." His mind's eye could see him drawing a line in the sand with a Civil War cavalry sword adorned with golden tassels.

Trying to gauge how much time was going by was of no use. His watch seemed to be going in reverse or jumping ahead minutes or hours. Maybe Soup could be their timekeeper. One of the previous visitors had returned to tell them he had some mighty good smoke to share. He produced a big, fat football joint saying it was all leaf, no stems or seeds. Someone lit it and handed it off. Wiggins took a hit and said it tasted strong. Rector took one and coughed and coughed. Dyson took what he thought was a small hit, held it and thought it tasted bad, too. When the joint was finally gone, the visitor busted out laughing. "That was tobacco, man. Tobacco!" He left, sometime, thankfully.

Dyson asked Soup what time it was. Midnight, he said. It still looked yellow, gold, and orange outside. How could it be midnight? Someone from another hootch came over and asked the guys to keep it down. D became conscious of the ringing in his ears. He had forgotten all about it until just now. He could actually hear it over the music. He could hear the high-pitched ring, a different tone in each ear, with pulses going up and down in each ear but not in time with each other. Then it was two differently toned buzzes. Then it sounded like dozens and dozens of songbirds outside, cackling away louder than any flock of birds he had ever heard before.

Someone was shaking him slightly and there was a bottle of Jack Daniels in front of his face. "Here, have some." What a huge nose the guy had. How long has he been holding it there? A minute? Ten minutes? An hour? D put it to his lips and took a swig. He couldn't taste it or feel it. He took another. Same thing. "Go ahead and hit that thing, man," said the visitor.

"No! NO!" Soup said. "Get that outta here, man. And quit fucking with those guys I said." The guy left, laughing on his way out. "Never drink that stuff when you're trippin', man," warned Soup. "It goes down like water, and you'll drink and drink and drink until it's too late, man. And you'll wonder next day how did you get this hangover, man." Even while tripping on powerful acid, Soup was still looking out for him.

"I'm gonna go lie down, man." It was the first time he'd stood up since they dropped the acid so many hours ago. Walking to his bunk was strange. Was he leaning, trotting, big steps, little steps, going fast, going slow? He didn't know, but he knew when he made it. He slipped off his sandals and got in bed. He was uncertain about everything. Time, tomorrow, what was now. How far away was morning?

Nope, this wasn't working. He got up, put on his fatigues and sandals and went outside. There was the expected monsoon cloud cover, but tonight the waning moon—three-quarters full—was a silver coin shining through the clouds. They swirled slowly and spun with reds and purples, some slower-moving, vortex-shaped vapor morphed into huge, graceful eddies and cyclones. Five- and six-pointed stars peered at brief intervals through the moving clouds that twirled, revealing planets with rings like Saturn. Hundreds and hundreds of red and green tracers drew a huge spider web over the entire sky. There was no wind to be heard that could be moving the clouds like that, and the silent tracers were just there, like artwork, not endangering anyone.

He lit a Camel. After a few drags, he looked at the glowing ember, used the cigarette like a pen and wrote his name in the air. The ember left a luminous multicolored trail. He laughed and looked around, hoping no one saw him. He had a notion that he was the only person up in camp. Then he looked at the flight line and saw the portable work lights streaming red, orange, and yellow beams onto the mechanics. Damn! The cigarette had burned down and scorched his fingers—that was cool. This is cool, man. He went back inside. He glanced at the man who lay completely exposed in the first bunk. He appeared burned beyond recognition—burned, charred, and seared black. Only broiled tissue covered his skull and face—no ears, eyes, nose, and his mouth was burned away exposing jaws and teeth. The tissue was burned off his hands and feet, exposing skeletal fingers and toes. Then the burn victim turned his head, looked toward Dyson and gave him a sinister smile. Add one more indelible image.

It's not real, he told himself, but the next guy lying down looked like he took the brunt of an explosion. One leg was gone below the knee, the other to the hip. He had tourniquets and field dressings on his limbs, a loud sucking chest wound, and Dyson could see a heart beating wildly inside the gaping hole. Slowly the guy turned his head toward him. This ain't real. Why am I seeing it? Another scene planted in his memory.

Turning, he stepped to the doorway and stopped short. Just

outside was a pile of people, villagers in black pajamas. They were tied together by lines of rope and writhing like snakes. Three of them tried to hang on to their weapons while untangling them from the mass of human limbs, gunshot wounds evident on many of them. They all froze, then looked his way. He recognized the same exact villagers tied together with the VC, the hostages, the ones he and Morgan had fired on. Their faces appeared exactly like they did when they had all looked up at their Huey. Jesus, what were they doing here in Long Thong? Why do they keep appearing in his mind?

Sit on your bunk and just stay calm. This stuff isn't real, but it sure looks real. It escaped out of his subconscious. Turning slightly, he saw Morgan sitting next to him, flight suit and bullet-shattered visor and all. "Hey, Mister D, long time no see." He stared at Morgan. "It's me, Soup." Soup's voice was coming out of Morgan's blasted face.

"You look like Morgan."

Soup shook his buddy a little, "No, man, it's me, honest. I'm not fucking with you." Now he could see Super Chicken in front of him.

"Let's just sit here and cool it." His friend was taking care of him again.

"This stuff started getting bad, Soup."

"Yes, it can if you let it. Most of it was good, wasn't it?"

"Yeah, it's good right now, but not a couple minutes ago." Soup looked like a rock star: long hair, beads, flower shirt. He knew Soup didn't look like that. D laughed. "It's OK now."

He felt like he could cope and go to work, but not flying. "What time is it, Soup? And don't lie to me, man."

Now Soup laughed a bit. "It's 5:25 a.m. and here comes the CQ." The CQ entered the hootch, said hi, and started waking everyone up for work.

Mr. D felt much better having Soup with him. Everything running vertically was still pulsating, and there was still a psychedelic glow to everything, but it was all under control. He would not do this stuff again in Vietnam. He looked at his calendar on the wall. It was Tuesday, November 25.

I III I

Thanksgiving

On Wednesday, word went out that both Alpha and Bravo Companies' ships would be on missions to deliver hot holiday food to the troops in the forward areas. Taylor let Robano and Dyson know they would be flying with Hines. It seemed like it could be a wonderful mission to fly Thanksgiving dinner out to the men.

That evening, the guys in the hootch were in Soup's area, listening to tunes and getting stoned. Even though it had been forty-eight hours since he dropped that acid, his trip had not completely worn off. Tonight, they were smoking some dynamite hash, supposedly from "way up north."

Of course, D was thinking of tomorrow's mission, out over hostile territory, bringing good food to the troops. What could happen on the mission? What happened on previous missions? Images from past flights rolled in his mind. The faces of the WIAs and the KIAs, of the villagers, the VC, the NVA, going through his mind like a slide show—Scene 1; Scene 2; Scene 3 . . .

Eleven days to go.

I III I

Thanksgiving morning, November 27, seemed so out of place. The quintessential American holiday transported to this tropical war zone, a juxtaposition of unimaginable irony. It would be strange enough to witness it here in Long Thong in their mess hall, but to move it out into the field was almost science fiction. And don't forget Thanksgiving in the Disney Land of Long Binh, in clean, sparkling, air-conditioned mess halls, white tablecloths, and all the trimmings.

Grunts thought crews and mechanics were REMFs, and they, in turn, thought the guys in Long Binh were REMFs. It all comes down to perspective. Then again, shit always flows and rolls downhill.

"I thought it would be great to have you two guys join me in flying Thanksgiving dinners out to the troops," said Hines as he and

Lewiston joined Dyson and Robano doing their pre-flight inspection on *102*. "This will be my third time, and it's a great feeling. I couldn't think of two better guys to help get the meals out there." Hines wasn't fatalistic like Dyson at this point. He wished the major's attitude would rub off on him.

The first leg of the mission was for *102* and *105* to land at Phuoc Vinh at 10:00 hours and pick up the mermites (insulated field cases for hot food), metal serving trays, and four cooks to serve the feast. The same cargo and cooks were then flown twenty-five miles out to 2nd Airmobile troops at LZ Barbara. This was a well-established and heavily defended LZ with an entire rifle company of two hundred fifty men. As they approached, it looked like all of them were out waiting for the delivery. When the two ships set down on the helipad, the troops practically swamped the Hueys getting the goods off the ships. These guys were really looking forward to a Thanksgiving—hoots and shouts, smiles and laughter, waves and handshakes, and peace signs everywhere. An outgoing mail sack and official correspondence were thrown aboard, and up and away they went back to Phuoc Vinh. Yes, it did feel fine to drop that stuff off there. The missions were timed so that the food was packed hot and delivered that way— hot turkey, hot stuffing, hot gravy, hot everything "just like home." Home. Would he ever see it again?

They went back to Phuoc Vinh, unloaded the mail and paperwork, topped off the fuel tank, picked up another round of Thanksgiving supplies and cooks, and headed this time to LZ "Dirty" Debbie thirty-five miles away. One of the cooks was obviously an FNG—brand-new dark green fatigues, white skin, and a bearing of bewilderment about him. He scrutinized every square inch inside the Huey, craned his neck to see into the cockpit, and minutely checked out Dyson and his weapon. Then he took in the countryside out both sides of the helicopter. The bunch at this LZ seemed even more eager than the men at LZ Barbara. They had their hands on the chopper before it even set down. A couple of them pulled the new cook out of his seat. Then *102* got on route to Lai Khe for yet another holiday run.

For almost a year now he had not seen so many men smiling. Hines was right when he said delivering the Thanksgiving meals was always a wonderful experience.

I IIII

LZ Dresden

It was 14:30 hours when *102* and *105* picked up the meals and cooks in Lai Khe and headed due north to LZ Custer, which was between Loc Ninh and the Cambodian border. LZs were usually given women's names or named in memory of a KIA soldier. Why give an LZ an ominous name, like "LZ Custer" or "LZ Doom?" Operations in Lai Khe advised Hines that LZ Custer was rocketed and mortared the previous night, so the enemy was active in the area.

The LZ was officially two miles from the border, the line everyone ignored. This LZ was on high ground, a sturdy outpost of massive bunkers, revetments, trenches, sandbagged walls, mortar pits, a helipad, and a high berm lined with bunkers and guard towers surrounding the camp. The perimeter was thickly defended, with miles and miles of razor wire, Claymore mines, and foo-gas barrels. It looked impregnable. And still there had been daring, almost successful attacks on the compound. This LZ was always waiting for "the big one."

The helipad could take only one ship at a time, so *105* went in first, set down, off-loaded, and headed back to Phuoc Vinh. Then it was Hines' turn to land *102*. This group of grunts were the red-tan variety, weary and war-wizened, looking much older than they were. They needed haircuts and shaves, wore faded, worn fatigues and boots ready for the scrap heap. A few of them grinned when off-loading the mess containers, a slight wave—not the enthusiastic bunch like at the other drop-offs. Hopefully, they could enjoy the entire day and not have to go out into the woods. No mail sack or correspondence was thrown aboard and Hines lifted off, climbed, accelerated, and arced southward. This was their last run. Other ships would pick up the cooks and equipment later in the day. They were headed back to

Long Thong for their own Thanksgiving dinner.

About five minutes into the flight, the radio spouted voices and static. A patrol from LZ Custer was returning to base when it was ambushed a mile from camp. There was one seriously wounded in need of Medevac. A rescue of the patrol had not been requested—yet.

Please let there be another ship that volunteers to go in and get him. Hines waited a few seconds, then radioed that *102* would Medevac. Meanwhile, there was a firefight going on with the out-numbered patrol. Here we go again.

After backtracking for five minutes the ship approached the Medevac site. This area was a forest of tall trees and triple-canopy vegetation—thick undergrowth, a dense layer of leaves, and thick blankets of vines draping the trees. From the ground it was almost impossible to see the sky above; from the air it was impossible to see the forest floor.

Hines and the patrol leader were talking now.

"The south slope, look for the highest trees. Over."

"We see your trees," Hines replied, getting his bearings. "Now over the site. Over."

"We see you, *102.* We see you. Look for yellow smoke, *102,* yellow smoke. Over."

And sure enough, a yellow smoke grenade billowed in the small space between all the giant tree trunks. It was a vertical shaft, like looking straight down a well. There wasn't time to sit, stare, evaluate, debate, and predict if the Huey could safely go down the shaft without blade-strike, where either the main rotor and/or the tail rotor comes into fatal contact with the trees. Hopefully the triple canopy would prevent the NVA from firing on *102.*

Errant tracers could be glimpsed deep in the vegetation. "OK, heads up, we're descending. We'll watch overhead, crew watch the tail. Watch the tail." and Hines and Lewiston started the ship sinking into the deep green shaft. The prop wash swirled the branches, shredding leaves and small limbs. "Yeow," said Lewiston into the intercom.

They dropped below the treetops. The vegetation was so thick, Dyson could only see a few feet into or beyond these forest giants. God, these trees are huge. He and Robano were assigned to watch the tail rotor, but he also kept a roving eye searching for any source of ground fire. The main rotor was trimming off some boughs. A good-sized branch threatened to hit the tail rotor. Robano advised Hines to pivot and turn the tail two feet starboard. "Go down . . . back . . . more . . . halt." The ship was halfway down the shaft. The branches were getting larger and closer, the leaves and vines so thick now it was hard to tell if they hid solid wood. The main rotor seemed in constant contact with the leaves and small branches. Shorter trees were now looming under the tail rotor. Robano advised Hines to move forward if he could, and Hines crept forward five feet. Dyson looked upward— it was like a mine shaft. To get out of here was going to take some maneuvering. He was amazed how dark it was in these woods.

At ten feet off the ground green tracers began zipping out of nowhere. He looked at the tail rotor. It was clear for now. Then he saw three grunts carrying a man. The landing site was covered by tree trunks and branches, so Hines had to hover with his skids resting on the highest point. The grunts hefted the guy up to chest level, then hoisted him above their heads while Dyson unhitched himself, moved to the edge of the deck and pulled the man in along the floor. He was heavily bandaged in bloody field dressings, and unconscious—or dead.

"Wounded on board. Wounded on board," said Robano.

As Hines lifted off, fire came at them from two directions. Dyson and Robano returned fire while Hines made a perfect stationary 180-degree spin and headed back up the opening. He had made a mental map of the descent. Now he was doing it in reverse.

"I got it, boys. I got it," he said into the headsets, and the guys kept up their returning fire. The foliage was so thick it was hindering both the crew and the enemy gunners. The ship continued up, and the sun was burning through the clouds. Level with the treetops, Dyson saw all the broken, splintered branches from the blades. Once above the treetops, Hines turned the ship southward, climbed, and accelerated. The guys stopped firing. Jesus. On Thanksgiving Day. Didn't matter. Over here, people died on Thanksgiving Day.

Dyson checked the man lying on the deck. The wounds were hidden by the bloody field dressings and his uniform. Dirty bandages covered one eye, the other appeared hazy. Dyson took his hand. It was warm, but no response. He moved the man's head from side to side for a response of some kind. Robano joined him, felt the carotid artery in the man's neck, felt his wrists for a pulse, then shook his head "no." Then he opened his mike. "I think this guy's still alive, sir." Never just write a guy off. You wouldn't want that done to you.

"We're headed for Lai Khe. They'll work on him there," said Lewiston.

Dyson looked at the glorious expanse of the sky, an unbelievable mix of blue sky and clouds. All this beauty and a dead man on their deck.

Alpha Company had Thanksgiving dinner at noon, Bravo Company at 17:00 hours. Hines set *102* down in Long Thong at 16:40 hours. They would eat in their flight suits, no big deal. Hines and Lewiston approached Robano and Dyson. "We made it, boys." He was beaming from ear to ear.

"That was a close one, sir," said Robano.

"Shhiiitt! You shoulda been with us when we was in the Central Highlands! We had rock cliffs *and* trees to dodge. Lot'sa times at night, too." He was a big, old, Ozark mountain man in a flight suit. "Now let's go have some turkey and maybe some fine sippin' bourbon." There he was with his baseball cap on the back of his head, his curly hair mussed up, and his big ears sticking out a mile. His four dogs came bounding up and swarmed him, jumping up on his chest.

▮ ▏▮▏▮ ▮

Isn't that something? Once they started delivering the Thanksgiving meals to the troops, he forgot all about Carol giving birth, maybe today. She said, "around Thanksgiving," months ago.

Months ago. So much had happened, so much reshaped him mentally. Did he get reshaped morally, too? Did he have a low regard for life, or was he just used to seeing all the death and maiming? Did he care about it? Did anyone care about it? It's like Vietnamese people didn't exist, didn't matter, didn't count, never even had names. And the Americans boys getting maimed and killed were only two dimensions—a number, a photograph.

Ten days to go.

I IIII

A reel-to-reel somewhere in camp was playing, "Lovely Rita, Meter Maid." Dyson thought about how much he loved that song. He remembered listening to *Sgt. Pepper,* the entire album, on a stereo at a friend's place a few times. He would be home in plenty of time for Christmas this year. Today was the last day of November. The waning half-moon hung over the woods. There were fewer clouds these days and nights. It was good to see the sun and stars again. The ponds and puddles were shrinking in camp; the mud turning back to hard soil.

Seven days to go.

I IIII

DECEMBER

Monday, December 1, had the first visible sunrise since the monsoon started. It almost made the entire camp stir with optimism, after all the gray mornings for more than two months, But the blessing of the break in the weather meant a surge in the number of missions. Good weather, more missions.

Word went out about another big commitment of ships, crews, and pilots from the 137th ASH for the next day's missions. Almost everyone was assigned to a ship. For some men, this would be their first mission in the air as a crew chief or gunner. The new guys were looking forward to it and most of the others were tired of it.

As hot and muggy as it was, it felt good to be out in the sunlight again. Dyson was working with three other mechanics on a ship that was written up for engine and vibration issues when Hines stopped with his jeep and his dogs. The dogs loved the men and the men loved the dogs, showering them with good-natured rough play that was returned with puckish, aggressive enthusiasm. Hines led Dyson away from the group to the tail end of the ship.

"We need everyone tomorrow and you'll be flying. You're going to be on the last standby ship in Phuoc Vinh. The last ship to be called if needed. You may not get called at all. We'll just see how it goes."

"We expected to be flying tomorrow, what with the commitment."

"We have been trying to spare you guys."

"Oh, we know, sir, and we all appreciate it. I know I do."

"Fuck this stupid war, Dyson." Man, that was totally unexpected. "In the beginning, it was different. We thought we were really doing something over here. It was hard enough losing men then, but now it's just so futile, a waste, a big fuckin' waste."

"I agree."

"I know you guys can see what's going on. I don't even feel patriotic anymore, like I did only two years ago. It's a big fuckin' waste of life, on both sides. I'll be mission commander tomorrow, so I'll be up there all day. You'll have two good pilots tomorrow, anyway. I made sure."

"I appreciate all you've done, sir. No court-martial and everything."

"Here—I feel like owe you at least a pack." He gave Dyson a new pack of Camels. "Hey, what do you like about those things?"

"Well, sir, not many people will bum one off you."

▌▐▐▌▐

On Tuesday, December 2, reveille was at 04:30 hours. All of Alpha and Bravo Companies were up and running—only five ships couldn't fly and that was a very low number. After morning chow, Dyson readied himself in the hootch, chitchatted with the guys, had a few tokes from some Marlboro Greens, lit a Camel, and headed out to the flight line. He and Robano were assigned to *107* along with CW2 Lewiston and WO1 Burke. The plan was for all the Alpha and Bravo Companies' ships to head over to Phuoc Vinh and remain there on standby.

At 06:30 hours, the cluster of ships lifted off from Long Thong and flew toward the sun, climbing to five thousand feet with good visibility. Gone were the low, gray, moisture-laden clouds. There was something about flying in a big swarm of Hueys, or even seeing a big swarm of Hueys airborne. Power and might in the sky, like a motorcycle gang riding Harleys on down the road. Mechanical ships loaded with living men on their way to ultimately crash and die. Stop thinking like that. Just enjoy the scenery. A verdant carpet stretched out before them, the beautiful Vietnamese landscape oozed tranquility, except, that is, for the damned bomb craters.

I III I

Standby

A few minutes into the flight, half the ships veered northwest to Lai Khe while their group remained on course to Phuoc Vinh. *107* and five other ships stayed in the air until the transport ships arrived to pick up the troops and set off. Then the six ships set down near the Operations hut, shut down, disembarked, and were put on standby status. Two Chinooks from the Division's CH47 Chinook Battalion were also on standby. The weather was nice and the sunshine made things more bearable. Enlisted crew members could remain in and around their shack, and the officers could wait in and around their luxury bunker, but no drinking allowed. They didn't say anything about smoking pot.

About twenty crew members were milling around the shack, smoking, drinking Cokes, exchanging info about the day's missions. Half the guys seemed to be new—new Nomex suits, new boots, not yet sporting a red-tan. A speaker mounted high in a corner was playing The Doors from an unseen source—"Waiting for the Sun."

"Dyson? That you, man?" It was Al Dwight. They'd met on the train ride from Hartford to the New Haven Induction Center.

"Holy shit!" said D. "Wow, good to see you." They shook hands. Then the stories began about where they went after basic training.

Dwight, too, had been in Fort Eustis attending Chinook Maintenance/Crew Member School, but they were in different battalions. He also was shipped up to An Khe to the 2nd Airmobile Division Replacement Center. While there, the Division needed twelve hundred riflemen for the infantry units. "They took everybody, the first twelve hundred they could get their hands on—clerks, cooks, motor pool mechanics, telephone linemen, everybody, no matter what their MOS. No one could believe it, man. Some of us wound up in the 2/5 Infantry. We kept telling them we weren't trained for this. They said, 'You went to basic training, didn't you?'" He was getting serious now. "We went out there. You know it's bad, man. The new CO was a captain on a list to be promoted to major. He was nuts. He got us attached to a mechanized outfit. We went out at night. The tracks made so much noise you couldn't hear what was going on, man." He was letting it all out. "The gooks were dragging big-ass mines right in front of the APCs and tanks. Then the shooting started." He lit a cigarette, hit it like a joint. "Lotta casualties. Tracks blown up. APCs with everyone inside killed. The CO up in his chopper directing the whole thing like it's some fucking chess game. Asshole should be fragged."

"Jesus."

"They have this thing in 2nd Airmobile, if you want to get out of the infantry you re-enlist for one year in the Army. When we got back to camp, thirteen of us went down to the CP and said we wanted out. We wanted out before that asshole killed us. I signed for an extra year and was assigned to the Chinook battalion." The 137th ASH had guys like that—re-enlisted, re-assigned, the guys with the CIBs. "The 2nd Airmobile Division has the highest re-enlistment rate of all the units in Vietnam. They brag about it, man." He exhaled smoke like a bull exhaling steam. That Division also had more congressional inquiries than any of the other Divisions.

"Yeah, that's us, too, man," two nearby crew members said. "We were in the 2/8. Same thing."

While the morning went on, word of mouth from the Operations CP had it that contact was made in both Binh Long and Phuoc Long, so things were heating up. 2nd Airmobile units in Binh Long were experiencing hit-and-run firefights with an elusive NVA unit, and in Phuoc Long they had heavy contact with entrenched NVA in the hills. Calls for Medevacs would be coming any time now.

About 11:30 hours, factory-rolled joints were passed around outside the shack. A row of wooden benches encircled the shack so men could sit in the shade as the joints moved. It was really smoking out in the open, but no one seemed to care. Lifers would walk close by sometimes. Nobody seemed worried about getting busted. He wouldn't mind it if he could spend the rest of his time in-country on fruitless standbys with no missions to go on.

Some guys drifted over to the Operations CP to listen to the chatter on the radios. The 2/5 was engaged with an NVA unit that had them hemmed in on three sides by raining down mortars. He remembered the time he lay down in the drainage ditch during a mortar attack in Long Thong. They can fall on top of you just as easily as they can miss you.

"So did you hear about the pro football players that were 'suddenly' in Reserve Army units back home?" one of the Chinook crew members asked, with an edge in his voice. "No spending months on a waiting list to get in. WHAM! They're in. No draft for them, man." Yeah, like fuckin' magic.

In the background, John Fogerty, drummer Doug Clifford, and their bandmates in Creedence were blasting out the Cajun-boogie-rock chord progressions of "Proud Mary." Little did the guys know then that back in 1966, when the two musicians got their draft notices, rather than taking the chance of being called up, Fogerty joined the Army Reserve while Clifford joined the Coast Guard Reserve. Fogerty said he wrote the song as the result of his high spirits after receiving his full discharge from the Army Reserve.

Boxes of C-rations were brought down to the standby shack. Some guys dug in, some ignored them. He thought about Floaty and Gator and all the times he pulled KP. He fished through the rifled boxes but none of the meals appealed to him. He had plenty of Camels.

At 12:50 hours, the radio chatter changed to dispatches on the battles in both provinces. So far, the ships in the forward areas were handling the emergencies. There were four in Medevacs heading to Phuoc Vinh with non-life-threatening wounds and Long Binh for serious wounds. Two other ships had been hit by ground fire and were heading back to base if they could make it. Two of the ships here on standby were called into action and off they went. Four ships were left in their group, biding their time. It never stopped. Ships replaced ships, men replaced men, day and night.

Another ship was needed at 14:10 hours when a ship was hit by ground fire. Luckily it was able to land miles away from the fight. That left three ships on standby. The radios continued monitoring the situations. In Binh Long, the enemy had broken contact and seemed to melt away, disappearing into the woods and tunnels. The big fight in Phuoc Long was still raging. Suddenly, at 15:20 hours, one ship on resupply was shot down, slammed into the ground, and burst into a fireball killing the crew and pilots. Twenty minutes later another ship was hit but made a rough landing and all hands survived. Two of the standby ships replaced them in the battle.

107 was the last ship on call. Just a matter of time.

Then word came out of the Operations CP that ships from Charlie and Delta Companies, 137th ASH, were called into the fight. Lewiston and Burke came over to the standby shack.

"OK, guys, we gotta go." The four of them began the walk to *107*. "The ship that crashed and burned in Phuoc Long? We must recover those bodies." Oh, Jesus. "Alpha Company recovery team will be there, too. They'll help you with the bodies while they try to salvage some of the ship."

"Do you know who was on it, sir?" asked Robano.

"No. No names yet." Walking close to Lewiston, Dyson could smell whiskey. Robano noticed it, too. Lewiston didn't seem drunk, and they couldn't tell if Burke had been drinking also. We smoke, they drink. "I know this sucks guys, but this came from Bravo Company. There's infantry out there providing security. We should be all right."

As they were getting ready to start their run-up, a jeep came speeding over and screeched to a halt. A little SP4 jumped out and hefted four black body bags onto the ship's deck.

"Any gloves or masks?" Robano asked. He had been on a few recoveries.

"Nope, sorry," and he sped off.

"REMF mother-fucker," Dyson muttered.

"Clear!" yelled Lewiston, and the engine and the blades started turning. The ship ran up, lifted off, cruised to the runway, and took off for the recovery. Dyson was bracing himself. He had seen a couple crew members burned beyond recognition, but he never had to handle any. Robano had asked for gloves and masks because he knew what it was like.

After twelve minutes into the flight, Burke announced the recovery was in sight. Dyson looked ahead as the ship descended. There were rice paddies in groups, islands of brush and woods, scattered huts, farmers, and water buffalo. The burned-up hull of a Huey sat on the edge of a paddy against a dike with human figures clustered beside it. The wreck was two hundred yards from a copse of bamboo and trees. Lewiston flew the ship to within fifty feet of the group. He set the ship down to a hover just above the water. The guys unhooked themselves and removed their flight helmets. Robano grabbed two body bags, Dyson grabbed two more, and they jumped into the water up to midcalf. Lewiston lifted off to cruise around the immediate area until they signaled for him to return. For now, their ship and the Alpha Company ship would remain aloft, within sight and circling.

The Alpha Company Recovery Team had gotten there earlier. They were joined by a squad of infantry from the 2/8 that was charged with securing the area for the night. They already had three of the blackened bodies lying along the dike, ready to bag. Dyson gave them a quick glance—it was bad. They didn't even look human. Who were they? Two of the grunts were helping, two grunts looked bored while smoking, and the other pair were on guard. One of the pilots was still in the cockpit.

"We'll bag these guys," said a recovery team member. "You guys get your pilot." ("*Your* pilot?") The recovery team casually lifted one body at a time with their bare hands while an opened body bag was spread underneath it, the remains were placed down, and the bag was zipped shut.

"Come on," said Robano. They walked to the scorched ship. The stench from burnt fuel and flesh was overwhelming. The pilot's door was missing, he was still strapped to his seat and still had his helmet on. It was seared, misshapen, and partially collapsed from the inferno. Amazingly he was still grasping the stick control with both hands. The tissue on his fingers had been incinerated, exposing all the bones up to his wrists. Maybe his hands melted onto the stick. Only shreds of his Nomex flight suit still existed. Meager fragments of his boots covered his feet, with the soles melted away. His facial features were gone. All that was left were empty eye sockets, an open nasal passage, exposed teeth, and jawbone. His dog tags were still around his neck. He was a ghost pilot steering the ship through the spirit world. Dyson leaned forward and read his dog tags without touching them. Reynolds! Lieutenant Reynolds! He flew with this man two months ago. All four of these KIAs were from Bravo Company!

Robano spread the body bag on one side of the dike above the water line. "OK, D, let's see if we can lift this guy out."

"Hey, it's Reynolds, man."

"Humph," was all Robano said as he reached in.

They were standing outside the cabin. Robano slid his left arm between the remains of the backrest, then moved his forearms under the pilot's armpits. D tried holding his breath. The smell was sickening. The only things he could wrap his hands around were the exposed shinbones above the remains of Reynold's boots. As they lifted the body the hands came off the control stick. Blackened tissue moved and some fell off.

"Let's try not to tear open his body cavity. Easy . . . easy, you clear?"

"We gonna take his helmet off?"

"No, man, let Graves Registration do it. I'm not messing with that."

They had him out of the cabin and still in a sitting position. A few hours ago, this was Lieutenant Don Reynolds. "God," Dyson said.

"Keep him like this. We'll set him down just like this on his back." Dyson walked backward and Robano forward until they reached the body bag. "OK, down." Robano still had his arms through the armpits. "OK, D, now you'll have to pull and unbend his knees and straighten him out." They both pulled until the legs straightened somewhat and the body wasn't bent so much at the waist. D could feel something coming up in his throat. "OK, man. Try zipping him up."

But before he could do anything, Dyson turned, bent over, and puked. The smell and the sight were just too much. He had never thrown up during his whole tour, no matter what he saw. "Oh, man." He had never touched anything like that in his entire life.

Robano zippered up the bag. "It's OK, D. You done?"

"Yeah." Together they carried the bag over to where the other three lay. The bags were ready for transport to Graves Registration. A SP4 recovery team member waved to the circling Hueys and Lewiston and the Alpha Company ship to close in and set down. The four bodies would be loaded on their ship and the recovery team would board the Alpha Company ship.

Dyson reached down and rinsed his hands in the muddy rice paddy. He shook the water off and sniffed. The stench was still there. He could see Reynolds's face in his mind: good-looking American boy, family man, defender of his country, burned beyond recognition for who-knows-why-anymore. Hope he was dead before the fire got to him.

Now the two ships approached, set down, and hovered on the water line. The Alpha team helped load the bodies onto the deck of *107* by laying them crosswise in the forward passenger area. Then the recovery team climbed and crossed over the dike to *107*. Dyson and Robano were donning their flight helmets and hooking up their lifelines when a bullet smacked into the ship.

"Fuck!" Dyson was turning and sinking down into his gunner's seat when two more rounds hit the ship. He looked at the six men on the berm running for their ship and the grunts crouching, lying either prone or behind the burned-out hulk, bringing their weapons up. Green tracers were coming from the bamboo copse two hundred yards away. The VC had waited for the right moment—two ships at a hover and a cluster of men with their guard down.

Here they were, a couple of Hueys in the open with no cover or concealment, a gunner's dream. The copse of bamboo and trees was only sixty to seventy feet across. Dyson could plainly see the sites the fire was coming from, so he opened up, working his tracers at the base of the trees from left to right and back again. Robano was on the far side of the ship and had nothing to fire at. The grunts were all firing and so was one gun on the Alpha Company ship. Lewiston was lifting *107* off while the other was still on-loading the recovery team members.

Six grunts and the ships' M60s were pouring fire onto the enemy gunners' positions, a good-sized fusillade, but the damn gooks were continuing the fight like nothing was going on. Lewiston raised the ship, banked, and turned up and over the recovery site, giving Dyson nothing but sky to shoot at. Then the ship descended to inches above the water and put the dike and the wrecked ship between it and the enemy. Now the VC had nothing to zero in on but the tail end of the ship, gaining distance the whole time. Looking back, D could see the Alpha ship following on the same course. Red and green tracers showed the grunts were still shooting it out with them. But it wasn't their concern anymore. *107* was bound for Graves Registration.

Five days to go.

▌▐▐ ▌

107 arrived back safely at Long Thong at 17:10 hours. Walking past the Operations CP, Dyson learned that the crash that killed Donald Reynolds also claimed the lives of Kenneth Gesso, the ship's co-pilot who was a warrant officer from Oregon, Ronald Stevenson, the crew chief, a SP5 who also came from Oregon, and Donnie Rhinehardt, the gunner, a SP4 who went almost all the way through Warrant Officer Flight School. Dyson knew all of them. More faces in his nightmares.

There was a letter on his bunk from his mom. It was resting right on the corner of his bunk where he had hidden his stash and the works Gray had left him. She was so glad this "was almost over." She said she ran into Mrs. Gibbons. Her son, Rich, who graduated a year ahead of him, had come back from Vietnam. She said Mrs. Gibbons couldn't believe how troubled he was now. He had nightmares, drank a lot, bought some guns, got arrested, never laughs, and in his room she found a bunch of pills and what was probably marijuana. "I hope you're not like that after you come home." Why did that old biddy, Mrs. Gibbons, have to say anything? "After you come home"? *If* you come home . . .

▌▐▐ ▌

He was the "shortest" man in Bravo Company—the guy scheduled to go home next. He carried the short timer stick Soup had made him, and Soup was beaming from ear to ear. Taylor in Operations told him on the side that he was done with flying, grounded for the rest of his time. Taylor told him he had earned eight Air Medals for his time crewing. Actually, he had earned more but some of his hours had been distributed to some sorry-ass lifers so they could get Air Medals without ever leaving the ground.

The Company clerk had told him that they hadn't heard anything about his Distinguished Flying Cross, nor his Purple Heart. In fact, everyone who was treated at the dispensary that night hadn't received their Purple Hearts either. Everything was still "in channels."

Dyson and many other guys knew the Awards and Decorations program was in shambles. They felt the medals didn't mean much anymore. Company and Battalion commanders were getting Silver Stars for leading their men in battle—from a helicopter. Distinguished Flying Crosses, DFCs, were given to field-grade officers just for piloting aircraft. Purple Hearts were awarded to lifers for getting hit with hot brass casings, tripping and falling during an attack, or not even being present during the action. Bronze Stars were handed out like M&Ms. But the men who earned and deserved medals never got them—never submitted, never received.

Wednesday, December 3, was a beautiful sunny day, and working would make the time go faster. Guys would wish him good luck and say that they would miss him. Some even insisted he take a toke of dope with them. He obliged.

One of the hottest topics was that Out-Processing for the guys going home now included piss tests for heroin use. Anyone testing positive would have to be detoxed before leaving the country. Everyone believed it was true. No one ever knew what to expect when they went through Out-Processing. This was the final deciding factor for Dyson not to shoot up with the stash and works Gray left for him.

That evening, Super Chicken gave him a small traveling suitcase for his personal things on the trip home. "It belonged to some guy that never came back from R&R to Hawaii." Soup put on *The White Album*, they smoked some hash, and went out and sat on the sandbags. The gorgeous sunsets had returned after the monsoon season. Oranges, reds, yellows, gold, and light purple glowed over the dark silhouette of the treetops. He was always struck by how fast the sun rises and sets in the tropics—not like at home. They watched as the colors faded and the clouds darkened. "Dear Prudence" was playing.

"Gonna miss you, man."

"I'm gonna miss you, too, Soup."

"Still got tomorrow."

"I hope so."

I III I

This was his last day, and night, in Bravo Company. Thursday, December 4. He spent the hot, sunny day walking back and forth to the flight line, touching base with guys scattered in different areas of Maintenance. FNGs had replaced many of the original guys he remembered from when he had first landed in Long Thong. It seemed like a century ago.

He stood for a while near the perimeter and remembered the daylight probe the VC sprung on them and the "Sympathy for the Devil" response they got from the defenders. And the rainy night the enemy breached the perimeter and made it into camp. That's when a wounded VC was gasping for breath and was shot dead, point blank in the face. He looked all over the flight line where ships and crews left on their last trips anywhere—officers and enlisted men, gone, their lives and names seemingly erased. His life had almost been erased a few times.

Long Thong itself was made of shacks, chicken coops combined with metal roofs and sandbags, bunkers of sandbags, barrels, timbers, steel panels, and the decrepit hangar riddled with shrapnel holes. God, what a dump, a real shantytown. Since the mud dried up, the dust devils were back. He would not miss living here. The guys, yes, but not living here.

It was time to turn in his uniforms and equipment to the supply room. Just leave with the fatigues on your back. Even the supply sergeant had been replaced. Penton had gone home. Reichhart, his replacement, slowly checked off every item of equipment and clothes turned in. At the armory, he turned in his M16 and .45 automatic. The M16 he'd rarely used, and the .45 was the one he drunkenly shot up the company area with. And at the dispensary he picked up his shot-record booklet. Even Galveston, that wonderful medic, had gone home.

Someone yelled his name, "Dyson . . . Dyson." It was Hines. He and the major saluted each other. "Hey, I got your home address from the orderly room. Hasn't changed, has it?"

"No, sir. Still the same."

"I personally checked on your DFC. It's still 'up there.' Division sent it to Awards and Decorations a long time ago. They're still waiting to get it back."

"Well, thank you, sir. I really appreciate it, believe me."

"I will hunt this down until it comes back, and I will make sure you get it."

"Sir, you know a bunch of us got hit in that mortar . . ."

"Yeah, I know. You guys just might have to kiss that one good-bye. There's no records of it. Like they just disappeared, damn it." He offered Dyson a Camel and they lit up. "It's gotten so goddamn rotten, from the top down. Everything is so screwed up now. It's not the same Army I joined years ago. Back then you felt like you were a part of something. I just want to go home back in the woods and hunt and fish."

Then Hines said, "Well, been great having you here." They shook hands as friends.

At 18:15 hours, Mister D and Soup entered the mess hall for his last evening meal—franks and beans. "Short!" Dyson announced with his short timer stick under his arm. Cooks, mechanics, and crew members all let him have their best wishes and good-byes. He and Soup took their trays and were called over to sit along the wall with a bunch of guys.

"Hey, D, we want to take a picture." They moved four tables together along the wall. What's going on? One guy had a picture of the Last Supper so the men seated and posed themselves to resemble the picture, Dyson being Jesus with Soup next to him and all others were the Apostles.

"Oh, man, I hope we don't get struck by lightning doing this."

"Or a mortar," said Soup.

"That's good. OK, close it up a little so I can get everyone in.

Ready. OK, everybody say 'FTA.'"

"FTA!" The 35mm camera flashed once, then three more times just to make sure.

"We'll call it the 'Unholy Supper.'"

"We'll send you a copy, man, promise."

After chow, Soup, Dyson, and several other guys went to the EM Club for a few beers. On the way, they had a couple tokes on some Marlboro Greens. He yelled, "Short!" as he entered the club. He still had his short timer stick under his arm. Guys slapped him on the back and shook his hand. He couldn't buy his own beer. "Born on the Bayou" was blaring over the speakers. Bowls and joints were passed around. There were laughs about Earlywhile and how he'd been Medevac'd with a bad case of the clap, "Stinky" Rivers, "Iron Cock" O'Grady, Hiller "the Killer," and a bunch of other one-of-a-kinds who had passed through the company. O'Grady, "the only one of his kind in captivity."

Someone broke out some Jack Daniels (forbidden in the EM Club and to enlisted men, period) for some shots in paper cups from the Dispensary. Mister D took one. He didn't want to, but he did because of the occasion. "Here's to all the guys that couldn't be here tonight." They raised their cups and beers. It got quiet. Even the music stopped.

"Morgan. Anderson. Harvey. Jonas. Patterson. McQue. Daniels. Muzzano . . ." More names were added and added. "Cheers, man!"

"Fuck this stupid war!"

"FTA!"

"FUCK THIS STUPID WAR!" some men bellowed, like an act of treason almost.

"Amen."

They stayed for a half hour before heading went back to their hootch. They smoked some more and then Soup and Dyson went outside, sat on the sandbags, and watched the sunset. There must have been twenty or so other guys scattered along the revetments doing the same thing.

"Robano extended for another six months," said Soup.

"Huh. I think he likes it here," said D.

"I just want to go home. I got fifty-five days left."

"You'll make it, Soup."

"You never know over here." He was right.

At 23:20 hours, he got in his bunk. He was stoned but didn't fall asleep. All night he stared up at the roof, the roof he dreamed of with mortar and rocket warheads sticking through, ready to go off any second. He thought of all the people he had seen—soldiers, civilians—pulverized, some mixed in with the earth, plastered to or hanging from trees, burned black beyond recognition, gone. His mind was a continuous slide show, scene after scene. Are these going to disappear on the trip home? Step from one dimension to another with no memory of this shit? It went on all night.

Two days to go.

▌▐▐▐▌

Friday, December 5, was the first morning he had showered and shaved completely in months, he usually did it in the evening. The whole company knew who he was and that he was leaving for out-processing in Long Binh and flying home Sunday, December 7—Pearl Harbor Day. He was bombarded with all kinds of well-wishes, handshakes, goodbyes, and nice-knowing-yous. Some of the guys he didn't know from Adam, but it was nice.

He skipped the morning mess. At sunup, he was packing his cameras, shaving gear, clean underwear and socks, Ho Chi Minh sandals, and Camels into the small suitcase Soup had given him. He and Soup sat on the sandbags outside until 07:45 hours, then went inside, and had a few tokes for the last time.

"How you getting to Long Binh?" he asked.

"Major Hines said I could ride with the cooks on their food run . . . in ten minutes."

"Well, good-bye, old friend."

"Bye, Soup." They shook hands. Dyson took his small suitcase, put his treasured short timer stick under his arm, and stepped out of the hootch into the sunshine of Long Thong for the last time.

I IIII I

Out-Processing

At 08:00, he climbed into a three-quarter ton truck with two soul-brother cooks—Artimus Lambert and Willie Loomis. A jeep in front of them was riding shotgun, and a deuce and a half behind them to pick up food in Long Binh. They drove out the main gate and began the seven-mile drive. As soon as they got out of camp, Lambert lit up a Marlboro Green. The three of them smoked that joint and then another before making it to Long Binh. The small convoy was waved through a gate and into the sprawling compound. Dyson lit a Camel to cover the pot smell. The jeep driver led them right to the out-processing center.

"Here's where you get off, Mister D," said Lambert.

"Goodbye, guys." They shook hands. "Thanks for the ride."

"Take care, Mister D." They gave each other the peace symbol.

"It's been real, man."

It was a permanent building with steel siding, glass windows, and super-market glass entry doors. An overhead sign said "U.S. Army RVN Out-Processing Center." Another sign over the doors said "Report Here." He entered and joined a short line to a counter with clerks behind it. When he got to an empty spot, a clerk asked him for his full name. The clerk then gave him a form to fill out. After he'd done that, the clerk looked it over and said to have a seat with the others and wait for his name to be called for an interview. After ten minutes, he was directed to sit in front of a desk occupied by a clerk. Like all the clerks, he was in khakis and wore only a National Defense Ribbon, a sure sign he was just out of basic training and AIT. He was Wonder Bread-white, like he never saw the sun.

Without even looking at Dyson, he asked, "Do you agree all the information on this form is correct, spelling and accuracy?"

"Yeah."

"Do you have your shot record with you?"

"Yes."

"OK, hang on to it. Sign here." Dyson signed. "OK, now take all your belongings and go through that door and have a seat."

He entered a gymnasium-size room with folding tables lined all around the walls. NCOs were running the show. They had the men stand between the walls and the tables with all their personal property on the tables in front of them. In the center of the room was an open wooden crate, four-foot square.

"OK, gentlemen, open your suitcases, valises, and bags so we can see everything. Spread it out, gentlemen." Everyone obeyed. Lifers began inspecting for contraband. "Now, we are going to have a 'mad minute' in which everyone will have a chance to turn in and throw away, in this crate, articles forbidden to be taken out of the country—no questions asked, no punishments. Understand?" Everyone understood. "Now, those items are as follows: no ballistics of any kind, no ammo, no grenades, no live rounds, no spent rounds, and no brass." The men began bringing all kinds of stuff to the crate and dumping it—stuff most people wouldn't even dream of taking home.

A lifer walking up and down the tables saw Dyson's short timer stick with the brass casing at each end and his Ho Chi Minh sandals. "The stick and sandals will have to go, buddy," the sergeant said. No argument, Dyson dumped them in the box—his two most valued possessions from his tour.

"Now, no pictures of dead or wounded personnel, friendly or enemy, none whatsoever. No aerial pictures of American compounds, bases, camps, fire support bases, or landing zones. No pictures of aircraft on flight lines. All those pictures must go in the box. You may, however, keep undeveloped film if you have it. Let's go, gentlemen." Then there were searches through pictures and snapshots, some moans and groans, and many pictures were dumped into the crate. Dyson discarded his pictures that were in violation. The lifers continued walking around.

"Well, now comes the big one, gentlemen. No illegal drugs

whatsoever. No pot, no opium, no heroin, no hashish, no pills, no powder. It all must go, NOW! No questions asked." And didn't some guys run up there and dump their dope. They'd brought drugs with them. "Very good, very good. A wise decision, gentlemen. If you are caught with dope beyond this station, you will not be going home soon. And that is affirmative!"

They seemed to be finished. But then . . . "All right now, gentlemen, has everybody dumped all their unauthorized material? Nobody's holding onto anything illegal? Everyone is done?" A couple guys looked nervous. "Going once, going twice . . ." He paused, "OK, one last chance, one last minute, no questions asked." And two guys made a dash for the box and threw their stashes away. "Very good! A very wise decision, gentlemen. And your time is up. We thank you for your cooperation."

They were assigned to barracks for the next two nights. The barracks had double bunks with mosquito nets, concrete and tile floors, ceiling fans, and an astounding shower room and latrine with indoor flush toilets in privacy stalls—the first one he sat on in a year. Some barracks were for guys going home Saturday and his group leaving Sunday. New arrivals came every day. Dyson could pick the grunts out even if they had on new fatigues—red-tan faces and arms, skin plastered with the scars of razor-sharp grasses and vines, hundreds of bug bites, and the red embedded dust of this country. Also, the general demeanor and attitude, the guys who were really screwed over by this war.

They were shown to the out-processing mess hall for noon mess. It was air-conditioned and beautiful: concrete and tile floors, stainless steel serving line, piping hot food, friendly cooks, cold milk, choices of desserts, and linen tablecloths. The guys began to socialize. There were a bunch like him wearing crew member wings.

After noon mess there was a formation in which they stood for twenty minutes for nothing more than roll call. Then more dead time, then they were told they would be going to the paymaster when called. It was a long, drawn-out affair waiting to be called to the paymaster in groups of twenty men at a time. Around 15:00 hours, when his name was finally called, they formed up and sat on wooden benches until a clerk called their name. At last he heard his name and he sat with a pay clerk.

"OK, Dyson. You only drew $35 a month and the rest accrued. So, with pay grades, flight pay $55 a month, and hostile fire pay $55 a month, you have accrued $5,560 to take home with you. Sunday morning you will receive a Government cashier's check for that amount to carry home. Does that sound right?"

"Yes, it does." Living was so cheap over here. He drew $35 a month from his base pay and was able to buy cigarettes, beer, PX items, and only a few times dope. He always had a little left over on payday. $5,560 sounded like a fortune.

"OK, sign here."

"Do you have any MPC on you?"

He did and exchanged the Military Payment Certificates for U.S. greenbacks and coins. They felt so strange.

Processing was done for the day. The men killed time at the out-processing EM Club, smoked cigarettes, and shot the shit until evening chow—wonderful fried chicken with the works. After that, he shaved and showered in that beautiful latrine. What a difference from the gravity-fed showers, sinks, shitters, and piss tubes in Long Thong. They could go to the PX until 19:00 hours, watch a movie in the outdoor theater, go to the EM Club (but don't get drunk and disorderly) or lounge in the barracks. It was restful, but no one seemed to have any pot.

The movie was "The Graduate," which he had seen twice back home and twice in Long Thong. In the EM Club, he bought a beer and sat with two other crewmen, SP5 Spate and SP5 Wiley. They seemed to be just like him. They had been crew chiefs in a 1st Cavalry Division Huey Battalion in Bearcat, just down the road from Long Thong. Reggie Spate was from Ohio, Frank Wiley from Washington. They were as worn out as Dyson.

After a few rounds of beers, they had enough of the smoke

and noise, so they went outside and sat on a bench. It was a nice evening, growing dark. Everyone was cleaned up, well fed, relaxed, and counting the hours. The out-processing center was on the southwest side of Long Binh, some three hundred feet from the camp's perimeter. Guys gathered on the road behind the perimeter or stood on CONEXes and bunkers, all looking southwest. Flashes could be seen in the distance and some faint explosions were heard. Then they got the word—miles away, Long Thong was under attack. Nothing to see from this distance.

The out-processing center had a policy of lights out at 22:30 hours, so almost everyone was in bed or at least in their area by that time. He was surprised how clean the sheets were and how comfortable the mattress was. Conversations faded away and he fell asleep after midnight. He restlessly dreamed a jumbled phantasmagoria of dancing GIs during a mortar attack, crews falling out of their ships, wayward tracers lacing through everything, a hootch of no return— men went in but never came out, and the sun stuck during sunset over Long Thong, the orange glow over the camp forever, all the men bewildered, frozen in time.

▌▐▐▐ ▌

Reveille was at 06:00 hours, morning chow at 07:00 hours, first formation at 08:00 hours. After roll call, more names were called. His group was sent to medical out-processing. Again, they had to wait for a clerk to call their name and sit with them answering questions. Their shot records were checked. Just about everybody had to get three or four inoculations to update their records. So now that part was complete.

More dead time until his group was sent to personnel out-processing. Again, they sat until their name was called to sit with a clerk. This time Dyson sat with a Staff Sergeant LeMonte who wore khakis, with a CIB, Bronze Star, and Purple Heart.

"Here is a manila envelope to keep all your papers together," LeMonte said. "Put your shot record and medical clearance in there.

RAY DYER AND STEPHEN DWYER

Here is your check from the paymaster for $5,560 and your 201 File." His Official Military Personnel File. He was handed a crisp, brand-new folder. Dyson opened it and was shocked to see it only contained his promotion orders to SP5, and travel orders to CONUS (Continental United States). The Central Summary Form had only his name, rank, and serial number, and listed Fort Dix, Fort Eustis, and B Co., 137th ASH, 2nd Airmobile Division. That was it. No Air Medals, no Purple Heart, no Distinguished Flying Cross, only the National Defense Medal he got from basic training. It was a poor comparison to the 201 File he handed in when he arrived in Vietnam. The one in his hand could have been slapped together this morning it was so new. Then he noticed in one box the words "Clerk Typist."

"What the fuck is this?" he asked the clerk.

"What's what?"

"What's with this 201 File? This ain't the one I handed in last December. This doesn't have shit in it! And I wasn't no clerk!"

"Yours was lost."

"Lost! How the hell could it get lost? I was in one Company for the whole damn year. How the hell could it get lost?" Another heated exchange was going on at nearby desk. It was also about a lost file.

"Look, I'm sorry it got lost, OK? But I didn't lose it."

Dyson leaned forward and lowered his voice. "Do you know I'm supposed to have Air Medals, a Purple Heart, and was put in for a DFC? I was a crew member, a crew chief, a gunner. Not a fuckin' clerk!"

LeMonte leaned forward and said, "What do you care? You're getting out of the Army." He could see Dyson was starting to boil inside. "When you get home, your local VA will help you find your medals. Believe me." He was nice about it, but he was passing the buck.

Dyson had heard empty promises before. He caught himself starting to tremble. The clerk thought Dyson was about to go off and braced himself. He had seen many guys get fucked out of their awards and decorations, but it was hard to tell if he cared or not.

"OK, Sergeant. We done?"

"Yeah." They both stood up. LeMonte offered his hand and, after hesitating, Dyson shook it. The clerk said he was sorry to see this happen so many times. Small compensation. How the hell do these files "get lost?" Jesus.

Dyson walked out into the sunlight and lit a Camel. He put the prized check in his wallet. The area was full of guys carrying new manila envelopes that contained all their necessary paperwork. He spotted the sergeant who had him turn in his sandals and short-timer stick, with the stick tucked under his arm. He was strutting around like he was hot shit. Lifers. Wonder who got his prized Ho Chi Minh sandals? Don't do anything that will jeopardize getting on that jet plane tomorrow. Just get the hell home.

After noon chow, Dyson joined up with Spate and Wiley. "Everything OK?" Wiley asked. Dyson showed them the new 201 File. Spate had a new one, too.

"What the hell do they do with those things? You hand them in and they lose the damn things."

"I think they burn the damn things."

"What is it? Fucked up clerks? Government policy to lose so many a month? What the fuck!"

"Then he says to me, 'What do you care? You're getting out of the Army.' Do you believe that?"

"Well, we're done processing until morning. Let's go have some beer."

Dyson was glad for their company, helping him maintain his composure right now. They would have cold beer and snacks instead of going to the noon mess.

That was cut short for a mandatory formation at 12:30 hours. The sole purpose of this was a headcount and roll call. There was one guy AWOL. Who in his right mind would go AWOL from out-processing? After the formation, the three men decided to have a look around Long Binh. Tucking their precious manila envelopes under their arms, they walked on cement sidewalks along paved streets lined with permanent buildings.

"Doesn't this seem surreal, somehow?" Wiley wondered. What did this say about the intentions of the war effort? All the mayhem and death "out there" and the order and comfort "in here." Did these huge Disney Land-like bases and all the other bases of camps, LZs, and FSBs work with each other in the war effort or did they have two different objectives?

"Imagine being stationed in this place for your entire tour? What kind of impression would you have about the war?" "This place is so isolated from the war—would you even see anything remotely related to what's really going on out there?"

Everyone had heard about the VC ground attack on Long Binh back in February 1969 during that Tet offensive. That was the night a C-130 "Spooky" gunship obliterated the woods just outside Long Binh and then Long Thong. But that was just one night in the long, long, peaceful history of Long Binh.

"Like right now. I'm having a hard time believing we're in Vietnam; it's so different here." Just then a Mustang convertible with two American civilian women drove past, radio blaring.

"Da Nang's the same way, and Cam Ranh Bay and Bien Hoa. Millions and millions of dollars to accomplish what?"

"You know, I haven't even heard a Huey for a couple hours. Or a Chinook."

"Amazing, ain't it?"

They met up with two GIs walking in the other direction. "Going home, huh?" They had spied the telltale manila envelopes.

"Yeah, buddy."

"You guys need a little smoke?" asked one. "I got a couple joints." Free pot from a REMF.

"Well," said Wiley, "I sure could use a hit or two."

One of them said he knew it wasn't too cool to smoke in the out-processing center, so smoke out here while you're walking and keep an eye out for MPs.

"How much you want for them?" asked Spate.

"Nothin', man. Nothin'." He had spotted their crew member badges. "Just somethin' from us to you guys. You guys musta been crew chiefs or gunners." He gave them two joints. They all shook hands with best wishes and continued their walk. Even now, it still amazed him how free and easy dope is over here.

"What do you say we walk that way back to the EM Club?" They smoked one of joints along the way back and got good and stoned. That was ass-kicking pot. They entered the EM Club, bought three Hamm's, sat at a table, and talked while listening to the music until it was time for evening mess and then walked across the courtyard to the mess hall.

"Isn't this unbelievable? Air-conditioned." said Wiley. They filled their trays with Salisbury steak, roast turkey, mashed potatoes, gravy, and whatever looked good. Dyson got some cold chocolate milk and sat with his two new friends.

"I still can't believe this food, man," said Wiley. "We had the worst damn mess hall."

"No, we had the worst mess hall," Spate insisted.

"Did you guys ever have grease-con-carne?" That got a few laughs.

This was their last dinner in Vietnam, and it was kind of pleasant. Well, pleasant physically, but inside his head were those damn images co-existing with his surroundings. Nice and not nice all at once. He wasn't going to spoil their meal. Maybe one or both of them were in the same mess mentally.

They decided to shave and shower tonight. Dyson watched over their manila envelopes while Spate and Wiley were in the sparkling latrine, then they watched over his.

They walked into the EM Club, a raucous stag celebration of everyone's last night in Vietnam. There was unauthorized hard liquor going around, but no one seemed worried. Men scattered around the club were smoking cigars to camouflage the smell of pot. Wiley produced the other joint they'd been given.

"Our last joint in Vietnam, on our last night. Fuck this place!"

Creedence began belting out "I Ain't No Senator's Son." The adrenaline and testosterone were skyrocketing. Good thing there were no women in here. Up next was "We Gotta Get Out of This Place," and that was it. It could have been a riot. The EM Club became an arena of celebration. No cadre or MPs came in to have them quiet down and behave. Some guys were way past drunk, but no one seemed to care. Next came "Give Me a Ticket for an Aeroplane." The singers were coming out of the woodwork. Like high school kids. A lot of them *were* kids. Somebody running the sound system was choosing these songs well.

After an hour or so, Wiley said, "Hey, you want to get out of here?" Sounded like a good idea.

Back out in the fresh air, the sun was setting on the silhouette of the sprawling camp's skyline. It could have been mistaken for a small city back home. They sat on a bench against a building, and lit cigarettes, still stoned with a few beers in them. "Man, those joints were great, man."

Yeah, they were, but they didn't have the magical mind-blowing high that smoking had when he first got over here, before the rotten, gore-ridden senselessness of the war invaded his mind, day and night.

The light was dimming from the orange glow of the sunset to blues and purples of twilight. Then it quickly got grayer and grayer, the last rapid and fleeting dusk of the tropics they would ever see.

"I've got a little boy five months old I've never seen," said Spate. "I don't know if I will be able to touch him or pick him up after touching some of the terrible things I touched with these hands." Could Dyson still smell Reynolds' burnt flesh on his hands? It was ghostly, another phantom.

Those scenes were always just under the surface. I may look like I'm listening, Dyson thought, but I'm not. I'm always back on some mission, with dead and wounded lying on the deck, the foot in the boot left on the ship, the pile of dead villagers and dead VC tied together with rope, Morgan's face all shot to hell, Reynolds burned beyond . . .

"One thing that will stick with me," Wiley said, "is when we were ferrying troops for an assault from Lai Khe to someplace—I don't know where, doesn't matter—and they were all lined up on the flight line for boarding and this Huey was over the camp at about two hundred feet up and some guy falls out of it, just falls out, screaming the whole way down and when he hit the ground the troops just laughed their asses off. Yelled 'Airborne!' and shit like that. What the hell, man."

How did this shit come up, anyway? It came up because it is always there.

It was lights out at 22:30 hours. Dyson was under the mosquito netting, arms up, hands behind his head staring straight up. The last night. Small groups of men talked softly here and there while Long Binh's artillery fired "out there" somewhere. He closed his eyes and stayed like that for a couple hours until he dozed off. Maybe everyone was having trouble sleeping. He woke and dozed, woke and dozed, sometimes remembering just the tail end of a dream.

| | | | |

Goodbye Vietnam!

A CQ runner was there at 05:30 hours. "OK, gentlemen, OK. Wake up. Wake up. Let's go. You're all going home this morning. Let's not be late. The mess hall is open. Get dressed. Have your last breakfast in Vietnam, last breakfast. Formation at 07:00 hours. 07:00 hours. Do not be late."

Spate, Wiley, and Dyson had themselves a big breakfast of eggs, bacon, and sausage, hot cakes, real butter, OJ, and hot coffee in the wonderful, wonderful mess hall. "Man, I still can't believe this place—or the food," said Wiley.

At 07:00 hours, four hundred men stood in formation, everyone with his manila envelope and suitcase. Roll call showed one man still AWOL, whereabouts unknown. Their group of two hundred boarded buses for the flight to Tan Son Nhut Airbase in Bien Hoa. The route from Long Binh to Bien Hoa was through the chaotic, stinking, smog-choking, no-rules-of-the road most populated area in South Vietnam. Then past the gates of their base and straight to the boarding area of American Airlines' Boeing 707s.

"Look at that beautiful fucking bird!" someone yelled, and everyone cheered. It was the cleanest aircraft he had ever seen over here—glistening, painted, no bullet holes or green tape covering something.

As they stepped down off the bus, their names were checked off a roster, their luggage turned in for the trip home. Then it was into a securely cordoned-off airport gate for final out-processing, which consisted of going through security check points, one man at a time through a supermarket-style checkout.

"Do you have anything to declare?" and the answer should be "no" as all contraband and unauthorized material were to have been turned in. Ahead of Dyson was a captain with a valise.

"Do you have anything to declare, sir?"

"No, I don't." A gun muzzle of some sort was peeking out of the case, making the top and bottom portions unable to close on it. Dyson recognized the front sights as a 9mm Chi-Com submachine gun—a war trophy. "Nothing to declare." Lifers.

They passed outside onto the tarmac and toward the 707, the "Freedom Bird." Guys were just plain giddy. At the base of the steel staircase, their names were checked off again. Then up the stairs, where they were welcomed by two good-looking stewardesses, and they started filling the plane from the back to front, seat by seat, directed by two other stunning stewardesses. Dyson got a window seat just aft of the wing. One last time, their names were checked off in the assigned seats. One seat empty for the AWOL asshole, wherever he may be. Had to be a heroin addict. Hey! Dyson just remembered, there had been no piss tests! It had been a rumor.

Seatbelts were fastened, and the stewardesses went over the emergency procedures amid roars and howls, catcalls and profanities, with the women taking it all in stride. The engines started. The jet taxied to the runway. His heart was beating hard; they were leaving this godforsaken place.

There were no other jets to wait for. When the 707 got to the runway, it was cleared for takeoff and they sped down the flight line, gaining speed the whole time.

"GO! GO! GO! Come on, GO!" He found himself yelling with the rest of them. The nose rose off the ground, the roar of the wheels on the tarmac ceased, and the one hundred ninety-nine men aboard yelled their fool heads off. "GOODBYE VIETNAM!" The jet climbed steeply up into the clouds as Vietnam disappeared from his sight. Gone.

THE
YEARS
AFTER

Gary Dyson didn't know that in twelve hours he would be in uniform in Oakland Airport and be set upon by five peace creeps who called him "baby killer" then spat on his back. Two Marines saw this and came to his side, sending the creeps away, and then helped him clean his uniform in a men's room. After that, on the flight from Oakland to O'Hare, a stewardess spilled a drink on him, and again on the flight from O'Hare to Hartford/Springfield another stewardess spilled another drink on him. It must have been a game they played.

His mom and brother, Len, hardly recognized him—gaunt and red-tan. The three of them hugged. Only Len didn't cry. His mom had aged so much.

"I was worried sick," she said, looking him in the eye.

That night Len had to go to work at the hospital, but before he went, he quietly gave his older brother two joints. At the kitchen table, Gary and his mom smoked cigarettes and drank Murphy's Irish Whiskey. He told her some of the bad things that had happened, but he kept the gore out of it, sticking to the story that he had been in a secure area away from the fighting.

Later on, around 2 a.m., he was in his own room, in his own bed. He dozed off uneasily, half awake, half asleep, dreaming of flying in a Huey at treetop level, while in the foliage KIAs and ghosts whizzed by, waving, and beckoning him to join them. First one, then another, then a whole lot more mortar and rocket warheads pierced his bedroom ceiling, every single one capable of detonating at any second. As he stared at them, they disappeared. Suddenly he was sitting at a large oak table, playing cards with KIAs who had open, untreated wounds. The dealer looked the worst with an exposed rib cage. His face was unrecognizable. The phantoms had followed him home.

In the morning his mom asked him how he slept. "I slept just fine, Mom."

After a big breakfast she gave him the keys to her car. "I know there's places you want to visit." He drove straight to a bank and cashed the government paycheck, keeping the cash in his bedroom.

He drove out to the old hunting grounds where they used to shoot pheasant, grouse, and woodcock. Some of the property had houses on it now, and some was posted with surveyors' stakes plotting the initial parsing of the development to be known as Kristine's Ridge. He began showing up at old watering holes and friends began calling him at home. Never once did he want to call Carol.

The nightmares continued wherever he slept, and soon the heavy drinking and the drugging began. He partied hard almost every day and night. The high price and low quality of the pot astounded him. It was nowhere near as good as the Golden Triangle dope he was accustomed to. Len took him aside and told him to get a handle on himself as his mom was starting to worry all over again, especially since he was letting his hair and beard grow, and not looking for work.

He bought a beat-up, 1963 Chevy Impala for $200 and moved in with friends. They could hear him talking and yelling at night, but they never complained or asked questions. He also bought a 1911A-1 .45 just like the one he shot up the company with. The $5,500 he returned home with was gone after six weeks. As a veteran, he was eligible for one year of unemployment compensation, which he quickly took.

One afternoon, Gary ran into his Uncle Roy who was shocked at his condition—his unkempt beard and hair down to his shoulders, rumpled clothes, and drunk.

"Look, Gary," he said. "You need some stability. Join a VFW or an American Legion. They're full of veterans and they help other veterans. That's their purpose. They'll help you."

With that in mind, Gary went to a VFW hall in Tolland County. There was a large dining hall with a bar along the side. It was lunchtime and four older World War II vets sat at a table eating burgers and fries. They stared at him. The bartender was busily drying beer mugs. Gary approached him and asked, "Can you tell me where I can sign up here?"

Then the bartender stared at him. "You're a veteran?"

"Yeah. I'm a veteran."

"And just what war are you supposed to be a veteran of?"

With a little snort he said, "Vietnam."

"Hey," the bartender called to his buddies. "He says he's a veteran. A Vietnam veteran."

"We don't want you guys from Vietnam in the VFW," piped up one old vet eating his lunch. "You guys were not in a declared war, like us. It was an undeclared war. And besides, a lot of you guys use drugs." Besides their lunch of burgers and fries, there were eight brown bottles of Budweiser and double-shot glasses of whiskey.

"That's right," said another old guy wearing a red Marine Corps jacket. "We don't want ya." Addressing the bartender, he said, "Jerry, do you want him or his kind in here?"

"No way," said Jerry folding his arms. "Not now, not ever."

The rage was surging in him, his heart pounded, blood pressure rose, and he clenched his fists so hard his nails dug into his palms. Gary left. Fuck it. He wouldn't even bother trying the America Legion. Whenever he saw VFW and American Legion activities or their pictures, they were always full of old men—*only* old men. "Undeclared war," the term became branded in his resentments.

At a bar one night, a drunken philosopher said, "No man is an island," and Gary remembered it was a line from a poem by John Donne. He had heard it years ago, 1965, in English class.

"Oh, yeah?" he said to himself. "Watch me." He didn't need anybody. His life was a mess, but he was going to straighten it out. But he continued to drink and get high all night. He missed his buddies back in Long Thong.

Then he found a job making wooden pallets in a dilapidated old mill in Colchester—unskilled labor in a sweat shop, three dollars an hour, and push, push, push. Everyone who worked there was miserable.

His routine consisted of smoking a joint or a bowl soon after waking, do a few shots of Jim Beam or brandy, then smoke and drink on the way to work. If possible, he would leave work at lunch time to drink and smoke. Maybe he would return to work after lunch, maybe not, so he got fired. Job after job with gaps in between and his drinking and drugging was giving him a reputation as another messed up Vietnam vet. Then a friend of the family, Don Montecelli, an old WW II veteran, heard about Gary and offered him a job at his farm cutting firewood, "Cut wood a few times a week and I'll give you $20 for every cord." That job he could handle—while still drinking and smoking. He began putting a lot of effort into the work, looking better, and feeling better since working outside.

One summer day, Don's niece, Leah Cairns visited the farm. Leah was drawn by Gary's rugged good looks. They talked. She had heard about this guy, she thought, but he didn't seem that bad. They began dating, which straightened him up somewhat, taking care of his appearance, cutting wood five full days a week, cleaned up his Impala, and tried to become a decent boyfriend to Leah, limiting his booze and drugs. They rented a flat together and moved in. They had a comfortable little life until his drinking and drugging surfaced full force. Montecelli had to let him go, for safety reasons. Leah vehemently objected to all the booze and drugs, the mood swings, the energy swings, the sudden blowups, the blackouts, the nightmares, and him sleeping with his loaded gun. When she wasn't around, he would put the gun to his head, rehearsing suicide. One time he came out of a blackout doing just that. He made a half-hearted attempt to attend college and work part-time. But the $260 a month the VA gave him to return to school went to fuel his addiction, not toward the rent or groceries.

Almost four years after Gary got home, he and Leah attempted a geographical cure to Wellington, Ohio, to make things better. Northern Ohio had automobile manufacturing, steel production, shipyards and many related industries. He got a good job in a fabrication shop so they bought a house and, in March 1973 had a little boy, Aaron Joseph. Biblical names like Leah's. Gary lived in that house in Ohio, and he was the father of the little boy but nothing got better. It was a bare semblance of stability, and it didn't last. His usage surged, he missed a lot of work, drained the checking and savings accounts, got a DUI, and was fired. In January, Leah left and took Aaron with her. As bad as their home life was, Gary felt worse alone; alone in the house with a broken-down furnace he couldn't afford to fix. Leah sued for divorce. Broke, Gary was driving illegally now—expired license, altered tags, no insurance. He appeared at the final hearing drunk and stoned, reeking of liquor and pot. "I don't give a fuck," he avowed to himself. As the alcohol and drug intake had increased the failures of his personal life it only added to his omnipresent haunting memories and nightmares. Suicidal thoughts entered his mind daily. His mental state became worse and worse.

His life bottomed out into unmanageability, shitty jobs with shitty hours, and he lived in dives with other drinkers and dopers for three years. He went into detox in 1976 to beat a DUI and fired up a joint the day he got out. He thought he didn't have a problem. He detoxed again in 1980 when he thought he actually *might* have a problem. This time too, he lit a joint within hours of discharge. He went back to his seedy apartment, found out he had been evicted, his possessions had been put out on the curb, picked over and scattered like trash. "Fuck it!"

When he slept in his car, he would be awakened by somebody, a police officer or property owner, and forced to move. One of his drinking buddies gave him a room in their big, ramshackle Victorian farmhouse. Everybody there was a party animal or outright addict; he fit right in. Two of them, Clam and Botch, were drug dealers. He got a mediocre, outdoor job dismantling heavy equipment. So began Gary's descent into a steady supply of LSD, painkillers, and speed on a long odyssey of working to earn booze and drug money, working under the influence, and weekends of all out drinking and doing acid. No paid vacation time, no hospitalization, no paid sick days. Gary now drank bottom-shelf whiskey, Kessler's, $5 a fifth. He would drink and smoke before work, would sneak tokes at work, drink and smoke at lunchtime, then drink and drug himself into oblivion and, many times, nightmares. Nightmares about the gooks with machetes chopping up his buddies, innocent-looking VC children rolling hand grenades under their feet or into their jeep, the "last bullet" dream, screwing a gook whore that turns into a corpse, shaking a guy's hand when his bloody arm comes off, mortar and rocket nose cones protruding through the ceiling, Hueys plunging onto a field loaded with mines and punji stakes, playing poker with corpses with ghastly wounds. The nighttime had a way of swallowing him into a maelstrom of amplified memories.

Clam and Botch both got fired for not coming back after their lunch break and they disappeared, ending Gary's drug connection. His head cleared up, somewhat, and he was back to only booze and pot. An adult vocational education program opened in town. He enrolled in the VA-subsidized welding class and found out he could weld under the influence. It came easy to him, and his mind could wander while he rhythmically pooled his molten metal in different modes of joining metals. He became state certified in structural vertical and overhead welding, giving him a small sense of accomplishment.

In 1984, Gary got a job as a welder at a nonunion steel service outfit that did not give drug tests to applicants. It was a rough place full of dirtballs, bikers, and felons. He made some new friends and ran with a crowd that liked to snort cocaine and drink. They would start right after work Friday, drink and snort all night until the bars closed, then party at someone's place, start drinking again when the bars opened at 5:30 AM, drink and snort all day Saturday until the bars closed, then crash and pass out all day Sunday and Sunday night, and be lucky to make it to work Monday. Fights, nightmares, failure to file income taxes, arrests for no license, no insurance, fleeing the scene, and a DUI for the wreck of his car finally kept him off the road. By sheer luck, Gary got a room for $25 a week in a notorious rooming house on 28th Street in Lorain, three blocks from his job— walking distance. The rooms were on the second and third floor over the Blue Danube Bar and Grill. His room, like all the others, was tiny—enough space for the bed, a small dresser, the closet, and not much else. From his window was a view of the steel plant. And he had a tab in the bar downstairs.

Gary called this arrangement his "Iron Triangle," after the Iron Triangle near Saigon, a Viet Cong stronghold, and the scene of many fierce battles. It became work, the bar, his room . . . work, the bar, his room . . . work, bar, room . . . work, bar, room. He drank before work, he drank during his lunch break, and he drank after work until he tried to go to sleep. Every Friday after work he would pay his bar tab and the rent. There wasn't a lot left over, and the cycle would start all over again. Only occasionally did someone turn him on to any drugs. He walked the three blocks back and forth to work through rain, snow, and ice, below-zero temperatures, and summer heat. He felt like a zombie; he was alive, but he wasn't. He had no idea how long this would go on and what would happen next. A constant feeling of dread took hold of him. He remembered the type of fear he had in Vietnam—ice cold, paralyzing, sick-to-your-stomach fear. But it would pass as the danger passed. Back there, they would retreat to the bottle and the bong, only to have the living shit scared out of them again the next day. Then party down at camp, over and over. But this dread he had now never went away. He knew he was headed toward something bad but he didn't know what it was or when it would happen.

In 1989, a co-worker let him borrow his car to run an errand but Gary got stopped and arrested for no license and DUI. By this time, he knew how to play the game so he went into a detox facility voluntarily. He went to out-patient counseling and cleaned himself up for the court appearance. The judge believed Gary was trying to better himself, and only fined him while suspending his jail time. As soon as he left the courtroom, he went right to the bar and snorted cocaine. He knew no other way of life other than being under the influence. That was his "normal" condition.

There were more months of fights and busts, bars and drug houses, dumps and rooming houses, and shitty jobs with shitty hours. He managed to get disability from the VA for his hearing loss, rated at 11 percent, but it was much worse than that. He received a monthly check for $220 and bought an old, rusty '79 Ford, all black except for the replaced yellow driver's door, and again drove illegally.

Practically all his money went to drugs and booze. He had become a piece of white trash, the kind of man he had despised years ago.

Gary had begun to have deeply disturbing out-of-body experiences. Cold, chilling encounters so real he thought he was entering the metaphysical realm of the spirit world. The first time happened while he was driving, looked in his rear-view mirror and saw Morgan sitting in the back seat, clad in his Nomex flight suit, the sun visor of his flight helmet shattered by bullets, his face a bloody pulp. "Hey, Mr. D," he said and he waved. He'd sometimes felt Morgan was nearby, and there he was now, sitting in the car with him. From outside and above of the car, he was viewing the two of them riding together, just like old times. Morgan was so real Gary reached over to touch his flight suit, but Morgan warned, "No-no-no, Mr. D," and he faded away, out of the hallucination, back to the spirit world.

"No! Morgan! Don't go, Morgan! Please . . . stay." Gary began bawling uncontrollably, chest heaving and pounding the steering wheel with his fists.

One night in 1990, he was passed out in the back room of a trailer he rented with a crack addict. It was in a seedy, mobile home court nicknamed "Crack City," next to the railroad tracks. He slept on a collapsed mattress with filthy sheets while the trains, just sixty feet away, roared by, shaking everything. The neighborhood was overrun with rats and feral cats that lived under the trailers.

Something woke him up—the sound of someone shoveling in the ground. He rolled on his side to the edge of the mattress and looked down at a five-foot hole in the floor. He got up and saw that the hole continued down into the earth. He pointed his .45 down into the excavated hole. Its sides were smooth with shovel marks. At the bottom, he saw himself, digging and throwing each shovelful up into the space under the trailer. He didn't dare say anything, and just stared at the digger until the images faded away. The next day he sold his 1911A1 to a guy in a bar for two hundred dollars and went on a coke and booze bender.

Sometime after that, on a sleepless night, he envisioned himself outside during an electrical storm with black clouds and a heavy rain, like the monsoon. Soaking wet, he was crawling on his hands and knees under high-tension lines between two steel transmission towers. A lightning bolt landed like an artillery shell and splintered a huge oak tree just feet away. He saw himself on the saturated grass in the gale-force wind, fearing at any second he would be zapped. Standing above him, unaffected by the storm, was his dad—bent over him with his hands on his hips, berating him unmercifully. "What the hell have you done with your life? Huh? What the hell have you done with your life, you stupid . . . fucking . . . kid! I tried guiding you in the right direction, you son of a bitch." He went on and on until he faded out. Gary came to in a cow pasture over in Wellington and had no idea how he got there.

In December 1991, upon the advice from a couple of other veterans, Gary admitted himself to the VA Alcohol and Drug Abuse Rehabilitation Facility in Brecksville, Ohio. The smell of urine from the medical wards permeated the place. He was assigned to a four-man room. Only one of the guys offered his hand.

"I'm McGinty. Travis McGinty. Keep your valuables on you. The stealing around here is unbelievable." He glanced at the other two roommates and went on to say that at night outsiders wander around the halls stealing shit while the security people watch TV. Somewhere a radio was playing "White Rabbit."

Looking around Gary could see dust bunnies everywhere, under beds and furniture. Only the main floor area seemed mopped at all. Waste baskets were full and there were two serving trays each with unfinished meals. It was hot in there and someone had cracked a window open.

The staff seemed aloof, standing and talking in a small group, ignoring the residents. Gary was told he could be in this place for sixty days and wondered what he had gotten into. Should he check himself out? No, it's winter outside and he had no place to go. He gave himself and his predicament some self-examination. "My life . . . will it ever be normal again? Will I ever be like I was before I got sent over there? Ever have a place to call home, have a family, a job I like, peace of mind of some kind, something to hold onto?"

"Keep your eyes open, man," McGinty advised him. "You'll see how the place runs, man. You know, you and I come here for help, right?" They both lit cigarettes. "We use it like a lifeboat, right? We want help, and that's all, man. A lifeboat." Travis exhaled heavily. "But we got guys around here, like those two guys over there, man," he nodded toward two older vets smoking in the lounge area. "Simmons, the white guy, and Baker, the black guy. Man, what a pair. They both have canes to make them look disabled. These guys are always in treatment, always in the hospital or the clinic, getting big, and I mean big, full disability checks—and there ain't a damn thing wrong with them, man. Not a damn thing! They use the place like a houseboat, man. A houseboat. Not a lifeboat like you and me, but a houseboat. There're thousands just like them, man. Bleeding the VA!" He lit another cigarette. "There's even a bunch they call the 'snowbirds,' man, because they go to treatment up here in the summer, and trot down South, like Florida, man, for the winter. They even tell the VA and Social Security where to send their next checks. Sick!"

At least, Gary thought, he could eat, get cleaned up, shower every day, clean sheets . . . "three hots and a cot." He felt like he had been sucked into another dysfunctional system and was powerless to do anything but remain here. His mind was naturally rebelling, but he would go with the flow of things.

"I sure could use a joint," Gary said and lit a Camel with his Zippo.

"Oh, don't be surprised if you smell pot around here at night," Travis said. "That's quite a lighter you got there." The dented Zippo had been with him in Vietnam through all those terrible times. And so was his dog tag, the one with the shrapnel hole.

A new term had started floating around the treatment centers—PTSD, post-traumatic stress disorder. Many vets were being diagnosed with it—and many weren't. This was a VA residential treatment and intensive outpatient facility. It sounded welcoming and hopeful, but now it didn't seem that way. Whenever he sat in a group therapy session, it was always the guys who had been in the infantry, artillery, and armor who felt they had suffered the most. Only *they* could have PTSD, no one else. The MPs and truck drivers who were ambushed in convoy after convoy and suffered great losses couldn't possibly get PTSD. Soldiers who worked in Graves Registration and handled the mangled bodies and then reassembled, cleaned, and hermetically sealed them in plastic couldn't possibly get PTSD. Crew chiefs and door gunners who flew sorties in and out of combat, they couldn't possibly get PTSD because they lived in the rear, "away from the action." Neither could medics in and out of combat who saved some guys and lost others ever possibly get PTSD either. The cooks, supply sergeants and helicopter mechanics pounded by enemy mortars and rockets—no PTSD. And skimpy, incomplete, erroneous or lost records only hindered their claims.

In one session, there was an Infantry Marine named Vallinez. When he arrived in Vietnam, a suspicious, overzealous officer discovered Vallinez was only seventeen—too young for RVN— and sent him back home the next day. Vallinez then began a life of alcohol and drug abuse and was eventually granted a PTSD disability, for serving one day in Vietnam.

Then a teenaged-looking kid, Jimmy Kindall, showed up. What was *he* doing here? It came out he had been in the Kuwaiti invasion of August 1990, drove an Abrams tank during a big battle with Iraqi tanks, and it was one of only a few American tanks that were blown-up by the enemy. He had been Medevac'd to a Navy hospital ship, transferred to Germany for further treatment, and was diagnosed there with PTSD—just like that. Dyson resented Kindall's brief time in the Army, his brief time in combat, and the very brief time within which he was determined to have PTSD. It was determined before he even got to Brecksville.

It was always the same bullshit in group sessions. Everyone was in the toughest unit, everyone killed the most Viet Cong and North Vietnamese, everyone had the most KIAs, everyone was in the worst area, everyone had someone's brains spattered all over them, everyone was out in the field the longest. The resentments and the war stories went on and on and on.

"We killed four-hundred gooks that night, dead in the wire . . . and in camp, man!"

"We was in the field for forty-five days. Forty-five days! Not one single night in the rear, man."

"At night, we could hear the NVA in the woods, talking and laughing. They even had fires we could see. They didn't give a damn, man. We was in their backyard."

"We suffered seventy-two percent casualties, like three out of four, men, dead or wounded."

"Our unit was the worst."

"No! Our unit was the worst, man."

Inside, Gary was a mess. But he was detoxed from the booze and drugs. One day, resentment, hate, and rage would boil up within him, and the next day it would be grief, sorrow, mourning, and loss. Any time one of his buddies had gotten killed, it was like a specter with claws had ripped something out of his soul, happening so many times there was nothing left. No one here was talking about their feelings—just war stories, over and over.

He and Travis stayed out of it. He'd feel like an ass contributing to this bullshit. A kaleidoscope of images scanned through his memory. What story should he tell? What difference would it make? What would it prove? Fuck it.

Gary would sit there all bottled up but at the same time bored. War stories, constant war stories, and very, very little rehab. Where was the rehab? Does anyone in this place get better? He saw new guys admitted to their ward and others would disappear. Were they cured? Did they gain anything in here? He couldn't see how anyone got better in this place. His only support was Travis. They sat side by side and elbowed each other when some asshole said something stupid.

In one group session the counselor spotted Gary's damaged dog tag peeking through his unbuttoned shirt. "Tell us what happened to your dog tag, Gary." He wasn't ready to share this with anybody, but the staff running the meeting insisted on maintaining its policy of "Get it all out."

"I was in the prop wash of a Huey helping get a wounded man aboard when the NVA fired an RPG at us. It hit . . ."

"Oh, bullshit!" said a stumpy Marine named Ballard, who dominated just about every session he sat in on. "Bullshit!" He laughed contemptuously, shaking his head no. "Ain't no way in hell a damn piece of shrapnel could do something like that, man. No, way. You're lying, man. Ha ha. Bullshit all the way!"

The reality was that no one could ever duplicate what had happened in those few seconds when the RPG was aimed too low, fell short of its mark, exploded, and sent a piece of shrapnel through Dyson's dog tag suspended in midair by the hurricane-like wind of the prop wash. It was one of those one-in-a-million things that happen in battle—a single millimeter this way or that, a millisecond early or late, and the life-and-death decisions of fate. Like in just about every war, the bullet that drills right through a man's helmet and misses his head. "It was his time to die" or "It was not his time to die."

Dyson sprang up, sent his chair tumbling with a backward kick, startling everybody. "Hey, fuck you, Ballard! Fuck you *and* your mom, you fuckin' son of a gook whore!" He meant them as fighting words. Ballard stood up, too, but he made sure to take position behind the staff standing between him and Dyson, acting all cocky like. He was just a short, loudmouthed bantam rooster of a Marine, ready to fight only when he had the advantage or back-up.

"OK, Dyson!" said the counselor, scribbling furiously on his clipboard, "You're outta here!"

A counselor had previously told Dyson in front of everyone that he was the type to keep all his problems to himself, with his emotions bottled-up inside, until one day he explodes, hurting and killing others or himself. And that's as far as it went. After the confrontation with Ballard, he was terminated from treatment as RMB (received maximum benefits) and cut loose in January 1992, his twelfth day of treatment, and was denied a PTSD disability. He was transferred in a VA minibus to a residential treatment center in Lorain County called Century House.

I I|| I

Century House was in an old rooming house, only a hundred feet from Lake Erie, which was frozen over and white in the bright sunlight. There were vast stretches of flat frozen lake water and jagged piles of broken slabs of ice amassed by the fierce winds and lake currents. It looks like Siberia, he thought.

It was a place for homeless/unemployed males—he fit the bill. He didn't have the opportunity to drink, smoke dope, or snort coke immediately after discharge this time, so he was clean and sober when he arrived at Century House. He was relieved to be out of the bedlam of VA rehabilitation, but now he was back in yet another rehab facility.

He had an admittance interview with his assigned counselor, Charley LeBlanc, but had to wait because LeBlanc was conferring with another resident, a guy named Abe. Gary could hear what was going on in the office.

"Abe, we don't think you have been looking for a job, have you?"

"No, man, I haven't."

"And why haven't you been looking?"

"God told me not to work," Abe said matter of factly.

There was a pause. "God told you not to work?"

"Yeah, during my prayer and meditation, he told me not to work."

"Well, now God is telling you to get your things and go. You're discharged."

He was gone in ten minutes.

After LeBlanc made sure Abe was off the premises, he motioned for Gary to come in and close the door behind him. They shook hands. LeBlanc was six-three, lanky like a basketball player. He reminded Gary of a college professor, looking over his glasses more than through them. He had salt-and-pepper hair and a mostly white beard. He could have been fifty or sixty. "OK, Gary. You are now admitted to Century House. During your seventy-five days here you are supposed to concentrate on your recovery, attend classes, obey the rules, help when asked, go to meetings, and look for a job and housing. Also, there's no smoking in the bedrooms. Understand? What's your sobriety date?"

"I'd say it's December 18, 1991. When I went into the VA at Brecksville."

LeBlanc started the intake interview, casually, one on one. Gary was forty-four now. He had been in treatment four times. He was pretty badly beaten by alcohol and drugs. He had an unruly beard and long unkempt hair. He wore ill-fitting clothes and old tennis shoes. He was out of Camels and his Zippo was out of fluid. LeBlanc gave him a smoke and a light.

"So how were things at the VA?" he asked.

"They are of no help, to anybody. The place is a zoo."

LeBlanc had heard it all before. "Forget the VA. The answer is here, Gary."

With that unexpected introduction, they began a conversation about the wreckage of Gary's past.

"Why do you think you use so much, Gary?"

"Because I went to Vietnam," the words he always hated saying. He felt foolish in front of LeBlanc, or anyone else, saying them. "And I got this condition, this PTSD they talk about. But they said I couldn't have PTSD because I couldn't have suffered enough shit over there. Bullshit, man, bullshit. I saw all kinds of shit over there. I was a crew chief, a door gunner. We'd fly out and participate in the war during the day, then fly back to camp and come under attack at night. One time the VC overran our perimeter and we shot it out with them in camp. The killing, maiming, dead civilians, oh, man, that . . . that . . ." Shit, he thought, here I am telling war stories like at the VA. He felt like such an ass.

"Gary. Gary." LeBlanc was interrupting and waving him off. "Listen, Gary, you need some acceptance." He was looking over his glasses. "You have to accept what happened. You don't have to approve of what happened, but you must accept it. That's what you'll learn here. Open your mind and forget the VA. Fuck the VA." LeBlanc had just shown Gary he was the most effective counselor Gary ever had. His explanation of acceptance made perfect sense and at this moment it brought on a sense of relief from a new revelation he never heard before.

Gary, like all the residents, was taken to the Welfare Department and routinely issued monthly checks and food stamps. These were transferred to Century House to help cover the cost of his care, but each resident received fifty dollars for his own expenses. With some of the men, once they got their hands on fifty dollars cash, they were gone, off and running, relapsed. For once, the money did not burn a hole in his pocket.

Century House had an assortment of donated clothing of all sizes, so he had some decent pants and shirts now. The first things he bought were a carton of Camels, toiletries, socks, underwear, and new sneakers. Then he went to a barber shop and got a haircut and beard trim that made him look and feel a little better, better than he had looked and felt in years.

The second floor of Century House was the dormitory, two men per room, bunk beds, twenty-four men, for a seventy-five-day rehabilitation (plus or minus a few days, depending on the individual). They were awakened at 6:30 to start the day with breakfast and a resident group discussion meeting and then two classes before lunch. In the afternoon, they had a group session and another class. After dinner, it was out to an AA meeting.

Gary's roommate was Derrick, a country boy who looked too young to have been in Vietnam. Gary had the top bunk and a small dresser for himself. The two men shared a clothes closet. Gary saw Derrick's lighter fluid and asked if it was all right to fill his Zippo. No problem, Derrick said. They sat down on a couch in the hallway and lit up. Six other guys were sitting along the hallway smoking and talking.

"Do you like it here?" he asked Derrick.

"Well, yeah. It's better than some places I've been in."

"Any of these guys veterans?"

"Giancola over there, he was in Vietnam."

Tony Giancola was a stocky little Italian, hefty, not soft. He looked like he could handle himself. Black hair and beard, olive skin, and possibly a farm boy like many of Dyson's boyhood friends, whose dads used to make hundreds of gallons of homemade wine, which the boys would steal and get drunk on. Gary liked Tony right off the bat for being such a reminder of those days.

The men attended discussion groups run by the staff as well as groups with residents only, no counselors. There were classes on addiction, powerlessness, and unmanageability. Participation was encouraged—remaining silent was not. Gary could see a difference between the older residents, like him, and the younger guys. Most of the men his age had been beaten up very badly by alcohol and drugs. A lot of the youngsters were cocky, know-it-all brash toughies. What a bunch they were—heavily tattooed, body piercings, neon-colored dyed hair; one guy had a Mohawk. They just hadn't been beaten up enough yet—the "not yets" was the term used in rehabilitation. There was a generational rift between the older and younger residents, but everyone seemed to get along. Gary missed the hippies of years ago.

Evenings after dinner, AA volunteers would drive them to meetings so they could talk to people and look for a program sponsor. He was happily amazed at the wide variety who attended—all ages, men and women, working people, bikers, high school students, retirees, housewives, and veterans wearing identifying baseball caps. There were coffee and doughnuts, tons of cigarette smoke, and all kinds of men to talk to. Gary recognized some old acquaintances from his drinking and drugging days. One guy, Theo Brennan, also a Vietnam veteran, remembered Gary from when they were both in treatment in 1989, when Theo had reached his bottom. He'd been clean and sober ever since. When taking seats, they were joined by Tony Giancola. They talked about what their addictions had done to their messed-up lives. Tony and Theo both had been in prison, Gary hadn't—yet.

The speaker at tonight's meeting was Allen C., who had been sober for two decades. He spoke of all his years of addiction to drugs and alcohol. He'd been dual addicted like Gary, Theo, and Tony.

"The menu doesn't matter, it's all the same. There was alcohol, drugs, and if there was a third realm of substances then I would have been into them, too." He talked about hitting his bottom. How his drug-related crimes landed him in Pickaway Prison in Orient, Ohio, for two years. Then he went out drinking and drugging again and wound up back in Pickaway for four years. He got high in there both times, no problem. After he was released, he continued robbing and stealing to support his habit, and when he got caught this time, he wound up in Ross Correctional in Chillicothe, Ohio. On his first night there, he was knocked to the floor next to an overflowed toilet and gang raped, his face in the water, piss, shit, and toilet paper.

"That moment, I realized, was my bottom. This is where drugs and alcohol had gotten me." Wow, man. "That's when I finally asked God for help, while those perverts were butt-fucking me and laughing their balls off."

If he was going to lick this thing, Gary started to see the importance of becoming spiritual—not religious like Roman Catholic, but spiritual. And no one would ever see him get down on his knees in the morning and pray, and again at night. First, he had to learn *how* to pray and meditate, and *what* to pray for. All he knew was he wanted the turmoil in his brain to stop.

After Allen finished, it was time for comments from the audience. This person and then that person thanked him. Then this enormous black guy stood up. He had to have been four hundred pounds, and his brother just like him was sitting next to him. After he thanked Allen for his lead, he said he was not only addicted to alcohol and drugs, "But I'm also addicted to cheeseburgers." Everyone laughed, but an addiction is an addiction, uncontrollable, and as Gary began to believe, a disease that controls a person's behavior. Many times, he had wondered what made him do the terrible things he had done when using. I'm not like that, he remembered thinking during or after some of that bad behavior. "In my last checkup," the big man said, "they found something in my aorta—a bacon double-cheeseburger." More laughter. Gary found these meetings could be very enjoyable, too.

Allen's lead and the black man's comment would be topics at the House in class and discussion groups—addiction taking many forms and reaching one's bottom. Now, Gary was seeing things differently without his alcohol and drug addled thinking. He realized he was sleeping better and his dreams, if he could remember them, were not always about the war.

Theo would arrive at the House after dinner and drive Tony and Gary to meetings. The three friends talked about the war, not so much about the combat, but about their shared personal defeat, hopelessness, frustration, disappointment in the VA, downward spirals, divorces, suicide games and rehearsals, firearms, sexual debauchery, homelessness, job loss, unemployment, abandonment, and isolation from family. They chain-smoked cigarettes as they talked, practically lighting them end to end.

"How do you smoke those things?" Theo asked Gary about his Camels.

"Hardly anyone will borrow one," he said. And it was true. He remembered Major Hines bumming Camels off him. He prayed the man was still alive and retired back in the Ozarks.

❚ ❚❚❚ ❚

At a meeting on Monday night in Lakewood, Gary, Tony, and Theo were making their way around the crowd, stepping sideways down the rows of tables and chairs, shaking hands, and introducing themselves to men and women seated along tables when Gary reached a man who he just knew must have been a veteran. This fellow had half a featureless face—his right side burned beyond recognition, complete scar tissue and skin graft surfaces, and a club of a right hand with only his index finger and thumb, the hand he offered to Gary. Immediately there was a spark of recognition between the trio and burn victim, an "I-know-you're-one-too" thing. Like drug addicts can spot one another, vets can spot one another, too.

"Hi, I'm Tim Glascoe." They all shook hands. "Want to sit here?" This guy acted like there was nothing abnormal about himself as they exchanged names.

Gary sat next to Tim. Theo and Tony sat across from them. Before any of the three could say anything, Tim said, "That's right, man. Napalm. Our own napalm."

"What happened?" asked Tony. "You guys getting overrun and you had to call it right down on top of you?"

Tim lit a cigarette—he smoked! "No, man. Pilot error. Asshole dropped his canisters way too early and hit us. We knew we were fucked. He flew so low over us I could count the rivets on the jet and those cans as they came tumbling over and over right towards us until they hit our position. The gooks even quit shooting just to watch us burn. Crispy critters! Hey, what were 'Crispy Critters' anyway? Anybody know?" This guy was laughing about it.

Gary, and maybe Theo and Tony, had seen burn victims over there—ghastly. He remembered when he and Robano had pulled Lieutenant Reynold's charred and blackened dead body out of his shot-down Huey. Those who weren't burned to death screamed in agony, suffering horrific pain, even too much for morphine relief.

"When did it happen?"

"Oh, shit. Way back in '66, up in Quang Tri. I was alcoholic before I got in the Army. In Da Nang all we did was drink and smoke dope. I would shoot up heroin when we weren't in the field." That was three years before Gary was there. He was still in college then, with beer, frat parties, cutting classes, sorority girls, heavy music, and whiskey, keg parties, pot, and not a care in the world. And look what happened after he flunked out of school. Whose fault was that?

"How long you been in AA?" Gary asked.

"Ah, like two years now." There was a mild smile with the lip-less slit Tim had for a mouth. He didn't have much of a nose, either. His right eye socket was covered by the skin graft technique the VA used back then—primitive by today's standards. It was very difficult for many people to look at him or shake hands. "I never thought I could feel this good. Never, until after I started becoming spiritual. You ought to try it sometime."

He felt the relief Tim himself felt in those words. Gary had been improving gradually, coming to grips with his past, developing his faith in a higher power, using prayer and meditation, believing his life would get better. Comparing his problems with Tim's, his seemed trivial and inconsequential. "So, what finally made you change?" Gary asked him.

"Your mind can be the worst prison you could ever be in," Tim said, and Gary identified with that completely. "I mean look at me, man. From the day I got burned I never had the opportunity to use and get drunk or high because I was bedridden in hospitals—no access to my booze or my drugs, but they did keep me sedated—heavily sedated, until the worst was over as they called it. No one coming to see me or get me high. I never even had a cigarette for months and months. No one even asked me if I smoked. They put us under anesthesia, so we were passed out for a good part of the time. I was miserable. It was hell. We would lie there for hours, man, no radio, no TV. The nurses came only when they had to change our dressings or bedding, not talking to us, changing us as fast as they could. When they left, they closed the drapes. I drank and was fed through a tube. Sometimes I'd shit myself, or my catheter would fill up and I would piss the bed, and they'd get mad at me. I was screaming inside, livid with rage, hate, frustration. I had the best excuses in the world to be resentful. But I found out later that an excuse is not a reason. I was bitter, really bitter, and I couldn't get high. No one would even look at me, I thought. But after I had been here in the program for a while, I saw that was because I was selfish, the center of the universe, as they say. I was preoccupied solely about myself, man." He took a breather. "I heard 'the bondage of self,' and 'take away my difficulties,' and something clicked, something clicked in my head, man." The guy was totally believable.

Gary felt a warmth and a clarity in this revelation, a way out of his misery. This was God working through people. Gary tried not to show his emotions. He would have teared up if he had let himself. Tim Glascoe was the real thing, a guy who once had huge amounts of bitter resentments and self-pity. But look at him now. Gary thought about his own problems compared to Tim's. "I thought I had been through so much . . . Piss on 'em," he declared. He felt weak and stupid for having dwelt on them for so long, squandering many years of his life, throwing them away.

"And you know what? There were guys in those burn units I was in that were worse off than me, man. Much worse. I'm only burned on half my body—they were burned much worse, their entire bodies burned. So bad they couldn't communicate with anyone, and they had no visitors. Their burn units were 'Off Limits,' and 'Authorized Personnel Only.' No communication, no radios to listen to. Nothing. No hope. When we were all finally shipped like freight from Japan to San Diego, I had family come see me, they didn't, and I bet they're still there today. I found out that my folks had unconditional love for me. There's always someone far worse off than you are. Always." He got closer to Gary. "Put your problems in perspective, man. Put them in perspective."

After the meeting they were saying their goodnights. "I'm here every Monday night," Tim said. "Let's go get something to eat sometime. Then we can really talk."

The four of them had bonded like Gary had never bonded before with any of his family and friends, a stronger bond in fact than with his buddies in Vietnam. At one class session at the House, the counselor said, "Many alcoholics and addicts are incapable of forming close relationships with anyone—their parents, their siblings, wives, sons, daughters—with no one." Gary realized that was him. He hated his dad, he only depended on his mom, felt indifferent about his brother, and had been in heat, not love, with any of his girlfriends, like Carol, who got pregnant by a friend of his soon after he left for Vietnam. He didn't suffer the loss of a loved one—his manly pride had been hurt, that's what it was.

In the evenings after all the group sessions and classes, Gary and Tony would continue their recovery, hooking up with Theo and, on Mondays, with Tim. That guy was a riot. The amazing thing was he had a big hearty laugh—loud, raucous, and contagious. The three of them had never met anyone like him in their lives, never. He was an amazing example of personal recovery from addiction.

One night before the meeting the four of them were talking when someone used the phrase "serving his country." At that, Gary's thoughts, and maybe the other guys' too, were jolted at the irony of the words. How the goddamned hell did we serve our country doing what we did? That glorious phrase is an ideological whitewash, a patriotic blanket of imaginary glory spread over that nightmare entanglement of bombing, shelling, and slaughter. "In Service to His Country" emblazoned on framed certificates, hung on a wall, collecting dust, not read anymore, eventually taken down and lost, forgotten like the man's name on the award. It was an intangible belief, out there somewhere, impossible for them to grasp.

Gary glanced at Tim. Look at this guy, he thought, a miracle—healed in his body and mind. I want the change this guy had, he thought.

Theo would drive Gary and Tony to some inner-city meetings in Cleveland which many homeless men and women would attend. One meeting on West 25th Street was full of street people—homeless men and women, along with their children, and homeless vets, some old from Vietnam and some young from Iraq and Afghanistan. Before the meeting would begin, the trio would contact the vets, shaking hands, making introductions, sitting with them, giving them cigarettes while drinking coffee. But some were there just for the coffee and donuts, and in winter, just to get warm for a while. Someone would yell, "Last call for coffee," and they would get more coffee, grab some donuts, and leave, not wanting to stay for the meeting. One guy stacked three donuts on a pencil and then split. They "didn't want to hear it," just like Gary, Tony, and Theo "didn't want to hear it" for years and years before.

Gary linked the passage of time with his new sense of acceptance, the things he could not control. Now he had to seek control of his life, no more unmanageability, and he realized he was powerless over the first drink or drug. One sip of alcohol, one toke on a pipe, one line of coke, one hit of speed, and he would be off and running, again. The results were the same, always.

It was time to reconnect with his mom, his brother, and his son, who was born in 1973 or 1974—Gary wasn't sure. But Aaron had to be twenty years old by now—an adult, not a minor anymore. He could not remember his birth date and he was his father. How messed up is that?

It took some doing on his part to reach his brother. Since he left and moved to Ohio with Leah, his mom's dementia progressed to the point Len had to put her in a nursing home. She didn't know anybody anymore. Even her brief periods of lucidity were gone now. Len was glad Gary was in treatment and doing better than ever before, so they would remain in touch and plan for some time together.

Leah's number was in the phone book. She was rattled to hear from her ex-husband. "What do you want, Gary?" She sounded cold, defensive. Gary had heard in treatment that no alcoholic/addict could take what he had dished out to family and friends. Suppose the tables had been reversed and Leah had been the problem—draining the checking and savings accounts, lying, not coming home all night, getting fired, jeopardizing the mortgage, wrecking the cars, ruining holidays. No wonder she didn't trust him.

"Leah, I'm sober now, and I'd like to see Aaron, that's all."

She gave him their son's phone number. "Do you think you can stay sober?"

"Well, I'm off to a good start here. I see things a lot different now, Leah . . . Honest."

"You do sound different, that's for sure."

Saturday afternoons at Century House were reserved for family visits. Aaron drove over to meet his dad. They hadn't seen each other since January 1974, when Leah had taken him and left—and here all this time they had lived in the same county! He had no recollection what his dad looked like. It turned out that father and son were the same height and weight. Both had dark hair combed straight back and trimmed beards. They gave each other a big hug. Gary was elated and so grateful. This was the best feeling he had in a long, long time, after years of nothing but hostile negative emotions, fueled by the drugs and the booze. He recognized only his sobriety had allowed him to reunite, and they agreed to spend days together when Gary was discharged.

Beacon House was a halfway house for the unemployed and homeless men who had completed their treatment at Century House. In June 1992, LeBlanc arranged for Gary to stay there until he first found a job and then a place to live. That permitted him to look for employment during the week and stay with Aaron on Friday and Saturday nights. Aaron helped his dad get his driver's license and paid the reinstatement fee. Gary also went through the weeks and weeks of red tape for getting his hearing disability upgraded from the VA. With the help of Disabled American Veterans, his hearing loss was rated at 50 percent, which resulted in his receiving a monthly check of $660. That was a big help.

He landed a job as a welder-apprentice at a manufacturing plant in Lakewood near Aaron's apartment and moved in with his son in September. "There's no rush, Dad, finding a place. It'll be a while before you can afford it," Aaron said. And that was true. His life got better in increments—his driver's license, a job, and a used car. He could now drive himself, legally, to work and meetings.

Living with Aaron was a spiritual godsend. Weekends spending time together—drinking coffee at the kitchen table, shopping for groceries, maintaining their cars, and all the while counting his blessings. Sometimes Aaron would go with him to the big open meetings and gain insight as to what his dad, and his dad's friends Tim, Tony, and Theo, overcame. Aaron did not abuse alcohol or drugs, but he was absorbing the messages of their program and changing his own outlook on life—especially the unique idea of "acceptance." He was also awed at the brotherhood between his dad and his dad's three comrades.

▌ ▌▌▌ ▌

Gary met Peg at a discussion group meeting in December 1993. For weeks they just shook hands and said hello, but then they wound up sitting next to each other and chit-chatting at the Wednesday and Friday meetings.

She was a natural beauty with reddish-brown hair in a ponytail, good muscle tone, and athletic looking. She wore no makeup and dressed in simple clothes, usually just blue jeans, and a pullover. She had a master's degree in education. But then her addiction had her spiral downward out of control, and absenteeism, poor job performances, and a reputation of unreliability blackballed her from work as schoolteacher or principal. Her parents had died years ago and she had no siblings. She had been recovering for eleven years.

"It's been a long haul for me," Peg said. She was holding her Styrofoam coffee cup with both hands. "And I'm trying to stop smoking, too."

One night, a mixed group of about twenty members, young and old men and women, decided to go out after the meeting for a bite to eat, so they joined them at an IHop. As the they filled up the seats in one area, Peg and Gary wound up by themselves in a booth. This was so different than going to a bar to socialize. Here their friends were clean, with clean clothes, pleasant, upbeat, with no hostilities or profanities—amazing. Then they talked about their loneliness, solitude, and isolation, having fallen away from family and friends in self-imposed solitary confinement, even feeling alone in a crowd, and agreed they now cherished their private times in sobriety. Peg would keep almost constant eye contact when they talked, even during gaps in their conversation. "I can tell you're a good man, Gary."

On a Saturday in March, 1994, Gary and Peg drove to Mill Hollow State Park to spend their first day alone together. It was time to reveal everything about themselves—all their growing up

years, all of their school, high school and college years, and all of
their years of addiction—just lay it all bare. They took long walks
through the Lorain County Metro-Parks, holding hands or arm
in arm talking. Many times, they would stop on a bridge over the
Vermilion or the Black River, Peg leaning on the railing and Gary
wrapping his arms around her from behind, resting his head on top
of hers. She smiled when he called her "Little Tiny Peg." They could
communicate without words, their thoughts drifting into each other.
But sometime soon, he was going to have to reveal to Peg that he had
a problem becoming intimate with anyone, and he was not looking
forward to that.

Then came the first time she invited him into her place. It was
a spacious apartment on the second floor of a Victorian house in
Bay Village. "This," she said, "is all second-hand, used, pre-owned,
left-on-the-curb furniture," described just like he would have said it.
She took him on a tour of the place—living room, kitchen, bath,
dining room, a parlor, and two bedrooms, one of which was her
office. Shelves were crammed with books. There was an electric
typewriter and a computer, stacks of folders, and spiral notebooks,
framed photographs and diplomas, and brass candle holders.

"It's an organized mess," she said. "Let's sit over here." The small
sofa faced large windows with a serene view of Lake Erie through
the trees and over rooftops. "My favorite place in the house." She
snuggled up to him.

They talked quietly about their feelings, certainly about their
pasts, and especially about their years of recovery, an ongoing,
never-ending progression. Both agreed their worst day in sobriety
was better than their best day drinking or drugging. "It is what it is"
was one of their mantras. Minutes of silence, a change of topic, some
introspection, an observation, common thoughts, one of which was
they were going to "take it slow."

It would be difficult for Gary to ask or have Peg stay the night at
his place because he lived with Aaron. And she had only a single-size
mattress since she "had given up on the idea of having someone." But

one Friday evening she asked him to have a weekend together.

Gary had longed for and dreaded this moment, but he stuck to their vow to be honest with each other. "Well, Peg," he started, "there's a problem here . . . with me."

Peg didn't miss a beat. "Whatever it is, Hon, we can straighten it out."

"It's funny you should say 'straighten it out' because that is the problem. I have this problem . . . with getting intimate . . . with anyone. It's started years ago, in the late seventies, off and on, then in the eighties the failures became more and more frequent until I never got hard again. And then after I sobered up, I've never even had an opportunity to make love to anyone . . . never."

She gave him an even bigger hug and, touching his forehead with hers, she looked into his eyes and said, "That's not a problem, Buster. Not a problem with me, not at all. We will stay together, you and I living here together. We will continue to get better together, and that's that. OK?" And that was indeed that. This moment could never have happened if they, individually, had not become clean, sober, and spiritual. They were now a couple.

Aaron married a lady named June and they had a son, Chase, and a year later another son, Adam. Gary couldn't believe how things turned out, how his life had improved, and how family now became all important.

Gary continued to work as a certified welder for Garrington-Ohio Fabrication, gaining skills, more certifications and better pay. Peg worked from home as a freelance editor. Almost two years later, they bought the old Victorian house they lived in and had the whole place to themselves. They went to meetings several nights a week and made many friends. They took nature walks and bought bicycles. And they quit smoking—good-bye Camels, for Gary. They made the most of all their time together.

"I love our little life," she would tell Gary.

Then came the shock of 9/11 and in its aftermath a rampant sense of patriotism swept the country. Thousands of young people joined the military to avenge the senseless attack on U.S. soil. Gary mused about it all. Many young men back in the sixties and early seventies had joined the military to fight the Communists in Southeast Asia. They had been praised only in private circles of family and friends and condemned by many more. But now the whole country was swept up in a surge of patriotism—"God, country, the flag, the girl next door, and apple pie" all over again. What a difference, he thought, being able to accept all this without the pain and resentments of the previous war. He prayed for the new wave of American forces fighting over there—and for the civilians who would get in their way.

Being a grandfather brought out warm feelings he never had before. Chase called him "Grampa Santa" because of his now white beard. He loved having a "gang hug" with the boys and Peg and even sometimes with Aaron and June, too, all embracing hello or good-bye. Times like these brought back his sensitivity and humanity, putting those dark days of the war behind him, ridding himself of the callous disregard for life he developed during the war—and he still detested mentioning out loud the name Vietnam.

Garrington-Ohio was getting crushed by foreign steel. When the layoffs came in June 2005, Gary was among the workers let go. It was only a bump in the road as far as he and Peg were concerned. Gary looked for another job, Peg continued working, while together they went to AA meetings. They saw Aaron and his family often. Gary's brother, Len, came and visited for Christmases 2006 and 2007, and was awed by the new sister-in-law and nephews he had. In 2009, Gary got a job welding for a new steel fabrication shop on East 28th Street in Lorain, the same street he used to live on during some of his worst years. There were the constant reminders—the drug houses, the seedy bars, abandoned cars, and deserted houses, rats and feral cats, derelicts looking for handouts—of everything that awaited him if he ever started drinking and drugging again.

He turned sixty-two when Peg was sixty. People told both that they didn't look like they were in their sixties. Gary shaved his head, kept that white beard trimmed, and weighed two-forty. Peg was still his "Little Tiny Peg," and he still rested his chin on her head when they hugged.

Tim Glascoe and Tony Giancola were still going to meetings, but Theo was gone, back into his addiction, gone, nobody knew where. Whenever Peg saw Tim, she gave him a bear hug and a big kiss on his bald head, and he would light up like a Christmas tree.

▌▐▐▐ ▌

In 2019, the astonishing Wall That Heals, the traveling three-quarter-scale replica of the Vietnam Veterans Memorial, came to Lorain County. Before, Gary could never have made a special trip to Washington to see the actual wall with the names of the more than 58,000 service members who died during the Vietnam War. But now he had twenty-eight years of life clean and sober, and he felt he was ready to go see it for himself, with Peg. He didn't ask Tim and Tony or any other vets he knew if they wanted to join them. He preferred to go just with Peg, the person whose support for him meant the most.

The traveling Wall had been erected outside a VFW Hall out in the farm country. He and Peg parked the car at 8:50 on a Saturday morning—the gate opened at 9 a.m. At least a hundred cars were already there. He was tearing up before he got out of the car. Even though this was not the real Wall, an aura of reckoning fell on him.

"Here it comes," he whispered.

"Hon," Peg said, "Just breathe deep and ask God for help."

Most of the people in the crowd were vets, and most of them his age. There were lots of gray ponytails and white beards. Many of the men wore black leather vests or jackets with badges, pins, and unit patches of all descriptions—1st Cavalry, 1st Infantry, 4th Infantry, 9th Infantry, 23rd Infantry, and others he couldn't remember. Combat Infantryman's Badges, Bronze Stars, Purple Hearts, and Air Medals gleamed in the sunlight. He never could get himself to wear those things, not even just a veteran's hat. And there were plain-dressed civilian men and women of all ages, searching slowly for the names, some talking quietly or sobbing into handkerchiefs, some carrying a portrait of someone. There were those who placed mementos on the ground beneath a name—small teddy bears, a flower and ribbon, toys, and even scale model cars, things that had meaningful personal stories.

Seated at a row of tables, VFW volunteers helped people to find the names of their loved ones, telling what panel and what row on that panel to look for. The names were in the chronological order in which they died, beginning with the first KIA and ending with the last man to die in Vietnam.

Peg held his hand tight, seeing him becoming emotional. So many other people there had to be feeling the same things. It could be sensed in the air. Gary asked a volunteer where he'd find the names of Randy Garland, the first man in old Bravo Company he knew was killed in a mortar attack, Andrew Morgan, his best friend back then, and Donald Reynolds, the last man KIA he'd known.

"Randy Garland is on Panel 15, Row 16, and Andrew Morgan is on Panel 19, Row 20. Donald Reynolds is on Panel 20, Row 15." Here it was, clean, concise, tidy, organized, categorized, and arranged. Just how many people here really knew how it happened and what it cost to earn a name on the Wall. Images he hadn't seen in a long, long time came to mind. Peg put her right arm around his waist and pulled his left arm over her shoulder, and that's when his and her tears started. They strolled among other people searching, some very emotional, some were putting their hands over the names they had sought. One lady sank to her knees, bawling, as husband and two others bent to help her. "Jerry . . . Jerry," she sobbed.

They were on Panel 15 now, thousands of names of thousands of guys beyond the beginning of the Wall. They counted down to Row 16. There he was: Randy Garland.

"Who was he, Hon?"

"He was a mechanic killed in a mortar attack on Long Thong, right at the beginning of my tour in Bravo Company. He was a black kid from Florida. Just got there." He'd seen Garland get blasted. He began to scan the other names, moving down and to the right, to the next panel. Across, down to the next row, across, down, across, down. He pictured hundreds and hundreds of faces and saw all those ghosts standing in one line, shoulder to shoulder. How long would it be? Seventy panels, the largest having 137 lines of names, five names per line, thousands, and thousands. Then there was the immeasurable amount of grief in hundreds of thousands of families. And what the hell had it all accomplished?

What felt like a physical weight was pushing down on him, the enormity of it all, each name a tombstone somewhere in a cemetery, thousands of cemeteries, thousands of funerals. He and Peg navigated their way around the people—hundreds of them—solo, couples, families, groups—all courteous to each other, doing their best to avoid being in anybody's way.

Then James Cott. "Shit!" Gary said, "I went to high school with him." He kept reading. Richard Pauley. Richard Pauley? "That's the guy that got killed when someone threw a .45 on the table, it went off and killed him," he told Peg quietly. What's his name doing here? What the hell, he thought, the Army couldn't keep track of anybody correctly. Was that friendly fire? No, he was killed by the actions of an asshole drunk. They kept reading.

Damn. Another high school friend, Al Marrodino. Then came Cochise Toohany, the Electric Indian, an enigma to Gary. Toohany and his people got screwed by the white man and his government, then he's drafted and killed in Vietnam. He put his fingers on his name and pictured him stumbling around camp, wearing sunglasses, and flashing the peace sign.

More names, familiar last names. "Is this one of our guys?" trying to remember full names. Only a last name becomes a man's identity in the service, last names or nicknames—Stinky, Super Chicken, Iron Cock, Iron Lung, the Creeper. Then Bob Anderson. "Hey, he was a gunner in our company." On the next row, Ronald Harvey. "He was another gunner. Oh, shit. Here's Chase LaChappell, the pilot. And Robert Berthal, co-pilot. All on the same ship." Now he couldn't remember the details of the crash and read some other names that didn't spark his memory.

Then he came to the name among them all he wanted to find most. His closest friend during the whole nightmare. Gary touched every letter in Andrew Morgan's name. And Giovanni Cavecchio, the pilot that day. The two men were hit by small arms fire. A big crowd was waiting for them back at Long Thong—lifers waiting for the pilot's body, enlisted men for Morgan's body. Fifty years ago.

"Miss you, man."

They kept reading. Don Vickers, the lazy guy no one liked, but he didn't deserve to get blown up like he did. "Not sure," he would say as they scanned still more names, from the top down, name after name. A single panel was horrendous in itself but seeing panel after panel was staggering. Then, "Oh, man . . . Kenneth Gesso . . . Dan Stevenson . . . Rob Rhinehardt." Gary and Robano had pulled Reynold's burned-beyond-recognition body out of the wreckage and put him in a body bag. He didn't tell this to Peg. He just said, "They all died in the same ship—shot down and burned." Peg tightened her arm around his waist and held his other hand. Without even knowing those men she was crying. He had put his bitterness behind him. He remembered it vividly, and he accepted it. It happened, it's over.

"That should be the end of them, the guys I knew." But they continued reading toward the bottom of the panel when he read the name Del Trone. "Oh, my God! Super Chicken. I can't believe it, Peg. Soup . . . he made my short timer stick for me . . . one of my best friends." And tears fell down his cheeks. "Soup, I miss you, man. I'll never forget." He must have gotten killed in an attack on Long Thong after Gary left. His number was up.

"Let's go, Hon." Gary had enough of reading the Wall. He and Peg started walked toward the car. He was breathing heavily.

"You OK, babes?" She hadn't let go of him the whole time.

"Yeah. I'm glad we came. I'm glad you were with me. It's more closure, I guess. More closure, more acceptance." Then they drove home through the beautiful Ohio farmlands, composing themselves along the way.

Once home, Peg brought the mail in. "Hey! There's a letter from your brother Len," who didn't correspond often.

Gary opened it, found a note and an unopened envelope inside. "This came for you right after you moved out. I forgot all about it. I found it yesterday going through Mom's stuff. Love you guys, Len." It was a letter sent to their old family home address and it was from Company B, 137th ASHB, 2nd Airmobile Division, APO San Francisco—it was from Long Thong!

"I don't fuckin' believe this!" He hadn't cursed like this in years.

"What is it?" Peg knew this was something big.

He slit the envelope with a letter opener and removed the contents. A note said, "Told you we would send this." It was a photo of the Unholy Supper scene in the mess hall the night before he left Vietnam. He was speechless.

"Oh, my God," said Peg. "Is that you? Oh, my God. Oh, my God . . ."

They sat on the couch and just stared at it. Next to Gary was Soup—Del Trone—his buddy, the last name they had read on the Wall. And it arrived today of all days. "It's like he's still here, looking after me." He was unsure of or could not remember at all the names of the others posing as Apostles. Then he said, "I have to see something, Hon," and he stood.

They went right to their laptop and logged on to Google Earth. Then he did something he had never done before and began flying around III Corps, the 2nd Airmobile Division Area of Operation where he spent his year in Vietnam. He wanted to see the places he'd been—the LZs, villages and provinces.

He found Nui Ba Dinh, Black Virgin Mountain, the area that was hotly fought over by the North Vietnamese and U.S. forces. He was shocked and astounded. The forests surrounding the mountain that had once been a zone of fierce battles had been cut down and replaced by hamlets, towns, agricultural fields, cashew orchards, and rice paddies. Instead of red-clay country roads, paved roads now ran everywhere. There was even an amusement park at the base of the mountain and a cable-car ride to the top. And nowhere could he find even a hint of LZ Grant, the closest LZ to the mountain, the site of three big battles when the NVA tried overrunning the camp. "I don't believe this shit!" he said out loud. Peg silently got behind him and put her hands on his shoulders to see what he was looking at.

He scoured the area where Long Thong was and could not find it, nor Bearcat, the neighboring camp, nor any hint of the bases at Phouc Vinh and Lai Kai. No rows of barracks, no airfields, no perimeters, bunkers or revetments, it was like they had never existed, never. When the North finally defeated the South in 1975, the Vietnamese population descended onto the old military installations, tore down the bunkers and buildings, salvaging whatever was valuable to construct new homes and businesses. They even pried up the PSP metal airfields and used the steel for that purpose. Even the sprawling bases like Long Binh and Ben Hoa had disappeared without a trace. All over South Vietnam towns, villages, farms, fields, and orchards crept into and swallowed up the deserted bases. The country he had known was gone. There was no more North and South Vietnam, it was just Vietnam, one country. The land was finally at peace. And so was he.

Spirituality and sobriety saved him and gave him the acceptance he needed to come to grips with the war. But he would never forget those sunsets—not the sunrises that began some of those terrible days, but the sunsets—orange, red, and liquid gold-yellow sunsets on a land that was a vast tomb where all those who died there would all be forgotten someday. Nor could he forget the scene of flying above the monsoon clouds at night, and the light from the basketball-sized full moon and millions of stars shining down on the silver and white cloud cover. The jungle, rolling hills of forests, secluded valleys of elephant grass, miles and miles of rice paddies and dikes, hamlets, and villages, streams, and rivers. And all its astounding settings for the war going on within. The sunrises, sunsets, and the nights never began or ended the battles, bombing, artillery, or fire fights. They went on all day and all night, all over, from the forests and jungle, in the rice paddies, on the waterways. Death, slaughter, maiming, and suffering had been everywhere.

And through it all were the men in Gary's life while he was there, the guys in Bravo Company. Super Chicken (Soup), "Iron Cock" O'Grady, "Stinky" Rivers, the cooks "Big Floaty" and "Gator," Kosski the mail clerk and Taylor who "ran" Operations, Kranicki and "RJ" Gray, Romano, Rector, Earlywhile, Alvarez, Rick Strickland (who heard incoming rounds before anyone else), Lieutenant Papp, Robano and Andy Morgan. All the long days either pulling maintenance and repair on the Hueys, flying into and out of the fighting, the rocket and mortar attacks, the night the gooks breached the perimeter, the Medevac missions. For all the bad things that happened, Gary was always with someone else, other guys, buddies. They worked together, flew together, shot it out with gooks, stood formations, filled sandbags, built bunkers and revetments, burned shit, pulled guard duty and KP, but they also found time to get stoned and drunk together, listen to the Doors, Joplin, Hendrix, Spirit, Procol Harem, Beatles, Zeppelin, Creedence, Simon and Garfunkle. They screwed Vietnamese whores, pulled practical jokes, and withstood mountains of Army bullshit. They smoked opium, hashish and Gold Triangle pot while theorizing on fate, chance, destiny, death, and the afterlife. Gary didn't realize how closely he had bonded with them until he left them behind and went home.

For all the time he was there, Gary knew very few of the Vietnamese workers by name. It was Tug, their hootch maid, who was able to make him see just how difficult life was for people caught between the Americans and the Communists. He remembered how genuinely grateful she was whenever he gave her things to take home with her for her and her kids—candy, combs, soap, cigarettes, and C-rations. One day, Tug just never came to work again—gone. If only he could have done more for more of her people. Fifty years later, no one can compare the here and now with the there and then. It is not possible. It was like Vietnam was on another planet, and he could not get there from here.

❙ ❙❙❙ ❙

Labor Day weekend Aaron and June had invited everyone over for a holiday picnic. Gary and Peg arrived at 2 p.m. and were amazed how many people were there—family, friends and neighbors. Gary's ex-wife Leah, Aaron's mom, was also there, and she had mellowed over the years. There were three picnic tables draped in red and white checkered tablecloths, one serving table with tons of food, a propane grill pumping out hot dogs, burgers, and chicken, and two coolers of ice-cold pop and beer. Retirement-age couples, middle-aged people, younger working people, teenagers, and kids everywhere. Adam and Chase were always glad to see Grampa and Gramma Peg. Mingling was easy and fun for Gary and Peg. "Not like the picnics in the old days," said Peg. Not at all like the drunken, loud, and profane beer busts of years ago.

The adults were in pairs and small groups, scattered around the grill and tables. Some sat in lawn chairs and at the tables chatting. The talk ranged from work, school, property taxes, the Cleveland Indians, and the highly anticipated NFL season with the Cleveland Browns. It was practically a Norman Rockwell setting. No one was getting drunk or out of hand, just the way it's supposed to be.

Around 8:00 that evening, their grandsons and other kids were in the back of the yard bent over or squatting to study something on the ground. Gary thought he would go over and see what they were looking at. It turned out to be a small green grass snake—it looked just like the bamboo vipers in the jungle, minus the large round eyes. Gary picked it up, and the boys were amazed. "He can't hurt you," Gary said and released it in the tall weeds.

"Grampa," said Chase, "would you tell us a story?" The boys had heard over the years, without being told directly, that Grampa had been in the war years ago, "somewhere near China." Ranging in age from six to ten or eleven, they all looked up at him. Gary could not refuse his first grandson, the special little guy.

"OK," he said, "everyone sit down Indian-style and I'll tell you a story." They were thrilled they were going to hear a story about the war and sat cross-legged on the ground in a rough semi-circle. "One night, our General called us into his tent and told us the enemy General, Ho Chi Minh, was in a camp way out in the jungle." The kids were wide-eyed. "Our General wanted us to catch the enemy General Ho and bring him back—alive." The kids were listening closely, hanging on every word. "He showed us a map of where General Ho was—along a big river full of crocodiles, and in the jungle full of cobras, scorpions, leopards, and tigers." A couple of the boys looked astonished.

"We started out before the sun came up, sneaking through the jungle. Not only did we have to look out for the wild animals, but the woods were also full of enemy soldiers on patrol. We couldn't let them see us. Sometimes we hid in the bushes and they would walk right past us. Sometimes they were so close, we could have touched them." Gary reached out with his arm to show the kids how close. Not one kid said one word. They were rapt with attention. "We found the big river. Then the sun set and it got dark. We followed the river until we saw a big campfire in the jungle. We hid in the trees and saw the enemy, General Ho, dressed in black pajamas, sitting next to the fire, and surrounded by five thousand of his fiercest soldiers, protecting him." Gary paused and let the scene sink in. "We waited a long time until all the soldiers and General Ho were sound asleep . . . Slowly and quietly we crept into the enemy camp, making no noise what-so-ever . . . silently creeping and creeping . . . stepping over the sleeping soldiers . . . closer and closer . . . until we were right behind the sleeping General Ho." Gary paused here. "Then one of my men slapped a piece of Gorilla Tape over his mouth the second we grabbed him. His eyes got this big . . . he couldn't yell for help . . . General Ho knew he was being kidnapped!" These kids were really into the story, believing every word. Gary didn't dare sneak a look at the dads listening. "We tip-toed as fast and as quietly as we could, stepping over hundreds of soldiers, out of camp and back into the jungle." The two dads listening were amused by the whole scene.

"Don't stop, Mr. Dyson," said one of the kids.

"We thought we made it, but just then . . . we heard a twig snap . . . Slowly we turned . . . and there, standing at port arms," Gary demonstrated port arms, "with their AK47s at the ready, was the entire five-thousand-man regiment—all of them looking right at us!" He let it sink in. "Someone yelled 'RUN!'" All the kids jumped. "And we took off running, dragging General Ho by his black pajama-collar!" Every young listener was bug-eyed.

"We took off running as fast as we could go. The enemy soldiers were shooting and screaming at us! We were scared to death . . . that's why we ran so fast—faster than the enemy behind us . . . We ran a mile . . . then two miles, then three . . . The enemy was lagging behind us. And then at ten miles not many soldiers were left . . . and then they pooped out . . . We kept running . . . We were at fifteen miles . . . Then we lost count of how many miles . . . no more soldiers were chasing us . . . We made it back to our old camp and finally stopped running . . . And you know what?"

"What? Mr. Dyson?"

"All we had left of enemy General Ho Chi Minh was his black pajama shirt. He had slipped out somewhere along the way . . . and escaped." The kids were amazed, still wide-eyed. "And to this day, the route we took is known as the Ho Chi Minh Trail."

None of the kids knew or ever heard of the Ho Chi Minh Trail, but the story had fascinated them.

Gary looked at the two grinning dads. Then they both stopped smiling and one said earnestly, "It wasn't like that, was it?"

"Nope," Gary said, "wasn't like that at all."

GLOSSARY

‖‖‖

COMMON TERMS AND ABBREVIATIONS

ARMAMENTS, MUNITIONS AND WEAPONS

MILITARY RANKS

WARRANT OFFICER GRADES

OFFICER RANKS

MISCELLANEOUS OFFICERS

I III I

COMMON TERMS AND ABBREVIATIONS

11B20—the Military Occupation Specialty (MOS) code for the Infantry, Rifleman. "11 Bravo" was a slang term for the rifleman's MOS—11B20, Rifleman.

201 File—a military member's personnel file containing all the information pertaining to their enlistment.

3.2 Beer—beer containing a low alcohol content (3.2%).

4-F—the Selective Service draft status of those deemed unfit for military service, usually for medical reasons. The 1A classification was for those eligible to be drafted. During the Vietnam era, college students received what was classified as a 2S deferment.

AAA—acronym for Anti-Aircraft Artillery.

A Shau Valley—one of the principal entry points to South Vietnam located in the Thua Thien Hue Province off the Ho Chi Minh Trail, west of the coastal city of Hue near the Laotian border.

A-Team—operational name of the basic ten-man U.S. Special Forces team who often led irregular military units that were not held responsible to the Vietnamese military command.

ABN (Airborne)—term referring either to soldiers who have qualified as parachutists or to paratroopers as a group.

AC (Aircraft Commander)—a first lieutenant, usually the pilot.

Agent Orange—an extremely powerful herbicide sprayed by the U.S. military forces on forests and vegetation in Vietnam to allegedly defoliate a "specific" area in order to eliminate any forest cover and crops for North Vietnamese and Viet Cong troops. Dow Chemical and Monsanto were the two largest producers of Agent Orange for the U.S. military, and along with dozens of other companies (Diamond Shamrock, Uniroyal, Thompson Chemicals, Hercules, etc.), were later named in a lawsuit brought by veterans. The Department of Veterans Affairs eventually recognized the formation of several types of cancer and other illnesses as diseases specifically associated with exposure to Agent Orange and finally approved veterans' disability benefits.

AHB (Assault Helicopter Battalion)—the organizational structure the U.S. Army Aviation employs is a parallel to that of its non-aviation units with brigades, battalions/squadrons (air cavalry), companies/troops (air cavalry), and platoons. The aviation battalions in the U.S. Army are generally attached to divisions, corps and armies and mostly consist of helicopters, both attack and reconnaissance. The helicopter battalions are often grouped into aviation brigades. A Combat Aviation Brigade (CAB) is a multi-functional brigade-sized unit that fields military helicopters, offering a combination of attack/reconnaissance helicopters, medium-lift helicopters, heavy-lift helicopters, and Medevac capability. These divisional Assault Helicopter Battalions (AHBs) were usually comprised of three "slick" companies and one gunship company. Unlike independent AHCs, each company was made up entirely of either "slicks" or gunships.

AHC (Assault Helicopter Company)—approximately 70 Assault Helicopter Companies served in Vietnam during the war. In 1961, the antecedents of these units began the helicopter war in Vietnam, long before the arrival of American ground troops and Air Cavalry units. The standard independent Assault Helicopter Company contained roughly thirty aircraft: approximately 20 Bell UH-1D/H models formed two slick platoons and 8 UH-1 gunships or Cobras formed a separate gun platoon. In most units, the slick platoons were designated the 1st and 2nd platoons and the gun platoon was designated the 3rd platoon. An additional 1 or 2 aircraft were often assigned to the maintenance or headquarters platoons for liaison and general support duties. The number of helicopters in a platoon depends upon the type of platoon and the helicopter used, but typically it is either four or five helicopters per platoon. Assault Helicopter Companies went on to serve in Vietnam until the last days of the American war in 1973, long after most American forces had already left.

Air assault—the movement of ground-based military forces by vertical take-off and landing (VTOL) aircraft—such as the helicopter—to seize and hold key terrain which has not been fully secured, and to directly engage enemy forces behind enemy lines.

Air Cav (Air Cavalry)—a helicopter-borne infantry or gunship assault team first introduced into combat during the early days of the Vietnam war. They were deployed to Camp Radcliff, An Khe, the Central Highlands of Vietnam and were equipped with the newest range of weaponry: the M16 rifle, the UH-1 troop carrier helicopter, UH-1C gunships, the CH-47 Chinook cargo helicopter, and the massive CH-54 SkyCrane cargo helicopter.

Air Medal commendation—the military Air Medal is awarded to any person who, while serving in any capacity in or with the armed forces of the United States, shall have distinguished himself by meritorious achievement while participating in aerial flight. Created in 1942, and awarded for single acts of heroism or meritorious achievement while participating in aerial flight, the Air Medal may be awarded to recognize either single acts of merit or gallantry in combat or for meritorious service in a combat zone. Award of the Air Medal is intended to recognize those personnel who are on current crew member or non-crew member flying status which requires them to participate in aerial flight on a regular and frequent basis in the performance of their primary duties. However, it may also be awarded to certain other individuals whose combat duties require regular and frequent flying in other than a passenger status for every twenty hours recorded as having been spent in-flight.

Airmobile—a reference to helicopter-borne infantry. The Vietnam-era 1st Cavalry Division (Airmobile) was not an actual "air cavalry" division, although it did contain air cavalry squadrons. The division was a new concept that was more akin to a modern version of "mounted rifles," owing to its helicopter "mounts," and carried the "Cavalry" designation primarily for purposes of lineage and heraldry, and not because of its then current mission or organizational structure.

AIT (Advanced Infantry Training)—specialized training given to soldiers after completing Basic Training based on their Military Occupational Specialty (MOS), (i.e., those with the MOS of 11B10, 11B20 received infantry training, while those with a MOS of 13E20 received artillery training).

Ammunition—projectiles, such as bullets and shot, together with their fuses and primers, that can be fired from guns or otherwise propelled; nuclear, biological, chemical, or explosive materials, such as rockets or grenades, that are used as weapons in offense or defense.

Ammunition Dump—the ammunition or ammo dump is the physical location where live or expended ammunition is stored.

ANZAC (Australian and New Zealand Armed Corps)—the U.S. allied countries of Australia and New Zealand provided military personnel and equipment to the South Vietnamese. A total of approximately 60,000 Australians—ground troops, air-force, and naval personnel—served in Vietnam between 1962 and 1972. 521 died as a result of the war and over 3,000 were wounded. When a military needs people to fight in a war, but there aren't enough volunteers, sometimes they'll begin conscription, which is a law that says if you are able to fight, you must fight. Of the conscripted national servicemen who served from 1965 to 1972, 202 were killed and 1,279 wounded.

APC (Armored Personnel Carrier)—the M113 series armored personnel carrier is a fully tracked APC that was developed and produced by the Food Machinery Corp (FMC) and was the most widely used armored vehicle of the U.S. Army in the Vietnam War. The M113 was usually armed with .50-caliber machine guns that had been used by mechanized units to transport squad sized patrols or supplies. The M113 introduced new aluminum armor making the vehicle much lighter than earlier vehicles; it was thick enough to protect the crew and passengers against small arms fire but light enough that the vehicle was air transportable and moderately amphibious. Largely known as an "APC" or an "ACAV" (armored cavalry assault vehicle) by the allied forces, it earned the nickname 'Green Dragon' by the Viet Cong as it was used to break through heavy thickets in the midst of the jungle to attack and overrun enemy positions. When mechanized units worked together, the APCs were referred to as Fords and the tanks as Buicks.

ARA (Aerial Rocket Artillery)—aerial rocket artillery is a type of armed helicopter unit that was part of the artillery component of the United States Army's two airmobile divisions. The Army experimented with strapping rockets onto helicopters in Vietnam and began using them as true helicopter artillery in 1962. This wasn't air support or close combat attack; this was artillery in the air. In order to make artillery more responsive, two new unit types were created: aerial rocket artillery battalions and aviation batteries. Aerial rocket artillery battalions, the true helicopter artillery, were UH-1 Iroquois or AH-1 Cobras modified to carry a load almost entirely composed of rockets. The aviation batteries were helicopter units that could pick up tube artillery, usually howitzers, and deliver them to firing points near the battlefield on short notice where they would then be used normally, even if they had been deposited by helicopter miles ahead of any artillery units.

Arc Light—the term refers to both the name of a specific operation as well as the code name for B-52 bomber strike missions along the Cambodian-Vietnamese border that were used as close air support against enemy base camps, troop concentrations, and supplies. Known to shake the earth ten miles away from the target area, their strike pattern would saturate an area of 1,100 by 2,200 yards and flatten the jungle.

Article 15—the section of the Uniform Military Code of Justice that is a form of non-judicial punishment in connection with a soldier's summary disciplinary judgment by a commander that could result in possible fines or confinement to the stockade or even, at times, incarceration in Leavenworth.

ARVN (The Army of the Republic of Vietnam)—the ground forces of the South Vietnamese military from its inception in 1955 until the Fall of Saigon in 1975; also refers to a soldier in the ARVN (pronounced "Arvin"), or the ARVN military itself; *aka* known as the South Vietnamese regular army).

ASH BN (Assault Support Helicopter Battalion)—U.S. Army Aviation employs an organizational structure parallel to that of its non-aviation units with brigades, battalions/squadrons (air cavalry), companies/troops (air cavalry), and platoons. The aviation battalions in the U.S. Army are generally attached to divisions, corps and armies and mostly consist of helicopters, both attack and reconnaissance. The helicopter battalions are most often grouped into aviation brigades.

A-Gunner (Assistant Gunner)—the Gunner's Assistant was responsible for carrying the miscellaneous parts required to operate his assigned gun properly. A bipod, belts of ammunition, an extra barrel and several spare parts made up the contents of a typical load, all this in addition to the soldier's personal gear.

ATC (Armored Troop Carriers)—often called "Tangos" from the phonetic alphabet for "T" signifying "troop," the armored troop carriers were LCM-6 landing crafts modified for use by the Mobile Riverine Force of the U.S. Army and Navy with many equipped with helicopter decks. The ATC, the most common variant, carried four M1919 Browning machine guns, two Mk 16 20mm cannons, and one Mk 19 grenade launcher. Some carried flamethrowers and were known as "Zippos" while another version was designed to be a floating tank and was nicknamed the "Monitor."

Automatic (full) mode—continuous firing, like from a machine gun where the gun would fire nonstop as long as the operator depressed the trigger and there was ammunition.

AV-Gas—a high-octane gasoline mixture specifically formulated for use in aircraft; *aka* aviation gas or aviation fuel.

AWOL (Absent Without Leave)—leaving a military post or position without obtaining prior official permission.

Banana clip—slang for the curved, banana-shaped standard issue magazine on the AK-47 assault rifle.

Bandolier—a webbed belt of machine gun ammunition.

Bangalore torpedo—a long connectable tube, typically made of bamboo saplings, containing enough explosives to clear a 10 – 12-foot-wide path through wire obstacles and heavy undergrowth. These were usually placed at night by VC and NVA sappers who were small in stature and only weighed about ninety pounds.

Barracks—the living quarters for enlisted men; *aka* hootch, bunker.

Base camp—a semi-permanent location for field headquarters of brigade- or division-size units, each consisting of approximately 20,000 troops, and a base for artillery batteries and air fields with a resupply base for field units. Base camps usually contain all or part of a given unit's support elements; *aka* the "rear area."

Basic—the introductory training period for new recruits; boot camp.

Battery—a U.S. artillery unit equivalent to a company and consisting of six 105mm or 155mm howitzers or two 8-inch or 175mm self-propelled howitzers.

Beans and dicks—derogatory nickname for C-rations consisting of hot dogs and baked beans.

Beans and motherfuckers—derogatory nickname for the unpopular lima beans and ham C-rations, hence use of this and other nicknames like "ham n' motherfuckers" or "ham n' chokers."

Bearcat—the U.S. base camp located on Route 15, about 16 km southeast of Bien Hoa, that took its name from its Special Forces radio call sign; see "Big Red One."

Beehive round—a 105mm artillery shell capable of delivering thousands of small projectiles, commonly described as being "like nails with fins," instead of misshapen shrapnel. Designed to repel ground attacks, the cannon would be leveled parallel to the ground and aimed directly into the attackers. After clearing the muzzle, the shell casing would "banana-peel" back and each deadly round released over eight-thousand-five-hundred tightly packed one-half gram stainless steel flechettes flying at three-thousand feet per second in a sixty-five-degree killing field.

Berm—the perimeter line of a fortification, usually made of bulldozed earth; a hedgerow or a raised dirt parapet surrounding an area; called a "dike" when used in the rice paddies.

Big Red One—the infamous nickname for the 1st Infantry Division, based on the red numeral "1" on the division's shoulder patch; *aka* "Big Red 1", "The Bloody First" and "Bloody Red One" among others.

Bipod—a two-legged, supportive stand attached to the front of the barrel of many weapons.

Bird—any aircraft, but usually referring to helicopters.

Black Virgin Mountain—Nui Ba Den (Black Lady Mountain) is located approximately 10 km northeast of Tay Ninh and 96 km northwest of Saigon. Covered with large basalt boulders and honeycombed with caves and tunnels, the U.S. controlled the top and the bottom while the VC controlled everything else in between.

Blooker or blooper—slang for the 40-millimeter M79 grenade launcher, a shotgun-like weapon that shoots spin-armed "balls" or small grenades; *aka* "Thumper."

BN (battalion)—use of the term and the size of a "battalion" varies by nationality and branch of the military. A battalion is comprised of three rifle companies, a combat support company, and a headquarters company. Three to five battalions, approximately 1,500 to 4,000 soldiers, comprise a brigade. Although American battalions in Vietnam were usually much smaller, the typical infantry battalion numbers about 900 people and an artillery battalion about 500 people. Battalions normally fight enemy forces they can see and engage. This is defined as an area extending from less than 100 yards in forests, urban areas, and other close terrain out to about two to three miles from the battalion's direct and indirect weapons-fire.

Body bag—a heavy-duty, black, zippered plastic bag with handles used to transport dead bodies from the battlefield.

Body count—callous term used by Washington and Saigon to indicate the number of the enemy killed, wounded, or captured during an operation. Although used by the military and government as a means of measuring the progress of the war, the figure was grossly inaccurate and often inflated.

Boom-boom—slang for sexual intercourse, often referring to having sex or "short time" with a prostitute who would typically charge just a few dollars.

Boom-boom girl—slang term for prostitute.

Boonies—Boonies—a general infantry term referring to the jungles, swampy areas, or any remote area away from a base camp or city in Vietnam; *aka* boondock, bush.

Boonie hat—a soft, round, golf-style hat worn by a boonie rat.

Boonie rat—infantryman, a grunt.

Bou—slang for the Caribou C-7A, a small transport plane utilized for moving light loads of men and material.

Break squelch—disrupting the natural static of a radio to send a "click-hiss" signal by depressing the transmit bar on another radio on the same frequency (i.e., to press the transmit button on the radio handset without speaking: twice for all-clear, once for the enemy is near); almost always used when actually speaking into the microphone might reveal your position.

Brig—slang for a military jail or stockade.

Brigade—traditionally, the brigade provides mobility, counter-mobility and survivability, topographic engineering, and general engineering support to the largest unit—the corps—and augments the corps' various divisions. The tactical and administrative military unit in Vietnam was composed of a headquarters with one or more battalions of infantry or armor and with other supporting units that was organized into three brigades, with each brigade consisting of approximately 2,000 people, generally three-plus battalions, commanded by a colonel.

Bronze Star—the Bronze Star Medal, unofficially the Bronze Star, is awarded to any person who, while serving in any capacity in or with the military of the United States after December 6, 1941, distinguished himself or herself by heroic or meritorious achievement or service, not involving participation in aerial flight, while engaged in an action against an enemy of the United States; while engaged in military operations involving conflict with an opposing foreign force; or while serving with friendly foreign forces engaged in an armed conflict against an opposing armed force in which the United States is not a belligerent party.

Brown Bar—nickname for a second lieutenant, referring to the single bar signifying the rank of lieutenant where camouflaged rank insignia while out in the field which was often brown or black instead of brass; *aka* "butter bar."

BAR (Browning Automatic Rifle)—a heavy .30 caliber shoulder fired magazine-fed automatic rifle previously used by U.S. troops during World War II and Korea.

Buck sergeant—a rank signifying a leadership role, equivalent to a Spec 5.

Bunker—similar to a bomb shelter, it is a defensive military fortification consisting of substantial items such as sandbags, logs, steel grating and were designed to protect people and valued materials from falling bombs or other attacks. Bunkers are mostly underground, in contrast to blockhouses which are mostly above ground. The bunkers are about twenty-six feet wide and up to eighty feet long and have enough room for between 10 to 20 people and can keep supplies for 12 months.

C-7—the two-engine Caribou, nicknamed the "Bou", was a small funny-looking, dark grey, cargo airplane manufactured by de Havilland Canada. It was used to re-supply fighting forces in-country because of its unique ability to perform short takeoffs and landings (STOL) thereby allowing it to fly in and out of camps on short, unimproved airstrips.

C-130—U.S. Air Force four-engine turboprop military transport aircraft designed and built originally by Lockheed (now Lockheed Martin) and introduced into U.S. service in 1956. Capable of using unprepared runways for takeoffs and landings, the C-130 was originally designed as a troop, medevac, and cargo transport aircraft. The versatile airframe found uses in a variety of other roles, including as a gunship (AC-130), for airborne assault, search and rescue, scientific research support, weather reconnaissance, aerial refueling, maritime patrol, and aerial firefighting. Used in the hauling of large bulky equipment, including artillery pieces and tanks, over long distances with an ability to land in tight spaces, slow to 125 knots for paratroop drops, and fly, if need be, with one engine; *aka* the "Spooky" gunship.

C-rations (Combat Rations)—a package of canned meals for use in the field that consisted of a can of some basic entrée course, a can of fruit, a packet of some type of dessert, a packet of powdered coca, sugar, powder cream, coffee, a small pack of cigarettes, two pieces of chewing gum, and toilet paper. The C-3 combat ration was composed of the same five menus of the C-2 but offered greater variety. In addition to new and improved "B" (bread) and "M" (meat) units, each menu contained an accessory packet, fruit, and cigarettes. There were six daily ration boxes per cardboard case; *aka* "C-rats", "beans and dicks."

Cache—a hidden storage area typically containing ammunition, weapons, and food.

Cadre—a cadre is the U.S. military complement of commissioned officers and non-commissioned officers of a military unit responsible for training the rest of the unit, group or member of a group of leaders, especially in units that conduct formal training schools. In U.S. Army jargon, the word is both singular and plural.

Call sign—a word and number assigned to the position of those who needed to communicate on the radio (i.e., "Little Bear" was the radio call sign for A Company, 25th Avn Bn, 25th Inf Div.).

Carbine—a short-barreled, lightweight automatic or semi-automatic rifle.

Caribou C-7A—a small transport plane for moving men and material.

Cav—nickname of the 1st Cavalry Division (Airmobile), it also referred to the armored cavalry using M113 APCs and other light armored vehicles.

Central Highlands—a plateau area at the southern edge of the Truong Son Mountains that was a strategically important region of South Vietnam. Known for its production of coffee, tea, and vegetables, in 1968, nearly one million people, mostly Montagnard tribesmen, lived in the Central Highlands.

Charlie—a shortened form of the radio phonetic spelling for VC or VICTOR CHARLIE; one of the many slang derogatory terms for the Viet Cong; *aka* "Mr. Charlie", "Charles", "Sir Charles", "Chas", "Chuck."

Charlie Company—the call sign used to identify "C" Company.

Cherry—slang for a soldier who has never been under fire; inexperienced; a virgin; a newbie; the NFG—New Fucking Guy.

Chicken Plate—the aircrews' protective body armor consisting of a front pocket and stretchable webbing sides with an overlapping waistband, similar to a WWII flak vest. The armor in the early models did more damage than good. A projectile entering an unprotected part of the armored vest would ricochet off the plates inside the vest like a pinball, causing major, usually fatal damage to the wearer. The design was improved in 1968 using ceramic armor and was capable of successfully providing protection against .30 caliber fire from a range of 100 yards.

CHICOM—term referring to either a Chinese Communist or to those weapons manufactured in Communist China. In addition to the Soviet Union, Communist China was an especially important strategic ally of North Vietnam during the war.

Chinook—the Boeing CH-47 Chinook is an American twin-engine, tandem rotor, heavy-lift helicopter developed by American rotorcraft company Vertol and manufactured by Boeing Vertol (later known as Boeing Rotorcraft Systems). At its peak employment in Vietnam, 22 Chinook units were in operation with approximately 200 of the nearly 750 Chinook helicopters in the U.S. and South Vietnam fleets lost in combat or wartime operational accidents. Chinook is from the Native American Chinook people in modern-day Washington state where the Boeing company is located; *aka* "Shit Hook" or "Hook."

Chopper—slang for a helicopter; *aka* "bird" or "ship."

Chu Hoi—a political initiative by the South Vietnamese in order to encourage the Viet Cong to defect and aimed at letting NVA and VC soldiers surrender to the South Vietnamese Government. Hundreds of thousands of fliers and cards were dropped all over South Vietnam encouraging the enemy troops to surrender without enduring any harm by chanting "Chu hoi, chu hoi" Vietnamese for "arms up." While many field units received their surrender honorably, other units didn't and some NVA and VC were interrogated and then disposed of—either shot on the spot or thrown from helicopters. The ARVN forces were notorious for their brutal treatment of Chu Hois.

CIB (Combat Infantryman's Badge)—the infantryman's badge of honor awarded to those combat veterans holding an Infantry MOS who personally fought on the ground under enemy fire in an active combat zone for 30 days or more, or for being wounded while serving as an Infantryman in combat while assigned as a member of either an Infantry, Ranger, or Special Forces unit.

CID (Criminal Investigation Department)—the investigative section of the U.S. Army provides the investigations into serious crimes such as robberies, burglaries, sexual offences, fraud, serious assaults, and murders. Crime investigation during Vietnam often involved incidents related to the fragging of officers, war profiteering, or racial incidents, particularly near the end of the war.

CIDG (Civilian Irregular Defense Group) (pronounced "sidgee")—financed by the Americans, these irregular South Vietnamese military units were typically made up of Vietnamese nationals or members of ethnic minorities and were led by members of Special Forces A-teams.

Civies—slang for civilian clothes.

Claymore—derived from the Scottish Gaelic words claidheamh ("sword") + mòr ("great"), it was a very popular anti-personnel land mine widely used in Vietnam for perimeter defense. Carried by the infantry, when detonated, it was designed to propel small steel cubes in a 60-degree, fan-shaped pattern extending out to a maximum distance of one hundred meters.

Close air support—air strikes against enemy targets that are close to friendly forces, requiring detailed integration of each air mission with the fire and movement of those forces.

Comics—slang for military maps, especially topographic maps; *aka* "comic books" or "funny papers."

COMM—either portable communication equipment or equipment set up inside a bunker that was usually included inside the last protected area of an established defensive position; *aka* "COMMO."

Company—the basic elements of all battalions; a military unit of 130 to 150 soldiers, commanded by a captain, consisting of four platoons, a headquarters unit, and some logistical capabilities. In the artillery corps, a company would be called a battery while cavalry units refer to this unit level as a troop.

Compound—a fortified military installation.

Concertina wire—coiled barbed metal wire with razor-type ends used as a defensive barrier manufactured in large coils that can expand like a concertina (small instrument similar to an accordion).

CONEX—a rectangular corrugated steel packing crate used for standard transport by sea, air or land vehicles, approximately seven feet high, six feet wide, and five feet deep with two steel security doors. Later recycled as shelters for storing weapons and other equipment on the flight line, thousands of these quasi-buildings were all over Vietnam and used for everything from offices to living quarters to clubs to PXs.

CORDS (Civil Operations and Revolutionary Development Support)—a pacification program created on May 9, 1967, that included the joint military and civilian components of the U.S. and South Vietnam governments in order to counter the effects of the insurgency.

Corps—the largest tactical unit in the U.S. Army, the corps is responsible for translating strategic objectives into tactical orders. It synchronizes tactical operations, including maneuvering, the firing of organic artillery, naval firing, supporting tactical air operations, and actions of their combat support, bringing together these operations on the battlefield. Each corps has between two and five divisions, and specialized brigades depending on the mission.

CP (Command Post)—the place from which a commander in the army controls and organizes their forces; the headquarters of the commander of a military unit.

CP (Control Point)—the point at which a potential hazard can be controlled.

CP pills (Chloraquine-Primaquine)—the large, orange, anti-malarial pills (the "yellow" in the phrase "two whites and a yellow") that needed to be taken in addition to Dapsone (*aka* the "whites") due to CP resistant malaria in the Central Highlands.

CQ (Charge of Quarters)—the officer officially in charge of a unit headquarters at night whose duty assignment was to answer the telephone in the orderly room from 23:00 hours until relieved at morning reveille.

Crew chief—the Huey crew member who performed a dual role by not only maintaining the aircraft, but also serving as an integral member of the helicopter crew during missions.

Cyclo—a three-wheel passenger vehicle powered by a human on a bicycle; a motorized rickshaw.

Daily Dozen—the core exercises during basic training were numbered one through twelve and the trainees were required to know the name and number of each exercise; Number One, the high-jumper, is often called "jumping jacks" while others included sit-ups, toe-touches, and the dreaded eight-count pushup.

Daily-daily—nickname for the small daily anti-malarial pill.

Dapsone—small white anti-malarial pills (the "whites" in "two whites and a yellow") taken regularly by U.S. troops and used in the Central Highlands with CP pills to counter falciparum-resistant strains of mosquitos (allegedly given to prevent malaria but actually it was to prevent leprosy).

DD214—the Department of Defense form for "Certificate of Release or Discharge from Active Duty."

DEROS (Date Eligible for Return from Overseas Service or Date of Eligible Return from OverSeas or Established Return from Overseas Service)—the date a soldier's tour in Vietnam ended and he/she could go home.

Deuce and a half—a two and one half-ton military truck.

DFC (Distinguished Flying Cross)—a U.S. military decoration for heroism or distinguished achievement while on aerial duty.

Dien cai dao (pronounced "dee en key dow")—Vietnamese for "crazy in the head."

Dink—a derogatory slur for Asians that originated from an Australian reference to the Chinese.

Dinky dow—slang phonetic Vietnamese term for "marijuana" and "crazy."

District team—those American personnel acting at the district level as advisors to Vietnamese military and civilian officials.

Division—military entity that performs major tactical operations for the corps and can conduct sustained battles and engagements. One division is made up of at least three maneuver brigades with between 10,000 and 20,000 soldiers, depending on the national army involved. American divisions are normally commanded by major generals and tend to be on the lighter side of the headcount. Divisions can have specialties such as light infantry, armored or mechanized infantry, airborne, and air assault. In other countries, division sizes vary widely.

DMZ (Demilitarized Zone)—the neutral area dividing North Vietnam from South Vietnam that was established at the Geneva

Convention in 1954; much later it was nicknamed the "Dead Marine Zone."

Donut Dollies—young, single, women recently graduated from college who volunteered to go to Vietnam with the Red Cross as part of the Supplemental Recreational Activities Overseas program. During Vietnam, their official title was changed to "Recreational Advisors" where they worked in the service clubs for the troops. Their jobs were to motivate and entertain and some were even known to visit troops in desolate areas out in the bush. Unofficially, they were called Donut Dollies, but they didn't serve doughnuts like during WWII.

DP (Displaced Persons)—those South Vietnamese who were forced to move their villages due to ongoing military operations.

Drill sergeant—the sergeant assigned to new recruits during basic training camp.

Drum—a container of live ammunition ready to be mounted on a weapon.

DSC (Distinguished Service Cross)—the second highest military award, behind only the Medal of Honor, for a member of the United States Army for gallantry and risk of life in combat.

Duffle bag—the large oblong olive drab (OD) bag used by soldiers to store their gear.

Duster—the self-propelled M42 40mm M2A1 Bofors automatic cannon was initially designed for an anti-aircraft role, only to prove very successful for firebase and convoy security when used against unarmored ground forces. The vehicle was also equipped with double radio antennas and either grenade launchers, a side-mounted 7.62mm M60 General Purpose Machine Gun (GMPG) or a .30 caliber M1919A4 machine gun.

Dustoff—while the dustoff term has been used to apply to all medical evacuation missions, GIs reserved the term for missions flown to pick up wounded soldiers in the field, usually while encountering ground fire. Many of the early helicopters used in Vietnam did not perform well in dustoff missions due to a lack of maneuverability and relatively slow speed, and small doors until later "Huey" models featured wide doors allowing troops to get in and out quickly. The term came into use in 1964 after the death of Lieutenant Paul B. Kelley while flying a medevac mission—"Dustoff" had been Kelley's radio call sign; *see* medevac.

Elephant grass—tall, razor-edged tropical plant indigenous to the highlands of Vietnam that covers hundreds of meters of jungle terrain and also grows in clumps under trees and alongside riverbanks.

Eleven bravo—slang for the Military Occupation Specialty Code used to identify an infantryman.

EM (Club Enlisted Man's Club)—a specific building or area whose clientele pertained to, or belonged to, that part of the armed services with a ranking below commissioned officers or warrant officers.

ETS (End Time of Service or Estimated Time of Separation or Established Termination of Service or Expiration of Term of Service)—abbreviation for the date ending a soldier's term of service date of departure from overseas duty.

Extraction—withdrawal of troops by helicopter from any operational area where they had been previously offloaded for a mission.

F-4—the McDonnell Douglas F-4 Phantom, a tandem two-seat, twin-engine, long-range, supersonic, jet interceptor aircraft/fighter-bomber. With a range of over 1,000 miles and a top speed of over Mach 2.2, it could carry payload on nine different external mounting points while the airframe would carry more than 18,000 pounds of weapons, including air-to-air missiles, air-to-ground missiles, and various bombs.

FAC (Forward Air Controller) (pronounced "fack")—the person responsible for directing air strikes and artillery fire on enemy positions identified from a light, low-level, low-speed aircraft, such as a single-engine Cessna O-1 Bird Dog spotter plane. The FAC identified Viet Cong or North Vietnamese positions and relayed the information to attack aircraft, helicopter gunships, or high-altitude bombers; *aka* "Oscar Deuce and Birddog" in reference to the O-2 style of airplane they used.

FAO (Forward Air Observer)—the pilot of a single engine spotter plane.

Fatigues—standard U.S. combat uniform in olive drab (OD) green.

FB (Fire Base)—a temporary firing position for artillery usually consisting of four howitzers and their crews and a company of infantry men used for fire support of the forward ground operations; *aka* a fire support base.

FFZ (Free Fire Zone)—any living thing within this area can be engaged and fired upon.

Field of fire—total area that a weapon or group of weapons can cover effectively when firing from a given position.

Fire for effect—the continual firing of all available ordnance aimed at the enemy. Often the platoon leader would give coordinates and the guns would "fire for effect" to determine their proximity to the target, but also to disrupt and confuse the enemy.

Firefight—an intense battle or exchange of small arms fire with enemy units.

First or 1st Cavalry Division—the nineteenth century horse-mounted cavalry units gave way during the twentieth century to armored personnel carriers and tanks. An innovation of the Vietnam War was the use of air cavalry units to move troops into battlefield positions by helicopters. The 1st Cav was the first full division deployed to South Vietnam in September 1965 and was almost immediately engaged in battle in the Ia Drang Valley where it won a Presidential Unit Citation. As the army's first airmobile division, the First Cavalry Division pioneered air assault tactics and suffered a total of over 30,000 casualties.

Flak jacket—a flak jacket/vest is a form of personal body armor, usually made from ballistic nylon mixed with a special protective material called Doron. Contrary to popular belief, flak jackets are not interchangeable with bulletproof vests, instead it is designed to provide protection against fragments from high explosive weaponry like anti-aircraft guns, land mines, grenades, some pellets used in shotguns and anti-personnel mines, and other lower-velocity projectiles. The term "flak" originated during WWII when the Allies had to fly over large enemy areas containing anti-aircraft guns. Known as the Fliegerabwehrkanone or "air defense gun," the German contraction for Fliegerabwehrkanone was "flak" and it was much easier for Americans to pronounce. The flak jacket was developed by Wilkinson Sword Company to address the need for body armor against these German shells and to protect the wearer from severe injuries and death. Doron was developed by Dow Chemical Company in 1943 and was created by bonding together glass filaments under high pressure that uses the resin methacrylate. A heavy fiberglass-filled vest was heavy and bulky and later designs incorporated pyro-ceramic plates to protect the back and chest from rifle-fire.

Flare—an illumination projectile that can be hand-fired or shot from artillery, mortars, even air dropped by helicopters.

Flechette—from a French term meaning "little arrow" or "dart," it was a very effective close-range anti-personnel munition consisting of a pointed steel projectile with a finned tail, for stable flight clustered in an explosive warhead. Attack helicopters had a similar warhead in use on their 2.75-inch "pecker-head" rockets, nicknamed "Nails" and containing 2200 flechettes that delivered thousands of small projectiles instead of shrapnel; *aka* grapeshot.

FNG (Fucking New Guy)—the most common name or designation for a newly arrived soldier in RVN who served as a new replacement soldier from the States; *aka* "cherry", "fresh meat", "newbie", or "new citizen."

Forward observer—a soldier or person attached to a field unit coordinating the placement of direct or indirect fire from ground, air, and naval forces.

Foo gas (fougasse)—a mixture of explosives and napalm usually set in a fifty-five-gallon drum that projects a burning liquid onto a target when purposely detonated by machine gun or rocket fire.

Frag or fragging—killing, murder, or assassination of fellow soldiers, usually officers, by a fragmentation grenade that typically happened by tossing a live grenade into a latrine or barracks occupied by the targeted individual in retaliation for an action or order that resulted in somebody getting needlessly hurt or killed. The grenade was popular with enlisted men because the evidence is immediately destroyed when the crime is committed.

Freedom Bird—usually an American Airlines Boeing 707 that flew soldiers back home from Vietnam.

Friendly fire—air, artillery, or small-arms fire from American forces mistakenly directed at other American or allied troop positions.

FSB (Fire Support Base)—although originally referring to a temporary firing base for artillery, many evolved into more permanent bases, or small forts. Their main components varied by size: a typical FSB had a battery of six 105 millimeter or 155mm howitzers, a platoon of engineers on station for construction and maintenance projects, at least two landing pads for helicopters, a tactical operations center (TOC), an aid station staffed with medics, a communications bunker, and a company of infantry serving as the defense garrison.

FTA—acronym for Fuck the Army.

"Fuck You" lizard—the Tokay Gecko is the second largest species of Gecko lizard. The female has a bluish or grayish body, with vibrant colored spots ranging from light yellow to bright red, while the male is even more brightly colored than the female. Their mating call during the night sounds like "faaa-cue" and is repeated about every 15 seconds.

Garand—although the U.S. M1 rifle 30-06 caliber semi-automatic rifle was issued as the standard U.S. service rifle during World War II and the Korean War, it also saw limited service during Vietnam.

Gooks—derogatory racial slur referencing Viet Cong, North Vietnamese soldiers and other Asians; it was derived from Korean slang for "person" and brought to Vietnam by Korean war veterans; *aka* "Chuck", "Charlie", "dinks", "gomers", and "slopes."

Gooks in the wire—a verbal alarm indicating enemy soldiers were trying to infiltrate a basecamp or firebase.

Green Berets—specialized U.S. soldiers trained in the techniques of guerrilla warfare; *aka* Special Forces.

Green line—the outer perimeter of the military position itself, consisting of a bull-dozed earthen berm surrounding the entire camp site with the unspoken acceptance that the area beyond the perimeter belonged to the enemy alone.

Green tracers—a colored flash left by specific ammunition intentionally fired from enemy AAA or AK-47s that allows the shooters to identify and track the path of their bullets.

Grenade—a baseball-sized metal explosive device thrown by hand for either detonation or for releasing a brightly colored smoke for signaling.

Grids—the thousand-meter square areas individually identified by number on a map. Maps were often referred to as "the comics" or "the funny papers."

Grunt—although originally referring to a Marine fighting in Vietnam, it later applied to any foot soldier fighting there and was supposedly derived from the sound one made from lifting up his rucksack; *aka* a "Boonierat", "Ground Pounder" or "Crunchie."

Gun trucks—deuce and a halfs providing support to convoys traveling through known hostile territory were usually fitted with a .50 caliber machine gun and one or two M60s, plus a variety of individual weapons for the typical crew of four to five men.

Gunship—initially a heavily armed helicopter such as a UH-1 Model B or C Huey Bell Helicopter and then later in the war an AH-1G Cobra, equipped with full artillery firepower consisting of pods of rockets and/or grenades with a primary mission of providing fire support; the UH-1C gunship was known as "the Hog."

H&I (Harassment and Interdiction)—artillery bombardment rounds used to deny the enemy access to any terrain they might find beneficial to their campaign; general rather than specific, confirmed military targets; random artillery fire into areas prior to closing down a base for the night; random artillery fire in order simply to keep the enemy in a state of unease.

Ham and lima beans—a common staple of C-ration packages where the entrees could be spaghetti and meat balls, pork and rice, meat and noodles, frankfurter and beans, pork and beans, or ham and lima beans (which nobody liked, hence the nicknames "ham 'n' motherfuckers" or "ham 'n' chokers").

Hamburger Hill—the most famous battle in the A Shau Valley was "Hamburger Hill," the battle that launched the first phase of *Operation Apache Snow* consisting of a coordinated attack by the U.S. Army and South Vietnamese forces against units of the northern People's Army of Vietnam (PAVN).

Hamlet—a small rural Vietnamese village.

HE—high explosive.

Helmet liner—typically made of fiberglass, it went inside the steel pot.

Highway One—the main route from the north into Saigon.

Ho Chi Minh sandals—primitive sandals worn by both the NVA and VC made from worn-out truck tires with soles made from rubber tire tread and the straps from inner tubes; these were routinely appropriated from the war dead by GIs as war souvenirs; *aka* "Ho Chi Minh Road Sticks" or "Ho Chi Minh slippers."

Ho Chi Minh Trail—the extensive complex of miles of narrow, unpaved supply paths throughout the jungles of Cambodia and Laos that traveled from North Vietnam to South Vietnam and served as the primary means of transportation toward Hue and Danang for funneling North Vietnamese Army and Viet Cong troops, supplies, and communications for the unit's operating in the I Corps area.

Hog—a UH-1C gunship manufactured by Bell Helicopter equipped with full artillery firepower consisting of pods of rockets and/or grenades; slang term for a M60 machine gun.

Hooch or **hootch**—slang term for a thatched hut or improvised living space (e.g., inside a sand-bagged bunker or improved "foxhole") for either the military or civilians that was derived from a corruption of the Japanese word for "dwelling places" and passed on by GIs who fought during the battle for Okinawa. The term also had several other meanings: barracks, house, living quarters, a native hut, weed, or booze—especially homemade "moonshine."

Hootch girl or **hootch maid**—a Vietnamese woman employed by American military personnel as a maid or laundress.

Hose down—directing a massive amount of automatic weapons fire, as from a minigun, Spooky or other high firepower gunship. Any basecamp perimeters suspected of infiltration by sappers would frequently be hosed down by gunships during "mad minutes."

Howitzer—a short cannon, aptly nicknamed a "Baby Howitzer" because of its relatively small size and portability. It usually refers to a 105mm towed howitzer with a relatively short barrel and the use of comparatively small propellant charges capable of firing medium velocity shells with relatively high trajectories and a steep angle of descent. The term "howitzer," meaning "sling" or "basket," was taken from the Prussians when the U.S. began producing howitzers in the 1830s.

Hue—located on Highway 1 about 420 miles south of Hanoi and 670 miles north of Saigon, Hue, for the Viet Cong and North Vietnamese, was the center of cultural and religious life with tremendous historical significance. Hue fell to the Communists during the 1968 Tet Offensive.

Huey "Hog"—the UH-1C gunship manufactured by Bell Helicopter came fully equipped with an artillery firepower package consisting of pods of rockets and/or grenades.

Huey "Slick"—the Bell UH-1 utility helicopter, called the "Iroquois" by the United States Army, served a multitude of roles. More widely known by the nickname "Huey," as derived from its initial designation of HU-1 for "Helicopter Utility," it was a ubiquitous icon of the Vietnam war where hardly a night passed without the evening news showing Hueys engaged in combat missions. For American troops in the field, the sound of the helicopter was perhaps the most iconic sound of the war; usually evoking positive feelings, since the helicopter almost always meant some type of relief be it additional troop reinforcements, supplies such as ammunition, food, and medicine, or evacuation of the wounded and/or dead.

Hump or **humping**—while carrying full rucksacks and supplies troops walked from one location to another over routes through dense jungle, along paths or trails, through streams and rice paddies and sometimes uphill/downhill on very steep slopes.

I CORPS—known as "Eye" Corps, it referred to the northernmost military region in South Vietnam and was one of four major military and administrative units of the Vietnamese government during the 1960s and early 1970s. The headquarters of I Corps was located in Da Nang and contained major cities such as Hue, Quang Tri City, Da Nang, and Chu Lai.

II Corps—the Central Highlands military region in South Vietnam.

III Corps—the densely populated, fertile military region between Saigon and the Highlands.

IV Corps—the southernmost military region in South Vietnam, including the Mekong Delta.

Incoming—verbal warning of the beginning of an enemy mortar or rocket attack.

In-country—the GI's slang term for a tour of duty in Vietnam.

Indian country—the U.S. often thought of Vietnam like images of the American West and cast the Vietnamese in the role of Indians during the early war years. American soldiers in Vietnam routinely called enemy territory and hostile areas outside of basecamps "Indian Country:" *aka* boonies, bush, field, or jungle.

I&I (Intoxication and intercourse)—a raunchy takeoff on R&R for "rest and relaxation."

Iron Triangle—War Zone "D." the Viet Cong and NVA dominated area between the Thi-Tinh and Saigon rivers, next to Cu Chi district.

JAG (Judge Advocate General)—the legal department of the U.S. Armed Services.

Juicers—those troops identified as being heavy beer and/or whiskey drinkers; alcoholics.

Jungle utilities—lightweight tropical fatigues.

KIA (killed in action)—a total of 58,220 soldiers died from a range of causes, including death from wounds, killed in action, accidents, and even self-infliction. There were 47,434 hostile deaths and 10,786 non-hostiles. Richard B. Fitzgibbon, Jr., a U.S. Air Force Technical Sergeant, was the first American soldier to die in the Vietnam war. He wasn't killed in action but was murdered by another U.S. airman and later died of his wounds on June 8, 1956. On October 22, 1957, the U.S. forces suffered their first battle casualties. Thirteen Americans were wounded in three terrorist bombings.

American troop strength in Vietnam got nearly as high as 540,000 during 1968, the deadliest year of all with 16,899 U.S. deaths. May was the bloodiest month of 1968 when more than 2,000 soldiers were killed. From the Tet Offensive through 1969 this number only continued to increase resulting in a total of 11,780 deaths in 1969.

The U.S. military administration estimates that between 200,000 and 250,000 South Vietnamese soldiers died in the war.

Kill zone—the radius of a circle within which 95% of all people therein will be killed when a bomb explodes; the area of an ambush where everyone will either be killed or wounded.

Kitchen police or **kitchen patrol**—mess hall duties, very often assigned as punishment.

Klick (kilometer) (1,000 meters/0.62 miles)—the military used both metric and Imperial measurement systems depending on the application, while weaponry size and the distance on the ground were measured using the metric system.

Lambretta—a versatile motor scooter that clogs the streets of Vietnam by the thousands.

LBJ—common nickname for the USARV Long Binh Stockade (jail) on the Long Binh Post by changing the last word to make a pun on the initials of President Lyndon Baines Johnson; whether that military post, also known as Camp Long Binh Junction, was also referred to as LBJ is still a hotly debated issue.

Lifer—term most often used in a derogatory manner in reference to a career military service member.

Lister Bags—also known as the Lyster Bag, it was a component of Field Feeding Equipment, such as the Mobile Kitchen Trailer, with Lister Bags supplied according to the unit size of the kitchen, issued approximately one per 100 persons. In 1913, Army physician, Maj. William J. L. Lyster developed a simple apparatus used to purify water quickly in the field by placing water into a linen bag and then adding calcium hypochlorite to kill microbes in the water. Lyster's method became the standard for U.S. ground forces in the field and in camps, implemented in the form of the Lyster Bag (also spelled Lister Bag). The Lister Bag was in common use from before World War I through the Vietnam War. The linen bags were replaced with large portable canvas containers. Every camp or base would have a proliferation of Lyster Bags. In addition to providing drinking water, the Lyster Bag was a water resource for cooking, showers, medical use, and many other general instances.

Lit up—firing upon a target with extreme force.

Litters—medical stretchers to carry the dead and wounded.

Little people—slang for the enemy.

LOH (Light Observation Helicopter) (pronounced "Loach")—usually the egg-shaped Hughes OH-6A Cayuse recon Light Observation Helicopter that served extensively with U.S. Army forces in Vietnam and replaced the OH-23 helicopter.

Lock and load—phrase originating from the rifle range exercises during basic training it seems to have acquired several meanings. "Lock" means mounting the magazine while "load" refers to chambering a round. Some have stated "load" meant putting the magazine in and chambering a round, and "lock" meant putting the safety on.

LP (Listening Post)—a two- or three-man position set up at night outside the perimeter of a fire base that was away from the main body of troops as an early warning system. Each man would lay out claymore mines and then take turns during the night listening, looking, and monitoring the one radio they had for communicating with the Fire Base; *see* Fire Base.

LRRP (Long Range Reconnaissance Patrol)—an elite team usually composed of four to eight men who go deep into the jungle without initiating any contact in order to observe enemy activity and gather intelligence; an experimental lightweight food packet consisting of a dehydrated meal that was most often issued to the LRRP patrols.

LURPS—slang for Long Range Reconnaissance Patrols.

LZ (Landing Zone)—generally, anywhere a helicopter can land, but typically a small clearing temporarily secured to allow for the landing of resupply helicopters that often became permanent and later base camps.

LZ cut—a jungle clearing technique performed from a C-130 aircraft and usually undertaken by rolling a large bomb attached to a 6-inch fuse out the rear of the aircraft. When the bomb exploded it blew horizontally, flattening everything, it didn't create a crater but instead made an instant LZ.

M11—a large, anti-malaria pill (Chloroquine) taken every Monday that produced almost immediate diarrhea.

MACV (Military Assistance Command Vietnam)—the main American command unit based at Tan Son Nhut assigned with responsibility for and authority over all U.S. military activities in Vietnam.

Mad minute—an order given to all bunkers to shoot a concentrated fire of all available weapons into the area across their front for one minute. This maximum rate of free-fire practice was to test-fire weapons and was intended to harass, pin down, interrupt or show the enemy our units were "at the ready"; *aka* "Mike-Mike" or "recon by fire."

Marker round—the first round fired by mortars or artillery that were used to adjust the following rounds onto the desired target.

Marlboro Greens—mentholated tobacco cigarettes bearing the Marlboro brand that were not available to GIs. The Vietnamese would remove the tobacco from each cigarette and replace it with marijuana by means of a bicycle pump. These new packs of mentholated marijuana cigarettes were then sold to the GIs for about $2 per pack.

Marvin the Arvin—derogatory term for the stereotypical South Vietnamese soldier derived from the abbreviation for the Army of the Republic of Vietnam—ARVN.

Medevac—the term refers to the evacuation of casualties by helicopter or occasionally by airplane during or after a battle. Dustoff became a synonym for medevac that was adapted for use after the death of Lt. Paul B. Kelley in 1964 while out on a medevac mission—"Dustoff" was Lt. Kelley's radio call sign.

Medivac—a medical evacuation from the field usually by helicopter; *aka* medevac.

Mermite—large, insulated food containers.

Mess—meals, food, chow.

MI team (Military Intelligence team)—an oxymoron—the Army intelligence investigative team from the Criminal Investigation Department who wore civilian clothes and sidearms.

MIA (Missing in Action)—a soldier reported missing while on a mission but whose death has not been confirmed.

Military Occupation Specialty (MOS)—the role or job someone has while in the military. There are over 10,000 different occupational specialties across the military that cover a whole range of skillsets and levels of responsibility.

Minigun—electronically controlled, extremely rapidly firing machine gun most often mounted on aircraft to be used against targets on the ground.

Monday pills—a large, anti-malaria pill (Chloroquine) that was officially designated M11 and taken every Monday by U.S. troops.

Mosquito wings—slang term for the stripes sewn on privates' uniforms to signify the rank of E-2, whereas no stripes or insignia signifies the rank of E-1 Private, Trainee.

MP (Military Police)—the Military Police in the Army are responsible for maintaining law, order, and discipline and they serve as the Army's law enforcement and security specialists by patrolling Army installations and supporting troops during operations.

MPC (Military Payment Certificates)—military currency script used in Vietnam because use of U.S. dollar "greenbacks" was illegal; *aka* "Monopoly" money.

MR (Military Region)—Vietnam was divided into four areas representing I Corps, II Corps, III Corps and IV Corps (North to South) that were later referred to as Military Regions (MR1, MR2, MR3 and MR4).

Mr. Charles—slang term for the Viet Cong; the enemy.

MULE (Multi Utility Light Equipment)—a small 4-wheel drive, gasoline-powered truck/tractor type vehicle originally designed to carry a 106-millimeter recoilless rifle, but it could carry up to a half ton and was usually used to transport equipment, supplies and the wounded within firebases; *aka* "Mule", "Military Mule", or "Mechanical Mule."

Nails—slang for a 2.75-inch anti-personnel rocket warhead. Not known for their accuracy, this warhead wasn't used near friendly troops and was attached to a spin-stabilized, folding-fin, aerial rocket fired from helicopter gunships. Weighing 9.3 pounds, the warhead contains approximately 2,200 twenty grain flechettes that are released by a base-mounted, fuze-ignited expulsion charge at rocket motor burnout. The U.S. Artillery units had a similar round called a Beehive round; *aka* flechettes.

Napalm—an incendiary defoliant and antipersonnel weapon used in Vietnam by the French and Americans. Nicknamed "maple syrup in a Zippo-track," it consists of a thickened, flammable organic solvent—usually gasoline—gelled by soap. Delivered by bomb or flamethrower it would ignite on impact, clinging to anything in its blast radius suffocating its victims by consuming all the available oxygen as it burned.

NDSM (National Defense Ribbon)—a service medal of the U.S. Armed Forces established by President Dwight D. Eisenhower in 1953. It was first intended to be a "blanket campaign medal" awarded to service members who served honorably during a designated period of which a "national emergency" had been declared during a time of war or conflict.

Newbee or **newbie**—a new guy in the unit or new at a specific job; any person with less time in Vietnam than the speaker; *aka* "cherry."

New Zealand—New Zealand's involvement in the Vietnam War was highly controversial, sparking widespread protest at home from anti-Vietnam War movements modelled on their American counterparts. More than three thousand New Zealand military and civilian personnel served in Vietnam between 1963 and 1975. In contrast to the world wars, New Zealand's contribution was modest. At its peak in 1968, New Zealand's military force numbered only 548. Between June 1964 and December 1972, a total of 3,890 New Zealand military personnel (volunteers) had served in Vietnam with a total of 37 killed and 187 wounded.

Next—the soldier claiming to be the next person to rotate home from Vietnam.

NLF (National Liberation Front)—officially called the National Front for the Liberation of the South, it was the name of the Communist political wing, and the military was called the People's Liberation Armed Forces (PLAF).

Nomex—flame-resistant, polymer material developed for aviators in 1968 that was used extensively in making flight suits and gloves.

Number One—Vietnamese slang for something that is either good, the best or great.

Number Ten—Vietnamese slang term for something that is either bad, no good or the worst.

Nung—idigenous tribespeople from the highlands of North Vietnam, some of whom moved South and worked with the U.S. Special Forces.

NVA (North Vietnamese Army)—either the army itself or a soldier in that army.

O2—a Cessna Skymaster airplane used as a Forward Air Controller airplane with twin engines, one fore and one aft of the cabin section.

OCS (Officer Candidate School)—educational facility where qualifying enlisted men would be promoted to Commissioned Officers upon completion of all studies and training.

OD (Olive drab)—basic green color used by the Army on practically every single item issued by the Army.

OP (Observation Post)—the location outside the base perimeter used by infantry personnel during the daytime as an early warning device.

Orderly Room—a room in the barracks of a battalion or company used as the administrative office of a small military unit for general administrative purposes.

P-38—a small metal collapsible can opener for canned C-rations, nicknamed a "John Wayne"—it was pocket-sized, approximately 1.5 inches (38mm) long, and consisted of a short metal blade that served as a handle, with a small, hinged metal tooth that folds out to pierce the can lid.

Parris Island—Marine training base located in South Carolina.

Peckerhead—2.75inch rockets, loaded with flechettes and painted white with a purple head, it detonates in a purple explosion soldiers called "purple haze," the title of the popular at the time Jimi Hendrix song containing the lyric.

Pedicab—a foot-powered cyclo.

Purple Heart—U.S. military decoration awarded to any member of the Armed Forces wounded by enemy action. Originating during the Revolutionary War, any soldier who was awarded three Purple Hearts was allowed to leave Vietnam.

Piss tube—a vertical tube connected to a fifty-five-gallon drum buried two-thirds in the ground and surrounded by a chest-high privacy wall for use a urinal.

Platoon—a platoon is the smallest military unit led by a commissioned officer. Typically, there are platoons in a company, consisting of four squads: generally, three rifle squads and one weapons squad, normally armed with machine guns and anti-tank weapons commanded by a lieutenant and a sergeant as the second in command.

Pogue—an American pejorative military slang for non-combat, staff, and other rear-echelon or support units. "Pogue" frequently applies to those who do not have to undergo the inherent risks and stresses of combat as the infantry men do.

Point man—the lead soldier or element in a combat patrol that often required cutting a path through dense vegetation where needed and was constantly exposed to the danger of booby traps or being the first soldier contacted by the enemy.

Port—left side of the slick or boat when facing forward.

PTSD (Post Traumatic Stress Disorder)—a psychological disorder development with characteristic symptoms brought on after experiencing a psychologically traumatic event or any events outside the range of human experience usually considered to be normal. Many Vietnam veterans suffered from PTSD upon their return from their tour of duty. The government and military denied for years the negative effects on those affected until they were finally forced to admit the connection. Meager payments began to be slowly distributed to those few who met the stringent requirements to qualify for any disability payment.

POW (Prisoner of War)—a soldier that has been taken captive by the enemy. No American POW escaped from North Vietnam and successfully reached friendly forces. All the men who escaped in North Vietnam were recaptured, usually, but not always, within the first day. American POWs did escape from camps in North Vietnam, some of them from camps in Hanoi. And at least five escaped twice from camps in North Vietnam, some from established camps, others from guards while en-route to Hanoi.

Following the Paris Peace Accords of 1973, 591 U.S. prisoners of war were returned during Operation HOMECOMING, but while the U.S. listed about 2,500 Americans as POW or MIA, only 1,200 Americans were reported to have been killed in action with no body recovered.

Captain Charles Frederick Klusmann, a United States Navy combat pilot, was the first American airman shot down (June 6, 1964) and captured by the Pathet Lao (Laotian guerillas). On August 31, 1964, Klusmann was the first to escape his captors. "First in, first out." This is notable because the U.S. government never negotiated for the release of any prisoners held in Laos, and so, not one American held in Laos was ever released

James Nicholas "Nick" Rowe was a U.S. Army intelligence officer who, on October 29, 1963, after only three months in country, was captured by Viet Cong elements while on an operation to drive a VC unit out of the village of Le Coeur. Sentenced to death, he was finally able to escape his would-be executioners and was rescued December 31, 1968, one of only 34 American prisoners of war to escape captivity during the Vietnam War.

PRC-25 (Portable Radio Communications, Model 25)—a back-packed lightweight FM receiver-transmitter used by infantry for short-distance (5 – 10 kilometers) communications in the field.

The range could be extended to 20-30 kilometers if it was attached to a special, non-portable antennae; *aka* "Prick 25."

PRC-77—a very heavy radio similar to the PRC-25, but with a cryptographic scrambling/descrambling encryption unit attached to provide transmission frequencies commonly known as the "secure net."

Province chief—the governor of a state-sized administrative territory, usually a high-ranking military officer province team consisting of American civilian and military advisors assigned duties at the provincial capital.

PRU (Provincial Reconnaissance Units)—an irregular unit organized within each province for the official purpose of reconnoitering guerrilla sanctuaries and collecting intelligence on guerrilla activities. These units operated under the auspices of the CIA and were also the operating arm of the Phoenix program.

PSP (Perforated Steel Planking or Pierced Steel Planking or Perforated Steel Plate)—first used in November 1941, the standardized, perforated steel matting material was primarily for the rapid construction of temporary runways and landing strips. Construction panels were about 3'X8', made of plate steel, punched with 2" holes, and having features on the sides for interlocking together. A small team of CB engineers could create a runway 200 feet wide and 5000 feet long within 48 hours.

PT (Physical Training)—the regimen of exercises and drills that are a part of basic training, called the "Dirty Dozen" by the trainees.

Puff the Magic Dragon—nickname for a propeller-driven C-47 helicopter armed with 3 miniguns or other rapid-fire weapons on the port side that were capable of firing 6,000 rounds per minute per gun for a total discharge of 18,000 rounds per minute. It is said that when firing a minigun while flying over a football field, a bullet will hit every square foot of the field. During a night attack, the string of tracers would be constant and sometimes looked like an imaginary urine stream. Leading some soldiers to reference Puff-involved attacks as "bringing piss" on the enemy or "pissing down rain"; *aka* "Spooky."

Pug marks—term used to refer to the footprint of most animals. "Pug" means foot in Hindi. Each animal species has a distinct pugmark and as such this is used for identification.

Punji stick/stake—a sharpened stake, usually of bamboo, with the point smeared with water buffalo and human feces as a poisoning element, planted with the point sticking up and hidden in the ground.

PX (Post Exchange)—the soldier's "store" on a military installation.

Quad 50s—a World War II vintage, anti-aircraft weapon used in Vietnam as an anti-personnel weapon. Used for firebase and convoy security, it consisted of four electric solenoid-fired, .50 caliber machine guns mounted in a movable turret and often put on the back of a deuce and a half truck.

R&R (Rest and Relaxation/Recreation/Recuperation)—every GI was entitled to take a three- or seven-day vacation from the war during his one-year tour of duty and fly on a free roundtrip to out-country locations like Penang, Kuala Lampur, Tai Pei, Tokyo, Singapore, Manila, Bangkok, Hong Kong, Australia, or Hawaii (only if you were married). The in-country R&R locations were at Vung Tau, Cam Rahn Bay or China Beach; *aka* "I&I" or "Intoxication & Intercourse."

Red tracer—a colored flash left by specific ammunition intentionally fired from U.S or allied AAA or long rifles that allows the shooters to identify and track the path of their bullets.

Regiment—a permanent military unit of an army typically commanded by a colonel and divided into several companies, squadrons, or batteries and often into two battalions. The U.S. Marine Corps still operate regimental units, comprised of five battalions—about 2,000-strong.

REMF (Rear Echelon Mother-Fucker)—an extremely insulting and derogatory slang term of derision used by front-line soldiers, especially during the Vietnam War, for those serving in the rear, including those military personnel employed in rear echelon support capacities. They are perceived to have a relatively safe job and good living conditions while in a war zone and are hated (because of envy) by frontline combat soldiers who have neither comfort, and wished they did. There are two basic types of REMFs: pencil pushing administrators, or combat support personnel. It is a myth that REMFs risked the lives of those in combat on the frontlines, in fact the opposite is true. Combat support REMFs kept the grunts alive by supplying "beans, bullets and blood."

Re-Up Bird—the Blue Eared Barbet, a jungle bird whose song sounds like "Ree Up" (as in "re-enlist") to those soldiers out in the jungle.

Revetment—an "L" shaped or parallel type of wall fortification usually made of sandbags or steel plating that gave some protection to any helicopters while they were parked on the flight line.

Reveille—traditional bugle musical arrangement used to wake up the troops in the morning.

RMB (Received Maximum Benefits)—the status given to those veterans determined to have utilized all the benefits available to them from the Veteran's Administration.

ROK/ROCK (Republic of Korea)—nickname for a soldier from the Republic of Korea, a U.S. ally.

Rotate—returning home to the U.S. at the end of a year's tour in Vietnam

RPD—a 7.62mm Communist light machine-gun with a 100-round, belt operated drum that fires the same type of round as the AK-47.

RPG (Rocket Propelled Grenade)—a long-standing misnomer for a Russian-made portable anti-tank grenade launcher that was the weapon of choice by VC / NVA for attacks on armor and against sandbagged bunkers. "RPG" is actually an acronym for three Russian words and not for "Rocket Propelled Grenade" as the U.S. soldiers called it.

RPM—rotations per minute.

RTO (Radio Telephone Operator)—the enlisted soldier who carried the communications radio, usually a PRC-25, for the small unit commander. Not only did it have a large antenna but the operator was the unit's link to support and coordination and made him a prime target for the enemy.

Saccharine—an artificial sweetener about 550 times as sweet as sucrose but with a bitter or metallic aftertaste.

Saigon cowboys—a derogatory term used to describe the thousands of draft-age Vietnamese men who should have been serving in the Vietnamese Army, in uniform and fighting for their country. Instead, many just hid out in the cities riding their motor bikes around like American cowboys riding horses and snatching purses.

Saigon Tea—very expensive colored water or soda purchased in very small glasses in a bar or nightclub that, when bought by a GI, signaled he would pay the managing hostess for the prostitute's company.

Salvo—firing a battery in unison or in quick succession.

SAM (Surface to Air Missile)—anti-aircraft missiles launched from the ground, often portable, one-shot units.

Same-same—although this phrase was first heard during the Vietnam War in the '60s, it is still used quite extensively throughout Vietnam by Vietnamese as well as by ex-servicemen from the U.S. and Australia. (i.e. How's it going? Same-same yesterday. All Vietnamese same-same . . . black hair, brown eyes.)

Sappers—highly trained and dedicated units of NVA or VC demolition commandos whose mission was to penetrate American defensive perimeters at night armed with explosives.

Satchel charges—a pack containing explosives usually more powerful than a grenade that is dropped.

SeaBees—nickname of the Naval construction engineer battalion derived from Construction Battalion (CB).

SEAL (Sea Air and Land)—a member of a highly trained Naval special warfare team.

Search and avoid—a derogatory term for an all-ARVN manned mission.

Search and destroy—offensive military operations designed to search out and destroy enemy forces and supplies or anything else the enemy might find useful; *aka* "Zippo missions" due to the soldier's use of the ubiquitous Zippo lighter when burning local villages.

Shaped charge—an explosive charge where the energy generated is focused in one direction (*i.e.,* a claymore mine).

Shell—a shell, or bombshell, is a payload-carrying projectile that, as opposed to shot, contains an explosive or other filling.

Ship—helicopter.

Shit burning—a daylong ritual at firebases where half-barrels filled with human excrement are pulled out from the enclosures and replaced with empties. A soldier or Vietnamese civilian was assigned to sanitize the latrines by burning all the waste with a mixture of kerosene and diesel fuel—continuously stirring the contents during the entire 10-hour process.

Shitters—outhouse-like enclosures usually located at firebases where 3 or 6 holes (3 holes wide with a hole across from each other) were cut in a wooden plank and suspended over 55-gallon barrels cut in half.

Short—the time when a soldier's tour of duty in Vietnam is almost complete—usually when less than 100 days remain. In the last couple of weeks, soldiers were so "short" they were invisible. Short timers carried notched walking sticks and most became extremely paranoid and tried to avoid taking any more risks.

Short-timer's stick—a long stick customarily presented to a soldier when he had approximately two months remaining on his tour in Vietnam. He would notch it for each of his remaining days in-country. Every passing day he would cut the stick off another notch until only a small stub remained on the day he finally rotated out to return to the World.

Shotgun—1) a method of smoking marijuana where the first person, after inhaling a large amount of marijuana smoke, would exhale and blow the smoke down the barrel of weapon for a second person situated at the other end of the barrel to inhale; 2) the armed guard on or in a vehicle who watches for enemy activity and returns fire if attacked. Term originated during the days of the stagecoach where a man equipped with a shotgun would ride up front with the driver as a form of protection (as in "to ride shotgun").

Shrapnel—pieces of metal shell casings sent airborne by the explosion of a munition.

Silver Star—military decoration awarded for gallantry in action.

Sit rep (Situation Report)—field units and firebase bunkers are normally contacted on an hourly basis by the company/battalion radio operator.

Six—infantry term for a Unit Commander, from the Company Commander on up; the area behind you, as in "watch your 6," referring to the 6 o'clock position and is derived from the use of a clockface to indicate a physical position where the area directly in front would be 12 o'clock.

SKS assault rifle—Simonov 7.62mm semi-automatic carbine used by VC and NVA forces.

Sky Pilot—nickname for a military chaplain. The British rock group Eric Burdon and the Animals released an anti-war song by that title in 1968 on *The Twain Shall Meet* vinyl record album.

Slant—derogatory term for a Vietnamese person.

Slick—the UH-1 helicopter did not have protruding armaments and was, therefore, "slick" when used for transporting troops in tactical air assault operations. Troops could ride in the wide doors of the aircraft, normally in two rows on each side, and could exit quickly when landing in a landing zone under fire. Often a UH-1 would not touch down during "slick" operations; instead, it would hover a couple of feet above the ground while troops evacuated the aircraft; *aka* Huey.

Sling load—cargo carried under a helicopter that is attached to a metal ring on the underside of the helicopter by a lead line and swivel.

Slope or **Slope head**—derogatory term for an Asian person.

Smack—heroin; *aka* "H."

Smoke grenade—a baseball sized, handheld metal object that released brightly colored smoke used for signaling.

SNAFU—slang for "Situation normal—all fucked up."

Snake—Snake-Eye bombs were used for close air support, as in "Snake n' Nape" (bombs and napalm); a nickname for the AH-1G Huey Cobra gunship.

Sortie—a sortie (from the French word meaning exit) is a deployment or—dispatch of one military unit, be it an aircraft, ship, or troops, from a strongpoint. The sortie, whether by one or more aircraft or vessels, usually has a specific mission.

SF (Special Forces)—U.S. soldiers trained in the techniques of guerrilla warfare; *aka* Green Berets.

SOP—acronym for Standard Operating Procedure.

Spider-hole—a very small narrow camouflaged enemy hiding place (typically foliage and grasses were used) similar to a foxhole that is so narrow and shallow the occupant could only stand up with difficulty.

Spooky—the call sign of the Douglas AC-47 fixed-wing, propeller-driven gunship (*aka* "Puff, the Magic Dragon"). Equipped with three 7.62 miniguns on the port side that are capable of firing 6,000 rounds a minute.

Squad—small basic military unit or organizational institution in the U.S. Army and Marine Corps usually commanded by a sergeant consisting of about ten men, generally composed of two teams of four men each.

Squadron—a cavalry unit whose size was similar to a battalion.

Stand-down—a military unit's return from the boonies to the base camp for rest, refitting and training during which all operational activity other than security is stopped.

Starboard—on the right side when facing forward.

Starlight scope—a night-vision scope weighing six pounds and filled with an image intensifying fluid that magnified both reflected starlight and the light given off by rotting vegetation. Although the field of vision was a yellowish-green color and any images were not clear, any movement could be plainly seen by both snipers and base camp defenders.

Stars and Stripes—the official U.S. military newspaper.

Stateside—term used to describe the strict Army regulations pertaining to just about everything—uniforms, personal appearance, barracks conditions, military courtesy, the adherence and enforcement of regulations—just about everything that was expected back home in the states, hence "stateside."

Steel pot—the outer metal cover on the standard Army helmet.

Stove-pipe—a potentially dangerous situation where an empty shell casing becomes stuck in the breech of the firearm.

Suzie Wong—*The World of Suzie Wong* is a 1960 British-American romantic drama film. The main characters are Robert Lomax (William Holden), a young British artist living in Hong Kong, and Suzie Wong (Nancy Kwan), a Chinese woman who works as a prostitute and is often seen dressed in a slinky red cheongsam, a full length body-hugging dress or gown worn by Chinese women with a high collar and long slits, one on each side of the dress.

Tarmac—material used for surfacing roads or other outdoor areas consisting of crushed rock mixed with tar and is often used generically to describe the apron or runway of an airport.

Tet—the Vietnamese lunar New Year that celebrates Buddha's birthday usually begins in January or February. Tet also refers to the nationwide NVA-VC offensive that began January 31, 1968, at the beginning of the Tet holiday.

Tet Offensive—a major uprising of the National Liberation Front, their sympathizers, and the NVA was characterized by a series of coordinated attacks against U.S. military installations and provincial capitals throughout Vietnam during the beginning of the lunar New Year, January 31, 1968.

The World—term used by soldiers when referring to the U.S.A. To the GI stationed in the jungles and highlands of Vietnam the United States was an entire world away.

Thumper or **Thump gun**—slang for a M79 grenade launcher; *see* "blooper."

Thunder Road—a term that was used repeatedly as nickname for various local roads. Similarly, there were many LZs from north to south that had the same names as they were built and as they were deserted—LZ Dot, Dolly, Barbara, Betty, etc.; 1) The main north/south highway in southern Vietnam from Saigon to Loc Ninh, it was known for having many mines, ambushes, etc. and stretches from the northeastern outskirts of Ho Chi Minh City, the commercial center of the country and once the site of the military academy of the Army of the Republic of Vietnam, towards the border to Cambodia; 2) National Route 13 from Saigon west to Quan Loi was also nicknamed Thunder Road by the 11th ACR who used the callsign Thunder. The enemy ambushed this road regularly resulting in many "battle of Thunder Roads." In one instance several 1st Infantry Division units responded, killing 73 NVA in two hours. Within a ten-day period, the enemy attacked the road three times and lost 110 men.

Top—another nickname for a unit's first sergeant.

Tracers—projectiles or ammo rounds that are built with either a small pyrotechnic charge in their base or are chemically treated to glow or give off red or green smoke so that its flight can be followed visually. The VC and NVA weapons used a tracer every fifth round that appeared green in color in low light or at night, while U.S. tracers were red.

Trip flare—a cautionary ground flare with a trip wire to signal and illuminate the approach of the enemy at night.

Trip glasses—thin metal eyeglass frames holding small rectangular lenses that are tinted in different colors; *aka* "granny glasses."

Triple canopy—jungle vegetation growing in three distinct layers: at ground level, intermediate, and high-level.

Tunnel rat or **rat**—an American soldier, who volunteered for training to enter enclosed spaces such as the VC tunnel systems in order to search them and eliminate and/or capture any enemy occupants.

Two-digit-midget—a soldier with less than one-hundred days left to serve in Vietnam.

UH-1H—Utility Helicopter-1 Huey helicopter; *see* Huey.

USARV (U.S. Army Republic of Vietnam)—the Command of operations unit for all U.S. military forces in Vietnam. Based in Long Binh, USARV controlled the activities of all U.S. Army service and logistical units in South Vietnam. The post was the largest U.S. Army base in Vietnam with over 50,000 women and men.

USO (United Service Organization)—the USO is a nonprofit, charitable corporation chartered by Congress that relies on donations from individuals, organizations and corporations to support its programs and to provide entertainment to the troops in an effort to raise morale. The USO troupes visited various bases in Vietnam, from the rear area to the front-line troops.

VC (Viet Cong or **Victor Charlie)**—slang based on the military phonetics for the letters "V" and "C" and refers to the Communist-led forces fighting the South Vietnamese government.

Vietnamization—the term was coined by President Richard Nixon's Secretary of Defense, Melvin Laird, for U.S. policy to end U.S. involvement in Vietnam.

War Zone "C"—the area in South Vietnam centered around the abandoned town of Katum near Tay Ninh Province on the Cambodian border there was a strong concentration of North Vietnamese Army (NVA) and Viet Cong (VC) activity. This area was reportedly the general location of COSVN, the headquarters for communist military and political activities in the southern half of Vietnam. War Zone C, located in the area designated as III Corps, was a section of South Vietnam with high strategic value due to its location in between Cambodia and Saigon as well as the fact that it was a popular jump off spot for NVA forces and supplies from the Ho Chi Minh Trail. War Zone C's boundaries followed the Cambodian border to the north and west, while its eastern boundary ran parallel to Highway 13. The area has been described as pathless jungles through mountainous regions and boggy swamps which made travel and transportation extremely difficult.

War Zone "D"—known as the Iron Triangle, the area was a National Liberation Front (NLF) stronghold 20 miles northwest of Saigon. Located between Saigon, Tay Ninh, and Song Be cities, the Triangle comprised about 125 square miles. It was generally bounded by the Saigon River, the Song (river) Thi Thinh north of Bien Hoa, and the Than Dien Forest. The area was thickly forested, consisting of jungle and rubber plantations and containing a few small villages and hamlets.

WIA (Wounded in Action)—through the use of the Huey in the battlefield evacuation of those wounded in action, nearly 98% of the soldiers would be alive when reaching medical attention.

Willy Pete—slang for White Phosphorus. Delivered by mortar or artillery, this substance burns extremely hot and generates a lot of light. It is only supposed to be used for illumination, as it should be considered a chemical weapon if used against people.

Zippo—the brand of lighter most commonly carried by U.S. soldiers during the war that were often engraved to show their personality. They were well-made with a perforated windscreen, and a cover that clicked shut with a trademark snapping sound; slang term for any tracked vehicle or boat with an attached flame-thrower.

Zippo raids—military operations involving the burning down of Vietnamese villages, typically using Zippo cigarette lighters to ignite the huts. Zippo Raids were infamously documented by renowned news journalist, Morley Safer, showing American GIs with shining, metal lighters igniting thatch-roof huts.

I IIII

ARMAMENTS, MUNITIONS, AND WEAPONS

One-O-Deuce—refers to the 105mm howitzer (even though it's actually 102mm).

105mm howitzer—towable or air-liftable short cannon that fires medium-velocity 102mm shells with relatively high trajectory.

107mm and 120mm—the two main types of Communist-made rockets the NVA and VC fired on the Americans by the thousands.

155—the U.S. 155mm howitzer.

175—the U.S. 175mm howitzer.

1911A1—a .45 caliber U.S. military handgun designed for close-up, hand-to-hand combat.

60 or M60—officially designated the M60A1, it was a 7.62mm machine gun carried by the infantry; *aka* "The Pig" or "The Hog."

81mm—the British-designed M252 81mm medium weight mortar is a smooth bore, muzzle-loading, high-angle-of-fire weapon used for long-range indirect fire in order to provide support to light infantry, air assault, and airborne units.

82mm—nicknamed the "eight-deuce," the M-37 (or 82-BM-37) is a Soviet 82-millimeter mortar.

AC-47—the helicopter gunship ("A" for attack) was first designated "Spooky" by the Air Force and was later given the nickname "Puff the Magic Dragon." The C-130 Hercules airframe was selected later on to replace the AC-47. "Spooky" was the call sign for any gunship in the area.

AK-47 or AK—the Soviet-manufactured Kalashnikov combat assault rifle (7.62mm) was both semi-automatic and fully automatic and was the basic weapon of the Communist forces. Known to the Chinese as the Type 56, it is easily identified by its distinct explosive "popping" sound.

B-52—the Boeing B52D Stratofortress is a long-range, high-altitude (30,000 feet), subsonic, jet-powered strategic bomber commandeered by an 8-man crew. It entered service to achieve penetration of high-altitude enemy airspace, a concept quickly rendered obsolete by the development of accurate Surface-to-Air Missiles (SAMs). The most effective use of the B-52 in Vietnam was for tactical support of ground troops. When B-52s were called in to disrupt enemy troop concentrations and devastate supply areas, the strikes often consisted of two-thousand-pound steel tipped delayed action bunker-busting bombs in an attempt to destroy enemy tunnels and underground facilities.

C-4 (Composition 4)—a common variety of the plastic explosive family known as Composition C, it is the type of explosive favored most by sappers. Lightweight with a texture similar to modeling clay or Play Dough, it can be molded into a charge of any desired shaped. Stable, easy to carry, it can only explode with a combination of extreme heat and a shock wave from a detonator even when dropped, beaten, shot, or burned and it cannot be destabilized by water, very important given Vietnam's climate. C-4 reduced the necessity of carrying a variety of explosive charges. Soldiers during the Vietnam War era would sometimes use small amounts of C-4 as a fuel in foxholes at night for warming hands and feet. Other troops broke off small pieces as the preferred fuel for heating water or C-rations because it will burn unless detonated with a primary explosive. However, burning C-4 produces poisonous fumes, and soldiers are warned of the dangers of personal injury when using the plastic explosive. The Army "jungle grapevine" operated by the field troops in Vietnam soon made it common knowledge that ingestion of a small amount of C-4 would produce a "high" similar to that of ethanol. Others would ingest C-4, commonly obtained from a Claymore mine, to induce temporary illness in the hope of being sent on sick leave.

C-130—Lockheed Hercules—an American four-engine turboprop military transport aircraft designed and built originally by Lockheed (now Lockheed Martin) it could fly faster, longer, higher, and carried increased munitions loads. Capable of using unprepared runways for takeoffs and landings, the C-130 was originally designed as a troop, medevac, and cargo transport aircraft. The versatile airframe has found uses in a variety of other roles, including as a gunship (AC-130), for airborne assault, search and rescue, scientific research support, weather reconnaissance, aerial refueling, maritime patrol, and aerial firefighting.

CAR-15 (Colt Automatic Rifle-15 Military Weapon System)— Colt Firearms first marketed, designed, and manufactured a combined AR-15 and M16 rifle to produce a cut down M16 featuring a telescopic butt and a short barrel for close quarters, it was used almost exclusively by Navy SEALS and the Special Forces.

M1—the World War II-era eight-shot, .30 caliber American rifle/ carbine that was replaced with the M14 and subsequently by the 18 shot .223 caliber M16.

M2—the Browning .50 caliber machine gun, nicknamed "Ma Deuce."

M14—a .30 caliber select-fire rifle with a wooden stock used during the early years in Vietnam.

M16—nicknamed the "widow-maker," it replaced the M14 and was the standard U.S. military rifle (5.56mm) in Vietnam after 1965.

M60—the American-made 7.62mm (.308 caliber) lightweight machine gun used by U.S. forces in Vietnam.

M79—U.S. military single-barreled, single-shot, break-action, shoulder-fired, hand-held grenade launcher that fires a 40x46mm grenade designed to keep recoil forces low; *aka* the "Blooper," "Thumper," or "Thump-gun."

M113—Armored Personnel Carrier (APC); a tracked vehicle.

I IIII

MILITARY RANKS

PVT—Private, Trainee, no insignia of rank; E1.

PVT2—Private, with insignia of rank; E2; "Mosquito Wings."

PFC—Private First Class; E3.

CPL—Corporal; E4.

SPC4—Specialist-4 or Spec-4 (pronounced "Speck 4") Specialist 4th Class; SPC/4; E4—the Army Specialist rank immediately above Private First Class that had no command function. Most enlisted men who had completed their individual training and had been on duty for a few months were Spec-4s, which was probably the most common rank during the Vietnam-era Army.

SGT—Sergeant or Spec-5; SPC (5) Specialist 5th Class; SPC/5; E5; the rank equivalent to a "buck" sergeant but usually with a specialist, rather than formal leadership role.

SSG—Staff Sergeant; E6; the second lowest rank for a noncommissioned officer.

SFC—Sergeant First Class; E7.

MSG—Master Sergeant; E8.

1SG—First Sergeant; E8; "First Shirt" is also a slang term for a first sergeant; *aka* "Top."

SGM—Sergeant Major; E9.

CSM—Command Sergeant Major; E9.

SMA—Sergeant Major of the Army; E9 Special.

▌▌▌▌▌

WARRANT OFFICER GRADES

WO1—Warrant Officer One. The copilot, nicknamed "Wobbly Ones."

CW2—Chief Warrant Officer 2.

CW3—Chief Warrant Officer 3.

CW4—Chief Warrant Officer 4.

CW5—Chief Warrant Officer 5.

CO—Commanding Officer.

CC—Company Commander.

I III I

OFFICER RANKS

2LT—Second Lieutenant; identified by the single bar of the rank of lieutenant, officers in the field wore camouflage rank insignia which was often brown or black instead of brass; *aka* "brown bar."

1LT—First Lieutenant; O-2; *aka* "LT" (pronounced "ell-tee").

CPT—Captain; O-3.

MAJ—Major; O-4.

LTC—Lieutenant Colonel; O-5.

COL—Colonel; O-6.

BG—Brigadier General; O-7.

MG—Major General; O-8.

LTG—Lieutenant General; O-9.

GEN—General; O-10.

GA—General of the Army; Special.

| |||| |

MISCELLANEOUS OFFICERS

NCO—Non-Commissioned Officer; usually a squad leader or platoon sergeant.

NCOIC—Non-Commissioned Officer in Charge; the NCO in charge of operations.

OG—Officer of the Guard.

OIC—Officer In Charge.

XO—Executive Officer; the second in command of a military unit.

CPSIA information can be obtained
at www.ICGtesting.com
Printed in the USA
JSHW062309150922
30581JS00002B/3